A RELUCTANT BRIDE

Virginia looked over at the room's lone bed, then her gaze flew back to Slade. "Where are you going to sleep?" she asked innocently.

"Why, in the bed, of course," he replied.

"B—but . . . what about me?"

He chuckled. "I imagine you will sleep there too." He reached out and gently touched her cheek. His voice grew husky. "Although I doubt that either one of us will get too much sleep. After all, this is our wedding night."

Virginia swallowed hard, her heart hammering rapidly in her chest, her eyes widening into black, fathomless pits. "It's tr̲ ̲ ̲ ̲ ̲ ̲ ̲ ̲ ̲ried, but we hardly know each other̲ ̲ ̲ ̲ ̲ ̲ ̲ ̲ ̲ ̲ ̲ ̲til it seemed she was tr̲ ̲ ̲ ̲ ̲ ̲ ̲ ̲ ̲ ̲ck of the chair. Desire ̲ ̲ ̲ ̲ ̲ ̲ ̲ ̲ ̲ ̲ ̲face.

"Then I do belie̲ ̲ ̲ ̲ ̲ ̲ ̲ ̲ ̲ ̲for us to become better

JEAN HAUGHT
PRISONER OF PASSION

ZEBRA BOOKS
KENSINGTON PUBLISHING CORP.

ZEBRA BOOKS

are published by

Kensington Publishing Corp.
475 Park Avenue South
New York, NY 10016

First printing: January, 1989

Printed in the United States of America

This book is dedicated to the memory of my best friend — my mother, Evie Eubanks. I'm so sorry for all of the times I didn't, and so grateful for all of the times I did.

Chapter One

A cool breeze rustled across the prairie and hushed whispers tittered among the cottonwood trees that lined the creek. The wind gusted, flapping the canvas that covered the huge Conestoga wagon and lightly swirling the dust from the milling horses as they cropped the sage and buffalo grass that still glistened with the early morning dew. The wind ruffled across the ground to where the young woman stood along the bank overlooking the slow-moving creek.

Thoroughly enjoying the fresh, sweet scent of the early morning, Virginia took a deep, satisfying breath. New Mexico mornings were the only time of day she actually enjoyed, since this land and climate were so different from the tall, piny woods to which she was accustomed. She basked in the refreshing coolness, knowing that all too soon the wind would blow hot and dry as it always seemed to do once the sun had climbed over the rugged horizon. She hated this sparse land and the desolate feeling that came with it.

Pulled from her reverie by the sounds of her father stumbling about in the wagon, Virginia rushed to the creek to fill the water bucket so that she could hurry and heat it over the campfire. She hoped plenty of hot water would entice him to wash and shave before they broke camp and pulled out. After his two days of hard drinking in those awful-smelling saloons in town, combined with the heat that would come later in the day, she hated to think about riding in the wagon with him if he did not wash first.

Carl Branson, a small, wiry man, shielded his eyes against the brightness of the early morning sun and climbed down unsteadily from the wagon. Glaring at Virginia, he hooked his thumbs under his trouser suspenders, stretched the elastic material, then allowed them to pop against his chest — a habit he displayed whenever he was annoyed about something. His lips settled into a thin white line and the muscles in his cheeks worked at a furious pace.

"Ginny, where in thunderation did you hide it?" he asked, his voice grating harshly.

Virginia set down the bucket of water near the campfire. She looked at him, quickly noting his bloodshot eyes, rough, whiskered face, and the angry tone of his voice. It was clearly evident he was in one of his typical foul moods. Not only was he cross from drinking too much, but he had apparently lost all of his money at the poker tables again. Any hopeful feelings quickly disappeared.

Not wanting to do or say anything to make his mood worse, she asked as casually as she could manage, "Hide what from you, Papa?"

"Don't get sassy with me, young lady," he grumbled in his usual discontented manner. "I want to know where you've hid the money."

"I wasn't being sassy." Virginia forced a calmness into her voice she did not feel as she swept back a lock of honey gold hair that had fallen across her furrowed brow. "The money is in the cigar box underneath that loose board in the wagon bed — where it is always

8

kept," she added, strongly reproachful.

His eyes narrowed and a dark expression crept over his face. "I've already looked in the cigar box! And you mean to tell me that that piddling amount is all we have to our names? Why, our merchandise is more than half gone and we only have a few dollars to show for it!"

Of that fact, Virginia did not have to be reminded. She struggled to keep control of her temper, biting back the angry accusations at the tip of her tongue. When they had left East Texas, the huge Conestoga wagon had been so full of merchandise there had scarcely been room for their personal belongings. The wagon had held piece goods, threads, ribbons, pots, pans, skillets, food flavorings, knives, harnesses—almost anything anyone on the western frontier could need or want. Now, their stock had been picked over until the best selections were gone. But what else could she expect? They had sold or traded something at nearly every farmhouse at which they had stopped. But ever since her father had traded for that homemade whiskey, he had been drinking heavily again. It never failed; every time they came to a settlement large enough to have a saloon, he would buy a bottle of cheap whiskey, then hunt a poker game. He seldom won and upon the rare occasion he did win, it was never enough to recoup his previous losses. Their money had steadily dwindled. Now, there was hardly anything left.

Spinning on his foot, Carl climbed back into the wagon and returned a few minutes later, brandishing the cigar box high above his head. "Ginny, you're lying to me! I know there was more than this in here yesterday!"

"I'm not lying, Papa. And you didn't look at it yesterday. You've been gone for *two* days, not one,"

9

Virginia staunchly reminded him, blanching at his unfair accusation, no longer caring if she made him angrier or not.

"I said not to get sassy with me, girl! You know what I meant. Last time I looked in the box there was more than this." He shook the box again.

Virginia raised her head defiantly, as if daring him to argue. Anger flared in her dark brown eyes, turning them to ebony, and her lips compressed into a tight line. "Yes, and you took most of it with you. I did spend a few dollars though. The horses were out of grain and we were out of flour and coffee."

"You mean you hitched up the wagon and drove it into town?" Furiously, he expelled a rush of air, deliberately disregarding what she had said about his taking most of the money with him. "Girl, you know better than to do a fool thing like that! Now that those town merchants have seen our traveling store, they'll be wanting us to move on, and I'm not ready to leave yet."

Part of his fear was justified. The times they had set up camp too close to the town stores, they had been asked—none too politely—to move on.

"You don't have to worry, Papa. I did not take the wagon. I *walked* the three miles to town!" Virginia lowered her gaze to hide her hurt and growing frustration over the fact that he was too concerned about the possible objections the town merchants might offer to worry about how she had managed to bring the heavy sacks of grain and flour back to their camp. Sometimes he was so unreasonable, she just wanted to throw her hands into the air and give up, but it was not in her to do that. There was still too much fight left in her.

"I see," Carl said, rubbing his whiskered chin while he appeared to think calmly about what she had said.

He walked over to the campfire and filled a cup from the coffeepot. His hands trembled so badly coffee splashed and made a hissing sound on the bed of glowing coals. Ignoring his daughter's anxious scrutiny, he sipped the scalding liquid while mulling over their financial problems.

After what seemed like an incredibly long time, Carl tossed the dregs from his cup onto the ground and walked toward where the horses were staked.

Virginia watched him with growing concern while he saddled his horse and untied two of the horses that helped pull the wagon. Just as he was about to mount his horse, she rushed to him, her brows drawn together in an agonized expression. Even though he had said nothing about his intentions, Virginia knew what he was about to do, and somehow she had to stop him.

"What are you doing, Papa? Where are you taking the horses? I thought surely we would be leaving this morning. We can't stay camped out here forever."

"I'm not ready to break camp yet."

"But . . . where are you going?"

"To town," he muttered tersely.

"Why? And why are you taking the horses?"

"To sell them."

"You can't sell them!"

Carl glared at her. "And just why in the hell not? They are mine. I'll do with them what I damn well please!"

Virginia had seldom seen her father so obstinate. She knew better than to argue when he was this adamant about something. He would just use the argument as another excuse, another reason to buy more whiskey. But she also knew she had to try to stop him from making such a terrible mistake. If he started selling off their equipment, it would be the beginning

11

of the end.

"But . . . surely you remember what the man said."

"What man?" he asked, squinting one eye.

"The man we bought the wagon from. Remember? He said a Conestoga wagon was so heavy, we would have to have either six horses or four oxen to pull it."

Carl thought about it for a moment, then disregarded her argument with a wave of his hand. "Pshaw, he meant when the wagon was loaded. And you'll have to admit, girl, it is far from being full."

Virginia made one last attempt to change his mind. "But, why do you have to sell them? We have plenty of grain. We could hitch up the wagon and push on." She blinked back tears that had suddenly threatened. "Why, in no time at all, we could be in the Arizona territory. I know the population isn't that much yet, but there aren't many mercantilists either. I'm certain we could earn enough from the goods we have left to see us all the way to California, I just know we could!"

Almost frantic now, she glanced at the horses and gestured helplessly. "Besides, you're taking the mares! What are we going to use for breeding stock when we reach California? Are you forgetting about the plans we made?"

Showing tenderness toward his daughter for the first time in weeks, Carl reached down and gently patted her cheek. "Now, quit your fretting. You need to have more trust in me. I haven't forgotten our plans. You just jumped to conclusions when I said I was going to sell them. Why, I'll buy them back before the day is over." His voice rose boastfully. "I'll also have enough money left over to fill that empty cigar box." A wide smile spread across his weathered face. "My luck has changed, girl. I can feel it in my bones. Last night I heard about the wealthy ranchers who are coming into town today. Seems they come every month just to play poker. I was told if a man had a high enough bankroll, he could sit in with them. And that's exactly what I plan to do. Now you go ahead and tend to your business and let me tend to mine." With that, he dug his heels into his horse's flanks and rode off.

"Papa, don't go! Please don't go!" she cried.

But he rode on without a backward glance. For all the attention he had paid her, Virginia might as well not have spoken. She knew everything was over, so many of her hopes and dreams had gone with him.

Completely dejected, she poured herself a cup of coffee and sat on a stool by the campfire. Tears scalded her eyes. Her father was forty-six years old, and she was twenty, but at times she felt as though their roles were reversed and she was the parent and he was the child. Once he sold those horses, he would never have the money to purchase them again. Then they would be stuck in this godforsaken place. And before long, their past would be repeated. He would once again be known as the shiftless town drunk, and everybody would judge her by his actions and deeds.

Virginia closed her eyes and wished herself a child again, when times had been good and life uncomplicated. She imagined herself standing in the shadows of the tall, whispering pines and the towering cypress trees in faraway East Texas, listening to the trill of the mourning doves, the lowing of the cow, and the chatter of squirrels as they scampered along the ground and through the trees. It was a pleasant feeling, but then those had been happy, carefree days.

With only the tiniest effort, she remembered how she used to stand on the bank of the Big Cypress River, its riverbed cutting a swath through the outskirts of town, watching and listening to the shrill screams of the riverboats' whistles just before they began their maneuvers in the Turn Basin at Jefferson. She recalled her wondrous daydreams about the *big* rivers, the Mississippi, the Missouri, the Ohio, and the magnificent paddle wheelers that navigated them, and how she had yearned to be able to see them with her own eyes.

Then, as Virginia became caught up in her past, she allowed herself to recall the other pleasant memories of her childhood.

Her father had owned a small farm and she supposed it could have been more prosperous if it had not been left to the full attention of a hired hand, but her father had been a riverboat captain by trade and their farmhouse had been merely a place to live when she and her mother were not steaming back and forth with him between Jefferson and various points in Louisiana.

The only time she could ever remember cross words passing between her parents had been when she had become old enough to go to school. Her father had not seen the necessity of a girl's attending school beyond learning how to read, write, and decipher numbers. He had claimed she could receive more of an education traveling on the riverboat than she ever could in a stuffy schoolroom. But her mother, usually a soft-spoken, gentle woman who rarely disagreed with her husband about anything, had staunchly insisted that their daughter should attend school and receive as much education as possible, even if it meant having to give up their life on the river.

But before doing anything so drastic, they were finally able to reach a compromise. It was decided that Martha and Virginia would live at the farmhouse through the school term and travel with Carl during the spring and fall. School was always closed during those seasons so that farmers' children could help with the planting and harvesting. Virginia had noticed, even at that young age, that their home did not come alive unless her father was there. With his boisterous laughter and his aura of strength, he was always the mainstay of their family. They had been so happy then.

However, that was before the freak accident that claimed her mother's life. It happened the spring Virginia was ten. The heavy winter and spring rains had swollen the river and when it finally began to recede, sandbars were left where previously there had been none. One night, on their way to Shreveport, the riverboat struck a sandbar, hard. Unbeknownst to her father, her mother had been strolling on the deck and she was thrown overboard. Her dress caught on the paddle wheel and she became trapped beneath the water and drowned.

It was almost as if Virginia had lost both parents in that tragic accident, for her father blamed himself for the death of his wife. He returned to the farm, never to set foot on another boat. As the lonely months slowly turned into years, he changed from a self-respecting, hardworking man into the shiftless town drunk. If they had not owned the small farm, Virginia doubted they could have survived. And as the years all seemed to roll together, her father became even worse. Tears glistened in Virginia's eyes at the memory.

The respectable townsfolk gradually forgot about the man he had once been and eventually came to look down on him with scorn. They noted his grimy clothing—even though she pleaded with him to bathe and change more often—his whiskered face, the smell of cheap whiskey on his breath, the way tobacco juice dribbled down his chin when he was drunk, and they would turn away in disgust. It became so bad, mothers actually threatened their naughty children with her father, referring to him as a bogeyman. And sadly, most people treated her with scorn too, even though she tried her level best to retain her pride and dignity and to show them she was different. She could seldom walk on any street of Jefferson without overhearing a snide remark or having to endure cruel children's taunts.

After she grew older, it became even worse. When other young women her age gathered at church socials or at tea parties, they would titter and giggle coyly about certain young men, but she was never included. What girl wanted to be friends with the town drunk's daughter? The few who tried were quickly discouraged by their parents. And it had been the same with the men. Oh, she had had several invitations from young men, and from a few of the older ones too, but it had not taken her long to learn what they *really* wanted. Then they had the nerve to attend church on Sundays and behave so piously! After awhile, some of the men boasted that they had been successful in having their way with her—even though they had not. Then she had had *that* to contend with too. It had not taken much gossip for her to become a fallen woman, a tramp, in the town's eyes, even though she was still innocent and had never known a man's gentle kiss.

Just thinking about the ridicule she had suffered because of her father's weakness made Virginia shudder. She pulled her worn shawl tightly around her shoulders, still lost in her deep reflection.

Not counting her mother's death, it was amazing how one other incident, seemingly unimportant at the time, had altered her life so drastically. Who ever would have thought such a simple thing as a tinker's stopping by their house one day last fall would change everything? She had had no utensils in need of mend-

16

ing, but since it was supper time, she had invited the old gentleman to eat with them. After supper, the tinker and her father had sat by the fireplace and had talked long into the night about the western lands and the many opportunities out there for the common man. She had been baking bread and had not paid much attention to them, believing their conversation to be nothing more than attempts by each man to top the other with boastful tales.

It was several days later when Virginia realized just how much her father had taken that conversation to heart. When he first began to talk about selling the farm, putting the money into a wagon and mercantile goods, and peddling their way through to California, she thought it was just another one of his drunken schemes. But the more he talked about it, the more earnest he sounded. And gradually, his idea began to make sense to her.

She had known beyond a doubt, if they stayed in Jefferson, he would always be the town drunk and she would never have a good name. And, in all likelihood, she would remain a spinster for the rest of her life. She had certainly received no respectable offers, nor was she likely to. After all, what decent man would want to marry her even if she had done nothing to deserve her reputation? But, in California, they could have a clean, fresh start, a new beginning. With all of that in mind, she soon began encouraging him to try to find a buyer for the farm.

During the time it took to sell the farm, buy a wagon, and fill it with goods, her father seemed like his old self again, and for the first time in years they were almost happy. He actually stopped drinking for several months. But when they finally left Jefferson, his sobriety barely lasted a few hundred miles. They had stopped at the house of a farmer who was badly in need of new harnesses for his mules. The farmer had no money, but he did have a five-gallon keg of homemade whiskey to trade, and that was all it had taken for her father to start drinking again. In a strange way, it was worse than ever before, perhaps because she had had a taste of what their life could have been if her father had been stronger.

Virginia stared once again at the dismal surroundings. This sprawling, desolate, desertlike land was a far cry from the exotic places she had once dreamed of visiting, but those places had been merely a child's fantasy. In spite of all her father's weaknesses, she still loved him. After all, he *was* her father. But she also doubted he would ever change and there was nothing—absolutely nothing—she could do about it. For the past few months now, she had had the strangest feeling that the so-called golden coast of California would be as elusive as the mythical pot at the end of the rainbow.

That was all they were doing, she thought sadly as tears slipped from her eyes. Chasing a rainbow. Her father would never change, and like it or not, it would be up to her to make a new life for herself—the sort of life she could be proud of.

A respectable life-style was what she wanted more than anything else. Since her father refused to change, somehow, someway, regardless of what it took, she would one day have people's respect. No one would ever have a reason to look down on her again.

Taking a sip of the coffee, she grimaced. It had grown cold, almost as cold as her heart now felt.

Giving a forlorn sigh, she muttered aloud, "I suppose there's not much sense in my sitting here feeling sorry for myself. Pitying oneself never accomplishes anything. I might as well tend to my chores and get them over with. "Who knows," she said cynically, "a miracle could happen and Prince Charming might ride up on his magnificent white horse and rescue me from this life of drudgery."

Hearing a whinny from one of the horses, Virginia turned around and blinked in surprise, then a self-conscious smile tugged at her pretty lips. "Well, well, speak of the devil," she said with a slight tinge of wonder as she saw a lone rider approaching from the distance, astride what appeared to be a white horse.

Chapter Two

Virginia's brows drew together in a puzzled frown as she searched for some kind of plausible explanation. It was a strange coincidence that she had just mused aloud about a fictional character carrying her away on a white horse, and now, out of the blue, a man was actually riding toward their camp, mounted on a *white* horse! It almost made her believe that his unexpected appearance stemmed from her wish. Shaking her head, she rejected such an idea as absurd. The man had not appeared from out of nowhere simply because of an overly active imagination. There had to be a logical reason for his presence. But still, it gave her an eerie feeling and it made gooseflesh pop up on her arms.

Her face clouded with uneasiness as she stared at the approaching rider. When he came closer, she could see black spots and blotches on the animal. "Well, at least the horse isn't completely white — that's one consolation!" she remarked, feeling a strange sense of relief.

Suddenly, the incident struck her as being extremely amusing. She seldom talked to herself and never about men or horses. She began to laugh, but her amusement was still laced with her previous cynicism. "I cannot imagine anything more romantic than being whisked away on a polka-dot horse. And more than likely my Prince Charming is a doddering old man with long gray whiskers all the way down to his knees, and he is probably as homely as sin." Sighing deeply, she feigned disappointment. "Oh, well . . . that's just my luck. Next time I will have to be certain to specify a handsome man when I conjure up a Prince Charming."

Virginia's amused expression quickly faded when the man rode into the camp. Even though his features were shadowed by the brim of his hat, it was obvious from his physique he was not old. Self-consciously, she smoothed her dress and pushed back curling tendrils of hair that had come unpinned, not as a flirtatious gesture, but as a simple feminine response to the presence of what appeared to be a reasonably handsome man.

When he spoke, she was caught completely off guard by the mellow vibrancy of his voice. "Good morning, ma'am. Name's Slade, Stephen Slade," he said, smiling his greeting while politely touching the brim of his black, flat-crowned hat.

He swung down from his saddle, pushed his hat back on his head, rested one hand on his waist, and gestured toward the creek with the other. "I saw that line of cottonwood trees and your wagon from the distance . . . and I . . ." He paused, frowning slightly at how the young woman stared at him. Her pretty face had suddenly flushed and a deeper color stained her cheeks.

Virginia realized she was staring, but she could not help herself. Undoubtedly, this was the most handsome man she had ever seen. He was tall, well over six feet, and his shoulders were so broad, she wondered if he ever grew tired from the burden they posed. The powerful muscles that rippled under his dark blue shirt quickened her pulse.

The characteristics of Prince Charming ran through her mind. They were the same qualities most women wanted in a man, and she was certainly no different. During the past few years, she had often daydreamed about the man she hoped to marry someday; he would have to be handsome, charming, but most important, a protector—a man who would take care of her, love her, treasure her, keep her safe from all harm. Until now, she had thought such a man could be found only in stories or in her imagination, because she had certainly never met a man like that, and from her past experience, she doubted one even existed. Perhaps it was merely her mood, or her imagination, yet if there were such a man in existence, it would be this man standing so nonchalantly in front of her. There was something about his manner that said he was different from any man she had ever known. That vivid impression surrounded him like a magical aura.

Judging by the way he wore his gun holster strapped low on his hip and tied to his thigh with a rawhide thong, he was obviously a western man—he just had that look about him—but not necessarily a gunfighter. She had read about gunfighters in dime novels and they always had cold, cruel eyes and such a mean look about them—and weren't eyes a mirror of one's soul? Even though this man fit a gunfighter's general description—lean, rugged features, dark, unshaved stubble on his face, a brilliant white smile, and coal black hair that curled from beneath his hat—his blue eyes were so gentle and compassionate, it seemed impossible he could be a *desperado*.

Stephen Slade, she silently murmured to herself. Why, even his name had a romantic but masculine sound to it.

Suddenly, Virginia blinked her eyes, then quickly lowered them. Her face blazed from humiliation. What in the world was she thinking? Why, he was a complete stranger! After he rode away, she would never see him again! She knew she was blushing and that embarrassed her even more. It served her right for having such foolish thoughts. Why, for a moment there, she had taken leave of her senses.

Feeling a little uneasy from her perusal, Slade shifted his weight from one foot to the other. Why was she staring at him that way? Had she recognized him? Had she seen his face on an old wanted poster? No, surely that was impossible. That had been over five years ago and, hopefully, all of it was behind him now. Then it suddenly occurred to him that her strange behavior could be stemming from apprehension. After all, he was a stranger passing through and she was a woman, apparently alone at the camp.

He began to speak softly. "Like I was saying, I wasn't sure how far it was to the next town, and since I gave my horse the last of the water this morning, I decided I should refill my canteens while I had a chance." His grin flashed briefly, dazzlingly against his sun-bronzed skin. "And, I guess, to be honest about it, I smelled your coffee long before I ever saw your wagon. Sure would appreciate a cup. I'd be happy to pay for it," he added in a sincere tone.

Virginia blushed and took a deep breath to steady her rapidly beating pulse. His request rescued her from her nonsensical thoughts. "F—Forgive my lack of manners. You are welcome to a cup of coffee . . . and you do not have to pay for it either."

She hurried to the box attached to the side of the wagon, which contained the graniteware, found a cup that was not chipped, and quickly filled it from the

23

pot.

Virginia seldom initiated conversation with anyone, much less a man, but she felt she had to do something to prevent her thoughts from returning to such dangerous ground as before. She chattered nervously. "Actually, you were in no danger of dying of thirst. Barkersville is only about three miles from here . . . but I suppose you did not know that, and like you said, a person needs to keep his canteens filled — especially out here in *this* part of the country," she added rather dryly.

Slade raised his heavy brows in surprise. "You're right. I didn't know I was that close to Barkersville. 'Bout three miles, did you say?" He blew on the coffee, then took a sip.

"Yes."

"Did I detect a note of sarcasm in your voice a minute ago? What's wrong? Don't you like this part of the country?" Slade was deliberately forcing her into idle conversation. He suspected she was a single girl, and a long time ago he had loved to tease the young ladies, enjoying their bashful giggles and their eager attempts to pretend they were grown-up. He stole a quick, appraising look at her and decided she did not have to pretend anything. She was definitely fully grown.

"No, I do not like it here!" Virginia stated in no uncertain terms.

"Then I take it you and your man are not settling here. My first impression of your camp was that you have been here for awhile." He did not really believe she was married, but he knew that by asking the right questions, it never took long to find out.

"Oh, I'm not married —" Virginia caught herself. It suddenly occurred to her she was being far too open with this stranger. It had to be obvious to him that

24

she was alone, and revealing too much about her circumstances might be a terrible mistake. She had been so caught up in her absurd daydreams, she had behaved foolishly by inviting him to stay. Just because he was handsome and had gentle blue eyes was no reason to trust him. Why, he could be a wolf in sheep's clothing, she realized and began to tremble as fearful images built in her mind.

When the girl abruptly began adding firewood to the campfire, it gave Slade the opportunity to study her more freely. He mentally wagered that the young woman was not a day over twenty. Her hair was the color of finely spun gold and her eyes were as dark as the centers of black-eyed Susans. She was so small, he knew his hands could encircle her waist; yet, even small, she did not appear to be fragile. He did not know where she had come from, but since she was unmarried, he assumed the men there must have been blind.

Nervously rubbing her hands together, she peered in the direction of town. "I don't know what could be keeping my father. He said he would be gone for just a short while." She looked at the man and stated firmly, "I'm expecting him back any minute now."

So, *he* was the cause of her uneasiness. The warmth in Slade's sudden smile was echoed in his voice. "Rest easy, ma'am. You don't have to be afraid of me."

"B—But . . . I'm n—not afraid."

"Yes you are. But I assure you, you have no reason to be frightened." He set down his unfinished cup of coffee and stood. His stance emphasized his powerful thighs and the slimness of his hips. "To put your mind at ease, I'll just be on my way."

Virginia suddenly felt ridiculous. Just because she had allowed her overly active imagination to carry her away, that was no reason to behave so rudely. If this

25

man had been old and doddering, or if she had not in her cynical mood conjured up a Prince Charming, she would never have given this man's visit another thought. He was simply a stranger passing through and there was nothing wrong with being hospitable. Besides, if he had intended to do her harm, he never would have volunteered to leave.

Pulling herself up to her full height, Virginia stated boldly, "Mr. Slade, I insist you sit right there and drink your coffee. Honestly, I'm not frightened of you."

Slade considered her offer. By rights he should mount up and ride on into town to look over the situation there. He had to raise some quick money and he had heard that Barkersville was the place to do it. But it was early in the day yet, too early for what he had in mind later on. Besides, sitting here by a nice campfire and talking with a pretty young woman was far more desirable than hanging around a saloon or being in a stuffy hotel room. He had had enough of four walls around him to last a lifetime.

"Well . . . since you insist, I'll be happy to, and by the way, I answer to the name of Slade, just Slade, that's all—no 'Mister' in front of it."

She acknowledged his statement with a pleasant smile and a nod of her head. "All right, S-Slade it is. And my name is Virginia."

"Ginny for short?" his mellow voice probed further.

"Well . . . at times my father calls me Ginny, but I prefer Virginia." Her eyes clouded with visions and cruel voices from the past. Too many children's taunts of "Jenny the mule" had ruined that nickname for her. She detested it now.

She blinked, then focused her gaze on him, pushing those unpleasant memories from her mind. This was the first time she could remember talking to a man

26

and enjoying it, and she did not want any dark thoughts spoiling their conversation. She told herself it was for that reason only as she tried to think of something witty to say.

Unable to summon forth a clever response, she picked up the coffeepot and said, "I imagine your coffee has gotten cold by now. Here, let me warm it for you." Her mind raced, for she was eager that their conversation continue. "I assume you are a stranger to these parts too?"

He held out the cup for a refill. "I've been through New Mexico before, but never this particular area." Wanting to change the subject before she had a chance to ask too many probing questions, he glanced toward the wagon. "That's a nice-looking rig your father has. It's been quite a while since I've seen a Conestoga. I thought most people traveled by railroad now." He felt safe in mentioning that. After his release from the federal prison at Fort Leavenworth, Kansas, he had sequestered himself at his brother-in-law's ranch with as many back copies of newspapers as he could find. His lips tightened at the mere thought of that hellhole of a prison and the five years he had lost from his life.

Virginia did not notice the grim expression that briefly crossed his face. "You are correct. Most people do, but the railroad is actually the purpose behind our traveling with such a large wagon. You see, we lived on a small farm in the far eastern part of Texas, and when my father decided he wanted to move to California—"

"I thought I recognized a slight Southern accent."

Accepting his statement as a compliment, she smiled and continued. "Papa bought a big wagon, not only to carry our personal possessions, but mercantile goods as well. He chose a route that was not served by the railroad, and we've been stopping at remote farms and ranches . . . just peddling our way through." Oh, how she wished it were as simple as she made it sound.

Frowning slightly, he shook his head as if genuinely concerned. "I don't want to alarm you, but since you are headed west, you ought to tell your father to be careful after you get into the Arizona Territory. There's been Apache trouble out there." He could have told her a lot more about the Arizona Apaches, especially since he was headed in that direction himself, but he had learned a long time ago not to be too free with information.

"Indians?" Her face blanched at the thought of uncivilized savages running wild on murdering sprees.

"Yes, ma'am. But from what I've heard, the army has been keeping them under control fairly well," he added quickly, after noticing the stark terror that flitted over her pretty face. "I don't want to frighten you unnecessarily, but since there is a lot of mining going on out there, if I were your father, I'd throw in with some ore wagons and travel with them as far as I could. I've heard they are always heavily armed and are seldom attacked. To my way of thinking, there is safety in numbers. Regardless, it wouldn't hurt to mention to him what I've said."

Not wanting to admit they might never travel another mile, Virginia chose her words carefully. "Thank you for the information. I'll be sure to tell him about your suggestion." Feeling slightly awkward and not knowing what else to do, she picked up the coffeepot. "More coffee?"

"Yes, please." Then he laughed. "But I suppose if I'm going to keep my conscience in good working order, I should be honest with you. You see, I wasn't entirely truthful a while ago."

Virginia's expression grew serious. "Oh?"

"What I said about not knowing how far it was to the next town was the truth, but . . . I wasn't out of water."

"Then, why did you . . . ?"

He grinned sheepishly. "I ran out of coffee two days ago, and my days don't seem to go right when I can't start the morning with several cups of good, strong coffee. When I bought my supplies, I miscalculated how much I'd need. And before you get the wrong idea, I wasn't looking for a handout. That's why I offered to pay."

He did not see the need to explain to her why he had miscalculated the amount of coffee to buy. He had always loved the taste of that hearty brew and had been limited to one weak cup a day during the time he had been in that Kansas prison. Without warning, his stomach tightened into a hard knot. He had vowed never to think about that place again, and yet it had crossed his mind twice now in the past several minutes. He was going to have to come to terms with himself about that time in his life, but one thousand eight hundred and twenty-five days filled with nothing but misery was hard to forget, especially since he was not guilty of the crime that put him there.

Virginia's dark eyes sparkled. "I think I understand. My weakness is lemon drops, but it has been quite a while since I've had any."

Slade forced a cheery tone to his voice and his smile brought an immediate softening of his features. "Now don't tell me that a pretty young lady like you isn't given candy all the time."

She blushed at his suggestion and lowered her lashes. "My father used to buy them for me often."

"Doesn't he still?"

"No, candy is for children."

29

By the tone of her voice and the shadow that flitted across her face, Slade decided it must have been a long time since she had considered herself young enough to indulge herself with candy and treats of that sort. There was something about her—perhaps an unspoken sadness—that touched him, that told him in many respects they were just alike. It was a shame the way life worked out at times. If his circumstances had been different, he would not have minded trying to put laughter in those pretty eyes of hers.

Then he shook his head slightly to clear away such thoughts. He had no business thinking about a woman, leastwise a woman like her, or *any* woman for that matter. There were too many things from his past to be resolved before he could think about the future. However, if the friend he had made while in prison had told him the truth, his future would be brighter than he had ever thought possible. But only time would tell if Ed had been lying or not.

Standing abruptly, Slade tossed the dregs from his cup. "I have enjoyed the company and coffee, ma'am, but it's time for me to push on." He touched the brim of his hat. "I'm much obliged for your hospitality."

"Wait . . . don't . . ." She colored fiercely. "I mean . . . it has been very nice meeting you." She wished for the courage to ask him to stay longer, but she knew she could not be so forward. For a few moments, she had almost forgotten that he was just a stranger passing through and she would never see him again. Suddenly, she was a woman facing the harsh realities of loneliness, and she could not help but wonder if it would ever change.

Slade started for his horse, then he stopped, spun on his heel, and, with a mischievous smile on his lips, sauntered back to where Virginia stood. Without saying a word, he ripped off his hat and, crushing her to him, he pressed his mouth to hers. Virginia was so startled, caught so unaware, she merely stood there mesmerized and accepted her first kiss without one word of protest or one move to respond.

Slade abruptly released her, ran and jumped on his horse, gave a two-fingered salute at the brim of his hat, and flashed a devil-may-care smile. "It's been a pleasure, ma'am. Don't forget to tell your father what I said about that Indian trouble."

"I — I w — won't . . . ," she finally managed to reply. But her words went unheard because Slade had already spurred his horse onward, leaving a cloud of dust in his wake.

Trembling, she touched her lips, which still burned from his fiery possession, then she slowly waved her hand and murmured a soft good-bye.

Chapter Three

Unable to sit still any longer, Virginia rose from the stool and began to pace restlessly around the camp. She opened the clasp of the pendant watch that had belonged to her mother and was amazed to see that only ten minutes had passed since she had looked at it last. But then, whenever she was this worried, time always dragged; every minute seemed as long as an hour and every hour seemed as long as a day.

Her father had been gone for five days now — five long days without hearing a single word from him. She supposed a stranger would have thought it terribly callous that she had not been overly worried until today. But back in East Texas, his long absences had always meant one of two things: either he was sleeping off too much whiskey at the home of one of his drinking buddies, or he had made a nuisance out of himself and had been thrown in jail for disturbing the peace. But now, after so much time had passed, other thoughts, other worries, had begun to nag at her. He was in a strange town and had no close friends that she knew of. And if he was not in jail, he might be sick. What if he was lying in some dark alley or beside an infrequently traveled road, too sick to call for help? What if someone had hurt him? Those were such sobering thoughts, she knew she could not sit still any longer. She would have to do something to ease her mind. But what? What could she do?

A gamut of emotions pulled at her heart. One minute she was filled with anger at her father for putting her through this needless worry, and the next minute she was afraid something terrible had happened to him. To a certain extent, it was no one's fault but her own for continuing to put up with this sort of nonsense, but what else was she to do? If she learned he had been unable to return to their camp through no fault of his own, that was one thing. But if she found him in a drunken stupor, or locked in a dirty old jail cell, that would be something else entirely. If she found that to be the case, he could just stay there until he figured out a way to be released. She certainly had no money to pay a fine.

Seeing a small plume of dust in the distance, she shielded her eyes from the sun's glare, and her heart leapt with anticipation. Could it be her father? Disappointment settled heavily upon her when she realized it was only a dust devil twisting haphazardly over the dry earth.

Virginia glanced at the timepiece again, then at the sky. Taking a deep, shuddering breath, she made a decision. It would soon be noon. She would wait fifteen more minutes and if he had not returned by then, she would go into town to see for herself what had happened to him. Needing something to do to pass the time, she unpinned her hair, brushed it, then drew it back and plaited it into one long braid.

Then she began pacing, her thoughts still on her father. Suddenly, she clenched her hands into fists and blinked the rush of tears from her eyes. "If he's on another one of his drunken sprees, I swear I'll sell two of the horses and buy a ticket on the first stagecoach out of town!"

The sun, high overhead, found Virginia marching staunchly toward Barkersville, a determined but almost fearful expression on her face.

Word of the marathon poker game had drifted around town, then out to the small surrounding farms and ranches. Before long, the area men had found one excuse or another to come into town to see if the rumors were true. Even though it was just past noon, and on a week day besides, Darby's Saloon was filled to capacity with the curiosity seekers.

Usually, the owners of the three largest ranches in the area met in Barkersville once a month, played cards for a good part of the day, then the winner would buy a round of drinks before everyone headed home. Occasionally, one or two of the more prominent local businessmen would sit in for awhile, then after a few hours they would leave the game and the ranchers would play until they became tired. But this time it had been different. When the businessmen quit, there had been two other men eager to take their chairs.

The ranchers were somewhat leery about allowing strangers to join their game. They had been suckered in by a slick cardsharp once and had learned a lesson that still galled them whenever they were reminded of it. That particular game had lasted for several days and the cardsharp had been a big winner. Finally, they had become so tired, they had agreed to take a three-hour break. However, when the game resumed, they discovered that the cardsharp was long gone and they had been cheated of the chance to win their money back. It was not the money; it was the principle of the matter. The cardsharp had made them look like fools in front of the entire town and they were not eager to have the same thing happen again.

Before they agreed to let the two strangers join their game, they laid down a few rules. If a man was losing and he decided to quit, that was fine, but if he was over five hundred dollars the winner, he would have to stay in for the duration of the game or until he was no longer winning. Also, if and when they took a break, all of the money and chips would be left on the table until the game resumed. When the strangers agreed to those stipulations, the poker game began in earnest.

After word of the high-dollar game filtered through town, men constantly drifted in and out of the saloon, curious to discover who was winning or losing. Eventually, regardless of whether it was the middle of the day or night, the poker players had a lively audience. There were even side bets among the men as to which players would last the longest, who would lose the most, and who would be the big winner. Everyone knew the game would have to end soon. The men had been playing in eight-hour stretches, then resting for two, for days now, and it was evident to everybody they were all near exhaustion.

It was only after Abe Harrison's foreman had sent a message saying there was a problem with his prize mare that was about to foal that Harrison agreed to play one final hand, then call it quits. He was reluctant to be the first man to drop out, but the mare meant more to him than any game of cards.

Abe Harrison studied his cards for a moment, then casually tossed two blue poker chips to the center of the table. "I'll see your bet and raise the limit one hundred dollars," he said to the man who had opened the betting. "And to make it more interesting, since this is my last hand, and since I am losing, I suggest

35

the limit be raised to . . . maybe five hundred? What do you men say?"

Harrison's entire manner reeked of impatience. He was a big, square-shouldered man, his hair just starting to turn, and eyes the color of steel, nose strong and wide, the nostrils in a perpetual flare. He usually gave the impression of a huge, unmovable boulder, but now it appeared that cracks had begun to etch the granite.

Justin Swandell, sitting to Harrison's left, tossed his cards face down on the table, blew a rush of air through his lips, and said, "Not me. I'm out. If you all decide to raise the limit, that's between you." He picked up the chips that remained in front of him and slid his chair back. "I'm tired. I'm going over to the hotel and sleep for a day before I head home." He glanced at his friends. "Abe, Virgil, a month from Saturday?"

Virgil Latham, sitting to Swandell's left, nodded his head and rubbed his bleary eyes. He folded his cards also. "Count me out too. I don't see any need to stay when I have nothing to draw to. Wait a minute, Justin, and I'll walk over to the hotel with you. A day's sleep before that long ride home sounds good." Standing, he added, "I'll say one thing, men—it'll be a different story next month. Why, I wouldn't be a bit surprised if I didn't go home with a couple of extra deeds in my pocket, so you had better come prepared." Chuckling over his friends' loud guffaws, he picked up his few remaining chips and walked over to the bar to cash them in.

Impatiently, Harrison looked at Carl Branson. "Well, speak up, man—are you in or out? I don't have all day."

Branson glowered at him. "Don't rush me! I didn't hurry you none when you took your own sweet time."

36

He jabbed a finger at his chest. "I dealt this hand. I have the last call and I want to have time to study my cards." Branson reflected silently that he had over a thousand dollars more in front of him than when he had first sat down. It was more than enough to give him and Ginny a good start in California, but still, he had a good hand going and the way his luck had been holding, chances were he could improve his pair of aces and treys if he called. But, if he wasn't careful, he might lose his butt and all its fixtures, because he had a feeling the betting would run high. Only thing was, would he have enough money to call if the stakes were raised?

Arching his brows, Harrison laid down his cards and drummed his fingers on the table. His manner clearly showed his irritation, not necessarily because he was a heavy loser, although that did grate at him; instead, it was obvious he had nothing but contempt for the man now studying his cards — and for good reason. There was an odor about him — sour clothes, cheap whiskey — and one could almost smell the stench of indecision oozing from his pores. He wished now that he had stood his ground and not allowed the man to enter the game. But neither he, Virgil, or Justin had believed he would be able to stay in this long.

It was evident the man was having a hard time making up his mind whether or not to call. That gave Harrison all the indication he needed. A cruel grin spread his lips. Branson must have a fair hand, he thought. A fair hand with a limited amount of money.

It was then that Harrison decided if the man called the bet he would run him out of the game. It would serve the drunk right for trying to step over the line that defined their social differences.

Finally, Branson reached a decision. An opportunity like this might never come again. "All right," he announced. "I'll agree to raising the stakes if this here man agrees too." When the man sitting to his left nodded in agreement, he reached for his stack of poker chips. "I'll call the hundred dollar bet, the hundred dollar raise . . . and I'll bump a hundred."

"I will see that and raise the pot two hundred myself," Slade said softly. His face revealed nothing to indicate how good his cards were. During the course of the poker game, he had at one time or another bluffed his way into a good pot. He had also bet heavily on several worthless hands, then revealed the cards to prove he had been trying to bluff. All of this served to keep the other players wary, to keep them from knowing when he was bluffing or when indeed he had a good poker hand.

Since a three-raise limit had been imposed on the game, the other two men called his bet.

Branson cut a chew off his plug of tobacco and popped it into his mouth. After wadding it into the side of his jaw, he glanced at Slade. "How many cards do you want?"

Slade allowed a trace of a smile to touch his lips, but it never touched his eyes. He placed a stack of chips on his cards and said, "I'll play these."

Branson raised his brows. "So, you're pat, huh?" Then he looked at Harrison.

Harrison grunted and before Branson could ask, he tossed one card, face down, to the side. "I want you to give me one—the *right* one," he added, his mouth twisting into a leering grin. He knew that that particular expression often intimidated other card players.

Branson, his cards face down, removed his top card and pitched it onto the discard stack, then added one to his hand from the deck. He picked them up and slowly spread the cards. It was all he could do to keep from smiling when he saw that he had drawn a third ace.

Then, raising his eyes, he slowly studied the other two men. There was no telling what the young gunfighter had, but a gut instinct told him the man was not bluffing this time, that he held a good hand. He was not sure about Harrison though. He had drawn only one card. If the draw had been to a straight, a flush, or a full house, Branson knew he had him beat—unless the man had made a straight flush. Yet when he considered the number of cards that had been dealt, he realized the odds were against Harrison's having made one. Branson took a deep breath, which gave him added reassurance. He had a full house, aces over, and it would be damned hard for either man to beat him.

Harrison glared at Slade, still intent on intimidating the other players as much as possible. "Do you plan on opening with that pat hand, or are you going to just sit there?" He laughed. "I'll bet you're just bluffing again."

By now, Slade was thoroughly familiar with Harrison's tactics. Coolly, his face devoid of expression, he placed a stack of blue chips in the center of the green, felt-covered table. "I guess we'll soon see, won't we? I'll open for five hundred."

Harrison shot him a hard look, studying him more closely. Then, shrugging, he counted out a stack of chips. "And I'll raise five hundred."

Branson looked down at his chips and quickly counted them. Cold sweat popped out on his face. "All I have is nine hundred." He pushed all but four chips to the side and added his chips to the larger pot. "I'm in for this."

Angrily tossing his cards down, Harrison cursed. "Damnit, either call or fold. I don't know where you came from, but we don't split the pot here. If you can't call, then you are out."

"To hell I am! You're not running me out of this game—not with me holding the winning hand." Branson turned and called to the bartender. "Darby, bring me a pencil and piece of paper."

Harrison eyed him coldly. "What for?"

"For my IOU . . . my marker."

The rancher shook his head. "Huh-uh. I only accept markers from my friends—and sometimes not even them. I don't know you. You're a stranger to me, and as far as I'm concerned, your IOU wouldn't be worth the paper it's written on. In this game it is cash money or poker chips."

Branson, his mouth dry, and with fear twisting his gut, looked at Slade. "Don't you have a say-so in this?"

Slade met his eyes. Not sounding cruel or callous, he simply stated his feelings. "I don't accept markers from men I don't know either."

The muscles in Branson's jaw worked at a furious pace. He was not beaten yet. "All right then, if that's how it is, give me ten minutes to raise the money."

Harrison started to shake his head, but something in Slade's voice stopped him when the man said, "That's a fair request."

But the rancher was still not satisfied. He caught hold of Branson's wrist as the man started to rise. "You have ten minutes to raise the money, but leave your cards right here on the table. I want them kept in plain sight."

Branson's mouth twisted angrily. "Are you suggesting I would cheat?"

"Yeah, I suppose I am," he drawled slowly.

Branson swallowed hard and shifted his eyes. He figured half the men in the saloon were Harrison's friends and it would not pay to try to make him take back his words. "How do I know you won't switch them?"

Harrison grabbed Branson's shirtfront and yanked the man toward him. "Listen to me, little man," he muttered through clenched teeth. "I could buy you with the money I have in one pocket and still have folding money left — so don't accuse me of cheating!" He roughly shoved him backward. "You have nine minutes left. I suggest you get busy!"

Harrison sat back down at the table, took a silver case from the inside of his coat pocket, removed a cigar, lit it, and watched Branson through a curling mist of gray smoke as he went from man to man, trying to raise money. "Serves me right for agreeing to let him sit in on our game. It just goes to show that's what happens when you let outsiders in. Damn bastards!" he muttered.

Slade stared across the table; he measured Harrison coldly. There were two ways a man could succeed in ranching out here in this harsh western land. Most men bought a small ranch and worked it from daylight to dark, and then some. Then there were a few who moved in and trampled over anyone who stood in their way, using whatever means they thought necessary, whether it was hired guns, poisoned water holes, or a well-thrown torch directed at a ranch house, a barn loft full of hay, or prime grazing pasture. And just by the blustering way Harrison acted, Slade could tell he had no respect for anyone but himself or men just like him — mean, strong, and ruthless.

Slade's mouth settled into a thin-lipped smile as he leaned back in his chair. Only his eyes betrayed any anger. "You know, I don't appreciate that remark. I'm not from around here either. I suppose, from your point of view, that makes me a bastard too? I guess I should have told you at the beginning, I don't like to be called names." Even though he had spoken softly, there was an implied threat in his voice.

Harrison whipped his head around and started to say something but immediately changed his mind when his eyes locked with Slade's. The big, hard-eyed rancher studied the young gunman with the same curious intensity as he had when the stranger had first joined the game. Even though he tried to push it to the back of his mind, he kept thinking about Slade's hands. They puzzled him. He had calluses on them, the kind a man developed by hard, grueling work. But the other day when the man had lit his cigar, he had detected unusual calluses that would come only from continually cocking back the hammer of a pistol. Were they old calluses or new ones? He did not think he wanted to find out by making a stupid move. In his opinion Slade was as tightly wound as a coiled snake, and he wondered just how far he could be pushed before he struck.

When Harrison spoke, his carefully chosen words did not hold fear, but they did contain caution. "You know as well as I do, you're not in the same class with him. That man is worthless scum, that's all, just worthless scum." Then he threw back his head and let out a great roar of laughter. He reached over and slapped Slade on his back. "Friend, you have grit! I can't remember how long it's been since anyone talked to me like that. For a minute there, I thought you were about to call me out." Suddenly his eyes narrowed and a harsh challenge filled his voice. "But let me give you a word of advice. Next time you want to get testy with a man like me, you should think it over—you should make sure you're not taking a bigger bite than you can chew."

Then, a shadow flickered across Harrison's face as his eyes moved to the worn but well-cared-for gun belt around the young man's waist. He slowly rubbed his chin. "Then again, maybe you did think it over." Abruptly leaning forward, he said, "I like your style. Would you be interested in going to work for me? I can always use a man like you at the Triple Bar."

Recklessly, Slade folded his arms. A part of him wanted Harrison to know he posed no threat, but another part of him wanted to lull the rancher into a feeling of false security. Since he had been released from prison, he had been practicing his fast draw, and he knew he was faster now than ever before. "Just what do you mean, a man like me? What kind of man do you think I am?"

Harrison laughed. "You know what sort of man you are. I have a feeling we are two of a kind."

Slade started to reply, but at that moment Branson returned to the table. "How tight do you have this town in your first, Harrison? No one is willing to lend me the money for fear of crossing you." He clenched his hands. "It ain't fair! Damnit, it just ain't fair!"

Harrison's mouth curled into a sardonic smile. "Quit your damned whining! Maybe it's not me, Branson. Maybe it's you. Maybe no one wants to lend you the money because they know it would be going down a rat hole, that they would never be repaid."

"But I've got collateral!"

Harrison shrugged. "So what? Collateral will not pay your way around here. If you can't raise the money, then you are out of the game." He looked at Slade, dismissing Branson without a second thought. "Now, where were we? I believe it is up to you to call . . . or to fold." He wanted to beat Slade. He wanted it badly.

Branson clutched the back of his chair, his face drained of color. He would have had to have been dead not to have realized Harrison was deliberately trying to run him out of the game.

Slade smiled indolently and turned his attention to Branson. "You said you had collateral. What kind?" Even though he believed he held the winning hand, he did not feel guilty over trying to help him raise the money. Carl Branson was a grown man and it was his business if he wanted to stay in or not. Poker was a gambling game and the man knew the risks involved.

"Now wait just a damned minute!" Harrison protested heatedly. He had not counted on Slade's accepting Branson's markers.

"You gave him ten minutes. I figure he has a few of them left. That is, unless you intend to go back on your word . . . but then maybe you are afraid he has you beat." Slade knew he was taunting Harrison and that suited him just fine.

The silence that quickly fell over the saloon was overpowering. It had been a long time since anyone had stood up to Abe Harrison, and every man in the building wanted to see his reaction.

Harrison's face darkened with rage. Neither the drunk nor the poker game seemed important any longer. Slade had pushed a bit too far. Now there was nothing he would like better than to make the smart-ass stranger eat his own arrogance. But he knew when to be cautious. It had been a long time since he had called a man out, maybe too long. His gun hand was too out of practice to make a fast draw. And only two of his ranch hands were in the saloon, and neither was fast with a gun. He realized this was not the time or the place to make a move. But later, maybe Slade needed to be taught a lesson.

Attempting to salvage as much of his pride as possible, Harrison forced a laugh. "Listen, I don't need the money one way or the other. I have lost at cards before and I imagine I will lose again. But I don't intend to sit here on my butt and jaw over a measly poker game when I've got trouble at my ranch. If you want to take the drunken son of a bitch's marker, it's your loss, not mine. But he has one minute left, so make up your mind."

Not intimidated by Harrison's one-minute deadline and eager to show his defiance, Slade did not push for information about the collateral. He counted his chips, then nodded to Branson. "Before I agree to accept your markers, do you intend to raise?" He needed to know if he would have enough money to cover both their wagers. He intended to raise again and did not want to find himself short if Harrison raised the pot the full limit.

Branson shifted his wad of tobacco from one jaw to the other, then spit a stream of tobacco juice into the brass spittoon on the sawdust-covered floor. "No, I'd like to, but I don't think it would be right, since I'd be finishing with borrowed money."

Slade quickly calculated the maximum amount of money he would need. "All right then, I'll accept your marker."

Breathing a deep sigh of relief, Branson hurriedly pulled out his chair and sat down. He looked at his cards just to satisfy himself that they had not been switched. He said to Harrison, his voice suddenly filled with bravado, "You heard the man. I'm covered. I call the raise." He added his chips to the pot. "That makes one hundred I owe you, Mr. Slade."

Slade added chips to the pot to cover what Branson was missing, then he shook his head. "No, not necessarily, because I raise four hundred more." He removed a short pencil from his vest pocket and a piece of scrap paper, tossed them to Branson, then picked up another stack of chips. "If you intend to call my raise, start writing out the IOU's."

"Wait just a damn minute!" Harrison said, his face a glowering mask of unbridled rage. Branson was forgotten as he directed his anger entirely at Slade. "Before you stop writing, there's one raise left." He quickly counted more chips. With his jaw clenched, his eyes slightly narrowed, he smirked. "I raise five hundred dollars." It would serve Slade right to lose every cent he had.

Slade never batted an eye. He merely looked at Branson and asked, "You want to call?" When Branson bobbed his head, Slade pushed the chips to the center of the table. "All right, Mr. Rancherman, the pot's right. What do you have?"

Harrison's smirking grin spread further as he revealed his cards, spreading them near the huge pile of chips. "King high straight."

Standing abruptly, Branson whooped with joy and revealed his cards. In his excitement, he knocked his chair to the floor. "I have a full house, gents! Aces over treys!" He started to rake in the pot, but Slade stopped him.

"Aren't you interested in seeing what I have?" he asked softly.

Branson's face crumbled. "B—But, I have a f—full house. Aces o—over."

Slade raised his brows and drew air through his teeth. "That's a good hand." Branson grinned and again started to pull the pot but froze when Slade added, "But it's not good enough." He slowly spread his cards in front of him. "I have four little fours."

Branson could only stand there with a numb expression on his face.

Harrison pushed back his chair and stood. The man had won the money fair and square, but he was still furious. His anger did not stem from losing—although that particular word was not part of his vocabulary. He was mad because a two-bit gunfighter had backed him down. Aware that almost every man in the saloon was watching him, waiting for his reaction, he quickly decided to shrug it off for now. He could always send some of his men back with instructions to cover the roads out of town. Then word would get around that he had taken care of Slade in his own way.

Pretending to be gracious, he said to Slade, "Well, I'll have to admit that was certainly an interesting game. If you're still around these parts when my friends and I play again, you are welcome to join us. It will give me a chance to get some of my money back."

Slade shrugged. "Who knows? I just might take you up on that offer."

"A word of advice though." Harrison nodded at Branson. "If I were you, and you intend to collect on those IOUs, I wouldn't let that fellow get too far out of sight."

"Are you saying I would run out on a debt?" Branson glared at him.

Harrison's lips formed a sarcastic smile as he answered curtly, "Yep." Then he spun on his heel and strode quickly from the saloon.

Slade turned his attention to Branson. His eyes swept over the man's patched clothing, his rheumy eyes, his stooped shoulders. He was usually not one to judge a man by his physical appearance, but Branson looked like he seldom had two coins to rub together. Slade stroked his chin thoughtfully. He wondered just how the man intended to pay off the thousand dollars in markers he now held.

Chapter Four

Slade was tired and he wanted a good, stiff drink. Even before serving time in prison, he had seldom drunk anything stronger than an occasional beer, but not being accustomed to sitting for so long at a time, he figured something stronger might help relax his tense muscles. After he settled his business with Branson, he intended to go to the hotel, order a hot bath, then sleep for a day or two before pushing on.

It was a relief that now he had enough money to repay Susie and Dale, his sister and brother-in-law, for his horse and the loan they had given him when he had been released from prison. In addition, he also had enough to pay them for what they had spent on detectives' and attorneys' fees, and for the money they had laid out for his personal needs during the past five years. Now that the worry of repaying them was resolved, he felt free to pursue the lead on that lost gold mine over in the Arizona Territory. It would probably turn out to be nothing but a wild goose chase, but Ed had been so adamant about the general location of the gold mine before he had died, that Slade was inclined to believe the man. One thing was certain: if Ed had been telling the truth, he would be set for life.

Seeing Branson leaning dejectedly against the bar, Slade called to him. "Buy you a drink?"

"Yeah," he said heavily, walking back and sitting down at the table. "I think I need one."

Slade turned in his chair to motion for the bartender and was surprised to see that the saloon had emptied so quickly. All that remained of the curious crowd were a few men sitting at two front tables, one man standing at the bar, and an old man sweeping the floor. Catching the bartender's eye, he said, "Bring us two glasses of your good whiskey."

Darby reached under the highly polished bar and pulled the cork on a full bottle. He filled two shot glasses, then walked quickly to the table and set them down. When Slade attempted to pay, the man waved his money aside. "Nope, your money's no good in here. Haven't done this much business since . . . well, I don't rightly know. And I figure I owe a good part of that to you."

"Oh?" Slade had too many things on his mind to be interested in the bartender's idle chatter, but he half-heartedly listened out of courtesy.

"Not all of those men came in to see that poker game." The bartender chuckled. "Some of them came in to see if you would shoot Abe Harrison or if he would shoot you before it was all over with. 'Course it's just my opinion, but I think most of 'em were hoping you would draw on him."

"Why? I thought he was a respected rancher?" Slade's interest was suddenly piqued.

"I suppose he is, but that don't make him well liked in these parts. Oh, don't get me wrong. Folks show him proper respect, all right, but they stay clear of him . . . just like they would a grizzly or a wild bull. And if by chance you don't know it, you really riled

Abe Harrison."

"That's his problem for having such a short temper," Slade replied indifferently and shrugged his shoulders."

"No, sir, it might be yours."

"How's that?"

"People don't make Abe Harrison mad and get by with it."

"Hell, I didn't say *that* much to him." Slade's voice did not sound concerned. He was merely making a statement of fact.

"It's not necessarily what you said. It's what you did." Darby began counting off on his fingers. "One: you beat him playing poker. He'd never admit it, but that man can't stand to lose . . . at anything. Two: you crossed him by accepting this man's marker. Harrison's used to having his way about *everything*. When he says, 'Jump,' everybody in these parts asks, 'How high?' Three: you weren't scared of him, and that galled him no end."

Slade snorted with disgust. "Harrison sounds like a loveable cuss."

The bartender leaned closer and lowered his voice. "You can take my advice with a grain of salt, 'cause advice is cheap. But if you're planning on hanging around for awhile, watch your step . . . and watch your back. If you're planning on leaving, I'd wait 'til some dark night, and I'd be damned careful which road I took out of town. Men who cross him have a way of . . . well, let's just say they have a way of meeting with accidents. Some are fatal; some are not. Regardless, Harrison always finds a way to get even with somebody who's crossed him."

Slade thought about what the bartender had told him, then he said slowly, "I appreciate your advice."

"There's just one other thing, mister." The bartender shifted his weight uneasily and it seemed as though he could not quite bring himself to meet Slade's eyes. "If by chance this conversation gets back to Mr. Harrison, I'll deny it ever took place. Sorry, but that's how it is. I have my business to think about." Having said his piece, he slowly ambled back to the bar.

"What he said doesn't seem to worry you any," Branson remarked, studying Slade's stony features. Reluctantly, he had to admit there was just enough arrogance about the man to command a certain amount of respect.

Slade gave an impatient shrug. "I try to deal with one problem at a time. Right now I'm concerned about these markers I'm holding on you." His blue eyes narrowed and hardened. "Might as well ask straight out, how and when do you intend to pay me back?"

Not wanting to make this man mad at him, Branson formed his answer carefully. "I'm sure you realized when you agreed to take my markers, I don't have the cash, so you're going to have to give me a little time to raise it."

"How much time?"

Branson rubbed his chin thoughtfully. Considering what he had overheard the bartender telling Slade, if he could stall, put him off for awhile, Harrison himself might solve his problem. And just maybe there was something he could do to help matters along. The way he saw it, it would be damned hard for a dead man to collect on a debt.

Slade's eyes were flat, hard, expressionless. "I guess you didn't hear me. How much time do you need?"

"Well, let's see now, I figure . . . uh . . ." He glanced toward the door, looked back at Slade, then he whipped his head around and stared hard at the slight figure standing just inside the doorway. "Oh hell, I've had it now!" he grumbled, sliding down in his chair as if trying to hide under the table. "If she sees me, she's going to give me what for!" Then he remembered all of the false promises he had made to Virginia and he swallowed hard. "For once, I reckon I'm going to deserve everything she has to say . . . and then some."

Slade turned to discover whom Branson referred to and was surprised to see the attractive young woman he had met a few days before on the outskirts of town. "You know that young lady?" he asked.

Branson snorted. "I reckon so. She's my daughter."

"I see," he said slowly, pretending to redirect his attention to his glass of whiskey. He never would have figured that soft spoken young woman to be Branson's daughter, and he never would have thought she would be the sort to walk brazenly into a saloon. Decent women did not enter saloons, but then most women didn't have fathers like Carl Branson either.

The bartender started toward the young lady, ready to protest her presence, but something in her expression stopped him.

Virginia patted her wet brow with her handkerchief as she stood near the doorway looking frightened and unsure of herself. Her eyes squinted as she made a slow search of the dimly lit saloon. Relief was evident on her face when she saw her father sitting at a table in the far corner of the room.

She rushed toward him. "Papa! I've been looking everywhere for you!" So greatly relieved was she that he had come to no harm, her first instinct was to run and throw her arms around him. Then anger stabbed like a sharp pain and her hurried steps slowed as she realized he was sitting at a poker table calmly drinking whiskey as though he had no care in the world.

A glazed look of despair had spread over Virginia's face by the time she finally reached the table. For a moment she could not trust herself to speak, but when she finally found her voice, it was laced with the terrible fear and worry she had suffered during the past five days. "Where have you been, Papa? Why didn't you send word to me? Didn't you realize I would be half out of my mind from worry?"

Not one to admit he was in the wrong, Branson avoided her accusing eyes. He muttered darkly, "Girl, don't speak to me in that tone of voice! And you know better than to come into a place like this. I'll not have your reputation sullied this way. Get on back to the camp and I'll be there directly. Now go on, get!" He waved her away with his hands. "I've got to attend to some business here."

Virginia's expression was one of incredulity. Her facial color turned from ash to a mottled crimson. "You mean after all these years you are *finally* worried about my reputation?" It's never concerned you before. Why should you start now?"

Carl roughly grabbed Virginia by her arm and jerked her toward him. "Hush your mouth! And I told you not to use that tone of voice with me, young lady! I am your father and you will show me due respect. Why, you will give folks the notion that I haven't gave you proper raising." He added between clenched teeth, "Now get on back to the camp before you make me lose my temper!"

Slade's hand tightened on his whiskey glass. He wished he were somewhere else. This altercation was between father and daughter, but still it galled him for a man to treat a woman in such a way. However, Branson was her father and she shouldn't speak to him in that manner.

Wrenching her arm from his grasp, Virginia stood

with arms akimbo and glared at her father. Never in her life had she been so angry. "Why should you care now what people think? You haven't given it a second thought in . . . how many years now, Papa? You haven't raised me—I've raised myself! When Mother died, I lost my father too . . . because you were too busy wallowing in a whiskey bottle!"

"That's enough, Virginia!"

"No, it isn't enough!" All of the hurt and frustration that had been bottled up over the years came pouring out. She gestured with a sweep of her arm. "Tell me, just who are you trying to impress with your sudden fatherly concern? The man standing at the bar? The bartender? Or this man here?" Her voice caught in her throat as she recognized Slade when she pointed to him. Her mouth went dry and her knees began to tremble. Naturally, her concern had been centered on her father, but why hadn't she noticed him before now, especially since the memory of him—and his stolen kiss—had invaded her mind several times over the past few days.

For a brief moment, their eyes locked and held, then Slade lowered his gaze, but not before he had seen the anguish and despair that lurked in the dark shadows of her eyes. Just a minute ago, he had thought her behavior terrible, but now he was not so sure. The Good Book said that children should honor their mother and father, and while he was not about to argue with that, it seemed to him that a father should also treat his children honorably. In his opinion, that meant respect too. But how could someone respect a man who did nothing to deserve it? Suddenly, Slade wished he had never met Carl Branson.

Branson glared at Virginia. "I'm not going to tell you again to hush your mouth," he warned.

Virginia spoke quite coldly. "All right, Papa, I'll

hush . . . and I'll go back to the camp. But when I get there, I will break camp, harness what horses are left, and hitch them to the wagon. Then I will pull out. If you are back by then, fine; if not, then I'm leaving without you!"

"You can't do that!"

"Oh yes I can, and I will!"

Not for one minute did Branson doubt his daughter would make good her threat, and what was worse, he really could not blame her. He knew how much she had been counting on going to California. It was all she had talked about for months now. And not only did he have her threats to worry about, but there was Slade to consider too. He had noticed how the man wore his gun strapped low on his hip. Hell, a man would have to be blind not to recognize him as being fast with a gun, he told himself. There was no way he wanted to tangle with him, and if Virginia did leave with the wagon, there was no telling what Slade would do when he found out he could not redeem his IOUs. Branson swallowed hard. It was something he did not even want to consider.

"You can't do that, Virginia," he repeated, only this time his voice held a desperate plea.

Unconsciously, her brow furrowed and she tilted her head. His tone had sounded so resigned, so beaten. It was unlike him. "Why not, Papa?"

Awkwardly, he cleared his throat, then, staring at his hands, he spread his fingers wide apart before clenching them into tight fists. "Because I don't have a cent left to my name and this man is holding a thousand dollars worth of my IOUs. If you take the wagon and the goods that are in it, I'll never be able to raise the money to pay him. Besides . . . you can't leave me all alone."

Slade squirmed uncomfortably in his chair. He did

not like the way Branson was placing him right smack in the middle of their problems. But still, he could not help but wonder why the fool had not stopped to think about the possible consequences his gambling would cause.

Virginia glared, burning and reproachful, at her father. Then the misery that washed over her became so acute, it actually felt like a physical pain. Tears suddenly blinded her as she grasped the chair for support. Dear Lord, what were they going to do now? How could her father have gambled away everything they owned without even considering her feelings? Her mouth moved, but no words came. She felt her knees grow weak, then the room started to spin.

Realizing the young woman was about to faint, Slade leapt from his chair and hurried to catch her before she could slump to the floor. "Bartender, bring the lady a glass of water, and a damp cloth!" he shouted, easing her gently onto a chair.

Virginia came to her senses as soon as Slade caught her. It was as though another human's touch had brought her back to consciousness, and just for a instant she resented it. Why couldn't he let her escape the painful reality, however briefly? Then, she felt searing shame for being so weak. It was humiliating that anyone should see her this way. Realizing his hand was still on her shoulder, she shrugged it away, ignoring its gentle touch. "I'm all right. J—Just leave me alone for a minute and let me collect my wits. I don't . . . know what came over me. I . . . I . . ."

Glancing toward the bar, Slade tightened his lips when he saw the bartender peering out the window. "Hurry up with that water and damp cloth! This lady needs it now!"

The man ran toward the table, his white apron flapping. "Sorry, Mr. Slade." He looked at the man warily as he set the glass on the table.

"Here, lean your head forward and press this cloth against your brow," Slade said, taking the cloth from the bartender and handing it to Virginia.

Tapping Slade on his shoulder, the bartender said, "I need to talk to you for just a minute — in private — and I need to talk to you now." Frowning, Slade followed him.

As soon as they were out of hearing distance of the table, the bartender said, "I may be seeing trouble where there ain't any, but three of Harrison's men just tied their horses to the hitching post in front of the saloon. He hasn't had time to get to his ranch yet, so he might have met them on the road. If that's the case, more than likely he's sent them in to see you . . . or to get you, 'cause they're his best hands. What I mean by that is, they are his fastest hired guns." He cleared his throat and shifted awkwardly. "To be frank about it, Mr. Slade, I believe there is trouble brewing and I can't afford to be caught in the middle of it. The way I see it, you're just a drifter passing through . . . and I live here. And I can't afford to have my saloon shot up either."

Slade nodded. He could not blame the man for feeling the way he did. And as for the bartender's sensing trouble, the hair on the nape of his neck had started to crawl — a sure sign of trouble developing — even before Harrison had left the saloon. "I'll be leaving in just a few minutes. I won't be the cause of trouble in here."

Darby scratched his head and muttered, "All right, I guess that's fair, but you won't have to do anything to cause trouble. Just your presence here is enough."

On his way back to the table, Slade quickly considered his options. Since Harrison's men were already in town, he would have to make some quick but careful moves if he was to stand a chance of collecting a portion of those markers he held. But if Harrison became too pushy, he might have to forget about them. Yet, before he wrote off a thousand dollars, he would at least try. It stabbed at his conscience that if he did manage to collect the money, it would be the young woman who suffered, not Branson. But still, a debt was a debt and the man owed it to him. And *he* owed it to his sister.

It also did not sit well with Slade that he was strongly considering slipping out of town. Normally, he would have stood his ground and dared someone to try to take what was his. But with his prison record, and being in a town that Abe Harrison held tightly in his fist, he would be a fool not to avoid trouble if at all possible. Now he knew how a raccoon felt that had just been treed by a pack of well-trained hounds.

Slade's mouth tightened when he neared the table and overheard Branson berating his daughter further for looking for him. Feeling sorry for her, he placed his hand gently on her shoulder and asked, "Are you feeling better now, ma'am?"

When she slowly raised her eyes to meet his, tears trembled on her thick, sooty lashes, and she hastily reached up and brushed them away. He knew then that she was trying hard to be brave, but it must have taken every ounce of willpower and courage she possessed. He silently cursed Branson.

"Y—Yes, I think so." She pulled her gaze from his, as color stained her cheeks. The man's careful scrutiny made her feel even more uncomfortable. "I'm s—sorry. I—I apologize for my behavior. I'm usually not the sort of person to create a scene or make such a fool out of myself by almost fainting."

Slade, while worrying his bottom lip, closely studied her. It was obvious she was not like most of the women he had known. This girl had grit and back-bone and he admired her for it. But, even the strong had their limits and he wondered just how close to that limit she was.

Struggling for control of her emotions, Virginia gestured with her hand for him to join them. "Please sit down, Mr. Slade. Perhaps we can discuss this . . . this problem and reach terms that are agreeable." After Slade sat down, she took a deep breath and continued. "My father was wrong to ask you to accept his gambling markers—"

"Now just a gol-durned minute, Ginny! There you go, meddling in my business again!"

She numbly looked at him and said, "Papa, I believe it also happens to be my business. What you did will affect my life too."

Slade gave Branson a cold look. "I want to hear what she has to say. All I was getting out of you were hem-haws and stammers. Go ahead, Miss Branson."

"I—I'm sure my father will admit that he sometimes drinks a little . . . more than he should, but that does not make him less honorable. . . ."

Branson sat a little straighter in his chair. Maybe he should let Ginny speak for him more often.

It was all Slade could do not to snort from disgust. Honorable, hell! He'd lay odds the only honorable Branson sitting at the table was the young woman.

"However, even the most honorable sometimes find themselves in an embarrassing situation. To be blunt, Mr. Slade, we have no money. . . ." Her voice trailed off when she realized she had lost the man's attention. Turning slightly, she saw three dangerous-looking men walking toward the bar, and she also noticed that Slade's eyes were riveted on them.

Slade could sense impending trouble. Whether or not they intended to jump him in the saloon, he did not know; but he had to do or say something to keep them off his back for awhile. Either he had to keep the men occupied or create some kind of disturbance.

Then, suddenly, an idea struck him. He looked at Virginia and said, "Look, there is a time and place for everything. Even though we need to get this settled, this is not the place. I don't like everybody knowing my business and I'm sure you don't either. Why don't we ride out to your camp where we can talk this over in private?"

He knew collecting on the markers was now out of the question, but he could not afford to get into trouble right now, and he would if he stayed much longer in Harrison's town.

She nodded her head eagerly. Her pride had been damaged enough, and she certainly did not want the people in the saloon overhearing the details of their latest financial predicament. The Branson name had been dragged through the mud on too many occasions, and she hated to add more fuel to such gossip. "I think that is a very good idea . . . don't you, Papa?"

"Yeah, I suppose so," he mumbled indifferently.

Slade helped Virginia from her chair and together they walked toward the door. He was extremely conscious of how the three men watched every move he made. "Just a moment," he said to the Bransons. "Let me make some arrangements before we leave."

Slade then stepped over to the bar, deliberately selecting a spot close to the three men. He leaned forward as if to take the bartender into his confidence, yet he spoke in a voice loud enough to enable the men to easily overhear everything he had to say. "Darby, I wonder if I could ask a favor of you." He hoped the bartender would realize what he was trying to do.

"That depends," he said, throwing a nervous glance at Harrison's men.

"It looks like I figured Branson wrong. Apparently he will be able to pay something now on these IOUs I'm holding on him, or rather his daughter will. But it's stashed somewhere out at their camp. Only thing, you know how long that poker game lasted and I'm dead on my feet. I need to go check into the hotel so I can get some sleep, but I'm afraid if I don't ride out with the Branson's now and collect the money, they won't be here when I wake up." He shrugged. "Hell, to be frank about it, I really don't want to let them out of my sight."

Darby frowned. "I wouldn't trust him any further than I could throw him either, but what is it you want me to do?"

"I was wondering if you would send your man over to the hotel, rent a room for me, and instruct them to have plenty of hot water ready when I get back." He reached into his vest pocket and removed a twenty-dollar gold piece and slid it across the bar to Darby. "This is for your trouble. Tell them to have the bath water ready in about . . . three hours. I figure that should give me plenty of time."

His intuition told him the men would not follow him if they thought he was coming back. But if they did follow, and they forced him into a showdown, there would be less likelihood of an innocent bystander's getting hurt than there would be here in town. More than likely though, the men would wait until they could catch him sound asleep or helpless in a bathtub. At least that was what Slade hoped they would do. Then if they followed him, he would have the advantage of a three-hour headstart.

"Why, sure. I reckon I can."

Slade smiled. "Good! I certainly do appreciate it."

The bartender chuckled, obviously amused over the clever way Slade was getting out of this tight spot. "No problem. Won't be any trouble at all."

Slade favored him with a slow grin, knowing Darby would catch the double meaning of his words. "That's sort of how I figured it." He touched the brim of his hat. "Be seeing you, friend."

Chapter Five

Virginia was beginning to think Stephen Slade never would finish his business with the bartender. Just look at him. He certainly doesn't fool me anymore, she thought. Strutting around so cocky and arrogant, pretending to be so noble, but he isn't. And I was foolish enough to think he was different. It doesn't matter to him that my life has been destroyed. He doesn't care! All that matters to him are the markers he is holding. And it wouldn't surprise me in the least if he claimed everything Papa owns; then he'll probably turn us out with just the clothes on our backs. I'm sure that's why he wants to discuss this out at the camp. He doesn't want everybody to know how ruthless he is. She bit her lip until it throbbed like her pulse.

Men! Men! Men! She hated them! In one way or the other, they always seemed to be the major cause of her problems. Even during these modern times when women were free to do and say anything they pleased, if a woman had the nerve to complain, her behavior was considered disgraceful. In fact, if a woman did anything that did not meet with a man's approval, she was treated like a fallen woman. That was just what had happened a short while ago when she had come into the saloon looking for her father—who had been missing for five days. The men acted as though she had committed a crime by invading their sacred domain. One of these days things would change and women would no longer be at their mercy. She found that thought very gratifying.

But deep down, Virginia knew she was lashing out and placing blame unfairly. It was so unlike her, but she was tired of trying to be reasonable. Just as she was tired of having to pay the consequences of other people's foolish mistakes.

Then, because her emotions were in such turmoil, her thoughts turned in a completely different direction. With huge dark eyes, she stared miserably at her father.

Oh, Papa, she silently cried. Why did you do it? *Why?* Surely you must have known you risked losing everything we owned! She threw a quick, accusing glance at Slade. And of all people, why did it have to be *him?* Then, she immediately felt ashamed of her thoughts. She could not in good conscience hold him responsible for her father's deeds. No one had held a gun to her father's head and forced him to gamble away everything they owned.

But still, why did *he* have to be the man involved? Her face colored fiercely as she remembered all of the vivid daydreams she had had about him. Now, those memories would be mixed with this terrible nightmare. Her father's foolish actions had destroyed not only her real hopes but her fantasies as well.

Finally, much to Virginia's relief, Slade left the bar and escorted them outside. Then, wordlessly, they began to make their way up the boarded walkway.

As they walked along, Slade had to shorten his long stride so that Branson and the girl could keep up with him. For that, he was glad. He did not want it to appear he was in too big a hurry to leave town. Only one man had followed them out of the saloon, which was a good sign, and he did not want to do anything to heighten his suspicion. But, whether he raised suspicions or not, he wanted to stop by the bank and make arrangements to send what he owed to Dale and Susie. That way, if Harrison's men did get the jump on him, he would have that obligation taken care of.

"I need to attend to a little business at the bank before we pick up our horses at the livery stable," Slade remarked casually.

Carl Branson's mouth twisted into an ugly grimace at the thought of all that money Slade was carrying in his pocket, money that should have been his. Then he glanced uneasily at his daughter. He had never seen her this mad before, and after she found out what else he had done, there was no telling what she would do.

Trying to delay the inevitable, Carl said, "Don't you realize my daughter just walked three miles to town?" He peered defiantly at Slade as if daring him to disagree. "Since you're in such an all-fired hurry to settle out business, I think you should be the one to rent a buckboard so she won't have to make that long walk again so soon."

Virginia glanced sharply at her father. How could he behave in such a beggarly fashion? Where was his pride? Swallowing her anger, she managed in a crisp tone, "Renting a buckboard is not necessary, Mr. Slade. My father and I can ride double on his saddle horse."

"No, we can't."

"I don't see why not, Papa. We've done it many times before."

"I said no, we can't!"

"Why?"

He had the grace to mutter somewhat sheepishly,

"Because I don't own ol' Pete anymore."

She stopped and stared incredulously at him. "You mean you sold Pete too?"

"Yes, I did," Carl answered, regret filling his voice for the first time. Pete had been his wife's horse. She had raised him from a colt. Frustrated, he slammed his fist into his open palm. Damn! Everything that happened was this gunslinger's fault! he told himself. If Slade hadn't accepted his markers, he wouldn't be in this situation now. His eyes narrowed and took on a suspicious gleam. Now that he'd had time to think about it, it seemed awfully strange that Slade had taken his side against that fancy rancher. Maybe it wasn't so strange though. Maybe Slade had somehow known he had the best poker hand. 'Course, he hadn't actually seen the man cheat, but some fellows were mighty slick handed when it came to cards.

Virginia swallowed the lump that rose in her throat and her stomach lurched violently. When would this horrible nightmare end?

The corner of Slade's mouth twisted with contempt. Though he was aware that everything Branson had done so far had been foolish, selling his horse, especially in a land with such wide open spaces, showed nothing but sheer stupidity. He glanced at Virginia. If his daughter had any sense at all, she would carry through with her threat to pull out and leave him behind. Slade believed that if Carl Branson would do this once, he would do it again. Of course, they had no idea he was merely going through the motions of collecting on those IOUs. However, if Harrison's men had not been on his tail, it would have been a different story. But even then, though Branson was a good-for-nothing, he never would have been able to take everything they owned, regardless of the fact that he had won it fairly.

Shaking his head in disgust, Slade stalked into the bank, his movements stiff with anger. After transacting his business, he came back outside, almost hoping Branson had taken this opportunity to flee, but he and his daughter stood right where he had left them. By the taut expression on the girl's face, he could tell they had had a heated argument while he was gone. Without saying a word, Slade started walking. Carl and Virginia fell in behind him.

"Well? Have you made up your mind? Are you going to rent a buckboard or not?" Carl asked impatiently when they reached the livery stable.

Virginia's face blazed hot with humiliation. "Papa, no . . . we have already discussed this! I told you I am quite capable of—"

"Hush, girl." His grip tightened on her arm. "We need a buckboard. 'Sides, I'm feeling poorly myself. Don't know if I could make that long trip on foot or not."

Slade's voice held an undertone of icy contempt as he flashed the young woman a pitying look and said, "That's all right, ma'am. I don't mind renting one for you. You can wait here. I'll make the arrangements and be right out."

After Slade disappeared into the stable, Virginia yanked her arm from her father's grasp. She turned on him furiously. "Papa, if I live to be a hundred, I'll never forgive you for what you've done!"

He grabbed both her arms and shook her. "I've had just about enough of your lip! I'll admit I was wrong to risk losing everything, but I had a good hand, Ginny. A damned good hand," he added in his whining voice.

"Yes, of course you did. That's why we are in this predicament," she replied coldly. Deep down inside, she had known this day of reckoning would come sooner or later. Why, then, did she feel so devastated? It was as if someone had squeezed the life out of her heart. It really was not just the loss of their material possessions; it was the realization that she now stood at a crossroads that would change the direction of her life. She did not know which way she would go or what she would do, but one thing was certain—she would definitely make a change!

Carl sighed heavily. "It doesn't matter now, does it? The point is, if I'm to have any hope of salvaging anything out of this, you're going to have to help me."

Astonishment transformed her pale face. Again, he was depending on her to pull him out of trouble while not allowing her a voice in making any decisions. "What makes you think there is something I can do to help?"

Swallowing hard, Carl grasped at what he considered to be his last straw. "Ginny, you are a right pretty girl. And from the way that man looks at you, he thinks so too. Now if you were to sidle up to him, flirt with him a bit, he might be inclined to forget how much I owe him."

Her brown eyes widened and her back became ramrod straight. A startled gasp escaped her and she wrenched herself from his grasp again. "I can't believe you would ask your own daughter to do something as despicable as that!"

His voice held a desperate plea. "If it weren't so important, I wouldn't. But you have to help me, Ginny . . . you just have to! If you do, I—I promise I'll never take another drink or gamble again. I k— know I've made that promise to you before, but this time I mean it! I swear I do!"

His promise came as no surprise; he had made the very same one often enough in the past. But the request he made with it was terrifying. *Just sidle up to him, flirt with him,* he had said. She had no intention of doing what he asked. But just suppose she did? Then, what in God's name would he ask her to do the next time he broke his promise?

The question died on the tip of her tongue when Slade, leading his horse by the reins, came from the livery stable, followed by a young boy walking out a horse harnessed to a small carriage.

"The man didn't have a buckboard available so I had to rent a carriage. You'll have until tomorrow to return the rig. If you keep it longer, you will have to pay the additional fee," he told Carl. "And I did make it clear to the owner that you are the man responsible," he added.

Carl's mouth twisted into an unpleasant grin. "What's the matter? You afraid I'd run off with the rig?"

For just a moment, Slade's eyes darkened. "I figured it might be a strong possibility."

Carl muttered something unintelligible, then climbed into the carriage without offering to assist his daughter, which did not surprise Slade. Glowering at Branson, he dropped his horse's reins, then placed one hand on Virginia's waist and the other on her hand.

"Here, let me help you."

The heavy lashes that shadowed her cheeks flew up as something intense seemed to flare through her. Once, while doing day work for a lady in Jefferson, she had walked across a wool rug in her stocking feet, then had touched something metal and it had shocked her. His touch had caused the same strange sensation. And judging by Slade's startled expression, he had felt it too. Even under these terrible circumstances, she once again found herself extremely conscious of his virile appeal.

"T—Thank you," she finally managed to murmur. Her head spun as if caught in a gigantic whirlwind. Regardless of what was happening, she was still attracted to him. Why? There was no logical explanation for it. After the day's end or tomorrow at the latest, she would not be seeing him again. Even if he were to remain in Barkersville, she would rather die than stay on as well. And if, Heaven forbid, something happened to force them all to remain there, he certainly would not want to have anything to do with her—not after everything that had taken place. Besides, her pride would never allow it. Virginia's bottom lip trembled as she struggled to bite back her futile feelings of helplessness.

Except for the turmoil of Virginia's agonized thoughts, the ride to their camp was uneventful. Slade rode beside the carriage, and every so often she could feel his eyes on her, as if studying her, but she deliberately kept her gaze riveted straight ahead. She felt as though she were teetering on an emotional cliff. One wrong glance or word might send her over the edge. Later, when she was alone, she would give in to her emotions, but for now she had to remain in control or she would never be able to face the ordeal that lay ahead.

Slade had already dismounted and stood waiting, his legs splayed and his arms folded, presenting a formidable figure, by the time Carl brought the carriage to a stop. Not wanting Slade to touch her again and knowing her father would never offer to help her, Virginia quickly climbed down from the carriage on her own.

Trying to alleviate the heavy tension that hung over them, Virginia masked her inner turmoil with a deceptive calmness and declared, "I can tell just by looking, both of you are completely exhausted. Would you

70

like me to make a pot of coffee? And I baked sweet rolls this morning in the Dutch oven." Now why did I say that? she wondered. I sounded like a babbling idiot. After all, this is far from being a social call.

Slade shook his head. "No, ma'am. Thank you though; it was nice of you to offer. I'd rather settle this so I can be on my way." He removed his hat and ran his fingers through his thick black hair. "Miss Branson, I've been thinking, trying to figure out a reasonable way to handle this, and naturally I remembered our conversation from the other day. . . ."

"You met Virginia earlier?" Carl interrupted, squinting one eye thoughtfully.

"Yes, before I rode into Barkersville." He deliberately directed his attention back to Virginia. "Like I was saying, I remembered our conversation—"

"Ginny, I don't think I like the idea of your entertaining men when I'm not here."

Virginia's embarrassment turned to raw fury at his innuendo. "Oh, Papa, I was not entertaining him! He merely stopped for water. . . ."

"Sure he did, and him only three miles from town." Carl rolled his chew of tobacco from one jaw to the other, then asked sarcastically, "Tell me, Slade, did you think you would die of thirst before you traveled those three miles?" A satanic smile spread across his thin lips. "I want to know just what in the hell went on out here."

"Papa!" Virginia protested, mortified.

Slade's blue eyes narrowed and an unamused chortle escaped him. "I know what you are trying to do, Branson, and it isn't necessary to slander your daughter's name or mine. You know as well as I do, she is a decent woman—only I'm not sure where she got that quality, because she damn sure didn't get it from you!"

Slade had intended only to fill his canteens and

71

obtain a few supplies from them, then move on. But after hearing Branson's insinuations, he decided the man needed to be taken down a notch or two. "After I found out you were her father, for *her* benefit, I was just going to forget about those IOUs," he explained. "However, after those remarks you made, you can forget about my being generous." He wagged his finger in Branson's face. "You are going to pay me every dollar you owe me!" He glanced at Virginia. "I could lay legal claim to everything you own, but for her benefit, I won't. It would hurt her more than it would you, because you don't give a damn about anything. I'm going to say this only one time, so you had better listen well. The other day she told me you were on your way to California, and from my impression, you intended to make a fresh start."

Carl tried to interrupt, but Slade would not let him. "Shut up. I'm not through talking! I'm going to give you a second chance. You don't deserve it, but I'm giving it to you anyway. You go on to California, and in six months time I had better have a payment, and I had better receive future ones on a regular basis, because if I don't, I'll track you down and take it out of your worthless hide! But before I let you go, I want a bit of added insurance. I want signed papers stating I own the horses." Slade, hoping the young woman would understand he was doing this for her, added a final warning. "I figure by doing that, you might think twice about selling them or losing them in another poker game. Out here, a tall tree and a stout rope have a strange way of discouraging one man from selling another man's horse!"

Carl swallowed hard. He was too scared to say a word. He merely stared at Slade.

Virginia was not the least bit upset over the way Slade had spoken to her father. Strangely enough, his threats had made her feel good. Perhaps he had even managed to put a fear into her father that would cure his thirst for whiskey and his need to gamble. Then too, she felt awed by the fact that Slade was really giving him a second chance because of his consideration for her. No one had ever done anything like that before.

"Now do you have any questions? Did I make myself clear?"

Carl quickly shook his head. "N — No, no questions. I understood every word you said."

"But I have one," Virginia said softly. "Where are we supposed to send the payments?" She ignored the reproachful look her father shot her.

He shrugged. "I plan on moving around for awhile, so I'll give you my sister's address, and when you get settled somewhere, he can start repaying me through her. But before we go any further, I want to make it clear that it isn't your responsibility to pay me; it's your father's."

"Yes, I know."

Carl looked at Slade skeptically. He was not the type of man to be satisfied leaving well enough alone. "Why are you suddenly being so agreeable?"

"It's my business what I do," he stated coldly. Then he turned to Virginia. "Ma'am, if you don't mind, would you pack me a small sack of supplies? Enough for three or four days would be fine."

"Why, yes, of course I will."

Carl peered at Slade through thoughtful eyes. Now that a few minutes had passed since Slade had issued those demands and had damn near scared him to death to boot, his courage was returning. There was something about what Slade had said that did not sit right with him. After Virginia disappeared into the wagon, he asked, "Why do you need supplies if you have a hotel room waiting for you back at Barkersville? Aren't you going back?"

"I just told you, what I do is my business."

"I don't think you ever intended to go back," Carl said slowly. "And it seems to me you're in a bit of a hurry to be on your way."

"Maybe it's the company I'm with," Slade retorted.

"Does your tucking tail and running have anything to do with Abe Harrison?"

Slade flashed him a contemptuous look. "I wasn't aware I was tucking tail and running."

"That's it, isn't it?" Branson chuckled. "Why, you are scared of Harrison!"

"Look," Slade muttered angrily. He didn't owe Branson an explanation but the man's accusation had rankled him. "It's been a long time since I was scared of anybody. I'm just using my head, that's all. I crossed Harrison by winning that last poker hand and by sticking my neck out for you. I figured it would be smart for me to move out before there was trouble."

In Branson's mind's eye, he could see all of those high money pots Slade had pulled. Several thousand dollars had to be involved. But Slade had put that money in the bank—or had he? Maybe his stopping at the bank had been a ruse. Maybe that was just what he wanted people to think!

Satisfied that he had shut Branson up, Slade remained silent until Virginia returned with a muslin sack filled with supplies. He fished in his pocket for the pencil stub it was his habit to carry. Finding the pocket empty, he asked, "Do you have a pencil and some paper? I must have misplaced mine."

"Yes, we have some in the wagon." She attempted a smile. "It so happens we purchased a large supply of school tablets before we left Jefferson and we still have several packages left. I'll be just a moment."

Virginia's heart pounded frantically in her breast as she searched the wagon for the tablets. She was elated that Slade had not held her father's atrocious behavior against her. Maybe she had misjudged him. Maybe he was not like other men.

Her thoughts raced boldly. Since she would have his sister's address, she would not have to lose contact with him. As soon as they reached civilization again, she could find employment; then when she was able to send a payment, she could casually make inquiry as to his whereabouts. And if she decided to change her place of residence — especially since one place was just as good as another to settle in — and if they chanced to meet in the future, maybe, just maybe, the attraction she felt for him could blossom into something much deeper, much more substantial. Suddenly, Virginia felt more hope than she had in a long, long time.

After finding the tablets, she started to climb down from the wagon. The smile on her face vanished instantly and her eyes widened in horror. Her mouth opened to scream a warning, but only a strangled cry escaped her lips.

Slade, who had been watering his horse from a bucket, heard the startled cry. He started to turn just as Carl brought down a heavy iron skillet on his head. Slade slumped to the ground, unconscious from the severe blow.

"Papa! What have you done?" Virginia shouted as she rushed toward them. She swallowed hard and stared helplessly at the sight of Slade's large, unconscious form, her mind and body numb. "Is he . . . is he dead?"

"Hell no, he ain't dead! Now get a move on and start hitching the horses to the wagon," he ordered gruffly, grabbing a rope from Slade's saddle. "But first, help me drag him over to the tree. If I tie him to it, he won't be going nowhere, at least not for a while."

Horrified, she started to back away.

Carl caught her by the arm. "Listen to me, girl. It's not what you think. I haven't done anything wrong."

"N—Nothing wrong?" She could hardly lift her voice above a whisper, but it echoed through her ears like a shout. "I saw you sneak up on him from behind and attack him—for no reason at all! My Lord, what if you've killed him?"

"No reason at all, my foot!" Carl snarled as he abruptly released her. He then hurried back to Slade and began searching his pockets. He cackled with glee when he found a huge wad of bills and several gold pieces.

Completely appalled by her father's horrendous actions, she protested vehemently. "Papa, you can't do that! You can't rob him! You'll be thrown in jail!"

"I ain't robbing him! While you were in the wagon, he stood out here and bragged to me how he cheated at the card game. It's no wonder he was going to forget about those IOUs. Hell, I never lost in the first place." Clutching the money in his hand, he began to smile greedily. "Hot damn! Look at all this money, Ginny—and it's mine! All mine!"

Very shaken, she stared at him. "N—No, Papa, regardless of what he did, you can't do this. It's wrong!"

Carl's rheumy eyes darkened angrily. "By God, I suppose what he did wasn't wrong. If he hadn't cheated, the money would have been mine to begin with!"

"B—But . . . if he . . . since he . . . was cheating, couldn't you go to the sheriff and let him take care of it the right way?" She could not raise her voice above a whisper.

"Just what good would that do? Likely as not, the sheriff in that one-horse town is just as crooked as he is. Now come on and get a move on." Carl dragged Slade over to the tree, bound him to it, then snugged the knot tightly on the rope. "We need to put plenty of distance between us before somebody happens along and finds him." He removed Slade's gun from his holster. "I ought to take this too."

Deep down inside, Virginia knew her father was lying. Slade just did not seem like the type of man who would resort to cheating. And, if that was true, what did that make her father? She had never felt such despair as she stared down at Slade. He looked so pitiful, helplessly tied to the tree, and the amount of blood that oozed freely from the huge lump on his head frightened her.

"Papa, we can't leave him—" Her voice broke off in midsentence as Carl yanked her to her feet and shoved her toward the wagon. She lost her balance and fell to the ground.

"God damnit, make yourself useful. I told you to start hitching the horses to the wagon and I meant exactly what I said! We don't have much time. We have to get out of here!" he yelled, waving the pistol about threateningly. His eyes were wide and spittle flew from his mouth.

Suddenly, Virginia was filled with more fright than she had ever known. Right before her eyes her father had become a raving, maniacal madman, so enraged he was now capable of doing anything, even murder. Realizing if she protested further, he might even take his anger out on Slade by putting a bullet in his head, she dragged herself to her feet, swallowed her tears, and stumbled blindly toward the horses.

Chapter Six

Slade awoke to brilliant sunlight streaming across his face. Instinctively, he blinked and tried to avert his eyes from the blinding light, but the sudden movement caused excruciating pain to shoot through his head. He could feel darkness hovering over him and it was tempting just to lie there and allow the blackness to reclaim him, but he was determined to fight against the dark pit of unconsciousness.

Squinting his eyes tightly and pressing both hands to either side of his temples, he waited for the pain to subside. It was then he realized that a heavy bandage covered the top of his head. Taking a deep breath, he slowly rose to a sitting position. His movements caused a renewed onslaught of pain. It gradually eased, and for a short while his vision was blurred, but after opening and closing his eyes several times, he was finally able to bring his surroundings into focus.

He was surprised to discover he was in a small room, sparsely furnished with only the narrow bed on which he sat, a large wooden rocking chair, a night table holding a pitcher and washing bowl, and a bureau over by the heavy oak door. A covered chamber pot had been placed near the bed, he assumed for his convenience.

There was one window, only about four inches wide but several feet long, and it was located high on the wall across from the bed, as though it had been placed there for the use of guns in case of an Indian attack. His keen sense of hearing along with his natural instinct told him he was in some sort of ranch house in an area outside of town.

"Where in the hell am I? And how did I get here?" he mumbled aloud. His voice seemed to echo harshly and just the sound of it sent pain tearing through him. Nausea suddenly rose in his throat, choking, almost suffocating him, and he became dizzy. Slade forced himself to remain calm, to take slow, deep breaths. He lowered himself back down on the bed.

After the choking sensation eased and the dizziness had passed, he slowly walked step by step through his disoriented memory, attempting to recall the events that had put him in this unfamiliar place.

There had been a poker game . . . and he had kissed a pretty young woman. No, that did not seem right. He had the sequence confused. But the memory of the girl was vivid — Virginia, yes, that was her name — and he could see her face in his mind's eye quite clearly. But there seemed to be an important detail missing, which concerned her. Maybe she was related to . . . one of the men he had played poker with. Yes, that was it! She was . . . Carl Branson's daughter!

After Slade remembered Carl, his memory opened like a floodgate. The more he recalled, the clearer his mind became. Then a muscle quivered at his jaw and his brows drew together in a frown. Something was still not right. His last memory was of a startled cry, a sharp stab of pain, then nothing but blackness. How then had he gotten here, to this small room? Who had brought him here?

Suddenly, the questions seemed too much for him as pain began to pound relentlessly through his head once again. This time, Slade did not fight the blackness as it began to close its arms around him like a comforting shroud. Instead, he welcomed it, knowing the next time it released him from its dark clutches he would win the battle that raged within his body.

When Slade awoke again, he sensed it was now morning and he had slept the night away. The sharp, stabbing pain he had experienced earlier had been replaced by a dull throb. It was an uncomfortable feeling, but it was something he could tolerate without too much difficulty.

He swung his long legs over the side of the bed and sat up. Not experiencing much dizziness, he then attempted to stand. For an instant, the room spun, then Slade quickly grasped the arm of the rocking chair and steadied himself. It was then that he realized he was wearing a pair of lightweight, drawstring muslin pants, which very much resembled women's drawers. He did not know if someone had put them on him for comfort, or to make certain he would not try to escape, for his own clothes were nowhere in sight.

Escape? Why had that particular word crossed his mind? Was his sixth sense trying to tell him something?

After attending to his personal needs, Slade eased himself back down on the bed and waited for what little strength he had to renew itself. Several minutes passed before he was able to stand again. Still unsteady on his feet, he walked toward the door. It came as no great surprise that he found it locked. He pressed his ear against the door and unable to hear any sounds on the other side, he quickly decided it would be a waste of his energy to pound on it, or to try to get anyone's attention by shouting. He assumed that whoever had brought him here would check on him sooner or later. However, Slade wanted to know as much as possible about where he was being held. Dragging the chair over to the window, he stepped up on it, and standing on tiptoe, he peered outside. He was disappointed to see nothing but an adobe wall on the other side of a small courtyard.

Another man might have panicked over finding himself locked in a strange room in an unknown location, but not Slade. The years he had spent in prison had conditioned him against such things and had developed his patience and tolerance in circumstances he could not change. Then too, he did not believe he was in any immediate danger. It seemed senseless for somebody to have rescued him if he intended to do him harm.

But still, he would have been less than human if his curiosity had not been aroused. Who had found him? Where was he? Why was the door locked? What, if anything, did that person want with him? There were several suspicions in the back of his mind, but he decided that with only speculation to go on it would be futile to make plans against the unknown. Why agitate himself unnecessarily?

One thing was definite, though. When the door was opened, if it was within his power, he would be ready for whoever or whatever faced him.

Wetting his dry lips with his tongue, Slade realized he was terribly thirsty. Seeing no glass, he merely raised the pitcher of water to his mouth and drank greedily. Then he sat down on the side of the bed, trying to decide if there was something in the back of his memory he had missed, something that might give him a clue to where he was or who had brought him here. Without warning, he began to feel groggy. He rubbed his face and reached out for the water pitcher, intending to pour the cool liquid into the washbowl so he could splash it on his face. But Slade felt himself sinking once more into that nameless black pit, and his last conscious thought was that the water must have been drugged.

The following morning, the sound of a key turning in the lock awoke Slade. Opening his eyes slightly and peering through heavy lashes, he forced himself to lie still. A plump, gray-haired Mexican woman holding a tray of food pushed open the door and stood there for a moment, studying him cautiously before entering.

He waited until she had reached his bedside before he reached out and clamped his hand tightly around her wrist, knocking the tray from her hands. "Where am I? Why are you keeping me locked in this room?" Although he shouted, his voice sounded like a rasping whisper.

Startled, the Mexican woman screamed and wrenched from his grasp. She fled from the room, locking the door as if the devil himself were chasing her. Slade had, in fact, attempted to catch her, but she had moved too quickly for him.

Weak and dizzy from his abrupt movements, Slade slumped down on the bed and sat there with his hands propped on his knees, holding his head. He took several deep gulps of air and waited. He had a hunch someone else would soon be paying him a visit.

A few minutes later, Abe Harrison opened the door and stood there, staring at Slade with a peculiar expression on his face. Then, leaving the door open, he crossed the room in two easy strides and eased his bulk into the rocking chair. "You don't seem surprised to see me."

Slade's mouth spread into a thin-lipped smile. "I'm not." During his brief moments of consciousness, he had concluded that Harrison was the most logical choice among people who might want to hold him captive. Though he really had no idea why, he was determined to find out. "Where am I?"

"At my ranch. You know, Slade, you are tougher than I thought. I really didn't believe it when the doc told me you would come out of this all right, but I guess the old sawbones was right. You cost me a five-dollar bet."

"Why are you keeping me in a locked room?" Slade asked. "And why was I drugged?"

"The locked room was necessary." He gestured toward the door. "But as you can see, it's not locked now. You are free to leave as soon as the doc says you can."

Being careful to do it gently, Slade shook his head. "That doesn't answer my question. Why was it *necessary?*"

Shrugging, Abe lit a cigar, inhaled deeply, then slowly blew out the smoke before he said, "It's not as sinister as it might appear, so just get that suspicious look out of your eyes. My men found you the other day with your head cracked open and you were trussed up to a tree like a Christmas turkey. Two of them brought you to the ranch and one went for the doctor. The doc came out, checked you over, and left strict orders to keep you as quiet as we could. But that first night you started thrashing around so much, Maria and I were concerned you would hurt yourself even worse, so we gave you a dose of laudanum. Then late the next afternoon, something came up and I had to leave the ranch. I didn't know how you would react or who you would blame for bustin' your head wide open, so I told my wife not to take any chances and to keep giving you that medicine until I returned. The explanation is just as simple as that. You can believe it if you want to; if not . . ." He shrugged again. "It doesn't make a damn bit of difference to me."

Slade rubbed his whiskered face. Harrison's explanation sounded reasonable to him, and he really had no cause to doubt his word. After all, he knew who was responsible for jumping him from behind. "It sounds like I'm indebted to you now."

Abe gave an indifferent wave of his hand. "Just a thank you will do."

"All right then, thanks."

Slade had the grace to look sheepish as he stared at the food that had been on the tray. "Do you think your wife would mind bringing another tray of food? I'm about to starve."

"I figured you'd be hungry," Abe said with a grin. "I gave Maria instructions to fix you another one when she told me what happened. Ah, here she is now."

Maria stood cautiously, as if she were not sure if it was safe to enter. But when Abe assured her everything was all right, she hurriedly placed the tray on the corner of the night table and removed the red-and-white checked cloth that covered it. After quickly cleaning up the mess from the dropped tray, she left the men alone.

Slade pulled the table toward him and hungrily attacked the tray filled with flapjacks, a pitcher of hot, thick molasses, fried eggs, bacon, a thick slice of ham, buttered flour *tortillas,* and a carafe of steaming hot coffee. He did not say a word until the sharp edge of his hunger had abated.

He took a sip of his third cup of coffee, then said, "The best I can remember, I've been here for at least three days."

"Four, counting the day they brought you in."

"That long?" He mentally calculated how much of a head start Branson and his daughter had gotten on him.

Abe nodded. "Yes, and from what the doc said, you are lucky. A blow like that usually kills a man." His eyes narrowed. "Do you know who bushwhacked you?"

"Yeah, I know him."

"Branson?"

Slade nodded his head.

"I figured as much."

Pushing back his plate, Slade said with a wry grin twisting his mouth, "No 'I told you so's'?"

Abe chortled. "Oh, I was just about to get around to that."

Slade threw back the sheet that covered him and stood. Seeing Harrison's sudden amusement at what he was wearing, his jaw tensed visibly. "If you will just give me my clothes, I'll be on my way."

Leaning forward in his chair, Harrison said, "I don't think you should. The doc said you ought to stay in bed for a couple of days even after you feel up to getting out and about. And judging by your condition when you were brought in, I tend to agree with him. You are in no shape to leave."

Slade scowled. It was baffling why the rancher was going to great lengths to pretend he was concerned about his well-being. It just didn't fit. It was almost as if Harrison knew something he didn't, and the man was obviously enjoying it to the fullest.

Quickly deciding two people could play the cat-and-mouse game, Slade said, "I think I should be the one to decide whether I'm able to leave or not."

"Maybe so, but I doubt it," Abe countered, giving his shoulders a shrug. "Even if you were able to reach the front door, I don't think you are in any shape to do much walking. And I'm damn sure not going to give you a horse. I'm not that generous, not after the way you cleaned me out at that poker game."

Slade's eyes hardened. "You mean my Appaloosa wasn't there when your men found me? My horse had been trained not to leave me." So that was what Harrison had found so amusing. During the poker game, the only personal thing he had talked about was his prize Leopard Appaloosa. Blue was not actually a unique horse, but with his standing seventeen hands to his withers and having a black-dotted coat instead of the usual Appaloosa blanket markings, he was extremely valuable.

"Nope." Harrison flicked the ashes from his cigar. "From what I was told, there were just a couple of buzzards circling around, and a flea-bitten livery-stable nag tied to a tree."

"That sorry son of a bitch!" Slade muttered angrily, clenching and unclenching his fists. He hated the thought of Blue's being at that man's mercy. Men like that did not treat horses well. And Blue was a good, well-trained horse. Not only had his brother-in-law invested a lot of time in training the stallion, but Slade personally had spent days on end getting Blue accustomed to his hand and vocal commands. Slade vowed that when he got his hands on Carl Branson, he would make the man wish he had never been born. "Then I'll buy a horse from you," Slade declared.

"With what? Branson even took your boots." Harrison thought it was so amusing, he had to bite his lip to keep from laughing aloud.

Not aware that his eyes had suddenly become glazed with unspoken rage, Slade chewed on the little tit on the inside corner of his mouth, not trusting himself to speak.

The steely-eyed rancher rubbed a little salt into

Slade's wounded pride. "I knew he was no-good. I tried to tell you, but you wouldn't listen."

"I'll kill that no-good son of a bitch!"

"I'm afraid you will just have to wait your turn. You can have him after I am through with him . . . that is, if there is anything left of the mangy bastard. Some of my men found him on one of the rarely used trails that runs across my land. He had cut two of my fences." Abe's mouth took on an unpleasant twist. "No one who crosses me gets away with it."

"You mean you have Branson here?" Slade had momentarily forgotten that he had crossed Harrison too.

"Yes, I do. He is locked up in one of my toolsheds until the sheriff gets here. But his daughter is here in the house . . . locked in a spare bedroom." He grunted doubtfully. "That is, *if* she's his daughter. For all I know, she's just some little tart he picked up somewhere."

"No, she's definitely his daughter. She certainly fooled me though. I thought she was different from him, but the little. . . ." When he thought of her big, dark, innocent eyes, honey-colored hair, and pretty smile, Slade gritted his teeth and his nostrils flared. "Hell, now that I think about it, they probably had it planned. Tell me, did he have my horse with him?" His tone demanded an answer.

"Well, there was an Appaloosa tied on behind the wagon." Abe stroked his chin thoughtfully. "But whether it is yours or not is a question the sheriff will have to decide. You see, I suffered considerable damages when he cut my fences, and I have to recoup my losses somehow."

Slade ground out the words between his teeth. "You know that horse is mine!"

"Can you prove it?"

"Hell yes, I can!"

"Do you have papers?"

There was a threat in the smoldering depths of Slade's eyes as he said, "Don't try it, Harrison. Since Branson stole my horse and apparently everything else that belonged to me, you know I don't have any papers on Blue. But I'll tell you one thing—it makes no difference that I am in your house, wearing nothing but sissified drawers, with no gun, and no boots. I won't let you get by with something like that. If you have a bone to pick with me, do it like a man! I never figured you for a horse thief."

Jumping to his feet, Harrison scowled with cold fury. "Don't get too testy with me, son," he uttered. "If it weren't for that head wound, I'd knock you clear into next week for making a remark like that!"

Slade stood and bellied up to Harrison. "Better men than you have tried."

"Good God Almighty!" an older, but definitely masculine voice said from the doorway. Both Slade and Harrison turned. "You men sound like two little boys arguing over who can spit the farthest! Young man, get your butt back in that bed! Abe, I thought I told you he wasn't supposed to be disturbed!"

Abe motioned. "That's the doc."

Doc Neckar, a short, balding man weighed down by a potbelly, stomped into the room. "Young man, I told you to get back into bed. I didn't make these long trips out here just to bury you!"

"No, sir, I can't do that," Slade said stubbornly. "I wouldn't feel right accepting his hospitality—not when I might have to kill him."

In disbelief, the doc looked first at Slade, then at Abe. Then he started laughing. "Aw hell, Abraham, get the man a pair of breeches. I can't do him any good. He's already had the sense knocked out of him. Has to be, the way he just talked to you." He scratched his head. "In fact, the way he bowed up there sort of reminded me of you 'bout twenty years ago." He reached up and clasped Abe's shoulder. "Walk me out to the kitchen and have a cup of Maria's coffee with me and let this young man get dressed. Surely you have something around here he can wear. Besides, the sheriff and your foreman rode out with me and they told me what was going on. I believe if we all sit down and discuss it like sensible men, your differences can be resolved without my having to dig bullets out of either of you later. I'm getting too old for that kind of nonsense. My eyesight is about gone, and who knows? My hand might slip one of these days."

A few minutes later, the doc stormed into the small room and threw a bundle of clothing down on the bed. "Listen to me, son," he told Slade, not even giving him a chance to speak. "If your brains didn't fry out there on the edge of town after you were jumped, you ought to consider putting them to good use. Abe Harrison has a hair-trigger temper, and if I hadn't interrupted you a while ago, you'd probably be meeting your Maker right about now. He can be a fair man when he has a mind to. But the important thing is, you are surrounded by *his* men and you are in *his* house, which is close to *his* town. If you have any sense left in that thick head of yours, you'll hold your tongue, and you just might be able to walk out of here alive! Now, I am going back out there to talk to him and try to soothe his temper as much as I can. And if you are as smart as I think you are, you'll swallow a little bit of your pride and offer him an apology.

Slade was just tugging on a pair of ill-fitting boots when Abe flung open the door. "If you are dressed, the sheriff wants to talk to you," he snarled. "We're

89

meeting in my study, so you'll have to follow me." He spun on his heel, starting to walk ahead, but Slade stopped him.

"Wait a minute, Mr. Harrison."

Abe visibly stiffened, then slowly turned around. This was the first time he could remember Slade calling him Mister.

Slade had taken what the doc had told him to heart. Even though he had to swallow the bile that rose in his throat with the words, he said, "I apologize for the way I spoke to you a while ago. I lost my temper and got way out of line. However, I'm not backing down when it comes to my horse. Branson is bound to have my money and my other belongings. If necessary, I'll use them to cover any damages he caused you . . . but Blue is mine."

Harrison's granite expression did not reveal any of his thoughts, but when he spoke, his tone of voice had softened slightly. "The sheriff is in my study. He is waiting for us."

Chapter Seven

Hank Rogers, the foreman, escorted Virginia, none too gently, into a large study, obviously furnished for a man's comfort. Never having seen such an elegant, masculine room before, she was filled with wonder. Remembering how rough, crude, and ill-mannered the rancher had been when his men had brought her and her father in, she was surprised by the tasteful elegance of his home.

The walls were covered with a rustic oak paneling that fairly glistened from wood-scented beeswax. Polished inlaid hardwood covered the floor. A massive oak desk sat in front of a bookshelf that ran the length of the entire room. And the shelves were so full, Virginia doubted that a single book could have been added to the collection. On the wall across from the desk was a huge gun rack filled with every sort of gun imaginable. In the corner was an enormous fireplace and hanging over it was a set of Texas longhorns that reached at least ten feet from point to point. A small but well-stocked bar had been placed in front of the room's only window. Directly in front of the desk was a long sofa covered with a colorful, Indian-designed blanket. The sofa was flanked by two huge leather chairs.

In awe, Virginia started to walk around the desk so that she could look at the books, but Hank stopped her. "Leave things alone. You sit down and don't do any prowling around. This is Mr. Harrison's personal room, and he doesn't like anything disturbed."

When he was satisfied that she would obey his order, he hurried to the door. "If Mr. Harrison comes in before I get back, tell him I've gone after your pa."

When he was gone, Virginia sank wearily to the sofa. She was not physically tired; her weariness stemmed from the turmoil that had engulfed her life. As she sat there, an icy sensation seemed to spread through her stomach. She could not shake the strange sense of foreboding that seemed to be hanging over her, and had since the first time she had seen Stephen Slade.

Just the mere thought of Slade made her shudder with remorse. As long as she lived, she would never forgive her father for the brutal way he had attacked and robbed him. Shaking her head adamantly, she brushed away the tears that suddenly filled her eyes. She could not allow herself to think about that horrible day. It was far too painful.

The study door opened and her father, taking short, shuffling steps, entered in front of Hank Rogers. They were followed by a man who wore a badge pinned to his vest.

Her father's hands, which were tied in front of him with a piece of coarse hemp, trembled visibly. In fact, his entire body seemed to be shaking. Even though his head was bowed, she could see that a huge bruise had swelled the entire left side of his face.

"Papa, what have they done to you?" In spite of all he had done, she still felt compassion for him. It would have been against her gentle nature to have done otherwise.

"Ginny!" Carl's sorrowful expression brightened. He attempted to embrace her, but the foreman stepped between them and forced Carl onto one of the chairs.

"Have they treated you all right, girl?"

Virginia blinked back tears as her bottom lip trembled. "Y—Yes, I s—suppose so. T—They haven't hurt me, though they kept me in a locked room. B—But, Papa, what have they done to you?" She started to rise, but the foreman pushed her back on the sofa.

"Those bast . . . they beat me within an inch of my life! And they've kept me locked up too!" Carl glared at the sheriff. "Is this how you keep the law? Can't you see that we are being held against our will? I want to press charges against Abe Harrison! He can't do this. . . ."

"Oh, shut up!" the foreman ordered.

Carl scowled. He felt somewhat braver in the presence of the sheriff. "I'm not about to shut up! Sheriff, ain't kidnapping against the law? That's what Harrison has done to me and my daughter—kept us against our will! And my face hurts! I demand to see a doctor!"

The stone-faced foreman stepped forward and said threateningly, "Look, Branson, you're in enough trouble without adding to it. Your face isn't hurt. You'd best sit still and keep your trap shut until Mr. Harrison gets in here and we can get this settled."

Virginia protested. "You don't have to talk to him so hatefully!"

Hank's face darkened angrily. "You shut your lip too!"

The sheriff spoke for the first time. "All right, Hank, that's enough. It's not proper to talk to a woman that way."

"That's right!" Carl agreed. "You've got no quarrel with her. And you had better not lay a hand on her either!"

Hank wagged his finger in Carl's face. "I've already told you twice to keep your mouth shut. If I have to tell you again, the other side of your face will be swollen too!" He then walked behind the chair where Carl sat and folded his arms as if to stand guard.

Virginia reached over to hold her father's tied hands, but Hank leaned over from behind the chair and yanked her hand away. "The boss said to keep you two separated so you couldn't get together and cook up a story."

Whirling around on the sofa, she glared at him. "And just how do you think we could manage that in front of you and the sheriff?" She defiantly took her father's hand again, and the expression on her face dared Hank to protest.

For all of her false bravado, Virginia was frightened. She had no idea what lay ahead for them, but every horrible thought imaginable had run through her mind ever since the rancher's men had found them cutting that last fence. No, that was not quite right. Her misery had begun the moment her father had brutally attacked Stephen Slade. Again, the thought of him, how helpless he had looked tied to that tree with blood dripping from his head, sent shudders of remorse through her. In a strange way that she could not explain, she felt responsible for what had happened to him.

Stealing a quick glance at the sheriff, Virginia wondered if he were here in part because of the assault on Slade.

Please let it just be assault! Please don't let him be dead! she prayed inwardly. Then, another terrifying thought struck her. What if they blamed her for the crime too? They might say she was her father's accomplice and place her in some kind of women's prison. She had heard they existed. And if Slade had died from his injury, why, more than likely, they would hang them both! *Oh, Papa, what have you done?* she silently cried.

Just then, the study door flew open and Abe Harrison stalked in. Virginia gave a sharp cry of relief when Stephen Slade followed him, very much alive. Except for the bandage on his head, he appeared to be in relatively good health. Without warning, Virginia realized that her relief went further than she cared to admit, as if it stemmed from much deeper feelings.

Slade visibly stiffened at the sight of them. He had tried to tell himself earlier that the girl had been in on it with her father, but from the relieved expression on her face, it seemed that either she was an expert at fooling people or she was innocent. Regardless, it did not matter that much to him. Branson was the one he wanted to get his hands on. He moved threateningly toward him.

A strangled sound seemed to catch in Carl's throat. Slade was the last person he had expected to see. He quickly scrambled from his chair and slipped from the sheriff's and the foreman's grasp. Not knowing if the sheriff and foreman were aware of Slade's murderous intent and what he would probably do if they allowed Slade to get his hands on him, Carl lunged for the sofa and squirmed in behind Virginia. "Keep that man away from me!"

The silence in the room was suddenly overwhelming. It was as though everybody, especially Virginia, realized he was shielding himself behind his daughter.

Carl nervously wet his lips. "I—I mean . . . keep him away from us!" He attempted to save face by leaning in front of Virginia.

Slade balled his hands into fists. He turned to Abe.

"His reaction just now should settle any doubts you might have had."

Abe held up one hand, a gesture that urged Slade to be silent. "Just hold on. We'll get to the bottom of this, but let's take it one step at a time. Branson, my men caught you, red-handed, cutting my fence, and I lost at least ten prize head of cattle because of it. What do you have to say for yourself?"

Carl jutted his chin defiantly. "I'll tell my story to a judge. I'll also press charges of my own! It's against the law to treat me like you did!"

The sheriff interrupted. "Look, Branson, that's your privilege if you want to use it, but the circuit judge won't be back in this area for at least three months. If you want to cool your heels in our jail until then, that's fine. But you'd make everything a hell—" Glancing at Virginia, he caught himself. ". . . a heck of a lot easier if you would do as Mr. Harrison asked. Your trouble with him might be settled if you would promise to repair his fences and reimburse him for the cattle that wandered away."

"Wait just a damn minute," Slade staunchly objected. "Sheriff, weren't you informed about what he did to me?"

"Are you the man Mr. Harrison's men found tied to a tree near town the other day?"

"Yes, I am. And Carl Branson is the man who tried to kill me, and not only that, he robbed me while I was out cold, then the dirty, low-down . . . stole my horse. I'm not about to wait three months for the circuit judge. If you don't want to do something about it, I will!"

The sheriff, chewing on a long sulphur match, eyed Branson warily. His voice rang with contempt. "That certainly puts a different slant on this. Don't you know we hang men for horse stealing in these parts?

If I let one man get by with it, word would soon get around and before long this area wouldn't even be safe for the local citizens. You're right, Mr. Slade, three months is much too long to wait."

Carl's eyes darted shiftily between Slade, Harrison, and the sheriff. He swallowed hard and ran his hand across his mouth. They had him dead to rights unless he could come up with a story that would convince them otherwise. "N—Now wait just a minute! It's his word against mine!"

Harrison rolled his eyes in disgust. "Cut the crap, Branson! You sat right there at the poker table and heard him tell us about his Leopard Appaloosa, and I know for a fact he damn near cleaned out every one of us during that poker game. That afternoon, when my men found him with his head bashed in, he didn't have any money and his horse was nowhere in sight. Later, when some more of my men found you cutting my fences, you had a horse in your possession that matched the description of his, and your pockets were filled with money."

"That still don't prove nothing!"

Abe continued as though he had not heard him. "After my men found Slade, I reported it to the sheriff and he did a little investigating around town. It seems Slade stopped in the bank and sent some money to his kin. That amount, combined with what we found on you, and taking into consideration he had some when the poker game started, equals about what we all lost. So . . . like I said, cut the crap!" He grabbed Branson by his shirtfront and yanked him from the sofa. "In my opinion, any man who would sneak up on another man and attack him is so low, he would have to stand on tiptoe to kiss a chigger's butt—but a no-account, worthless horse thief is even worse! I personally intend to have the pleasure of putting the rope around your scrawny neck!"

Tears welled in Virginia's eyes. There was a lump in her throat so large, she thought it would choke her. Nothing in her life had prepared her for anything like this. What her father had done was despicable, but surely it did not warrant taking his life. She could not sit idly by without saying something in his defense. She wedged her body between her father's and the big rancher's and began clutching at Harrison's shirt. "No! Please! He didn't know what he was doing! It was as if he . . . temporarily lost control of his mind! You can't h—hang him for that! You can't! It's inhuman!"

"That's right!" Carl was quick to agree. "It's just like she says . . . I lost my mind there for a while! I couldn't help myself!" He desperately grasped any excuse to save himself. "When I saw what he was trying to do to Ginny . . . why, I went *loco!* Yeah, that's what I done all right. I went *loco!*"

Harrison stepped back, frowning. "Exactly what do you mean, *when you saw what he was trying to do to her?*"

"W—Why, I . . . you see . . . it was like this." He threw Slade a nervous look, and deciding it was safer, sidled close to Harrison for protection. "He demanded I make good on my gambling markers—why, he was even going to take my wagon and my horses right then."

"I what?" Slade was dumbstruck at Branson's incredible lie.

Carl glared at him. "Don't pretend you have no idea what I'm talking about!" He turned his attention back to the other men. "As I was saying, we were at our camp and after he demanded almost everything I owned, I went inside the wagon to pack what I could—he said we could keep our personal possessions—and it took longer than I thought it would. I finally got the trunk packed and was carrying it out and I saw him. He was. . . ." He paused, pretending to be too overcome by his emotions to continue.

"What was he doing?" the sheriff demanded.

Staring at the floor, Carl muttered, "He . . . he . . . had Ginny down . . . on the ground . . . with her dress twisted up . . . around her waist . . . and . . . his hands were all over her body."

Virginia gasped at her father's outrageous lie. Her mind reeled from the injustice he was doing to an innocent man, yet an inner voice screamed that this was his only chance to escape the hangman's noose.

"That's a damned lie!" Slade lunged for Branson, but the sheriff and Harrison's foreman pulled him back.

"Go on, Branson, tell us what happened next," the sheriff urged. Only now, it was Slade who received a cold, contemptuous look.

"Well . . . since I had been in the wagon for quite a spell, I didn't know if he had already . . . got to my little girl. And, I admit, I went crazy, but I had enough good sense about me to know he would gun me down without blinking an eye if I didn't get the drop on him first. So that's why I jumped him from behind."

Virginia wanted to scream at her father to stop what he was doing, but she could only bow her head in shame.

"I grabbed an iron skillet and banged him in the head. I knew he'd come after me as soon as he came to, and I knew he would kill me. Then there would be no telling what kind of misery he would put my little girl through before he satisfied his lust. So, I tied him up as best I could, took his boots . . . and yes, I admit I even took what money he had on him. For one reason, I didn't know if my daughter would have to see a doctor or not . . . with her being violated so bad. And yes, I even tied his horse on behind the wagon so he wouldn't have a way to come after us."

Wild-eyed, he looked at Harrison. "That's why I cut your fences, Mr. Rancherman. I was only trying to put as many miles as I could between us before he found a way to come after us." He pulled himself up to his full height. "Now, if it's still in you to see me hang . . . well, so be it. But under the circumstances, I'm sure you realize why I didn't say anything until I was forced to. But, if I had it to do all over again, I wouldn't change a thing. A man has to protect his family the best way he can."

"What do you have to say about this, Slade?" Harrison asked.

Slade's brows had drawn together in a scowling frown, a muscle quivered at his jaw, and his eyes had narrowed into furious slits. "That is the biggest cock-and-bull story I've ever heard in my life! It's obvious the man is lying just to try to save his own mangy hide!"

"No I ain't lying either!" Carl grabbed Virginia by her arm and commanded her to look at him. His rhemy eyes held a desperate plea. "Now, daughter, you have to tell them what really happened. I know it's painful and I wouldn't ask you to shame yourself this way . . . but you have to tell the truth. If you don't, they are going to hang me."

"Oh, Papa," Virginia gasped quietly upon hearing his request. She felt a wretchedness that tore into the depths of her soul. By swearing to a lie, she could grant her father his life, but in the same breath she would be destroying another man. But still, she really had no choice. A sob tore from her throat. "M—My father is telling the t—truth," she finally managed to rasp.

Amid curses and flying fists, the sheriff and Abe's foreman quickly subdued Slade as he shouted a furious oath and started for the Bransons. At that moment it did not matter which one he grabbed hold of first.

A belt was produced, seemingly from out of nowhere, and in a matter of seconds, Slade had been thrown to the floor and securely tied.

"Boss, I think your rope had the wrong man's name on it," Hank Rogers muttered darkly. "I'm for taking him outside and stringing him up right now! A man who would treat a woman like that is nothing but an animal."

"Damnit, she's lying! They both are!" Slade strained at his bonds.

Hank placed his boot over Slade's mouth and declared coldly, "Shut up, you animal. One more word out of you, and you won't ever be able to talk again!"

The sheriff looked anxiously at Harrison. "I hate to hang a man without positive proof, but once word of this gets around, I'll never be able to hold him for the judge. He'll be dragged out of my jail and lynched inside of a day."

All of this time, Harrison had been rubbing his chin thoughtfully. He had always prided himself on being a good judge of character, and while he figured Slade to be too brash, too arrogant, and a little too independent, it was hard to believe he was the kind of man who would take a woman by force. Hell, he mused silently, if anything, as handsome as the cuss was, he probably had to fight the women off.

"Now, men," Harrison drawled slowly, "let's not be too hasty here. Just a few minutes ago I was ready to hang one man; now it seems we are getting ready to hang another instead. I think we ought to use a little reason before we make a wrong move. Let's start at

101

the beginning and look at the facts." He pointed to Carl. "We have a man here who is accused of assault, robbery, and horse stealing. He claims he is guilty of all those crimes because Slade attacked his daughter. Now, in my opinion, a man who would mistreat a helpless female is about the most low-down piece of scum walking the earth — even worse than a horse thief. And if Slade is guilty of that despicable act, then hanging is too good for him. But, on the other hand, my opinion of Carl Branson isn't too high. I think he is a liar and a cheat, and I don't think it is necessary to remind all of you that I am a good judge of character. But, is he lying about Slade?" He gestured toward Virginia, who stared at him with large, frightened eyes. "Branson's daughter backs up his claims . . . but it's important we remember that she *is* his daughter. She knows if she doesn't support her father's claim he will hang. So, just whose story are we supposed to believe?"

Hank slowly removed his boot from Slade's face and helped him up from the floor. "You know, Boss, I never thought about it that way. It's like you say, though — who are we supposed to believe?"

Virginia swallowed hard when all eyes turned to her. The young woman could see she would get no help from any of them, and the tiny flicker of hope that had flared in her breast when the rancher had come to Slade's defense died before it had a chance to take flame. Then she drew herself up with some semblance of dignity and tried not to let the men see how frightened she really was. She floundered in an agonizing maelstrom. She could not deny that it all came down to two basic facts: if she told the truth, her father would hang; if she did not, an innocent man would lose his life.

"Well, young lady," Abe said, finally breaking deafening silence, "looks like it all comes back to you."

Her eyes were dark and unfathomable as she looked first at her father, then at Slade. Her father's expression was pleading and remorseful, as though he were begging her to spare his life, while Slade now stood with his arms akimbo, his handsome face defiant and bitter — and with good reason.

Drawing a deep breath, she squared her shoulders. "M — My father told the truth . . ."

Carl breathed a deep sigh of relief and Slade uttered a strangled curse.

"But he told the truth only as h — he saw it."

"What do you mean?" Abe asked.

"Th — That really wasn't the way it happened."

"I think you had better explain."

Slade folded his arms and his voice carried a sarcastic, mocking tone, "Yes, I'm interested in hearing what you have to say too."

Virginia nervously wet her lips. A man's life depended on something she abhorred and something she had never been able to do well — to tell a convincing lie. Her voice barely rose above a whisper. "I first met Stephen Slade well over a week ago. He stopped by where we were camped, several miles from Barkersville. . . ."

"Go on," Abe urged.

"Papa wasn't there, and —" Her voice broke and she humbly bowed her head. "This is so very difficult." That was certainly an understatement. Lies did not come easily to her and considering what was at stake, she simply did not know what to say next.

"It will be difficult for one of these men, too, if he has to hang from a rope, so I suggest you continue," Abe declared gruffly.

"I know, I know, it's just . . . so embarrassing to admit how . . . shamelessly I behaved. You see, Papa

103

has always been very strict with me and he has never allowed me to have any beaus. When Slade stopped . . . I'm afraid I led him to believe he would be able to . . . to . . . take liberties with me. I—I never meant for it to go so far . . . but I was curious about . . . men, and he was so . . . so handsome. Later . . . after we . . . after we . . ." Tears glistened in her eyes when she stared at Abe. "Perhaps I never would have allowed him to . . . if he had not been so handsome and charming, but Mr. Harrison, in all honesty, he did not force me to do anything. It just seemed like everything got out of hand. Then later, I suppose he thought he would never be able to collect . . . what my father owed him and that is why he demanded that the debt be satisfied immediately. But I'm positive Slade didn't know he was my father or he probably wouldn't have made that demand, because . . . well, after Slade found out who I was, he was so considerate, he even rented a carriage so I wouldn't have to make the long walk back to camp."

Even though Virginia deliberately kept her eyes averted from Slade, she was acutely aware of how incredulously he was looking at her.

"When we reached our camp, neither Slade nor I could very well tell Papa what had happened between us, and when he went inside the wagon to start packing our trunks, Slade and I had a . . . rather heated discussion. I became quite angry and whirled away from him . . . and lost my balance and fell. Everything happened so quickly, but when I realized I was falling, I must have grabbed hold of Slade . . . and he fell on me. Then, when Papa came out of the wagon, he apparently got the wrong impression. Naturally, after he hit Slade over the head, he became very frightened, because even you will have to admit that Slade gives the impression of being an extremely dangerous man. And when Papa started going through his pockets, there was nothing I could do! I couldn't very well tell him what had happened between us. So, I held my tongue and hoped we could make good our escape. And . . . you know the rest," she murmured, her face blazing with shame.

"Why in Heaven's name didn't you tell us this earlier?" Abe shouted.

Virginia sat straight, her eyes staring directly ahead. Only the tremor in her voice gave any indication of her shame. "B—Because I didn't want my father to know . . . what I had done. But when you said Slade would hang, I could not let an innocent man die . . . no matter what all of you think of me now."

She could feel her father's eyes burning through her. Obviously, he knew she had lied, but she also believed doubts were eating at him. He had to be wondering if portions of the story were true. She could tell he was brooding about it, probably wondering if there was a way to turn it to his advantage. And Slade—Lord, there was no telling what he thought of her. Yet he would be a fool to deny her story.

The sheriff coughed, ill at ease. "Mr. Harrison, if it is all right with you, I need to be getting back to town. Under the circumstances, I don't think there are sufficient grounds to press any charges. It would just be a waste of the taxpayers' money."

"Wait around for a few minutes, George. There're a few details that still need to be settled. Hank," he addressed his foreman, "you might as well go on back to work. And I appreciate all of the extra trouble you've gone to today. I'll make it worth your while come payday."

"Yes sir, Mr. Harrison, and thanks."

After the foreman had left, Slade spoke up emphat-

105

ically. "I agree there are a few details that need to be settled—small details, like my horse, my money, and my personal belongings. I want them now. I am anxious to get the hell out of here. That is, unless somebody has any other objections?"

Abe shook his head. "I don't and the sheriff has already stated his feelings." He walked over to a small safe and began opening it. "I have your money in here and your horse is in the stable. I suppose any personal effects you had are in their wagon." His resentment toward Slade had long since disappeared. After the way everything had ended, revenge was the last thing on his mind. He just wanted all of them off his land, the sooner the better.

Slade accepted the money and started toward the door, but he stopped abruptly and turned. "Before I go, I have a few things to say. Miss Branson, I'm sure you will know exactly what I mean when I say you are definitely your father's daughter!" Then he stepped over to Branson and muttered between clenched teeth, "And as for you, I strongly suggest you sleep with one eye open in the future, and don't ever make the mistake of letting down your guard."

Carl scrambled for safety behind the sheriff. "Did you hear him threaten me? Did you?"

Slade shook his head and chuckled sardonically. "I didn't threaten you, Branson. I made you a promise." Thoroughly enjoying seeing the man squirm, he added, "You can consider it an obligation I feel honor-bound to keep."

Branson knew Slade was not making an idle threat. Thinking quickly, he blurted, "And what about your obligation to my daughter?"

"I don't owe her a damn thing!"

"Like hell you don't! We all heard her say—these men are witnesses—that you took her innocence. And

106

not once did you deny it either! I am flat busted, so it looks like we're going to have to stay on in Barkersville until we get the money to move on, and it sure won't take long for word to get around. Virginia's name will be dragged through the mud by the end of the week. And, what's more, what if you put a baby in her belly?" He shook his head adamantly. "I ain't taking on the responsibility of a squalling brat—'specially one of yours! Looks to me like it's my duty to see that you make an honest woman out of my little girl." He did not really want Virginia to marry him, but he believed if he pushed for a wedding, Slade might decide to leave well enough alone. And hell, he reflected, Slade might even give him a few dollars to get him off his back.

"Papa, no!" Virginia gasped.

"Shut your mouth, girl!" Carl shouted without ever taking his eyes off Slade. "Mr. Harrison and the sheriff seem like decent men, and I believe they would be honor-bound to help me make you do your duty toward her! She's always been a decent girl and I knew she never would have done anything like that if you hadn't filled her head with pretty words."

Carl pleaded his case with Harrison and the sheriff. "If either of you had a daughter and were faced with the same situation, wouldn't you want her to be protected by a Missus in front of her name?" Seeing the expressions on their faces, Branson suddenly hoped he had not pushed too hard. Just the thought of having Stephen Slade for a son-in-law was enough to twist his gut.

It was all that Abe could do to prevent a victorious smile from spreading across his face. What Branson proposed was the perfect way to obtain revenge.

Sighing heavily, Abe got to his feet. "I suppose if we leave within the hour we'll be able to reach Barkersvile before the preacher sneaks off to somebody's house for supper."

"No! I'm not about to marry him!" Virginia stated adamantly.

Abe shook his finger at her. "Little lady, if I were you, I'd do exactly like my papa said and keep my mouth shut. You are a pretty little filly, and once my foreman goes into town and opens his big mouth, you won't be able to walk down the street without being approached by some cowpoke intent on having a good time."

Virginia paled at his words. Any further protests died on her lips as she shuddered inwardly at the thought of what he had just said. If she had ever had any doubts about striking out on her own, they had disappeared in the wake of her father's infamy. But a single woman traveling alone was unheard of; whereas, a married woman—even one unaccompanied by a husband—was always accepted with no questions asked as long as she behaved respectably.

"What if I refuse to go along with this nonsense?" Slade asked coldly.

Abe shrugged indifferently. "The way I see it, you have two choices: either you can come along willingly, or else you can ride with a hair-trigger shotgun at your back. It's your decision to make."

Slade ran his fingers through his hair, wincing when he inadvertently touched the tender spot on his head. He had his back pressed against the wall, and what infuriated him the most was knowing that Harrison had seen through all of the lies and knew the truth. Slade had seen the undisguised triumph that had flickered through the rancher's eyes. It was at that moment he had realized it was Harrison's way of getting even with him for accepting Branson's markers at that damnable poker game. It was ironic that by doing so he would end up being that bastard's son-in-law!

"We're waiting for an answer, Slade," Abe stated flatly.

Shrugging, Slade shook his head. "Looks like I have no choice in the matter."

"That's right, you don't."

Slade glared at Virginia with hate-filled eyes, his mouth curled into a sneer. "I promise you will regret this day more than I will!"

Chapter Eight

No one ever would have known by their expressions how tightly strung were the emotions of the people who formed the small procession that approached Barkersville. The sheriff rode alongside the Conestoga to the right, and Slade rode at gunpoint in front of Abe Harrison on the left-hand side of the wagon near where Virginia sat.

Virginia's backside ached from sitting so ramrod straight on the wagon seat and her neck was beginning to get a crick in it from holding her head so stiffly, but she was determined not to glance to either side of her. She would have died before allowing anyone—especially Slade—to see her despair, and there was no doubt in her mind that it had been etched permanently on her features.

Her mouth felt raw and parched from the dust raised by the horses' plodding hooves and her eyes watered continuously from the grit. But her physical discomfort was nothing compared to the emotional pain that wracked her soul. Everything seemed so preposterous, it was difficult to comprehend how she had gotten herself into this terrible predicament. How desperately she wished she would wake up momentarily and find this was nothing but a horrible nightmare; she would still be a child, her mother would still be alive, and her father would once again be a man who carried himself with pride and dignity — not some sniveling coward who always blamed others for problems that were of his own making.

But, unfortunately, Virginia knew it was not a nightmare; it was actually happening. Soon she would be forced to marry a man who hated the sight of her. Oh, she supposed she could refuse, but what would happen then? Abe Harrison could very possibly decide her father had lied earlier and order him hanged. Or, he could turn his wrath on Slade and demand his life. He was such a powerful man, no doubt his wishes would be quickly carried out. Or, just suppose she refused and nothing happened to her father or Slade. What, then, would happen to *her?* Even though men claimed that women were gossips, she knew from past experience that men gossiped as much as women, if not more. Mr. Harrison's foreman would certainly repeat the lies she had told and more than likely embellish them, and then others would stretch them even further until she became known as the biggest harlot ever to set foot in the West. How could she begin a new life with a past like that? Whether she liked it or not, she would have to marry Stephen Slade. There was simply no other way.

Virginia clenched her hands into tight fists from frustration. All of this was her father's fault! That day at the camp, Slade had been more than reasonable. If only her father had left well enough alone, none of this would have happened. They would have gone their separate ways, yet, later, maybe their paths would have crossed again and the tiny spark of attraction that had existed between them might have flamed into something very dear and precious. Now, everything was ruined. Just the thought of all the misery her father had caused made her blood run cold. After his humiliation was over, she never wanted to see him again.

And she could only imagine what must be going through Slade's mind. Most likely, he believed she was as guilty of that malicious attack on him as her father was. He probably had no idea that she had been horrified by the atrocious deed. Virginia raised her chin stubbornly. He would just have to take her word that she was innocent. The only other person who could corroborate her story was her father, and Slade certainly would not believe him, not now, not after those outrageous lies he had told.

What about the lies *you* told, Virginia? a small voice asked. If you had not lied, they would not be forcing him to marry you. Virginia paled at that thought. But surely he would be reasonable; surely he would realize she had had to take such desperate measures in order to save her father's life — and to save his life too!

She sighed heavily, realizing no amount of *"what if's"* could answer the numerous questions hammering through her mind. At this point, any speculations would only be another feeble attempt to delude herself. Unfortunately for her peace of mind, only time would tell whether Slade hated her or not.

As the grim procession entered the town limits of Barkersville and passed by the first few stores, Virginia's brows drew together in an agonized expression. She realized that word of their coming — and probably their purpose — already had reached the town, for she noted the attention they drew from curious onlookers. Even storekeepers hurried from their shops to stand on the boarded walkway, staring as they passed by.

Virginia's mouth became drier and her stomach knotted into a tighter ball of apprehension. It took all of her self-control to keep from bolting from the wagon when they finally came to a stop in front of a small, whitewashed church on the far side of town.

"Sheriff," Abe called, stretching his legs in his stirrups. He motioned with his head toward a small adobe house located next to the church. "Why don't you go over to the parsonage and see if the preacher is home. And if he is, go ahead and explain the situation." He laughed and cradled his shotgun across one arm. "I'll stay here with the bride and groom, just in case the groom has a change of heart. I wouldn't want to see such a pretty little lady left standing at the altar."

"Sure thing, Mr. Harrison."

Abe, gesturing toward the church, spoke to Virginia. "Little lady, you should feel honored to be able to marry in such a fine house of worship. Most towns this size don't even have a church, much less one that's not used as a school too." He pushed his hat back on his head and wiped the sweat from his brow with his shirt sleeve. "I donated a considerable amount of money to have this church built. First one in these parts that is constructed of wood instead of adobe," he boasted. "The stained-glass windows were specially made in a glass factory back East. And to the best of my knowledge, your wedding will be the first one performed here."

Virginia chanced one quick look at Slade to see his reaction to this information, and the glance was enough to make her heart beat so rapidly, she thought it would leap from her breast. Never had she seen such anger, such hatred, on a man's face.

113

The preacher hurried from the parsonage while still attempting to fasten his collar. The sheriff followed close behind.

"Afternoon, Reverend." Abe nodded his head in greeting, then he swung down from his horse and extended his hand, still careful to keep the shotgun aimed in Slade's direction.

Reverend Kolb grasped the rancher's hand in a hearty greeting. "It's good to see you, Mr. Harrison." His expression grew serious when he saw for himself that the rancher held a gun on the young man still astride his horse. "The sheriff said that you needed me to perform a wedding ceremony . . . and that all of the parties involved were not agreeable to this marriage. Is this true?"

"That's right, Preacher." Carl spoke as he climbed across Virginia and jumped down to the ground. He then pursed his lips and spat a brown stream of tobacco juice, unaware that some dribbled from the corner of his mouth. The spit landed right at the preacher's feet and splattered on his shoes. "We need you to set things right in the eyes of God between my daughter and this . . ." He looked at Slade, his lips curled into a contemptuous sneer. "This young man here."

The preacher looked down at his shoes, and his mouth tightened minutely, but he said nothing about the man's ill-mannered behavior. Glancing about, he noticed they were quickly drawing an unwanted audience. "I—I see. May I suggest we go inside, where we can discuss this in private?"

Carl swore under his breath, then uttered sarcastically, "You can suggest all you want, but there is nothing to discuss. You are a preacher and these two need to get married before they commit any more

114

sins, and that's all there is to it."

Reverend Kolb stared hard at Virginia, then shook his head and clicked his tongue as if shaming her. He ran his finger around the inside of his ill-fitting collar and said, "Then the sooner they right their wrong-doing, the better. Come, let us go inside the Lord's House and wash away their sins."

Virginia was aware of standing beside Slade in front of the pulpit, and of the preacher's soft, mono-tone voice, but the words he spoke did not penetrate the barrier she had erected to shield herself from the actual ceremony. She wanted no memories of it. A girl's wedding day was supposed to be the happiest day of her life, but how could that be when she was marrying a man who hated the sight of her, who was being forced to take her as his wife?

A loud roar reverberated through her ears, her knees trembled, her hands shook, and she felt as though her entire body would soon shake apart com-pletely. To steady herself, she grasped hold of some-one's arm — Slade's — and fastened her gaze to a speck of lint that clung to the lapel of the preacher's black frock coat.

"Virginia Rose Branson, do you promise to take this man, Stephen Michael Slade, as your lawful wed-ded husband? To love, honor, and obey, in sickness and in health, until death do you part?" He waited expectantly for Virginia's reply.

When she did not answer immediately, he cleared his throat and, as was his nervous habit, ran his finger around the rim of his collar. His foot began to beat an impatient staccato rhythm against the wooden floor.

"Did you hear me, young lady?" he asked, peering over the wire rims of his spectacles.

Is he speaking to me?

Carl poked her in the ribs with his elbow and hissed, "Answer him, Ginny! Tell him you do!"

"I—I do."

Lord, when will this be over? I cannot stand here much longer without fainting.

"I now pronounce you man and wife. And . . . may God have mercy—" He quickly corrected his slip of the tongue. "May God bless this union."

Then, before Virginia could fully comprehend that the ceremony was over, they were all standing in front of the little church.

Abe Harrison's mouth curled into a contemptuous sneer when Carl extended his hand in an offer of thanks. "No, I don't like the feel of vermin next to my skin." He clasped the sheriff on his shoulder. "Come on, I'll buy you a drink. Perhaps whiskey will wash the bad taste from my mouth." He nodded at Slade. "Boy, I hope you learned your lesson. Next time you had better think twice about who you tangle with." He reached into his saddlebag and handed Slade's gun and holster to him. "Here, you can pick up your rifle at the sheriff's office when you leave town. And if I were you, I wouldn't tarry too long here in Barkersville."

"I don't intent to stay any longer than necessary," Slade replied bitterly. His eyes were flat, hard, and gave no hint of what he was thinking as he strapped on his gun. Only the tensing of his jaw and the white line around his mouth betrayed his deep-rooted anger and humiliation.

As soon as Harrison and the sheriff were out of hearing distance, Carl muttered darkly, "Damn high-falutin bastard thinks he's too good to shake my hand!" He hooked his arm through Virginia's. "Come on, Ginny, let's go find a place to camp outside of

116

town. It's past my supper time."

"No!" she cried angrily, yanking her arm away. "I'll never go anywhere with you again!" Rage flooded through her when he blinked at her uncomprehendingly, as though bewildered by her outburst. "And I don't ever want to see you again either!"

He was momentarily speechless in his surprise. "N — Now, G — Ginny," he finally managed to stammer. "Don't be like that, hon. I guess I can't blame you for being mad at me . . . but I had to make that . . . that . . . him marry you. I couldn't let him ruin your good name and then leave you behind so other men could . . . well, it would soon be common knowledge that you were damaged goods and no decent man would ever want to marry you."

If she had not been so distraught, she would have laughed at his ridiculous statement. Instead, she muttered through clenched teeth, "I told you to leave me alone, and, so help me God, I meant it!"

Again, he reached out for her hand, but she took several steps backward. In spite of his attempt to remain calm, a tinge of exasperation crept into his voice. "Now come along before I lose my temper and take my razor strap to you. I'm your pa and I've had enough of your disrespect. And you might get a taste of my damned razor strap anyway — admitting your harlot's ways to those men the way you did! Shamed me something fierce!"

Slade folded his arms and his legs splayed in an obstinate stance. Since Virginia was adamant about not going with her father, he would deal with her later, but first he needed to settle his quarrel with Branson. "If you'll shut your trap for just a minute, Branson, I want to ask you a question."

He whipped his head about. "What in the hell do

you want?"

Although he would have liked nothing better than to have hit Branson hard enough to knock him across the street, Slade held his temper. "Tell me, just what do you propose to camp in?"

Carl blinked as though Slade's question was absurd. "Camp in? W—Why, in my wagon."

"Huh-uh, I don't think so." Slade fished in his vest pocket and removed two small pieces of paper. Earlier, when he had retrieved his personal belongings from the wagon, he had been surprised to find Branson's IOUs still among them. The fool had not had enough sense to destroy the papers, and now he was going to call in the debt.

If he gave Branson the whipping he deserved, the pain would not last long enough to satisfy him. If he killed him, there was a strong possibility he would get in trouble with the law, for he knew what lengths Abe Harrison would go to when crossed, and he had had enough of the inside of a jail to last him the rest of his life. Slade decided he could hurt Branson more by taking everything he owned.

Slade shrugged indifferently. "Looks like we're right back where we started. Only thing is, I am now a wiser man. I learned my lesson the hard way. Either pay up or get your gear out of my wagon."

"You know I don't have any money."

"Then you had better start packing."

Slade grasped Branson by his arm and escorted him, none too gently, to the wagon. "Just in case you get any smart ideas, I'm taking the . . . excuse me, *my* horses and wagon down to the livery stable and, by God, they had better be there when I check on them, or . . . I'm sure you remember what the sheriff said they did to horse thieves in these parts. After all that you've done, it would be a pleasure to watch you hang."

His expression narrowed, and his voice became stern with no vestige of sympathy in its hardness. "I'll probably live to regret it, but I'm going to give you a chance to save your hide. I am going over to the hotel, rent a room, then eat supper. I may even have a drink while I'm there, but don't count on having extra time. Then" — Slade's voice turned deathly cold — "if you are still in town, I'll kill you."

Branson gulped. He knew Slade was not issuing an idle warning. He hurriedly crawled into the wagon, and a few minutes later tossed a small leather bag to the ground and climbed down. He looked anxiously at Virginia and gave a halfhearted shrug. "You will have to pack your own belongings. I don't know what you'll need." He was too worried about Slade to take Virginia's threats too seriously. After all, he reasoned, she had no place to go but with him.

Branson gave a nervous cough. "How am I supposed to get out of town if I'm afoot?" he asked Slade in a whining voice.

Slade was amazed at the man's gall. His first impulse was to put an end to Branson's misery. But the man was not worth the price of the bullet it would take to shoot him. He calmly peeled fifty dollars from his roll of money, crumbled it in his hand, then dropped it at his feet. "That ought to buy you a horse. Now you don't have any excuse."

"Fifty dollars! Why, that ain't enough!"

"It's all you're getting out of me, except maybe a bullet." Slade inched his hand toward his gun. "If you don't want a chance to clear out, maybe we ought to settle our differences now. I'll be glad to find you a gun. And you don't have to worry; the fight will be

119

fair. I am not the kind of man who waits until some-one's back is turned."

"N — No, no, that's all right. I'll take the money."

Branson's mouth was tight, grim, and deep lines of fear were clearly evident on his face. He knew Slade meant every word he had said. He glanced nervously at Virginia. "Come on, girl, let's go."

"No! I don't know how many times I have to tell you; I never want to see you again!" she muttered vehemently.

Branson raked his hand through his thinning hair. "Now, come on, girl, quit your nonsense! You heard what he said. We have to get out of town or he'll kill me!"

Her voice was cold, like an echo from an empty tomb. "Then I suggest you hurry."

Branson clenched and unclenched his hands and his face grew mottled with rage. When he saw that Virginia was making no attempt to move, he threw Slade one dark, fearful look, picked up the money and his belongings, then ran in the direction of the livery stable.

Slade watched, waiting until Branson turned into the livery stable, then he spun on his foot and headed toward the hotel, which was located farther up the street.

Virginia stared at Slade's retreating form. Suddenly, she knew she could not allow him to simply walk out of her life. Swallowing hard, she drew from the very core of her soul every ounce of courage and bravado she possessed.

"Wait a minute!" She planted her hands on her hips and spread her legs apart in imitation of the stance she had seen Slade take a short while before.

Slade stopped in midstride and turned around

slowly. "Are you talking to me?"

"Yes, I am."

"What in the hell do you want?" It was apparent to him that she had no idea she was reacting exactly as he had hoped.

Virginia took a deep breath, feeling the sudden rush of courage start to abandon her as his glacial blue eyes raked her contemptuously.

Then she thought: I have nothing to lose, not even my pride. I was stripped of that long ago.

"What about me?" she asked bravely.

"What about you?" he repeated with a significant lifting of his brows.

"I'm your wife. Are you just going to leave me standing here in the street?"

Slade stalked back to where she stood, and for a moment he looked at her intently. A probing query passed through his mind when he saw a frightened young girl pretending to be brash and brazen. He felt a twinge of compassion, but his bitterness quickly pushed it away. So, she wants to be my wife, does she? he asked himself wryly. All right, then so be it. I'll be happy to accommodate her. Two can participate in her scheming little game as easily as one.

Not knowing if his continued silence was acceptance or rejection, she lifted her head defiantly. "I do have some pride left, Slade. I will ask, but I will never beg."

He extended his hand and a mocking smile touched his lips. "Allow me, *Mrs. Slade*." His voice rang with undisguised sarcasm.

She studied the hand for what seemed like an eternity, though in reality her perusal lasted only a moment. It was a strong hand, yet curiously gentle. Fire seemed to spread from his touch, sending a scorching wave of heat up her arm.

Virginia could only hope she was not making a dreadful mistake as she squared her shoulders, raised her head haughtily, and looked him straight in the eye. "I believe you mentioned something about supper? I am famished."

"Well, I certainly can't allow my sweet little bride to go hungry, can I?"

Ignoring his sarcasm, she threaded her arm through his, and together, they walked toward the hotel.

Virginia had no idea what lay in store for her. She only knew the future had to be better than her dismal past.

Chapter Nine

Too upset to eat, Virginia pushed the food back and forth on the plate with her fork, acutely aware that Slade did not seem to have a similar problem. He had attacked his food enthusiastically, as though it had been the first meal he had had in days.

How could he have such a hearty appetite? she wondered. Or, for that matter, how could he even eat after what they had just been through? Didn't he realize they had pressing matters to resolve? Of course, they needed privacy to discuss many of the issues, and a hotel dining room was certainly no place for that. But why did he have to savor every bite? Were all men alike? Did all of them think of their stomachs first? Oh, why couldn't he hurry?

Hearing her impatient sigh, Slade smiled devilishly. Speaking in his most courteous tone, he asked, "What's wrong, dear? You're not eating. I thought you were famished." He was determined to hide his true feelings for her, even if he had to talk and behave like an imbecilic milksop to do so.

Intent on her thoughts, Virginia was surprised by his sudden question. She dropped her fork and winced as it clattered noisily against the plate. "I—I guess I lost my appetite," she replied nervously.

"Then may I have your apple pie? It's delicious—better than my mother used to bake."

Good Lord! she exclaimed inwardly. He wants *more* food? Where is he putting it? She wanted to throw up her hands in frustration.

"Of course if you want to eat your pie, that's all right. I will just order another piece." He half rose from his chair and craned his neck, trying to catch the attention of the lady who had served them their food.

"No, please don't bother. You don't have to order another piece. I don't want this." She pushed the desert plate toward him.

Not only was Virginia impatient to get things settled between them, but she was also beginning to feel more and more at a disadvantage, bewildered by her conviction that this man should be furious. He should be treating her with resentment, righteous indignation, *something* other than this well-mannered politeness. She had expected contempt and had received civilized behavior. She had braced herself for an assault upon her defenses and had met with disquieting courtesy. His behavior was so confusing, she was actually beginning to feel annoyed. It was as if he were deliberately trying to antagonize her.

Finally finishing the last bite, Slade signaled for another cup of coffee, settled back in his chair, and watched as Virginia grew increasingly uncomfortable under his careful scrutiny. Allowing his imagination to run rampant, he was unaware of the slow grin that spread across his mouth. In the olden days, he reflected, the pagans would prepare a feast before they sacrificed a virgin, using a roasted suckling pig complete with an apple in its mouth as the main course. He chuckled aloud, thoroughly amused by his thoughts. Not only would he be the pagan, but she would be the sacrifice and the suckling pig as well.

However, he seriously doubted that she was a virgin — not as experienced as she had sounded when she had told that outlandish lie. Oh well, he mused, shrugging indifferently, and still chuckling, a slightly used sacrifice would have to do.

"Is s — something funny?" Virginia asked uneasily, squirming on her chair.

Slade quickly altered the amused expression on his face and decided he should not seem too agreeable or she would become suspicious.

"No . . . well . . . yes, in a strange way, it is. This morning when I woke up, I never thought I would be married and sharing the evening meal with my wife. It is something that never entered my mind. Now, I'm wondering what I am going to do with you." His last statement was stretching the truth slightly. He *knew* what he was going to do, and he intended to enjoy every minute of it.

Pretending bafflement, he shook his head and drawled with distinct mockery, "I realize when your father tried to flatten my head with that iron skillet, it could have affected my memory, but I never thought I would have been able to forget anything as vivid as the seduction you described. It's too bad I can't remember it. It sure must have been nice."

Hearing the heavy dose of sarcasm in his voice, she lifted her chin and boldly met his gaze. "That never happened and you know it!"

"It didn't?" Slade feigned surprise.

Virginia looked about anxiously, afraid that he was merely baiting her, that he would lose his temper and create an ugly scene. Heaven only knew they already had given the citizens of Barkersville enough to gossip about without offering them more. "We need to discuss the circumstances of our . . . of this marriage, but please, show me the courtesy of discussing it in private."

"Oh, I definitely agree, it needs to be discussed, but first I intend to sit here and enjoy my coffee. If I remember correctly, you know how much I like it," he said smoothly, recalling the morning he had stopped at the Bransons' camp.

"Yes, I do," she said, settling back against the chair, trying not to show her impatience.

As Slade sipped his coffee, his face darkened as he became deeply immersed in thought.

For awhile back there at the ranch, he had barely given Virginia a second thought. He had believed her innocent of any wrongdoing. Even though her lies had cost him dearly, under the circumstances, lying had been about the only thing she could have done. If she had not agreed with her father, no doubt the old man would have been hanged from the highest tree. Then, the lie she had told about him . . . about them . . . well, at least it had kept him from hanging.

But as they had ridden into town, that shotgun aimed at his back had cleared his mind considerably. Having had time to think about everything that had happened, he had come to the conclusion that he had been the victim of an elaborate scheme, a sham they must have pulled all the way from East Texas — or wherever they were from — to here.

At one time, he had had an acute sense of good judgment, but perhaps those years he had spent in prison had dulled his wits. After giving it considerable thought, Slade realized he should have been suspicious when Virginia appeared at the saloon immediately after the poker game had ended. That should have tipped him off, because it was simply too much of a coincidence. Gullibly, he had believed her when she said she had been waiting at their camp for all of those days without knowing where her father was.

Hell, if it had been *his* father, he would have been searching after the first . . . second day at the most. But, like a fool, after she had cried a few tears and twisted her pretty face into a pitiful expression, he had believed every word she said.

The truth of the matter was she had probably been in town almost from the beginning, waiting to make her move when the time was right. Each time they had taken a break from the poker game, Branson had probably filled her in on what was happening. The victim of their scheme could have been any of the men, though. It was the big winner they had been after. That man had been marked for robbery from the very beginning.

He had played right into their hands by suggesting they go out to their camp to discuss the problem of the money Branson owed. They had performed their respective roles well. She had jumped at the opportunity, while Branson had seemed indifferent. Slade had to admit it was a smart move on their part. It had kept him from suspecting anything.

Then, at the camp, it had been her job to keep him occupied and to play on his sympathy so that her father could get the jump on him. She had done a damn good job of it too. Again, a few tears from those big black eyes . . . spider eyes—yes, that's what she was, a venomous female spider, and he had walked right into her well-spun web with both eyes open.

The only problem was, they had not counted on Abe Harrison. That man had immediately recognized Branson for what he really was. Slade now realized he had been too intent on whittling Harrison down a notch, on showing the rancher he was the better man. Harrison had pegged him right when he had called him a "cocky, arrogant bastard."

The Bransons' first mistake had been cutting across

127

Harrison's land and destroying his property. If they had taken a different route, more than likely they would have gotten away with it completely.

Then, during the meeting in Harrison's study, it had been lies on top of lies. And, for awhile there, he had actually felt relieved that Virginia had had too much of a conscience to let him hang for something he had not done.

Slade drew an invisible pattern on the tablecloth, still deep in thought. He had overlooked one angle. Now he was not so sure it had been her conscience. She could have told the last lie for a very different reason. It seemed to him that Virginia had switched loyalties very quickly after the ceremony—almost too quickly. Could it have been part of a larger plan? It was quite possible she had decided that the game she and her father had played was no longer worth the risk. After Harrison had given him back his belongings, maybe she had concluded that he would be easy pickings again. He had certainly given her no reason to think otherwise.

Slade reminded himself not to carry too much money on him until he left town. There was no need to tempt fate.

Virginia broke into his thoughts. "Your coffee cup has been empty for at least the past five minutes. Do you want another cup, or are you ready to . . . have our discussion?"

Smiling, he pushed his chair away from the table. "Oh, I am definitely ready."

Slade courteously held open the door for Virginia while she stepped inside. Even though the hotel room was quite ordinary, after being confined to the cramped quarters of the wagon for months now, Vir-

128

ginia was impressed with the roominess, and with how fresh and clean everything looked.

Against one wall stood a tall, golden-oak princess dresser with a beveled plate-glass mirror. In one corner was a brass tub shielded by a sandalwood screen for privacy. A clothes-horse and small dressing stool stood beside it. Lamps with milk-colored globes sat on night tables on either side of the huge, highly polished brass bed. The bed was strategically located so that anyone lying on it could benefit from whatever cool breeze happened to stir through the two open windows. Two comfortable-looking armchairs had been placed catercorner in front of the windows. It was a very nice room, especially considering Barkersville's size and location.

Virginia glanced at the bed and her face clouded with uneasiness. Never having thought about *that* particular side of their marriage, she quickly averted her eyes. She wondered, if they were able to resolve their differences, just how much Slade would expect from her. She became acutely aware of a flush stealing over her cheeks at the thought.

Nervously worrying her bottom lip, she took a deep breath and said, "Slade, I—I . . . really don't know where to begin. . . ."

"Why not start at the wagon when your father tried to cave my head in?" Slade did not want to sound too angry, but he knew he was dealing with an unscrupulous woman and if he suddenly seemed too agreeable, too eager to forgive, it might raise her suspicions.

Her eyes widened with innocence. "Slade, I swear I had no idea what he was going to do!"

"And you expect me to believe that?" he asked, his voice grating harshly.

Her mouth worked, but no words came. She twisted her hands nervously. Finally, she said, "No, I suppose not . . . but it is the truth." Her eyes clung to his, analyzing his reaction.

Deliberately, Slade allowed his features to soften, just enough to let her think he might believe her. "Well . . . what about those outrageous lies?"

She squared her shoulders, her nervousness intensified. "What was I supposed to have said?"

"The truth would have helped," he muttered with a minute ring of sarcasm.

"If I had told the truth, Mr. Harrison would have hanged my father. Regardless of what he's done, I couldn't allow that to happen."

"Even if it meant their stringing me up?" he scoffed.

Virginia moistened her lips. "That's why I said we had been . . ." She paused, embarrassed. "That's why I said what I did. I could not let that happen either."

"But you could have refused to marry me. Why didn't you?" he asked staunchly.

"B—Because I was a—afraid . . . they . . . Mr. Harrison would decide my father and I were lying . . . and I had no idea what they would have done then." She shook her head, and her voice gathered strength. "That's not true! I did have an idea. I was afraid they would go for a rope. And I would have done anything to prevent that!"

Slade took a deep breath and said, noncommittally, "I suppose, under the circumstances . . . you had to save your father's life."

"And yours too."

Chuckling sardonically, he shook his head. "I'm sure you'll forgive me if I find it hard to believe you were that concerned about me."

"But it's true," she whispered.

Before he could conceal it, a look of disbelief claimed his face. "Why? Because you care for me so much?"

Virginia stared at him hard for a long moment. Although he had every reason to be angry, she was becoming weary of his sarcasm and cutting remarks. Perhaps she should tell him the entire truth. It could not possibly make matters worse than they already were.

He folded his arms and splayed his legs into an arrogant stance. "I'm waiting for an answer . . . and it had better be a damn good one."

"The truth is" — she boldly met his gaze — "I *could* care for you." He made a rude, scoffing sound, but she could tell from his expression that she had piqued his interest. Even though her cheeks blazed from embarrassment, she pressed on, but she could not bring herself to keep her gaze leveled on his face. "That day when you first stopped by the camp . . . I thought then that you were the most handsome man I had ever seen. Then, after we talked for awhile, I decided you were also the nicest man I had ever met." She swallowed the hard lump that had suddenly formed in her throat. "I — I realize I probably sound very foolish — maybe even silly — but I was very attracted to you."

"So the shotgun wedding was a convenient way to trap me, huh?"

"It was never my intention to *trap* you. And I'm not telling you this for sympathy. I'm merely trying to explain why I did what I did. You saw how my father is . . . but he wasn't always that way. There was a time when he was a respected man, but after Mother died he just didn't seem to care anymore."

"I can't see what that has to do with me . . . with us."

"It has everything to do with us." Her chin jutted defiantly. "Do you have any idea how it is to live in a town where your father is known as the town drunk?

131

To be pointed at with ridicule? Not to have any friends? To be the subject of gossip, whether warranted or not. To be the object of cruel taunts? To be the subject of men's ugly boasts? To have your reputation sullied ruthlessly and your name bandied about on every street corner in town, even though you've never done anything to deserve it? To be stripped of pride and any feeling of decency?" Her bottom lip trembled from the memories. "I think not. So perhaps, deep down inside, I didn't want to say anything to stop the wedding. Perhaps I saw it as a way to escape. Perhaps I thought you were an understanding man . . . and that you were attracted to me too. And that maybe our feelings could grow if given half a chance."

Slade pulled his gaze away from her, realizing he had been entranced by the sadness on her face. Damn, he raged inwardly, for a minute there she had almost been convincing. But his father had had a favorite saying, and it was something that had stuck with him for many years:

> If somebody makes a fool out of you once,
> Shame on him.
> But if makes a fool out of you twice,
> Shame on you.

With the exception of what she had said about the lies she had told, Virginia's story was nothing more than a highly imaginative fabrication, he decided, and he was not about to be duped again. But, if he had any hopes of getting even with her, he could not reveal his true feelings.

Slade knew he had to be convincing. His brows knotted into an incredulous frown. "I had no idea your earlier life was that bad . . . but I don't know if this changes the situation between us or not."

"I don't want your sympathy, Slade," she was quick to say. "And I really didn't expect it to change anything between us. I just wanted you to know how I feel . . . and why I reacted the way I did."

He ran his fingers through his hair, wincing slightly when they brushed against the tender spot on the back of his head. "I need some time to think about this. I guess we can . . . or perhaps we could. . . ." He shrugged and sighed deeply. "I don't know, Virginia. I just don't know what to do." He pretended deep consideration. "Maybe it would be best if I went for a walk . . . to think about what you have told me. Besides, there are some pressing matters I need to attend to, and—"

"What pressing matters?" she asked fearfully, remembering the threat Slade had made against her father. Regardless of what he had done, she did not want to see him dead, or see Slade get into any more trouble. There had been enough of that already.

Even though Slade now lounged casually against the door frame, his words were crisp and to the point. "If you are worrying about your father, don't. I'm sure he has already left town. But I will give you fair warning: I won't underestimate him again. I'll be careful which way I turn my back."

"I—I cannot blame you for feeling that way." Again reminded of what her father had done, she glanced away, unable to look him in the eye. She knew her father's shame would haunt her always.

Slade's eyes held a deliberate touch of amusement as he allowed his gaze to drift slowly over her. "Since I am going to be out, I won't mind getting a change of clothing for you from the wagon. Is there a particular chest or trunk you keep your belongings in?"

She nodded, glancing at the brass tub with longing.

What she would give for a refreshing bath in a real tub instead of having to use a creek or merely sponging off with a wash pan. "My dresses are in a small brown trunk at the front of the wagon; that is, unless Papa moved it while he was getting his things. And there should be a reddish colored carpetbag near it that has my . . . my . . . personal belongings in it."

Slade wanted to laugh aloud at her pretense of shyness. Anyone who could spin such an incredible yarn as she had earlier, especially using such graphic detail, could not be embarrassed over such a simple thing as instructing him to fetch her undergarments.

"A brown trunk, did you say?" he asked nonchalantly.

"Yes." She looked away, blushing.

He reached for the doorknob. "I'll be back soon." Then he paused and turned to face her. "I couldn't help but notice the way you looked at the bathtub. If you want me to, I'll stop at the desk and have some bath water brought up."

"Would you?" Her dark eyes brightened at the thought of a refreshing bath.

"Sure. It's no problem at all." Virginia seemed so genuinely pleased and thankful, his conscience prickled at her reaction. She had no way of knowing that his motive, went deeper than simply wanting to be nice to her.

After Slade left, Virginia walked over to one of the chairs, sat down, and wearily rested her head against the back. She could not remember ever being so tired. The confrontation with Slade had been emotionally exhausting. She felt limp, wrung out. Then too, it had been nearly a week since she had had a decent night's sleep. At first she had worried about her father; then, later, she had worried over whether or not he had killed Slade.

134

She closed her eyes for a few minutes and tried to relax, to push all of her troubles from her mind, but Slade's image and how he had looked at her earlier with such hatred and anger kept torturing her.

Feeling perspiration bead on her forehead, Virginia got up to raise the window and caught a glimpse of Slade just before he disappeared from view. Pain stabbed through her heart, and tears formed in her eyes. She felt she had lost something very precious, something she had never really possessed, though under different circumstances she might have. She could have loved Slade—or did she already? Just the brief glimpse of him had caused blood to rush heatedly through every portion of her body. She was reluctant to admit it, but his recent behavior had given her so much hope. Perhaps he believed her. Perhaps he would hold her blameless for all that had happened. And perhaps he had the same feelings for her as she had for him. At least that was how it would be in a fairy-tale romance when a handsome prince rescued a fair damsel from a life of drudgery and whisked her away to live happily ever after.

But theirs was not a fairy-tale romance. Slade was a flesh-and-blood man. He had his own dreams and desires, which most likely did not include her. It was true he was treating her far better than she had expected, but treating her well and loving her were two different things entirely.

Intent on her worrisome thoughts, Virginia began to pace restlessly. Then she stopped abruptly, her eyes wide with alarm. She knew absolutely nothing about Slade's private life. What if he already had a wife? No, surely he would have said so. But what if some of the hatred she had seen earlier stemmed from the fact that he already had a lady, a woman whom he loved? Frustrated, she clenched her hands into fists.

Then, hearing a knock at the door, she rushed to answer it, hoping it was Slade. But, instead, a stooped-shouldered old man and a young boy entered, each carrying two large wooden buckets of steaming water.

"Your husband ordered bath water for you."

"Oh, yes, he said he was going to, but I had no idea it would be sent up so quickly."

"We don't dally around here. This ought to be enough, but if you want more, it'll cost extra." He nodded toward the dresser while emptying the buckets of water into the tub. "You'll find towels and a face-cloth in the bottom drawer, and here's a fresh bar of soap in the holder. Soap is so expensive, most hotels don't supply a new bar to every guest, but we do."

"T—Thank you."

As Virginia started to close the door behind them, she could hear the young boy saying, "Grandpa, she didn't look like Ma did before Albert was born."

"What do you mean, Sonny?"

"I overheard Ma telling Aunt Tilly that that woman had to get married—she called it a shotgun wedding—cause she was in the family way. But she looks awfully skinny to me. I looked real good and her belly was flatter than one of your flapjacks."

"Sometimes different women fleshen up quicker than others. But you be careful and don't let your ma hear you talkin' like that. She'll tan your hide and wash your mouth out with lye soap."

"But why, Grandpa? I was just saying what Ma said. Is she gonna wash her mouth out too?"

Leaning her forehead against the door as their voices grew faint, Virginia stood helplessly as a feeling of shame washed over her and stains of scarlet appeared on her cheeks. If a young boy was already commenting on her predicament, what was everyone else saying? Suddenly, the room looked less cheerful. Her need for a bath became overpowering, not just to wash away the grit and dust from her body, but to cleanse the stain that had spread much deeper.

Opening the drawer to remove the towel and face-cloth, Virginia caught sight of herself in the beveled mirror. The reflection showed a girl so slender she could have passed for a young boy if it had not been for her breasts. Her blue gingham dress was faded and wrinkled, and covered with dust from the wagon ride into town. Wisps of dull hair—no longer honey gold in color, but instead a mousy brown—straggled from her thick braid to cling to her moist, dust-smudged face, and there were dark shadows under her eyes from her fatigue and restless nights. She looked a fright! It was no wonder Slade had suggested she take a bath and don fresh clothing. How embarrassed he must have been to have been seen in her company. She looked like a homeless waif.

Determined that Slade would not see her looking so dreadful again, Virginia quickly unfastened the many buttons on the bodice of her dress. After disrobing completely, she stepped into the tub of hot water and gradually lowered her aching body into its warmth. A contented sigh escaped her lips. This was magnificent! Sheer paradise!

Removing the bar of castile soap from the holder beside the tub, Virginia worked it into a rich lather between her hands and soaped her hair again and again, letting the silken foam slide down her soft shoulders and across her rose-tipped breasts. Despite her earlier despondency, she found herself sighing with delight at how good and refreshing the hot water felt. She scrubbed herself carefully, inch by inch, then lay back, luxuriating in the comfort of a real bathtub, the delicate scent of the soap, and the feeling of being

137

fresh and clean again.

Finally, the water began to cool. Virginia rinsed the last traces of soap from her hair. She stood up with a lithe grace and allowed the droplets of water to slide unerringly from her body. She squeezed the excess water from her hair by drawing the golden strands over her shoulder and twisting them around her arm. Then, she shook her head to and fro, causing the tangled tresses to whip stingingly against her flesh, before allowing her hair to fall to its full length just below her waist.

Reaching for the towel she had placed beside the tub earlier, she stopped, frozen.

Good Lord, what has happened to my mind? she thought. Have I taken leave of my senses? What am I supposed to put on? Not those filthy clothes! But I cannot let Slade return and find me naked either! His opinion of me is probably already next to nothing and it certainly won't improve if he thinks . . . if he thinks . . . why, he might think I am deliberately trying to seduce him! Oh, dear, what am I going to do now?

She picked up her dirty clothes, but her nose wrinkled with disgust. She simply could not bear the thought of donning them again, not after that cleansing bath.

Then, an idea struck her. It was not the best solution, but it was better than having Slade return to find her wearing nothing but a towel wrapped around her. A look of dismay crossed her face as she unfolded the towel. It was a skimpy one at that! Wrapping it around her, she dashed across the room to the bed, stripped the top sheet from it, and quickly wrapped it around her, securing it by tucking the corner into her cleavage.

Then, hurrying back to the tub, she knelt beside it and washed her clothing in the bath water. Then she hung the garments near the far window, hoping that the light breeze would dry them before he returned.

Having nothing else to do, not even possessing a brush to groom her hair, Virginia uneasily sat down on one of the chairs. "If he comes back before my clothes dry, I'll just run behind the screen where he can't see me. Yes, that is exactly what I will do," she declared aloud.

She sank deeper into the soft cushions, and waited. The minutes passed quickly and before long, exhausted from her ordeal and thoroughly refreshed after the pleasant bath, she fell fast asleep.

Chapter Ten

The room was shrouded in darkness, and for a brief moment Slade thought it was empty. His emotions ran the gamut from relief that Virginia was gone to disappointment that he could not use her as she had used him. However, there was also something else, something he could not quite put his finger on. But before he had time to dwell on it, a cloud scudded from the face of the moon and brilliant light shone through the window. He saw her curled up asleep on a chair with a sheet wrapped around her.

His eyes widened with awe and his breath came in a ragged gasp. She was beautiful. Her skin reminded him of shimmering gold next to the stark whiteness of the sheet, and although her hair was disheveled, it fairly glowed under the pale moonlight. A sudden rush of desire raged through him. He longed to caress her tawny skin, to tangle his hands in the long, silken tresses fanned out before him. He had been too long without a woman, and the need was suddenly overpowering.

Walking very quietly, Slade crossed the room and sat down on the side of the bed, unable to take his eyes off her. A wry grin tugged at his lips. So, the spider continues to spin her web, he mused. Only this

140

time, instead of using false tears and wide, innocent eyes as bait, she has become a golden temptress.

His eyes narrowed knowingly. She's not asleep; she's only pretending. She knows all too well how beautiful she is. She also knows her loveliness is intensified by the moonlight. Since she has gone to all this trouble to seduce me . . . hell, I would be a fool to disappoint her. But this time, the spider will be snared in her own web. I'll show her how it feels to be used, he thought ruthlessly as he tugged off his boots, then removed his shirt and carelessly tossed it aside.

Stealthily, Slade knelt beside the chair. He took up a strand of her hair, letting it curl confiningly about his fingers for a moment before releasing it, watching with bemused eyes as the silken strand with its golden highlights covered the tip-tilted roundness of her breasts. Then he moved back slightly, eager to see what her reaction would be. He was not disappointed.

Virginia awoke with a start. "Oh!" Then, seeing Slade kneeling close by, she stammered, "Y—You s—startled me." Rubbing her face with both hands, she added, "I m—must have f—fallen asleep."

Her mouth suddenly became dry when she noticed that Slade was without a shirt. He looked so manly. His appearance was almost hypnotic, she decided, becoming mesmerized by the way his broad, muscular chest rose and fell with each breath he took.

"I started not to disturb you, you looked like you were resting so well. But I was afraid you would get a crick in your neck if you slept in that chair all night." He lied easily, without a pang of conscience.

His gaze drifted over her approvingly, lingering on the swell of her breasts. "By the way, I like your dress."

Immediately, her hands flew to her bosom to clutch the sheet tightly to her. Her heart pounded out an erratic rhythm. Suddenly, she was very frightened.

Her fear stemmed from the way his intense eyes beheld and caressed her with sensual appreciation.

Feeling the need to offer an explanation, she stammered, "I—I took a bath . . . and I didn't want to put my dirty dress back on. I washed it out . . . it should be dry by now." Growing increasingly uncomfortable with the dark gleam in Slade's eyes, she swallowed hard and added, "If you will excuse me, I—I think I had better get dressed." Virginia knew she was babbling, but she felt powerless to stop.

She started to rise, but Slade caught her hand.

"Why get dressed? It's bedtime."

"Oh . . . yes, I suppose it is." She looked at the bed and her gaze flew back to Slade. "B—But where are you going to sleep?"

"Why, in the bed, of course," he replied with feigned innocence.

"B—But . . . what about me?"

He chuckled. "I imagine you will sleep there too." He reached out and gently touched her cheek. His voice grew husky. "Although I doubt that either one of us will get too much sleep. After all . . . this is our wedding night."

Virginia swallowed hard, her heart hammering rapidly against her breast, and her eyes widening into black fathomless pits. "It's true, we were married, b—but I thought from the way you . . . talked earlier . . . we would . . . Why, we don't even know each other!" She inched backward until it seemed she was trying to burrow through the back of the chair. The look of desire was so evident on his face, he reminded her of those men in Jefferson who had tried to have their way with her.

Slade pursued her, giving her no chance to escape as he placed his hands on the arms of the chair. He trailed his lips along the soft line of her jaw, gently

142

murmuring, "Then this will be an ideal way for us to become acquainted." Slipping his hands underneath her, he rose and lifted her easily from the chair.

"N — No, we can't. . . ."

"We can and we will," he said, his husky voice cutting inexorably across her protests as he placed her on the bed and pressed his body close to hers.

His mouth descended on hers with an urgent heat, twisting, searching for its sweetness. Virginia tried to turn her head, but his body pressing against hers gave her little room. She delivered hard, frightened blows to his naked back, but it seemed they made very little impression on him.

Nevertheless, Slade took her face and held it in a vicelike grip. He whispered forcefully, "Will you please stop acting like I am trying to rape you? It's not my habit to force women! Just relax and enjoy it."

He lowered his mouth once again, eager to taste the honeyed nectar of her lips. His tongue slipped past her defenses in an intrusion so intimate it made her draw in her breath sharply. Somehow, she found the strength to wrench herself away from him.

With a smothered gasp, she scrambled over the smooth surface of the bed, but her desperate flight gained her nothing. The tumbled silk of her hair was caught under his elbow. Before she could pull it free, Slade shot out a hand, dragging her to him. Forcing her onto her back, he clamped his hands around her wrists and pinioned them high above her head.

"Damnit, stop fighting me, Virginia! I am not going to hurt you."

She set her chin in a stubborn line and her voice choked up with defiance. "You might say you don't force women, but your actions certainly prove differently!"

Slade stared at her hard, finding it difficult to believe her struggles were real. He had to give her credit; she was playing her virginal role to the limit of her ability. But didn't she realize he would *know* she was not a virgin the moment he entered her? He sighed heavily. Perhaps that was the problem. Maybe that was why she was struggling so. If that was the case, he would just have to be stern and demand his husbandly rights. Hell, if pretending to be a virgin was all that important to her, he could always pretend later he hadn't realized the difference. Since she thought he was a fool, he did not see the harm in acting like one.

Then, a different thought occurred to him. What if Virginia really was unwilling? Then how far should he go to obtain revenge? He had already considered several alternatives and the best way he could think of to get even with her was to use her, to humiliate her as badly as he had been humiliated, then cast her aside as though she were nothing. But how much satisfaction would he get out of it if he had to rape her? Revenge was one thing, but rape was something else entirely. Winning the battle would not be enough if he had to lose the war to do so. He was not cut from that kind of cloth and held men in contempt who tried to force themselves on women. He would try one more time, and if she was still unwilling, then he would simply mark off the past week as a lesson well learned and forget about it completely.

Although Slade still held her pinioned to the bed, he relaxed his hold. His tone was apologetic. "Perhaps I was too . . . forceful. I suggest we get this settled between us right now. Since we are married, we might as well try to make the best of it. However, I refuse to be married in name only. I expect you to be my wife . . . to the fullest extent of the word. If you are willing to do this, fine. If not, then I'll leave. I'm sure, under the circumstances, you would have no problem getting this marriage dissolved."

Virginia exulted at Slade's words. If only he had said them at the beginning instead of coming at her like a rutting bull, she would not have resisted him. But he had been so rough, so callous, uttering barely a word of tenderness, that he had frightened her half out of her wits. When he had left a while ago, she had not known if he would return. Then to be awakened abruptly by a Slade who wanted to make love to her . . . it was little wonder she had fought him. Placing all of that aside, her heart soared at the thought: *He wants me to be his wife! His real wife!*

Her voice was soft but unsteady as she said, "I do not believe in having marriages dissolved. But . . . what if I am not the kind of wife you want me to be?"

"What do you mean?"

Her eyes came up to study his face, and she suddenly wished for more light so that she could see his reaction better. Feeling awkward and very embarrassed, she could only manage a hoarse whisper. "You said that you do not force women. And . . . it seems from what I have overheard, most men know several women intimately before they marry, so I am not passing judgment," she was quick to explain. "But I know very little about men. My mother died so long ago, and no one has ever told me what to expect. I only know what I have overheard other women say, and they were always vague." She bit on her lower lip, then stated, "To the fullest extent of the word, I have no idea how to be a real wife."

Slade resisted the urge to laugh scoffingly at the lengths she was going to carry out this pretense. Instead, he merely chuckled and played her game. "Sweetheart, that is something you don't learn. It just comes naturally. It has to. That part of married life has been around since Adam and Eve. The most important thing is, I'm willing to give it a try. Are you?" He noticed a dim flush race like a fever across Virginia's pretty face.

Virginia moistened her lips. Unable to form the words, she merely nodded her head.

Lying on top of her in such an intimate way had taken its toll on Slade's woman-starved body. Those five years he had spent in prison had been a long time indeed. The two times he had sought relief in the arms of a saloon whore had been less than satisfying, and now his body demanded release.

Now secure in his victory, Slade released his pent-up breath and murmured softly, "Just relax, sweetheart, and do as I say." Once he started making love to her, he wanted no interruptions, no hindrances such as stopping to remove clothing. "First, we get rid of this damn sheet." He rose back on his knees and slowly removed the fabric that had become crumpled around her. His eyes widened in wonder as her silky flesh was revealed. The brief glimpses he had caught earlier were nothing compared to the wondrous sight of her mounded breasts, the dusk-colored nipples, her flat stomach, and the satiny curls surrounding her womanhood.

Giving a strangled cry, he wadded the material in his large hands and tossed it over his shoulder. Swallowing hard, he said, "And now, we get rid of these." He quickly unbuttoned his trousers, slipped them from his body, and kicked them off the foot of the bed. Then, lying down beside Virginia, he gathered her in his arms, his face dark with passion.

Virginia wanted to speak, to urge him to please be gentle, to tell him that in spite of her willingness she was frightened. And to be stripped bare for a man's admiration was something she had never experienced.

She opened her mouth to whisper her sudden rush of fears, but it was too late. He was already kissing her half-parted lips, his tongue darting in and out of her mouth, exploring every inch of softness that trembled beneath his demanding lips. Her eyes widened in fearful wonder when she felt his manhood growing, probing at her flesh.

He sensually ravaged the sweetness of her mouth until he was moaning with pleasure and panting for breath, so intense was his loving assault.

Virginia's flesh blazed as Slade's mouth burned its way across her cheek and up to one temple, where he buried his face in her hair and huskily murmured tender words, scandalous words, of love and sex. A moment—or was it hours—passed and she began answering his kisses timidly. Then her arms tightened around his neck and she kissed him back feverishly, as though swept away by some wild, wanton wind, much like the elusive dust devils that abounded in these arid spaces.

His hands found her breasts. His fingers cupped the full mounds possessively, fondling them teasingly, tauntingly, before he bent his head and covered one dusky crest with his lips, sucking it, sending sparks of fiery flames racing through her veins as his tongue swirled about the nipple caressingly, and his teeth nibbled gently. Virginia had never known that such raw, primitive pleasure existed. She was so caught up in the strange sensations he was producing in her body, she was only dimly aware of the soft moans of delight emerging from her throat.

His heavily matted chest rubbed against her breasts, the downy hair that trailed down his chest to the hard, muscular flatness of his stomach teasing her flesh provocatively. Then his hand inched down, past the rounded curve of her hip. He squeezed and ca-

ressed her gently, yet his touch had a savage roughness about it. His fingers sought her womanhood; he
stroked the silky velvet tenderly, rhythmically, tugging
at the satiny curls and tracing the swell of her silky
skin until she found herself brazenly arching forward,
eager for his hands, eager for his touch.

His mouth found her lips, and again he explored
her sweetness. But he did not linger long. He trailed
sensual kisses down her throat to her breasts, then to
her stomach. His tongue flicked in and out of her
naval until she tingled with desire. Somewhere in the
dark recesses of her mind she understood they had
gone past the point of sanity, that there would be no
return to any form of innocence, but she did not care.
There was a burning deep inside that screamed for
release, but she did not know how to obtain it.

Suddenly, Slade rasped hoarsely, "Touch me. I want
you to touch me."

Virginia was too startled by his demand to offer any
objection. She knew what he meant, but she was unsure of what to do. Slade took her hand and guided it
to his maleness, gasping when flesh touched flesh.
The noise drowned out the heavy thudding of her
heart. Her brows rose in amazement at his enormous
size, when with his urging, she closed her hand
around his shaft. Her hand traveled slowly from the
base to the very tip, which was moist with desire. She
drew in her breath sharply and her eyes widened with
wonder at what was still to come.

Deep in that soft, secret place between her thighs,
Virginia felt a slow, hot ache flicker like a smoldering
ember, then take flame and race through her body
like a raging wildfire, burning out of control.

Then, in one swift motion, she was flat on her back
and Slade had his knees planted between her thighs,
spreading her legs farther apart as he knelt, and,

taking her hands, he pulled her upward, guiding her fingers over his body.

She threaded her fingers through the dark mat of hair upon his chest, touching, caressing, marveling at his hard, sinewy muscles. Her senses were assaulted, her mind filled only with the mesmerizing effect his body had on hers. Then, vaguely aware that the hard strength of his thighs was pressing against her, Virginia gave a sharp intake of breath when she felt his maleness probing at the entrance to her femininity.

Slade thrust forward, and his mind was momentarily confused by the tight barrier that barred his body from seeking the release it so desperately needed. As he probed harder, her virginal barrier broke, sheathing his maleness with moisture and enabling him to press onward toward the titillating journey's end. He was aware of Virginia's sharp cry of pain as she tried to burrow into the feather mattress to avoid his impaling sword, but no power in the universe could have stopped him, not even if he had wanted it.

Tears filled Virginia's eyes, and she thought she would surely be split asunder. Her cries of pain and protest were abruptly cut off as his lips covered hers. His tongue shot into her mouth, probing deeper and deeper into that crevice while his manhood slowly filled the other. Her fingernails dug into his back and they grasped his buttocks as she tried to stop him, but her feeble attempts were useless. She could feel the invasion inch by inch. His toes dug into the mattress for added leverage while his hands gripped the bars of the brass headboard, pulling, straining, until he was completely buried within her. His buttocks tensed and trembled beneath her hands, and only then did he pause.

When Slade had entered her, Virginia had thought she would never be able to bear the pain, but now, as her body became accustomed to the feel of him, the pain — although still present — seemed to fade as would a few drops of water evaporating under a merciless, burning sun. She could feel him throbbing deep within her, and one lucid portion of her mind gave thanks that this onslaught was almost over, while another portion wanted it to last longer so that the first delightful feelings would have time to rekindle. There was something building in her she could not explain, an unquenched thirst or an unfulfilled yearning.

Sensing Virginia would no longer cry, Slade raised his head and his eyes gazed intently into hers. He knew his expression was triumphant, perhaps even gloating, but he wanted his face burned into her memory so that she would never forget who had completely possessed her first.

He could feel himself swelling, growing even larger, and he praised those pagan gods for endowing him so generously when he saw Virginia's eyes widening with astonishment. Knowing her tight sheath would soon drain him, he began making small, darting motions.

He first moved with rhythmic, evenly timed thrusts, but as the need for release became overpowering, his breath grew rapid and ragged, his teeth gritted together, perspiration shone on his skin, and his face became set in an almost demonic expression. Finally, he threw back his head, arched his back, and plunged himself to the hilt as the night exploded into red-hot ecstasy.

Chapter Eleven

Breathing heavily, Slade eased from Virginia. With gentle fingers he smoothed the fine but tangled strands of her hair from her face, releasing the tension where the tresses were caught beneath him and under her shoulders. He then sat up on the side of the bed, removed a match from its holder, and lit the lamp nearest him. Then he sat there, his head slightly bowed, his arms resting on his legs, deep in thought.

He felt torn by conflicting emotion. He was annoyed with himself for being so aggressive and for losing his self-control. It grated on his conscience. No man liked to leave a woman unsatisfied. He still felt confused over his discovery that she had been a virgin, yet he was strangely elated as well. But how could she have expected him to know. Though Virginia had been shy at first, she had responded passionately. She had not behaved like a virgin. He had believed her shyness was just an act and that she desired him as much as he desired her. Had he ever been wrong! He sighed heavily. Regardless of what he had thought at first, the fact remained that she had not been satisfied by their lovemaking; and now, for his plan to succeed, he would have to proceed very carefully, even if it meant having to show extraordinary patience.

Women! he grumbled to himself. Just about the time a man thought he had them figured out, they would do something to yank the rug out from under his feet. Slade's brows drew into a knotted frown. Since he had been wrong about her innocence, was it possible he was mistaken about the attack on him? Could she be innocent of that too? Slade shook his head adamantly. No, he was not about to let doubts creep into his mind now. The pieces fit together too perfectly for him to be wrong.

Biting back tears of frustration, Virginia drew away a small space, desperately wishing for something with which to cover herself. Too embarrassed to parade naked in front of Slade to retrieve the sheet he had tossed aside, she awkwardly covered her breasts with one arm and tried to strategically cover the lower region of her body with the other.

She felt tormented. There was a burning ache deep inside her that was almost as painful as the moment she had lost her virginity. It was a strange sensation, as though her body was in great need of something—a hunger, a yearning, a desire that had not been fulfilled. She looked at Slade with his arms propped on his legs and realized something troubled him too. She watched the steady rise and fall of his back each time he took a breath, yet for all his nearness, he seemed remote, lost in thought.

Not wanting to attract his attention but tired of keeping her opinions to herself, she said bitterly, "So that part of marriage is just for men's satisfaction too." Her bottom lip trembled as she struggled not to cry.

Slade turned slightly and peered over his shoulder. "What do you mean, it is just for men?"

Unable to speak for fear of crying, she could only shrug.

Gingerly, Slade lay down beside her and urged her to look at him. He spoke, gently cajoling her. "That was a profound statement you made. And I think my question deserves a better answer than just a shrug."

"It's just that . . . it seems so unfair." She clenched her jaw to quell the sob in her throat.

Moving closer and cupping her chin in his hand, he brushed his lips against her cheek. "What's so unfair?" he asked softly, extremely aware of her beautiful nudity and the effect it was having on his body. It was hard for him to believe he was already experiencing the stirrings of new passion when he had just been so thoroughly satisfied.

Virginia could feel his growing ardor pressing against her side and hear the huskiness of desire in his voice. She had no intention of falling victim to his kisses so soon after her devastating disappointment. He had raised her to the heights of ecstacy, then had allowed her to fall back to earth with a terrible yearning deep inside her. Wrenching from his grasp, she was fully aware of how his eyes lingered hungrily on her as she quickly crossed the room and slipped her now-dry chemise over her head. She then picked up the sheet, walked back to Slade, and spread the covering over him before sitting on the edge of the bed.

"A woman's role in life is unfair," she stated simply, folding her hands together in her lap and holding up her head with pride.

Slade lifted his hands to lock them behind his head and turned to lie back with his long form stretched at ease like a huge cat's, his amused gaze turned in her direction. "That's another profound statement," he said, struggling to keep the laughter from his voice, though he was not quite successful.

"You can laugh at me if you want, but it is the truth."

"Don't tell me that you are a Susan B. Anthony follower?"

"I am not referring to politics, Slade," she said haughtily. "I am talking about basic right and wrong, and women are treated unfairly."

He commented wryly, "I always thought they had it pretty good, myself."

"That is obviously a man's point of view," she sniped.

Amusement returned to his voice. "All right, tell me straight out why you believe women are treated unfairly."

Virginia was eager to express her viewpoint. She believed if she could engage him in a lengthy conversation, it might cool his ardor. "Mind you, I am not an expert and some of my childhood memories are fairly dim, but I do remember how hard my mother used to work."

Interrupting, he remarked sarcastically, "With her being married to your father, I can see why."

Virginia shot him a withering glance. "I know you find it difficult to believe, but there was a time when my father was a good, decent man." Firmly shaking her head, she said, "But I don't want to discuss him. The point I am trying to make is that my father provided a decent living for us—he worked hard, but when his chores were finished, he would sit in his comfortable chair with his feet propped up and would never offer to help Mother, regardless of how she was feeling or if she had had extra chores that day. Then when I grew older, I worked for a few ladies in town, and their husbands treated them the same way. There was one woman in particular with whom I stayed each time she had a baby, which was fairly often. Mrs. Matthews had seven small children — all within nine years," Virginia added pointedly.

"During the course of a normal day, Mrs. Matthews would rise several hours before dawn, prepare breakfast, wash dishes, bake bread, wash clothing, make beds, clean house, scrub floors, take care of the children, cook the noon meal, iron, mend clothing, and work in the vegetable garden. At times she would have to milk the cows, and before the boys got bigger, there were a few times she even had to chop wood. Then she would have to cook supper, wash the dishes, and get the children ready for bed. And in her spare time she would sew for the wealthier people in town. Her husband, even when he was not busy, never offered to lift a finger to help with any of the chores, and what's even worse, she did not expect him to! She claimed it wasn't proper for a man to do women's work, that her husband had enough to do to support them. And maybe he did, but she helped him support their family by taking in sewing, so why couldn't he help her when she needed it?"

Virginia sighed heavily, and not expecting an answer from Slade, she continued. "I realize a marriage is not all lilt and laughter, and if you think I object to hard work, you are wrong. I strongly believe the only way the common person will ever accomplish anything in life is through perseverance — and a lot of hard work! But what galled me was that Mrs. Matthews was not allowed to make any decisions because it was not her place, it was her husband's. He told her when, what, and how to do anything. Why, Mr. Matthews even refused to let her visit her brother and his family. And do you know why? Mrs. Matthews's brother married a woman he did not like — she was a fine, decent woman, and his own brother married the biggest harlot in town! The point is; any single solitary thing he wanted to do was perfectly fine, but she was not allowed to do anything because she was a *woman* and had no voice whatsoever in the matter!"

Her anger became a scalding fury. She folded her arms together adamantly and said, "Ooh, it makes me furious just to think about it!"

There was a faint glint of humor in Slade's eyes and an amused grin overtook his features. Then he quickly straightened his face, strangely relieved that she had not seen his expression. Sensing there was a definite reason behind her tirade, he decided to try to find out what it was.

"What brought all of this on?"

She turned her head away and muttered softly, "I — I'm really not sure."

Virginia knew that was not true. The answer to his question was simple: it did not seem fair for men to dominate women — even during their personal relationships. She knew very little about the intimate side of marriage, but why should a man be the only one to enjoy such intimacy? She did not know where she had gotten the incredible idea that being with one's husband was one of the most wonderful experiences in the world, but she had been badly mistaken.

She realized their relationship was very shaky, to say the least, and being too blunt with him might harm it even further. But if Slade's lovemaking was any indication of what she would be faced with for the rest of her life, perhaps she did not want a husband. She did not know if she could live a lifetime experiencing this gnawing, unfulfilled feeling each time he claimed his husbandly rights.

A sob caught in her throat. No, that was not entirely true. She wanted love, marriage, and respectability, but most of all, she realized with a sinking feeling, she wanted Slade.

"What's wrong?"

"I—I don't know."

"Do you think it would help if I held you?" he asked huskily, rising up on one elbow. He reached out and trailed his fingers sensually down her arm.

Finding his nearness disturbing yet exciting, she looked at him cautiously. "Y—You're not going to d—do that to me again, are you?"

"Do what?" he teased, knowing exactly what she meant.

"M—Make love to me."

"Oh, I don't know," he said, brushing his lips teasingly against the soft, silky curve of her shoulder. "Do you want me to?"

"N—No."

"Why not?"

A wild rose flush glowed on her cheekbones, but her ebony eyes remained steady. "Because . . . it hurt."

The purpose behind her story suddenly occurred to him. Tilting his head slightly, he asked, "Does the story you told me about Mrs. Matthews have anything to do with your not wanting to make love?"

Her outburst was unplanned. "Yes, it does! It seems to me that a man thinks a woman has no other purpose on this earth except to satisfy him!"

"Is that what you really believe?"

Hurt and frustrated, she lifted her chin defiantly. "What else am I supposed to think?"

Slade threaded his hand through his hair. He had no one to blame for Virginia's reactions but himself. He should have been more patient with her, but her idea about men and lovemaking was sheer nonsense, and if he wanted his plan to succeed, he would have to convince her she was wrong. A sly smile tugged at his lips. And if he was able to get pleasure out of it, then so much the better.

Rising up behind her, he slipped his hands up her arms, and firmly but gently grasping her shoulders, he brought his lips down to the back of her neck, brushing it with tender, featherlike kisses. "I guess I can't blame you for being angry with me," he murmured against her silky skin.

"But I am not angry with you."

"Yes you are, and it is my fault. I didn't take enough time to make sure you were satisfied too."

Moving forward slightly in an attempt to avoid his kisses, she asked, "Are you going to make love to me again?" Her face paled at the thought.

"Yes," he replied softly, still applying gentle kisses. "I intend to prove that you are wrong. Although very few women will admit it, they enjoy lovemaking just as much as men do."

"E—Even though it hurts so much?" That was difficult to believe.

"It was painful because you were a virgin. To turn your own phrase, I'm not an expert, but very few virgins enjoy lovemaking the first time. They are usually too tense, or too frightened, or the initial pain is too distracting. But, if she has a thoughtful, considerate husband, the second time is sheer pleasure." He nipped teasingly at her shoulder, then added, "And sweetheart, you'll never meet a more thoughtful, considerate man than me. But you can't be tense. You will have to promise to relax."

Wanting so desperately to believe him and to please him, Virginia took several deep breaths of air to steady her nerves. She swallowed hard, then slowly nodded her head. "I will try," she whispered hoarsely.

He slipped the chemise straps from her shoulders,

then alternately kissing, nipping, teasing with his tongue, he covered the line between her shoulders.

Then, laughingly he said, "Before we go much further, we are going to have to do something about all of these clothes you are wearing." When he made love to a woman, he wanted bare skin against bare skin. It was far more sensual.

"A—All I have on is a chemise," she stammered.

Giving a throaty chuckle, he quipped, "Yes, I know, but it's too damn much."

Tugging the chemise from beneath her buttocks, he slid his hands under the fabric and began the long, sensuous journey over her slender hips, gently caressing her tiny waist, then when he reached her breasts, he moved his hand around to her front and skillfully lifted the material past the rounded globes. In a matter of moments, he had the chemise crushed in his hands and was carelessly tossing it aside.

Then, still raining sweet, gentle kisses on her shoulders, he placed his hands, fingers spread wide apart, on her abdomen and brought them up tantalizingly slowly to cup her satiny breasts. He fondled them teasingly, tauntingly, before lowering her to the bed.

There, he positioned himself by her side and, starting at her forehead, trailed kisses down past her temple, to her earlobe, gently teased at her mouth, down the slender column of her throat, then his mouth paid homage to the swollen buds he had recently caressed.

Tiny shivers of delight raced through her as Slade gently outlined the circle of her breast with his hand, then he again lowered his mouth and teased the pointed nipples, which had swollen to their fullest. She curled into the curve of his body, feeling the overpowering need to be as close to him as possible.

Her flesh tingled against his hair-roughened chest.

She moaned aloud with erotic pleasure as her passion once again smoldered and took flame.

Virginia was no longer frightened or reluctant. It was as though her sexuality had been unlocked with a golden key and now her body stood in a doorway concealing some great treasure of unimaginable value. And all she had to do to obtain the riches was take one step forward.

She felt as though she were clay and he the master artist, molding her, shaping her, into a great piece of art, for suddenly it seemed she had no bones, no will of her own. There was only Slade and what he was doing to her, the feel of his body pressed so close to hers enveloping her, binding her to him. She was like quicksilver in his hands, growing hotter and hotter, melting beneath him, while molten rivers coursed through her veins as though they had broken from a dam.

His arms tightened and he crushed her to him. She twined her arms around his neck, holding tightly, allowing her breasts to be flattened against the broad hardness of his chest. Their mouths clung hungrily, twisting, turning, with the sweet flavor of desire on their tongues.

"Oh, Slade, Slade," she murmured feverishly, pulling her lips from his, threading her hands through his dark mane of hair, then caressing the strong tendons at the back of his neck. "Love me, love me now!"

Slade needed no further urging. Although he wanted to take her with the same wild abandon as before, he willed himself to draw from his store of self-restraint and proceed slowly. He positioned his knees between her thighs, lowered his body onto hers, and gently ravished her mouth while the tip of his maleness teased the outer folds of her woman-hood.

She was soon writhing with ecstasy. She thought she would go mad from wanting him so badly, for each time he teased her with his manhood, she would arch up to receive him and he would draw back. Finally, she gasped, "I cannot take much more of this loving torment!"

At that moment, Slade arched forward and entered her gently, and his unhurried, deliberate movements did not cease. He thrust slowly, languidly, moving within her as if she were a delicate rose unfolding fragile petals.

She drew a quick gulp of air and her eyes grew wide with wonder as she felt her loins start to churn tumultuously, like a mass of rumbling clouds building to a thundering peak, before a blaze of lightning struck within her, blinding her, shattering her to the very depths of her soul.

Then she lay still, taking short, panting breaths while caressing the corded muscles on his back.

Slade, his voice thick with passion, asked huskily, "Now, sweetheart, do you still think lovemaking is just for men?"

"Ooh no, it was . . . wonderful!" she murmured contentedly between breaths. Tears of joy and satisfaction glistened in her eyes as she ran her hands over the entire length of his back. Then her eyes widened in concern. "But . . . you didn't. . . ."

He chuckled and whispered hoarsely, "That's right, sweetheart, I didn't." His hips began moving in a slow, circular, thrusting motion. "But I will, and you will too . . . again. Then, if I have my way about it, we will again . . . and again . . . and again. . . ."

Chapter Twelve

Just as the sun burst forth over the distant horizon, the wind from the purple-tinted San Andres Mountains, which stood majestically to the east moaned through the thickly studded *piñon* and juniper trees. It swept down the mountainsides and began its precarious journey across the prairielike desert, swirling and gusting, forming dust devils and lifting loose sand. If ever there was a lonesome sound, it was that of the wind's voice as it rose and fell, calling, searching, losing velocity until it seemed as gentle as a baby's fragile breath, then gaining strength, becoming a wailing banshee. The wind was constant, like the earth, the sky, the moon, the stars; it would last throughout infinity.

Dawn spread like a pale blush on Virginia's cheek as the early morning breeze gently stirred through the window curtains. One minute Virginia was asleep and the next minute she was awake, though her chest still rose and fell with an even cadence and her lashes rested like fans on her cheeks.

She opened her eyes and turned her head to face Slade. He was sound asleep on his side, one arm folded under his head, and one hand outstretched, curled around her golden-tipped breast. Except for the dark stubble on his face, his restfully slumbering expression reminded her of a little boy who was having mischievous dreams. Then she smiled, remembering the previous night. He had not *behaved* like a little boy. He was definitely a man—a virile, passionate man. Her countenance blazed at the memory of all the delights they had shared.

He had definitely proved that her perception of men was wrong. The second, thoroughly satisfying time they made love was unequivocal proof of that fact. And, not only was he an expert lover but a compassionate, gentle man as well. Not once did he make her feel foolish or ignorant, even though she had had no idea how to please a husband.

Virginia's eyes were hooded as her thoughts wandered. Was every woman as naive as she on her wedding night, or was she a rare exception? If other women's husbands were as considerate as Slade, the trite expressions she had heard during the years such as "a lady is not supposed to enjoy *that* part of marriage," or "the best thing a woman can do is merely lie still and pray that he hurries," would soon be forgotten. Bless their hearts, those women had no idea of the joys they were missing. Since she had been mistaken about Slade and the intimate side of marriage, maybe, just maybe, he would also be different from men like Mr. Matthews.

Stretching languidly, a contented sigh escaped her. She had never dreamed she could be this happy or this deeply in love. Was it only yesterday that she had felt her life was over when it had scarcely begun? How strange it was that her life had been changed so drastically in such a short time. A small smile of enchantment softened her lips. And Slade was responsible for all of this happiness. If he had been a lesser man, what would have happened to her? Not many men would have accepted her as a wife; not after what her father did at the camp; then there were all of those horrible lies, and being forced to marry her at gunpoint. Without a doubt, he was an amazing man — in more ways than one. Love for him swelled her heart and tiny shivers of delight played havoc up and down her spine as she remembered just how amazing he had been.

Impishly, she curled a tress of her hair around her finger and trailed the tip of it along the line of his upper lip. When he wrinkled his nose, she clamped her lips together to keep from giggling. After he snugged back down into his pillow, she trailed her hair along his lip again. His eyes opened, widening in immediate recognition.

"Good morning," he mumbled in a sleep-mellowed voice.

"Wake up, lazybones. Do you plan to sleep all day?" she asked playfully.

Laying his head on her arm, he slid his arm around her waist and snuggled closer. "Have mercy on me, woman. I didn't sleep much last night."

"Neither did I, but you owe me one more *again,*" she murmured.

He cocked one eye open. "I owe you one more what?"

"You owe me one more *again,*" she repeated huskily. "Or at least I think you do . . . that is, if I did not lose count. And I think you should be forced to pay your debt."

Not able to resist such a tempting morsel so close to his mouth, he flicked out his tongue and drew an invisible line to her nipple.

"Ah ha, so you know what I meant?" she said, sensuously arching her body to give him easier access to her breast. Strangely, even though this was their first morning together after such an intimate, passionate night, she felt no shyness with him. It was as if she had known him for a lifetime.

"No," he drawled teasingly. "I suppose I'll have to admit to being dim-witted . . . but then, sweetheart, you have a way of making a man lose his senses."

Virginia pushed him supine on the bed and rested her breasts against his furred chest. She set her face with what she hoped was a sincere expression. "I am surprised at you, Stephen Michael Slade! Last night you promised we would make love again . . . and again . . . and again . . . and again. And we never took care of the last *again*." She made a clicking noise with her tongue. "I never thought you would be one to go back on your word."

He stared at her for a moment, then burst out laughing. Threading his hands through her tangled mass of hair and pulling her closer, he said, "Oh, I assure you, sweetheart, I am a man of my word. In one way or the other I intend to keep every vow I ever made."

"Then prove it!" Although her words were a challenge, her beckoning arms signaled her complete surrender.

He lowered his lips to hers and soon they were on another sensual journey toward paradise.

Much later, Slade swung his long legs over the side of the bed, stood, and started searching for his clothing, which had somehow become scattered all over the room.

Virginia sat up in bed with her chin propped on her knees and her arms wrapped around her legs. She watched him through a fringe of lowered lashes. "Do you know what you remind of?"

His grin flashed briefly, dazzling against his bronzed skin. "No, what?"

"A peacock strutting around the barnyard with his tail feathers spread into a colorful fan."

"Look," he said with mock severity as he turned to face her, unashamed of his nudity. "I am fully aware that I have a hairy backside—"

"And a hairy front side too, but that was not what I meant."

Enjoying their lighthearted banter, Slade held up his hands in a helpless gesture and looked down to inspect himself. "Are you insinuating I have bird legs?" He dodged just in time to avoid the pillow that came hurling at him.

"I'll have you know, I think you have pretty legs," she snipped.

Slade winced as if in deep pain. "Sweetheart, you shouldn't tell a man he has pretty legs. That fits into the same category as asking to borrow his parasol or lace-trimmed handkerchief."

Virginia giggled at the thought of his walking down a street wearing snug-fitting trousers, blue shirt, soft leather vest, his gun strapped low on his waist, and carrying a woman's frilly parasol.

Reading her thoughts behind the giggle, he chuckled good-naturedly. "Now, wouldn't that be a sight to see?" Placing his hands on his hips, he asked, "All right, you have raised my curiosity. Why do I remind you of a peacock?"

"It's not the bird you remind me of; it's how he walks, how he carries himself."

"And how is that?"

Chewing thoughtfully on her bottom lip, she pondered his question. Finally, she said, "I guess *arrogant strut* would describe it best. You carry yourself very proudly—and with self-assurance. I admire that very much." Sensing she had suddenly made him feel ill at ease, she quickly changed the subject. "My goodness! How did your clothes get scattered all over the room?"

Looking puzzled, he shrugged his shoulders and said, "I have no idea." Then he gazed at her with his most pitiful expression. "Sweetheart, I know it usually takes women a long time to primp and arrange every curl just so, but unless you want to see your husband die of starvation, I suggest you hurry and get dressed while I still have the strength to reach the dining room."

As Slade slipped his feet into his boots, he had to remind himself not to become too emotionally involved with Virginia, regardless of how pleasant it was to be with her. Just remember, Slade, he told himself, she's not what she appears to be. Her looks of adoration are merely part of her act to trap you in her web. Go along with her, humor her, pretend to be a considerate, devoted husband, but be wary of those beautiful ebony eyes and her loving arms. If you are not careful, she will hook the biggest fool who ever lived!

Virginia waited in the doorway of the dining room while Slade stopped and spoke to the man at the hotel desk. After a highly animated conversation, he grabbed the man's shirtfront and drew back to hit him, then, regaining control of his temper, he released the man, slammed some money down on the counter, and stalked toward her, his mouth set in a hard, angry line.

"Slade, what's wrong? W—What did that man say to you?" Virginia asked, concerned.

"Let's get our belongings and get the hell out of

167

here!" He grasped her by the arm and took long, hurried steps toward the stairs.

"Why?"

"I'll explain later," he grumbled, taking the stairs two at a time, half dragging Virginia as she scrambled to keep up with him. Reaching the top of the stairs, he strode down the corridor, and upon reaching their room, he opened the door and kicked it back against the wall. Stomping inside, all the while muttering curses under his breath, he began cramming their belongings into Virginia's carpetbag and into his saddlebag.

Bewildered, Virginia just stood and watched with openmouthed astonishment. He had a fiery, angry look that resembled the expression he had worn most of the previous day, but this burst of anger had happened so quickly it had taken her completely by surprise.

"W—Why are we leaving, Slade?" she asked, finding her tongue. "What on earth did that man say to you? Did he ask us to leave?"

His eyes flashed imperiously. "No, he didn't, but I told him we would not stay another minute in this paper-walled flea trap!"

"Why?" She wondered if it had anything to do with the conversation she had overheard the day before between the old man and his grandson.

His blue eyes pierced the distance between them. "Because I said so, that's why! I don't like to be questioned about everything I do or say!"

Her mood veered sharply to irritation. "You don't have to take your anger out on me! I haven't done anything!" She watched as his outraged expression gradually took on a semblance of calmness.

"You are right," he said, running his hand through his hair. "I shouldn't have taken my anger out on you." Placing the bags under one arm, he reached for her with the other, only more gently than before. "Come on, let's get out of here."

Not wanting to argue with him but feeling he was behaving unreasonably, Virginia asked in a small voice, "Where are we going? Isn't this the only hotel in town?"

By the expression on Slade's face, it was obvious he had not considered that fact.

"Come to think of it, I suppose it is." His jaw flexed and his eyes widened with determination. "But I still refuse to stay here!"

"I h—have a suggestion," she said hesitantly. "We could get the wagon from the livery stable and set up camp out at the creek." She really did not want to go back out there—it held too many unpleasant memories—but it seemed to be the only possible solution until they could make different plans. All of this had happened so suddenly.

"The creek?"

"Yes, the creek—where Papa and I were camped."

His blue eyes sharpened, then narrowed thoughtfully. "All right," he suddenly agreed, removing some money from his vest pocket and thrusting it into Virginia's hand. "Go over to the general store and buy some food and whatever else you think we'll need while I settle up at the livery stable. I'll stop and pick you up on the way out of town. The sooner we get out of this pesthole, the better I will feel!"

Virginia placed her hands on her hips and slowly looked around the camp, recalling the old adage: The more things change, the more they stay the same. Her life had been completely altered, yet she had set up the camp with such a practiced ease, it

169

seemed nothing had changed. The only difference was that Slade had at least tried to help, whereas her father never had. But, bless his heart, he had gotten in her way too much to be of any real assistance, except that he had gathered wood and built the campfire — chores her father never would have considered doing.

"Do you want me to slice the bacon?" he asked after he had the fire blazing and a pot of coffee on to boil.

She looked at him with surprise. "Yes, thank you. That would be a great help." While vigorously stirring the pancake batter, she allowed a bemused smile to tip the corners of her lips. Apparently he had paid closer attention to her furious tirade than she had thought — unless he was merely trying to prove she was wrong about that too. Or maybe he was so hungry, he was more than willing to help. She shrugged indifferently. Whatever the reason, it was an extremely nice gesture and one she deeply appreciated. She wondered if he had any more surprises in store for her.

Virginia waited until they were through with breakfast and Slade had his third cup of coffee in front of him and his cheroot lit before summoning ample courage to question him about what had happened at the hotel.

"Slade, what did that man say back there to make you so angry?"

He shook his head. "It doesn't matter. Just forget about it," he replied with a wave of his hand.

"I don't want to forget about it," she pressed stubbornly. "You promised to tell me . . . and you always keep your word. You said that yourself."

"Don't you ever forget anything?" he asked, squinting one eye while raising the other, yet not in an

170

angry manner, although it was obvious he was slightly perplexed.

"Very seldom. Now please tell me what he said."

"I see right now you'll hound me to death until I do," he remarked dryly.

Virginia walked over to him, sat down on his lap, and wound her arms around his neck. She lightly brushed his lips. "I didn't mean to hound you. I'm just curious, that's all."

Slade stared at her intently, a faint glimmer of amusement reflected in his eyes. "It sure didn't take you long to learn how to use your wiles to charm a man."

Virginia did not recognize the cynicism in his voice. Instead, she smiled and said, "I was not aware I was using my wiles."

"Humph, any time a woman comes at a man with sweet talk and hugs and kisses when she's wanting something, that is using her wiles." Even though Slade protested, he reached around her waist and pulled her closer to him.

While nibbling at his earlobe, she murmured teasingly, "Poor dear, you are so mistreated." Virginia was amazed at how open and carefree she could be with Slade. She felt so comfortable, so at ease, with him. "But I am not going to leave you alone until you tell me what that man said."

"It will make you mad if I tell you."

"Tell me anyway." She ran her hands over the muscles that were beginning to cord in his neck.

Slade mumbled reluctantly, "He made a few insinuations about the circumstances surrounding our marriage. Ugly insinuations," he added emphatically.

"Oh," she said simply.

"Now see there, I told you it would make you mad."

"But I'm not angry."

"You're not?"

"No."

"It damn sure made me mad."

"Well, it doesn't me."

"Why not?"

"Because it made you angry."

Baffled, he shook his head. "There is no reasoning behind that kind of logic."

She was keenly aware of his scrutiny. "I think my logic is very reasonable. The man insulted me and you came to my defense. I think that was probably the first time anyone has ever done that."

Suddenly uncomfortable with her gratitude, he moved her off his lap, knelt down, and busied himself with the camp fire. A tumble of confused thoughts assailed him. He had actually lost his temper because a man had made an ugly remark about Virginia. Why? She was a treacherous woman who would go to any means to get what she wanted. He knew that to be a fact. Yet, he was ready to defend her honor without giving it a second thought. A moment ago he had accused her of using her wiles against him. He had said it in jest, but apparently it was the truth. He had been so caught up in her charms, he had almost forgotten his plans for revenge. If he weren't careful, she would soon have him so ensnared he would never break free.

Standing abruptly, Slade spun on his foot, slung his saddle over his shoulder, and started walking toward Blue.

"Slade? What are you doing? Where are you going?" Her eyes widened fearfully. She was afraid he was going back to the hotel to beat the man senseless.

Slade tensed and stopped short. Damn! he raged

silently. Did she have to know every move he made? What did she intend to do, smother him? He took a deep breath. Keep a civil tongue in your head, he told himself. This will all be over soon.

Turning slowly, he smiled and offered the first excuse that came to his mind. "I'm just going to ride Blue for awhile. He hasn't been run in a few days and he tends to get mean when he has been penned or tied up too long. And tied behind the wagon on the way out here, he didn't get the exercise he needs. I'll be back in time for supper."

Disappointment swept over her. The thought of having to go so many hours without seeing him was almost painful. She walked over and stood beside him while he saddled his horse.

"S—Slade . . . when you get back, do you think we can talk?"

"Aren't we talking now?" he asked, pulling the cinch tight.

"Yes, but I mean about the future."

The smile on his face became brittle and his eyes hardened. "What about the future?" he asked just a little too harshly.

"We need to make plans." As the words began to flow, she gathered the courage to speak her mind. "I am not eager to stay in this area and I believe you feel the same way. And then, there is the wagon. I don't mind living in it . . . for awhile. But we need to plan ahead. I realize it is just barely summer, but winter will be on us before we know it."

Masking his true feelings, Slade cupped his hand under her chin and raised her face to meet his gaze. "I agree, we do need to make plans . . . but not today. I have a few things in mind, but I would rather discuss them . . . tomorrow." His eyes narrowed thoughtfully and a grin toyed with his lips.

"Yes, tomorrow will be a good day to talk about the future."

The sun was a steady decline in the western sky when Slade finally rode back into camp. One quick glance around the camp told him Virginia had been busy while he had been gone. Most of the loose sand and dirt had been swept from the immediate area and only the hard, packed earth remained. Freshly laundered sheets were hanging from low tree branches to dry. A white cloth had been spread over the battered old cook table and it was set with what he assumed were the best dishes and utensils from the storage box. There was even a bouquet of wildflowers in the center of the table. Corn bread had been cooked to perfection in a dutch oven, a delicious smelling stew simmered at the camp fire, and a pot of coffee sat warming near the fire.

Hearing Slade ride up, Virginia hurried from the wagon. She had taken pains with her personal appearance as well as having made the camp as comfortable as possible. She had carefully coiffed her hair, and she wore the best dress she owned, a lilac jaconet cambric trimmed with plum-colored piping, collar, and cuffs. Her tawny complexion and the honey gold of her hair were enhanced by the soft colors. The skirt was full, the bodice formfitting, and the sleeves fell to mid-arm.

She wiped her hands on her apron, then quickly removed it and tucked it into the utensil box. Smoothing the worry from her face, she waited until Slade had dismounted and had tied Blue to a cropping rope, then greeted him with a welcoming smile and a warm embrace.

"Supper is ready. You must be starved." He had

174

been gone so long, she had started to worry, but she was determined not to scold him, realizing he was accustomed to being free without having to be concerned about anyone. It would take time for him to adapt to this marriage too.

"Yes, I could use something to eat." He sniffed the air appreciatively. "Supper sure smells good."

Slade mentally cursed himself, for he doubted he could hold another bite of food. After he had left the camp, he had decided to keep riding, to forget about Virginia and the entire affair. He had ridden at least fifteen miles before he realized he had left his saddlebag behind and had no supplies at all. The next town was a ride of four or five days and he did not want to go without coffee and bacon for that long. Certain items in his saddlebag could be replaced easily, he had returned to Barkersville. And, while he was there, he had decided to eat before heading out again. While having his meal, he realized he was behaving like a coward, allowing his fear of being trapped by Virginia's charms and pretty face to stand in the way of his obtaining revenge. With thoughts of her treachery uppermost in his mind, he had come directly back to the camp.

He should have known she would behave like the "perfect little woman" and have supper prepared. Now he would have to eat again unless he could figure out a way to avoid it. Then he grinned. There was a perfect way to avoid it. All he had to do was preoccupy her with something other than food.

Slade caught Virginia by the hand and pulled her into his arms. "That's what I thought," he said, nuzzling her hair. "Supper isn't the only thing that smells good. You do too. I like that perfume; it smells like roses."

The even whiteness of her smile was dazzling. "It's

175

my favorite fragrance. I always thought Mother marked me somehow when she chose Rose for my middle name." Perhaps later she would tell him how she taken the small bottle from the goods they were selling and had hidden it for her personal use. But not now. The less Slade was reminded of her father, the better.

An adoring look came into her eyes. "I can have supper on the table by the time you wash up. I also did some laundry today. You have a clean suit of clothes lying across the tailgate."

So, he thought suspiciously, she rummaged through my belongings while I was gone. I wonder how disappointed she was when she didn't find anything of value?

"Is something wrong?" she asked, noticing his pensive expression.

He brightened instantly. "Oh, no, everything is fine. I was just thinking about a bath. Do you think supper will hold while I take a quick dip in the river?"

Disappointment swept over her. If they did not eat soon, supper would burn. Instead of expressing her true feelings, she complied with his wishes. "Yes, I am sure it will. There is a towel, facecloth, and a bar of soap on the tailgate too."

Nodding, Slade walked over to the back of the wagon and within a few moments he returned, barefoot and naked to the waist, with a towel slung over his shoulder.

"Want to join me?" His eyes were bright with merriment.

"Oh, no," she replied, suddenly feeling wistful. "I washed earlier."

Slade gently grasped her shoulders and pulled her closer to him. He lowered his head, and his lips quickly found hers. It was a slow, thorough kiss. With his gentle prodding, her lips parted and his tongue flicked in and out of her mouth, searching, seeking, exploring its mystery. Then, with deliberate slowness, Slade trailed teasing kisses down the slender column of her throat until he heard her moan of pleasure.

He spoke with mock sincerity. "I sure wish I could persuade you to join me. Why, I would even volunteer to undo the buttons on your dress."

Amused, she retorted, "My, that is a generous offer."

He feigned a heavy sigh and sadly shook his head. "I don't remember the last time my back received a good, thorough scrubbing."

Laughing aloud, she wound her arms around his neck and murmured, "I knew all along you were a scoundrel. All right, I'll join you, but I'm warning you now, if supper burns, it will be all your fault."

Purple shadows caressed the distant mountains and the sun on its final plunge set the sky ablaze. Silhouetted against the crimson sunset, Virginia stood on the banks of the river and gingerly tested the warmth of the water with the tip of her toe. Modesty prevented her from stripping as Slade had; instead, she wore her thin camisole and a pair of old-fashioned pantalettes.

Slade's breath caught in his throat as he stood admiring her. "Come on in; the water is fine. It isn't cold at all." He wondered if his voice had sounded as strangled as it had felt when he had spoken.

"It's not the water I am worried about." She looked about anxiously. "What if someone rides up and catches us like this?"

"We can always hide in the bushes," he teased, his voice soft and mellow.

She picked up the facecloth and bar of soap and waded through the water toward him. Her tone of voice was merry and lighthearted. "Oh, no, Mr. Stephen Slade, you are not about to get me in the bushes. I've heard that too many naughty things happen there."

He grinned mischievously. "Yes, I know. I've heard the same story."

Feeling his eyes stripping her bare, Virginia lowered her lashes as a warm flush stole quickly across her satiny skin. She briskly rubbed the bar of soap between her hands and vigorously worked it into a lather. "You will have to turn around if you want your back washed."

His gaze raked her approvingly. He especially liked the way her nipples shone darkly through the sheer fabric of her camisole now wet from the rippling water. "What about my front? Will you wash that too?" he asked in a deep, husky voice.

Recognizing his tone as a prelude to passion, Virginia moistened her lips, thinking about the pleasures that would soon come and realizing how fortunate she was to have a husband like Slade. Without saying a word, she ran her lathered hands over his chest, gently massaging, stroking, caressing. Then, cupping water in her hands, she rinsed the soap from his muscular chest in a slow, tantalizing manner. Her ebony eyes darkened even more as she looked at him, naked and gleaming from the rivulets of water beading on his bronzed skin, and her heart started pounding rapidly against her breast.

Seeing the pulse pounding in the hollow of her throat, Slade whispered as he crushed her against his chest, "I think we need to forget about the back washing temporarily."

"Yes, I think we should," she murmured hoarsely.

Lifting her with ease, Slade waded back to shore. In a matter of moments he had placed her on the feather mattress in the back of the wagon and with deft, sure hands was quickly removing her wet clothing.

His touch set her aflame with desire. Her earlier timidity disappeared as she met his searing lips eagerly, not caring that his kisses were ravaging, almost violent, for she recognized his driving need as her own. It was a hunger that demanded to be satisfied, a thirst that required quenching.

His lips slid across her cheek to her ear, and he flicked his tongue in and out of that crevice with a deftness that drove her into a passionate rage. Flames of fiery desire burned out of control as they blazed through her body. His teeth nipped hungrily at the silky skin that joined her nape in a slender curve. She moaned and writhed wildly beneath him, arching her hips in a maddening quest. His manly hardness pressed against her wet thighs and the crisp, curly hair on his chest teased and tickled as he continued his sensual onslaught on her sanity. The urge to have him within her quickly reached a feverish pitch.

"Now, my love, now!" Her arms sought him frantically. For one fleeting moment, it seemed as though he would resist her pleas, and his denial further inflamed her.

With a muffled groan, he penetrated her swiftly with a sharp thrust that made her gasp aloud and cling tightly to his broad back. His powerful muscles flexed beneath her hands as she held on to him, locking her lithe legs around his waist to keep him from escaping.

Slade could feel his manhood pulsating wildly as he plunged farther and farther, deeper and deeper, into the tight, moist recess. His eyes found her lovely face and he noted that she was watching his face cord and tense with their driving passion.

Virginia thrust upward, lifting her hips in a gyrating motion. Endlessly, he plunged into her, over and over again, withdrawing almost completely, then slamming full force into the depths of her burning desire. She anxiously answered each questing thrust with raw, animalistic passion. Slade was a strong, lasting man, and Virginia was woman enough to strive in unison, to match his voracious hunger.

Their loins began to churn tumultuously, like masses of swirling clouds about to swoop down and wreak havoc upon the land. There was intense sensation, ardent, strong. Lights flashed brilliantly as lightning stabbed across a darkened sky. Then, as though following in the wake of a violent, thrashing tempest, fulfillment poured forth, bathing their souls with satisfaction.

Dawn came like a curtain rising on a great stage. Golden shafts of light danced and shimmered, then spread majestically across the wide, open spaces.

Virginia stretched lazily and for a brief moment fought to remain in the pleasant depths of sleep. Then, smelling the heady aroma of early-morning coffee boiling on an open fire, she opened her eyes, struggled sleepily into her robe, and deftly plaited her hair into a single braid.

Stepping from the wagon, she yawned and stretched and, seeing Slade kneeling by the campfire, she walked over to join him.

"Good morning, love," she said softly, bending and placing a gentle kiss on the top of his head. "Why didn't you wake me? I would have been more than happy to build the fire and put on the coffee."

She began to gently massage the muscles at the back of his neck, but Slade tore himself away from her touch. Abruptly moving away from her, he whirled and stared at her bitterly. Loathing shone from his eyes and his lips curled into an ugly snarl.

It was difficult for Virginia to believe what she was seeing. "W—what's the matter, Slade? Did . . . have I done something wrong?"

"*You* are what's wrong, Virginia. You have no idea how many times I wanted to just ride off and forget you ever existed, but I didn't want to deny myself the satisfaction of seeing your face when I told you exactly what I thought of you!" He sneered contemptuously.

Her pretty brow creased into a frown and cold fingers of fear clutched at her heart. "I—I don't . . . understand. What have I done to . . . make you so angry?" She reached out to touch him, but he flung her arm aside.

"Drop the innocent act, Virginia." His eyes glittered coldly. "I'll have to admit you had me fooled for awhile, but I soon wised up. I know what you are, Virginia." He ran his hand through his hair, wincing when he touched the lump that still remained. "How well I know!" he added bitterly.

She felt as if a hand had closed tightly around her throat. "W—What exactly am I?"

"A scheming, treacherous bitch!" With arms akimbo, his legs splayed in a powerful stance, he glowered at her. "Just how big a fool did you think I was? Didn't you have sense enough to know I would realize sooner or later you were in on that scheme with your father to rob me, and to leave me for dead?"

"You mean you think . . . but that's not true! As

God is my witness, that's not true!" She shook her head adamantly as though trying to find some reason in this madness. She hurtled back to earth as reality struck. Swallowing hard, she was devastated to hear her voice echo her realizations. "You mean . . . you never loved me?"

"Love you? Ha! Don't be ridiculous! I can hardly stand the sight of you."

"How . . . can you say such a thing . . . after what we've shared?" She clenched her hands until her nails bit painfully into the palms of her hand, but the pain was nothing compared to the shame and bitter humiliation that ripped through her heart.

Tossing his head, he laughed sardonically. "Shared? We haven't shared a damn thing . . . except a few good times in bed. That's all it meant to me, just a good time." He shrugged indifferently. "I suppose I could have gotten the same thing from a paid whore . . . but you were a hell of a lot cheaper, sweetheart."

Gasping, she recoiled as though he had brutally slapped her. "I'm not a . . . whore! You know I was a virgin!"

He gave her a hard, cold-eyed smile. "Yes, I know. That's what makes my revenge all the sweeter. You and your old man tried to rob me, but I ended up taking something from you that can never be replaced," he boasted triumphantly. "So next time, sweetheart you might think twice before playing a man for a fool. The price could be higher than what you bargained for."

Virginia's mouth moved wordlessly as she merely stood there, not wanting to believe this was happening to her. He had never believed a word she had said! her mind screamed. He had used her! This rejection . . . this humiliation had been his intention from the very beginning!

Turning slightly, Slade motioned toward the wagon. "I'm not as coldhearted as you think, sweetheart. I've decided you can have the horses, the wagon, and all its contents. If you are as smart as I think you are, hell, you can have a profitable little business going in no time at all. If you don't mind a suggestion, up in Colorado, whores travel from mining camp to mining camp in wagons to service the miners. Hell, you might as well join up with one; it would be safer than bushwhacking men." He chuckled lewdly, deliberately being as crude and callous as he could possibly be, thoroughly enjoying the shattered expression on her face. "But, as hot-blooded as I *know* you are, it'll probably take an entire mining camp to keep you satisfied. Only thing, sweetheart, if our paths cross in the future, you'll have to promise me a free night's ride . . . that is, if I want it." One corner of his mouth twisted upward. "But, who knows, you may be so worn out and used by that time, I might not want any part of you—especially that part!"

Virginia was so hurt, so crushed, so furious, she could only take shallow, gasping breaths. Her face ashen, her eyes wild with fury, she muttered vehemently, "So help me God, I never thought I could feel such deep hatred for anyone! You had better hope our paths never cross again, Stephen Slade. If they do, I'll—I'll make you wish you had never been born! Just get out of my sight! I never want to see you again—not as long as I live!"

"I'm happy to oblige," he muttered coldly, turning to walk toward an already saddled Blue.

Rage like she had never known before raced through her. She had not completely had her say. The words to tell him just how contemptible she thought he was flashed through her mind. Hurrying after him, she shouted, "Wait a minute, Slade! You can't leave me like this! I—I won't let you!"

Shrugging off her hand, he stepped into the stirrup and swung his leg over Blue's back. "I can't?" he sneered mockingly. "Just watch me, sweetheart." With that, he spurred Blue in the flanks and rode off without once looking back.

Chapter Thirteen

Virginia, her face grim, her black eyes lethargic and dull, had sat rocking to and fro for hours, her arms folded close to her breast. At times she had felt as though she were on an emotional pendulum. One moment she hated Slade; the next moment her loss seemed so great, she found it difficult to draw the next breath.

She knew she had retreated into her own mind, much like a wild, wounded animal seeking shelter in its lair to lick its wounds, to become strong again, or to regain its courage before facing its enemy once more. Her enemy had become all the painful memories involving Slade. It would take courage to face them; it would take courage to accept what had happened. But for now she had none. She needed time to grieve for what she had lost, although it was difficult to understand how she could have lost something she had never had.

Staring listlessly at the campfire, Virginia watched it burn until only one tiny spark remained. Having no fuel on which to feed, it flared briefly, then belched a small gray plume of smoke that was quickly carried away by a wanton wind. It seemed that tiny spark represented her own life, her hopes, her dreams. They too had vanished so swiftly, leaving only an empty, withered feeling. But for that emptiness, they might never have existed.

Why had Slade done it? If he had believed her guilty of the vicious attack on him, why had he not just said so and been done with it? Why had he felt it necessary to use her, to make her feel so soiled and dirty that no amount of soap or scrubbing would ever thoroughly cleanse her again? He had unjustly accused her of being treacherous, a thief, and much, much worse. But what was he? Not only had he ruthlessly stolen her innocence, but he had captured her heart, then had carelessly tossed it aside as though it were nothing. Absolutely nothing!

It had to be some sort of horrible mistake! Surely it could not be true! Surely Slade was not guilty of deliberately trying to destroy her. But, as the image of his face, twisted with hatred and contempt, flashed before her, she realized it was not a mistake. God help her, it was not!

Numb from shock and grief, she threw back her head and moaned. She could not endure any more pain and heartbreak. It was too much to ask of her; it was just too much! She wished she were dead! Or was she already dead? Any person feeling this much anguish already had to be in the fiery pits of hell, doomed to an eternity of torment!

Suddenly, she was struck by the absurdity of such thoughts. "What am I doing? Why am I torturing myself about Slade? I heard with my own ears what he thinks about me. He never loved me; he only used me. I meant nothing more to him than would a saloon whore—probably not even that much. Where is my pride? I should be furious instead of feeling sorry for myself like some whimpering, weak-minded. . . ." Her eyes widened and her mood veered sharply to outraged comprehension. "Why, it's little wonder men treat women the way they do! We let them! We calmly sit by and allow them to do anything they please, and then feel guilty and believe it is our fault! Damn Stephen Slade! Damn him to hell!"

Virginia straightened her shoulders and lifted her head with renewed determination. "I shall never allow myself to be hurt by a man again!" she vowed adamantly. "And if there is any justice in this world, somehow, someday, Stephen Slade will get what's coming to him . . . and I hope and pray I am around to see it happen!"

Now girded with firm resolution, she began to pace about the camp, making plans for the future.

Remaining in or near Barkersville was out of the question. Why leave herself open to needless ridicule and gossip? Instead, why couldn't she carry out the original plans she and her father had made? Almost half of the mercantile goods were left. If she was careful and drove harder bargains with the ranchers and farmers, there was no reason she could not continue on to California and arrive with a tidy little nest egg, enough to start a new life for herself.

"Wait a minute," she muttered slowly. "That plan is not as simple as it seems. Slade said there was Indian trouble farther west; that means the cavalry will be making regular patrols and I doubt they would allow a woman to travel by herself—and with Indian trouble, I really don't want to. It would be foolish even to try. So, I will have to wait somewhere safe until the Indian trouble is over. But, my goodness, that could take months . . . and I don't want to wait that long." Then her eyes narrowed thoughtfully. "What did Slade say that first day we met?"

187

She snapped her fingers. "I remember! He suggested that Papa join a group of teamsters hauling ore. That's what I can do!" Then logical reasoning took over once again as she realized that plan, too, had weaknesses. "Oh, I am sure they would be very agreeable about having a lone young woman accompany them, but I doubt their wives would be too willing." She sighed and said firmly, "There has to be another way. There just has to be! I am beaten only if I allow myself to be beaten."

Sitting down at the table, she placed her chin in her hand and impatiently drummed her fingers on her cheek. Her mind raced at a furious pace. "There would be no problem if I were a man. The soldiers certainly wouldn't object to a man's traveling alone. Oh, they would call him a fool, but they wouldn't stop him. And there would be no questions asked if a man joined up with the teamsters for protection. It's not fair. It's just not fair!"

A slow, crafty smile tugged at the corners of her lips then, and excitement flared in her eyes. "Why not become a man? I have clothes. Papa left most of his in the wagon." Unconsciously, her brow furrowed as she ran her hand over her face. "No, I would never fool anyone. I'm simply not masculine enough." An unexpected warmth surged through her when another thought raced through her mind. "But perhaps . . . I might pass . . . for a young boy. If I bound my breasts, and with the proper clothing, and if I watched what I said and how I talked, I might . . . just might be able to pull it off! The plain and simple fact is, I have nothing to lose and everything to gain."

A short while later Virginia was in the wagon, wearing a pair of her father's patched trousers, a faded denim shirt, a badly worn pair of boots he had intended to have half-soled, and an old, battered hat. She studied herself in the mirror with a critical eye. Shaking her head, she raised the shirt and wrapped the breast bindings more tightly, then used an extra safety pin for added protection against the binder's inadvertently coming loose. Adjusting her shirt, she looked in the mirror and shook her head again. She still did not look masculine enough. Perhaps if she smudged her face with dirt . . . ? Then she swallowed hard. Dirt was not the answer. It was her hair. Young boys simply did not wear their hair in long braids down their backs. It would have to be cut.

Virginia slowly removed her scissors from her sewing basket, took a deep breath, and before her courage failed, she grasped her long, lovely braid and snipped it off at the nape of her neck. After swallowing hard, she opened her eyes and looked once again into the mirror. The reflection that stared at her was that of a stranger.

It was several long moments before she could find her voice, and when she did speak aloud, her tone held no remorse. Instead, it indicated acceptance. "Well, you are certainly not *Virginia* anymore. But you had better choose a name that is similar so that you won't unconsciously ignore people when they speak to you. How about Virgil?" She shook her head disapprovingly. "No, I am not particularly fond of that name." Her expression grew thoughtful. "Since Papa usually called me Ginny, perhaps 'Jimmy' would be close enough to have a familiar sound to it." She nodded affirmatively. "Jimmy is as good a name as any."

Turning, she stopped short and with trembling hands picked up the long golden braid. A wave of nausea swept over her as she stared at it, and she felt as though her breath had become lodged in her throat. Her hair had only been cut twice in her lifetime and she had always cared for it with pride. And now, it was gone. Her bottom lip trembled. Then, gathering her courage, she started to throw it from the wagon, but the voice of common sense stopped her. Hopefully, she would not have to pose as a young boy for long, and until her hair could grow back, with pins and combs, the braid could be used as a sort of wig. No one would ever have to know her shame.

Solemnly, Virginia placed the braid in her keepsake box, a box that contained treasures and mementos that were precious only to her.

She started to leave the wagon, then her gaze fell to the bed she and Slade had shared. The indentation his head had made on the pillow was still visible, and using only the tiniest bit of imagination, she could smell his masculine scent. Without warning, tears began to stream down her face. Her shoulders heaved and shuddered as her tears turned into violent sobbing. Collapsing onto the bed, she buried her face in the pillow and allowed herself the luxury of giving in to her pain and sorrow. But deep down inside, she knew this would be the last time she would shed a tear for Slade, or for the past.

"Whoa team, whoa," Virginia said, pulling back on the harness reins. Removing her floppy hat and wiping her brow with her shirt sleeve, she stepped down on the lever of the wagon brake before reaching behind the seat for the burlap-covered canteen. Opening it, she poured a small amount of water on a cloth, took a drink, then ran the cloth over her face and the back of her neck, in hopes this would help ease her discomfort from the terrible heat.

The Arizona valley stretched out like a wide, endless corridor edged by the heavily timbered Graham Mountains to the left and the more barren Gila Mountains to the right. After the arid desert of western New Mexico, this land looked fertile and green, and it was more densely populated than she had thought it would be. She supposed that was because the Gila River wound its way through the valley. And wherever there was a good, steady supply of water, people settled.

Lately, business had been very good. She had to admit, though, for the first two or three weeks after she had left the Barkersville area, it had looked bleak. Farms had been almost nonexistent and the ranches had been spread so far apart that often days passed without her selling a dime's worth of merchandise.

Once, feeling so downhearted and desperate, she had decided to abandon her idea. After reaching that decision, she had approached a storekeeper in Virden, near the territorial line, to see if he would buy her entire stock, but he had only offered her twenty cents on the dollar. His proposing such a pittance had made her so angry, she had vowed to burn her stock before selling it at that price. However, that bargaining encounter had given her confidence that her disguise would work. She had fooled him completely. And now, after reaching a more populated area, she was making good sales at almost every place she stopped.

At first it had grated on her conscience that some of the sales had come about because she was pretending to be a young orphan boy. There was something about a homeless waif that seemed to tug at most women's heartstrings, and more often than not, the women would end up buying more than they wanted. But there was one thing about which Virginia was adamant: she refused to place an unfair price on her goods. She refused to take advantage of people in that manner.

Virginia squinted up at the relentless sun, thinking that if her luck held, and if she had calculated correctly, she would reach the safety of Fort Grant several hours before nightfall. It was something she was eager to do. While spending the previous night in the small town of Solomonville, she had learned that not too long before, General Crook had held parleys with Geronimo and had finally persuaded him to surrender. But apparently the bloodthirsty old savage had had a change of heart. He had escaped from the garrison and had taken to the hills again and was proving to be more dangerous than ever before. Information varied about the size of his warring band. One report set the number at fifty warriors and another account rumored there were closer to three hundred. It did not matter to her which story about the renegade Apaches was correct; one could kill her as dead as five hundred if she was caught out by herself. God forbid that should occur and they discovered *what* she was, death would be the most merciful thing that could happen to her.

Realizing she was wasting time unnecessarily, Virginia released the brake and snapped the reins. "Yo, horses, get a move on," she yelled. The horses strained at their bits and the wagon lurched forward.

Fort Grant loomed ahead like an oasis. But it was nothing like the fort Virginia had envisioned. Instead of being behind a stockade, the fort was out in the open, built in the same manner as a town square sprawling over several acres of land. But judging from the number of troopers milling around the yard, Virginia thought it seemed well protected. A huge flagpole displaying a United States flag stood in the center of the square. Most of the buildings were a combination of wood and stone, and only a few were adobe. One building, the quartermaster's store, was over two hundred feet long and forty feet wide. It was constructed of solid stone. The nearby Post Creek supplied the fort with water. A fairly large civilian settlement had been built close to the fort and, at first glance, Virginia noted about thirty Apache *wickiups* a few hundred yards behind the garrison.

Three young lieutenants standing at ease on the porch of the fort's headquarters eyed Virginia curiously when she stopped the wagon. She knew the soldiers were lieutenants by the insignia on their shirts, but each looked so young, Virginia wondered just how long it had been since they had graduated from West Point.

She crossed her fingers, and said to herself, 'My disguise has succeeded so far. I hope it continues to work.' Trying to act as nonchalant as possible, she wrapped the reins around the brake handle, stepped down on the front wheel, and jumped to the ground, sending up a fine cloud of dust. One of the men, obviously impressed with his own status, marched haughtily toward her.

Quickly deciding flattery would be her best course of action, she spoke in her worst backwood Texas drawl. "Howdy, General. You must be the man in charge around here. My name's Jimmy Branson." She extended a grimy hand. "I cain't tell you how glad I am to make it here all in one piece."

The lieutenant disregarded the friendly greeting

193

the skinny young boy had made. Instead, he pushed past him and, not seeing anyone in the wagon, looked for a rider. "Where is your father?" he asked. "Doesn't he know this area is crawling with renegade Indians? Doesn't he know it's foolhardy for people to travel alone?"

Virginia blinked her huge black eyes and answered solemnly, "I don't reckon he knows much of anything 'cause I ain't got no pa. Leastwise not anymore. He took sick over two months ago and died."

"Where's your mother then?" the lieutenant asked, his youthful face suddenly grim.

She slowly shook her head, sniffed loudly, and wiped her nose on the back of her shirt sleeve. "My ma's dead too. We lost her and the new baby . . . not more than an hour apart. But she passed on a week 'fore Pa did." The line of her mouth quivered, giving the appearance of a brave attempt not to cry.

The lieutenant's eyes widened incredulously. Hastily, he stepped up on the wagon wheel and peered into the wagon. "Are there any more children?"

Virginia shoved her hands into her front pockets and toed the ground with her shoe. "Nope, it's just me. But General, you're mistaken about somethin'. I ain't no youngun! I'm a grown man . . . well, almost a grown man!" She rubbed her smooth, soft face. "I've been shavin' for almost a year now!" The thought crossed her mind that the young officer probably hadn't been shaving much longer.

The expression on the lieutenant's face bespoke his doubt about the lad's claim to maturity, but he was too interested in what the boy had said to comment. "You mean you have been traveling through Indian country all by yourself?"

"I reckon so. I'm here, ain't I?" Virginia jutted her

chin defiantly.

"Where are you headed?"

"California."

"Where are you from?"

"Northeast Texas. Jefferson, to be more exact."

The lieutenant stroked his chin thoughtfully. "Why didn't you return home after your parents died?"

"I ain't got nothing to go back home for. Pa sold our farm back in East Texas and put all the money into mercantile goods. He said we would be able to peddle the goods on the way to California and have a nice little nest egg when we got there." She sighed hard. "I reckon it was a good idea . . . or it would have been if Ma and Pa hadn't took sick and died. It cost every dollar we had to put them away proper."

The young officer once again allowed his gaze to sweep quickly over the skinny young boy. "When was the last time you had something to eat, son?" His tone of voice was now much more compassionate.

"Oh, I've been eatin', General. You don't have to fret about that none." Her face broke into a wide grin. "I'm a fair-to-middlin' cook. My ma taught me how . . . 'cause it's been several years since she was in good health." She looked down at herself and shrugged defensively. "Guess it might appear that I don't eat regular since I'm so skinny. But I was feeling mighty poorly myself there for a while."

The lieutenant shook his head sympathetically. "It sounds like you have had a rough time of it." Then upon remembering his authority, his voice grew gruff. "But, young man, with as much Indian trouble as we are having around here, you should consider yourself lucky to have reached the fort. Just pull the wagon over there out of the way. I'll tell the camp commander of your plight and he can figure out what to do with you."

Virginia straightened her back and glared at the officer. "What do you mean, he can figure out what to do with me? I know what I'm gonna do. I stopped at a ranch back aways and Mr. Mowlds suggested I come here and hitch up with some teamsters or freighters on their way to Phoenix. That seems like a good idea to me." She slowly glanced about. "But I don't see none around."

"No, and I seriously doubt there will be any more through for another month or so. You just missed a caravan of twenty wagons. They left two days ago."

Virginia spun on her foot and hurried for the wagon. "Exactly which way were they headed?" she called back over her shoulder. "Maybe I can catch up with them by the end of the week."

The officer caught her by the back of the shirt and the seat of her pants. "Oh, no, you don't, sonny boy. The commander would have my hide if I let you go."

Swinging her arms and kicking her legs, Virginia was aware of the boisterous laughter coming from the other two officers as she struggled to free herself from his grasp. "You let me go! You ain't got no cause to keep me here if I don't want to stay! This here is a free country, and I ain't done nothing wrong!"

"What seems to be the problem out here, Lieutenant Culpepper?" a gruff voice asked angrily.

The lieutenant quickly released his hold on Virginia, which sent her sprawling to the ground, and he came smartly to attention. "There is no problem, sir! Everything is under control, General Crook, sir!"

While Virginia quickly scrambled to her feet, she noticed that the other two officers who had been laughing at her had come to attention also. To her, that meant one thing: the man who had spoken was a higher-ranking officer. What had the lieutenant called him? General Crook? One corner of her mouth twisted upward. I'll show that pompous lieutenant not to be so bossy, she thought to herself.

"It shore don't seem like everythin' is under control to me," she grumbled, slapping the dust from her trousers with her hat. " 'Course I guess that depends on who got grabbed by the seat of the britches and who did the grabbing!" She glared at the much-older officer standing on the porch with his hands behind him. With a toss of her head to indicate the lieutenant, she said, "It appears your general don't know how to treat civilians properly."

"*My general?*" He glared at Culpepper.

The lieutenant's face flushed. "Sir, I never said—"

"That's quite enough, Mister Culpepper! Be in my office in one hour. I think perhaps you need a refresher course in the proper order of rank and what happens to a green lieutenant when he tries to pass himself off as a general!" He turned to Virginia. "Now, young man, suppose you tell me what all of that ruckus was about?"

"I don't rightly know," she replied, eyes wide with innocence. "I just told your general that I was gonna try to catch up with those teamsters who left a couple of days ago, and he grabbed me by the seat of my britches!"

One of the other lieutenants stepped forward. "Request permission to speak, sir."

"At ease, Lieutenant Beene. Permission granted."

"Sir, Lieutenant Culpepper never intimated he was a general. Apparently this young boy does not know which insignia belongs to which rank."

"I am well aware of the probability, Lieutenant," the general grumbled dryly. Trying hard not to lose

197

his patience, he added, "I am attempting to find out why one of my officers thought it was necessary to restrain a civilian by the seat of his trousers!" His voice had risen higher with each word he spoke.

After Lieutenant Beene related Virginia's story, the general dismissed the officers and turned his attention to the ragged young boy standing before him. Ordinarily, he would have dismissed the young lad as well with a few stern orders, without giving him a second thought. But there was something about the boy's courage, the hardships he had borne, that commanded his respect.

He placed his hand on the boy's shoulder and spoke in a gentle tone. "How old are you, son, twelve, fourteen?"

"I'll be fifteen my next birthday, sir."

"That's mighty young for a boy to be on his own. I've met quite a few ranchers and farmers in this area, and I'm sure I could ask around and find a nice family for you to live with. . . ."

Virginia's eyes widened fearfully. That would never do! "Oh, no, sir, I thank you kindly, but I believe I'll head on out to California. You see, that was a dream of my pa's. That's all I 'member us talkin' about when I was young . . . and I think it's only fittin' that I do as he wanted."

The general was impressed by the young boy's determination. "Well, I won't try to change your mind, but you will have to stay here for awhile. And you will also have to give me your word that you won't become impatient and try to slip away from the fort in the middle of the night. The newspapers back East have painted Geronimo as a hero who has been driven from his native land by land-grabbing white settlers. That statement is a far cry from the truth. Actually, the Apaches are as much invaders in this land as the white people are. And, in reality, Geronimo is a ruthless old savage and until he is brought under control, the Apache people will not make peace with the whites. Unfortunately, we have had to bury too many people who believed the newspaper accounts. And whoever told you to join up with the teamsters or freighters knew what he was talking about. Banding together in large or heavily armed groups is the safest way to travel right now."

Virginia eyed him warily. "What do you reckon would happen if a body was too stubborn to listen to your advice and tried to slip away in the middle of the night?"

With a solemn expression, the general said authoritatively, "My troopers would scrape together what pieces they could find of that person and bury him . . . or if that person were lucky, my troopers would bring him back to the fort and I would have him thrown in the guardhouse until he grew some common sense between his ears."

"You mean to tell me you've got the right to do that to a civilian?"

The general smiled, though the expression held no amusement. "Yes, Jimmy, Arizona is a territory, not a state. We are at war with the Apaches and I am a military commander. I *do* have that right."

Virginia took a deep, shuddering breath. The way it looked to her, she had no choice. She slowly extended her hand. "Well, since I don't have a hankerin' to be butchered by the 'Paches, and since I don't think I would take too kindly to being locked up in your jail, it looks to me like I had best give you my word."

Chapter Fourteen

Virginia rested against a wheel on her wagon and stared up at the sky in awe. It looked to her as if an artist had dipped his brushes into a special palette and had flung the paint into the sky and across the mountains. It was the time of day when the sun was a fiery red sliver in the west, bathing the land in multiple shades of scarlet and gold, while the sky directly above was still a brilliant blue. Then, to the far east, night advanced like a legion of Roman soldiers piercing a black-velvet, jewel-bedecked sky with their spear tips.

Watching nature's magnificent performance, Virginia was overcome by a melancholy feeling as she heard the lonesome cry of a harmonica drifting softly through the night.

There were other sounds, too, which came from the fort as well as from the settlement located just outside the garrison's perimeter. Dogs barked, a child cried, and boisterous laughter came sporadically from the saloon, but still, it was the lonely wail of the harmonica that seemed to stand out above all the other sounds. It threw her into a pensive mood.

So many things had happened. Her life had changed so drastically, and each time it appeared she was about to work out a difficult problem, another seemingly insurmountable obstacle suddenly loomed in her way.

It had taken so much courage for her to set out across the rugged, western New Mexico desert, but she had squared her shoulders and had bravely placed one foot in front of the other because it was something she had to do if she was to hold on to her hopes of having a normal, respectable life. And now, the setback of her having to stay here at the fort until another caravan of teamsters came through was yet another crushing disappointment. Why did it seem that happiness—or, at the very least, contentment—was just an elusive dream, dangling in front of her like the proverbial carrot prodding a stubborn mule?

Without warning, Slade's image flashed before her and it was only through fierce determination that tears did not spill down her cheeks. Struggling for self-control, she made herself remember every hateful word he had spoken. She thought it strange that she could have given her heart to him so freely, yet felt so much hatred for him now. She sighed heavily. How could a woman love a man so deeply one moment and hate him the next? Perhaps she did not hate him. Perhaps she had unconsciously formed a barrier around her heart and her thoughts so that the memory of him would not be a constant ache. Perhaps that was why each time the memory of him tried to steal into her mind, she closed it off, as though slamming an iron door on her emotions. Despite her inner feelings for him and the unwanted memories that crept into her mind, his treatment of her had been so cruel, she now felt as if he had snuffed out a light that had shone within her. One thing she felt certain of: she would never be able to love or trust another man as long as she lived.

Virginia pushed all such thoughts from her mind, for she realized there were other worries she should be considering instead of torturing herself with memories of the past.

Her most important goal was to maintain her disguise as a boy so that she would be able to leave Fort Grant when the teamsters came through again. And, in order to do that, she would have to stay on guard and not relax her vigil for one moment.

Virginia knew she would have to be careful with every word and even how she uttered it. Not only her grammar, but her actions and manners as well, would have to be those of a backwoods farm boy. Yet she would not appear ignorant or behave like a buffoon, for a person did not have to be highly educated or live in a city to be smart or have common sense. Nevertheless, she would have to be conscientious about her behavior. Then too, her complexion could pose a problem. Having always worn a bonnet in the sun and having faithfully used a rose-scented lotion to prevent her face and hands from becoming excessively dry and chapped on the trek west, she had maintained her soft, feminine skin. She hoped a bit of soot or ashes would help conceal it now.

Also, there was the problem of supporting herself until she could leave. While she had plenty of supplies, there were the horses to consider. Grain was very expensive and she hated to spend what few precious dollars she had without finding an immediate way to replace them. The owner of the general store in the settlement probably would not take kindly to her selling goods from her wagon. Of course, she had just as much right to sell merchandise as he did, but if she could find a few jobs to sustain her, it might prevent trouble. The less attention drawn to herself, the better off she would be.

While Virginia prepared for bed, she planned her next day, mentally listing the most logical places to seek employment in the settlement. Some of the possibilities were quickly discarded. "Virginia" could have done laundry, mended clothing, darned socks, or even baked cakes and pies for the soldiers, but "Jimmy" would never be able to do those sorts of things without raising suspicion. And also, there were many chores a boy Jimmy's age could do that she would not physically be able to accomplish.

Sighing heavily, Virginia plumped her pillow and covered herself with a thin sheet. Perhaps being a male would not be as easy as she had at first thought.

Early the next morning, Virginia quickly dressed and went to the commander's office to inquire about a job feeding horses. Having had sole responsibility for her own team, she thought Jimmy could handle the job of tending horses without too much difficulty.

The clerk informed her she would have to see the man at the settlement who held the contract to care for the horses. He further explained that granting a contract to a civilian was a procedure the military often practiced whenever the troops were engaged in Indian skirmishes. After obtaining the man's name, she hurried over to the livery stable with high hopes of finding a job.

Seeing a big, burly man standing in a wagon filled with hay, Virginia hitched up her trousers—a gesture she thought Jimmy would make—and called to him. "Hey, Mister, I'm lookin' for a man named Cyrus Jones."

"You found him, sonny. What can I do for you?" He never missed a beat in the steady cadence he had developed for pitching the hay from the wagon up to the barn loft.

"My name is Jimmy Branson, and I was told you're in charge of the army's horses and that you might be needin' some help." She thumbed her chest. "I figure I'm just the man you've been lookin' for."

At that brash statement, Cyrus stopped, leaned on the handle of the pitchfork, and stared at the young boy with amusement. "Son, I don't know where you are from—"

"Northeastern part of Texas."

"—but if you are an example of the men they grow there, I'd hate to see what the boys look like." He chuckled. "You must have been the runt of the litter."

Virginia bristled as if rubbed the wrong way with a burr. "Don't let my size fool you none." She snorted derisively. "My years might not tally up to what you think makes a man, but I'm a hard worker and I'll do an honest day's work for an honest day's pay."

Cyrus jumped down from the wagon, folded his arms, and leaned against it. He studied the boy for a moment. He badly need help. When he had bid on the army contract, he and his nephew had planned to do the work themselves, but until his nephew finished cutting the low-meadow hay fields, he was being forced to do all the work himself, and it was too much for one man.

He spat a dark stream of tobacco juice, then asked, "What do you consider an honest day's pay?"

Virginia shrugged noncommittally. "Well, don't

rightly know what wages run around these parts, so I'm willin' to talk that over. But I'll tell you straight out, I need keep for my horses too. I've got four of 'em. And as long as you pay me enough for my own grub, I really ain't in no need of anythin' else." Virginia figured it would not hurt to bargain for a small salary. If she could save what little money she had, so much the better.

"I don't know," he said, rubbing his chin. "You look awfully puny to me. Taking care of over two hundred horses is a mighty big job."

Two hundred horses! That many! Virginia thought with dismay.

She took a deep breath to bolster her flagging courage. "I suspect it is a mighty big job. But, I'll tell you somethin', mister. I might be puny, and I might not be strong enough to lift a full bag of grain or do some of the other heavy lifting, but I ain't lazy, and I ain't afeared of hard work. Don't imagine I could carry a full sack of grain at one time, but I betcha I could tote grain in buckets until I was able to carry the sack. Besides that, I could put out hay and water the horses, help curry and groom them, and keep the stalls and barn clean." She jutted her chin defiantly. "I know I could do that as good as anybody."

Cyrus had heard about the spunky young boy who, after losing his parents, had crossed the western part of New Mexico by himself. And after actually seeing and talking with the little cuss, he was even more impressed.

"You say you have four horses that need stabling?"

"Yes, sir." She slipped her hands behind her back and crossed her fingers.

Cyrus scratched the bristled whiskers on his leathery face. "Are you looking for a permanent job?"

A momentary look of discomfort crossed her face. She had always detested a liar, but if she told the truth he might look for someone else to hire. Although her pretense of being a boy was a deception, she believed it would hurt no one. However, to tell a deliberate lie that could possibly cause problems for this man was something she could not do in good conscience.

"Well," she said with a heavy sigh, "I got to be honest with you. I ain't lookin' for nothin' steady. As soon as some teamsters or freighters come through, I'm gonna hitch up with them and go on over to the Phoenix area. So I don't think it would be right for me to promise to stay with you for any length of time when I've got other plans. But I do need the work, mister. I really do."

He regarded her with a speculative gaze. "I'll tell you what I'll do. Since it's the soldiers' duty to curry their own mounts and to check for any hoof injuries when they come in from patrol, I'll pay you fifty cents a day and keep for your horses. Your duties would be to water the horses, put out hay in the morning and grain at night. You will also have to keep the stalls raked out and the barn clean."

Breathing a sigh of relief, Virginia asked, "When do you want me to start?"

"Hear me out first. You may want to look further before you make a decision. The job might not last as long as you need it to. I have a partner—my nephew—and he is tied up with other business matters right now, but when he finishes, we won't be needing you." He looked at the lad expectantly. "Now, are you still interested?"

Virginia glanced up at him sharply. His frankness had surprised her. Most men would have hired her without ever saying anything about a nephew. Apparently he was honest, and that attribute immediately won her respect.

"Yes, sir, I am still interested. Just like I asked before, when do you want me to start?"

"Right now," he said with a smile. "You can pull your wagon over here by the barn and turn your horses in with my own livestock out back in the smallest pen. The horses have already been fed and watered this morning, so as soon as you are through taking care of your personal business, you can start filling the water barrels—they only need to be filled once a day. There's a yoke in the barn with two buckets attached to it, and the well is out behind the main corral. After the barrels are filled, start raking the stalls. The officers' horses are stabled on the left side and they want them kept clean. I try to keep the right side open for sick horses and *I* want them kept clean. Do you have any questions?"

"No, sir, leastwise not yet."

"Well, if you have any later on . . . even if they appear foolish, I'd rather have you ask than make a mistake."

"Yes, sir." She turned and started for her wagon, then stopped and slowly turned around. "If you don't mind, Mr. Jones, I do have a question, but it don't have nothin' to do 'bout my chores, though."

"What is it?"

Obviously puzzled, she pointed toward the Apache *wickiups*. "If we're at war with the Indians, what are they doin' here at the fort? It just don't seem right to me."

"I know. I've had the same thoughts from time to time myself. Those are called "Reservation Indians," supposedly tame. And I guess the military's reasoning is, if they're here, they're not out raising hell against the settlers. But a lot of us have suspicions that they occasionally sneak off and join up with Geronimo or one of the other warring chiefs . . . like they did back in '71." He peered at Virginia intently. "Ever hear of the Camp Grant massacre?"

"No, sir, I haven't."

"Let's go get your wagon and while we're doing that, I'll tell you about one of the bloodiest happenings in Arizona history. Now, the present-day Fort Grant is not to be confused with Camp Grant—although they are actually the same, just in different locations. The living conditions became so unhealthy at the old fort, General Crook was forced to relocate it after he took command.

"Back in the late sixties and early seventies, the Indians were successful in arming themselves with rifles by frequently attacking emigrants' wagons and freighting outfits; they kept themselves supplied with ammunition by raiding lonely ranches or by jumping prospectors and lone travelers. After the Apaches became well armed, their atrocities against the whites just got worse. No one was safe then. For a long time it had been suspected that the Indians wintering on the government reservation at old Camp Grant—at the taxpayer's expense, I might add—were the culprits responsible for the numerous raids over in the vicinity of Tucson. It was hard to convince the authorities that such was the case. Then the Apaches made the mistake of attacking the Wooster ranch near Tubac. They killed Wooster and carried off his wife. Since she was never found, their friends could only hope she'd been killed and left somewhere in the desert. Needless to say, when the news of the bloody attack reached Tucscon, there was a cry for instant revenge. But the authorities dragged their feet, as usual, so the white men in Tucscon held a meeting and took matters into their own hands."

Cyrus shortened his normally long stride so that Virginia could keep up with him. "To the best of my recollection, Mayor De Long, Bill Oury, John Cady, and three other white men, along with three Papago Indian trackers, rode out to what remained of the Woosters' ranch. The Papagos began tracking and soon found a trail that led as plain as daylight to the Indian settlement at Camp Grant. They went back to Tuscon, rounded up over a hundred men, and set out for Camp Grant with blood in their eyes. They attacked just at the break of dawn. Before the startled Apaches could fully awaken to what was happening or the soldiers could gather their wits together, eighty-seven Aravaipa Apaches were killed. Of course it was later suspected that some of the soldiers moved mighty slowly, but no one was ever able to prove it. Back in Washington, when General Sherman learned about the massacre, he issued orders that the men be arrested and stand trial for murder.

"They were tried in Judge Titus's Territorial Court, but to the dismay of the military and General Sherman, who, of course, knew nothing about the events that had led up to the massacre, not one man could be found for jury duty who was impartial. The men were set free, but one thing that made their acquittal more certain was the fact, brought out at the trial, that a dress of Mrs. Wooster's and a pair of her husband's moccasins were found on the bodies of two of the Indians who had been killed. Nevertheless, a cry went up in the East that Arizonians were more savage than the savages were."

Cyrus shook his head sadly. "Things haven't changed much in all these years. The Apaches keep killing the whites, the whites keep killing the Indi-

209

ans, and the innocent die right along with the guilty. Makes a man wonder when it will all end. I usually try to keep my opinions to myself, but I really don't believe that saying, 'The only good Indian is a dead Indian.' There is good and bad in all people, I don't care what their color is." Cyrus clasped Virginia's shoulder. "Son, I told you about the massacre for a reason. And I'm not just referring to Indians either, but unless you have good cause, don't ever trust anybody too much. It simply doesn't pay."

Virginia looked up at him with huge, sorrowful eyes. "You don't have to worry about that none, Mr. Jones. I've done already learned that lesson . . . perhaps I have learned it too well," she added sadly.

Sensing the boy was referring to something else entirely but not wanting to pry, Cyrus slapped his hands together and declared, "Well, boy, we're burning daylight. Let's get to work."

It was well past supper time before Virginia finally finished her chores. Her arms and shoulders ached so badly, she could have cried. How many buckets of water and grain and wheelbarrows of hay had she carried? How many times had she reached for dirty straw with the heavy rake? And the smell! After raking forty soiled stalls, she was certain the odor had permeated her hair, clothes, and flesh. All she wanted was a hot bath and a good, soft bed until it was time to feed the horses. But how was she to take a bath and still maintain her disguise? Separate bathing facilities had been erected for emigrant travelers' needs, but she could not use either the men's or the women's. For now, a facecloth, soap, and a pan of water would have to do until she could figure out some other method.

After she had washed and put on clean clothes, Virginia became aware of a gnawing sensation in her stomach. It was then she realized she had not eaten since early that morning. Too tired to cook, she decided to go over to the settlement and find a place that served food. Arriving at the restaraunt just as it was closing, she was told the saloon sometimes served meals. After being cautioned not to confuse the settlement's only real saloon with the *hog ranches* — filthy pestholes that boasted cheap, rotgut whiskey, diseased women, and frequent murders — Virginia saw no reason why "Jimmy" could not go to the saloon to eat.

Pausing at the entrance to the saloon, Virginia took a deep breath, then pushed open the swinging doors and entered. She slowly glanced about. The bartender stood talking to a large group of soldiers who were lined up in front of the bar. Eight of the ten tables were occupied. A piano stood silent against the far wall, and in the back of the room four men stood around a large billiard table. Suddenly aware that she had caught the attention of several of the men, Virginia hurried to the end of the bar nearest the door.

George Adkins, the bartender, grinned and gave an exaggerated wink to the soldiers before ambling over to where Virginia stood. He folded his arms, resting them on his rounded belly, and teetered back on his heels. "Tell me, sonny boy, does your ma know where you're at?"

Virginia was too tired and hungry to be the butt of this man's joke. Without thinking of the consequences, she retorted in a surly tone, "Does yours?"

Noting the look of anger that swept over the bartender's face when the soldiers started howling with laughter, Virginia quickly decided that if she wanted

211

any supper she would have to change her tactics.

She bowed her head humbly. "I'm sorry, mister. Don't reckon I was too polite, and my ma taught me better than that. It's just . . . people have been funnin' me about my size and how young I look ever since my folks died and left me on my own. I realize you probably don't get many customers my age in here, but the lady over at the restaurant was closing, and she told me, next to her, you served the best meal in the settlement."

One of the soldiers nudged the man next to him and guffawed. "Apparently Mrs. Adams didn't tell him this was the *only* other place that served food." Lowering his voice, he added, "That's the kid who got Lieutenant Culpepper in trouble with the general."

Ignoring the soldiers, Virginia looked directly into the bartender's eyes. "I sure would appreciate it if you'd sell me my supper."

Apparently satisfied with the boy's apology, George pursed his lips and nodded. "Well . . . since you got a more respectful tongue in your head, I might be able to scrape up a plate of red beans and a couple of chunks of corn bread. But next time, boy, you watch your mouth. You hear?"

"Y — Yes, sir."

While Virginia waited for the bartender to return, she once again looked about the saloon, paying closer attention to small details than she had before. Her gaze fastened on the mirrored painting hanging behind the bar. As she took several steps sideways to get a better look, her face suddenly blazed. The painting was of a naked lady lying on a bed of pillows. Not realizing the men standing at the bar had been watching her reaction, she heard them begin to hoot and holler.

"What's the matter, kid? Haven't you ever seen a naked woman before?" a soldier asked.

Virginia sheepishly ducked her head and shook it.

Although not malicious, the soldier obviously enjoyed teasing the boy. He chortled, then raised his voice. "Men, the little runt hasn't ever seen a naked woman. I think we ought to pass the hat and take up a collection so he can go visit Dovie when she gets here." His suggestion received several boisterous chuckles.

Another soldier remarked dryly, "Hell, while you're at it, pass the hat for me too. I've been walking around with a *big* hurt for the past three months. Don't you remember? I was out on field patrol the last time and completely missed Dovie's visit."

"Yeah, but since tomorrow's payday, you can bet your last dollar that Dovie and her soiled doves will be here tonight or first thing in the morning."

The soldier sighed dreamily. "Yeah, I know it, and I can't hardly wait!"

Virginia's eyes widened when she suddenly realized what the soldiers were referring to. Apparently Dovie was a madam who made regular visits to the fort with her girls. That reminded her of what Slade had said about traveling prostitutes. Evidently, some women did do such things! And she had thought he was merely trying to be cruel and deliberately hurt her—which he had. Undoubtedly, there had been truth to his statement.

A soldier standing at the other end of the bar cackled with glee. "Look at his face, Sam. Why, he looks scared to death."

George came back carrying a plate heaped with beans and two large wedges of corn bread. "That's enough, men. Leave him alone. He's just a kid."

"Thanks, mister," Virginia said gratefully. Picking up the plate, she turned to take a seat at one of the empty tables, but the bartender stopped her.

"Wait a minute, boy. Don't take up a whole table. They are reserved for drinking customers." He pointed to the corner. "Pull over one of those stools and eat here at the bar."

Complying with his request, Virginia climbed up on the stool. She started to ask for a fork instead of the spoon she had been given but thought better of it. "Jimmy" would eat with a spoon and he would not have good manners. Leaning forward, she grasped the spoon with her entire hand and coiled her arms around the plate, then began shoveling in the food.

"Want something to drink, boy?"

"You don't have to call me boy. My name's Jimmy. And yes, sir, I would like something to drink." Lowering her voice, she leaned forward even farther. "I know this is a saloon, but . . . you don't have any milk, do you?"

George nodded. "Yeah, I've got some." His belly burned something fierce at times, and he tried to keep a crock of cool milk on hand. When he placed the glass of milk on the bar, the soldiers started laughing again.

"Look there, Sam, what the youngun is drinking! Hey, kid, wouldn't you rather have a shot of red-eye, or a mug of beer? Either one will put hair on your chest."

George glowered at the men. "All right now, I think that's enough! Need I remind you what can happen to a man for riding a kid too hard?"

A chorus of groans went up from the soldiers standing at the bar. One man grumbled, "You gonna tell us that yarn about Billy the Kid . . .

again?"

"Gawdamnit, it isn't a yarn! Cahill's grave will attest to that!"

A new recruit piped up, "What's this about Billy the Kid?"

That was the opening George had been waiting for. He thoroughly enjoyed retelling how the Kid had gunned down a man in his saloon. He began talking while refilling the soldiers' empty beer mugs. "It was back in '77 when Billy was here at the fort. Only thing is, most people refer to him as William Bonney, but his real name was Henry McCarty. Bonney was his stepfather's name. Anyway, F. P. Cahill kept riding Billy just like you all have been doing this kid here. One day, Cahill got a little carried away and he started slapping Billy around. First thing we knew, Billy got his craw full. He pulled his gun and shot Cahill. When the man died the next day, Billy was arrested for "criminal and unjustifiable" murder. The Kid escaped from jail a few days later." George shook his head. "From all accounts, Cahill was the first man he killed. I often wonder if Billy's life would have been different if Cahill had just kept his mouth shut."

Not aware that three young lieutenants had entered, George glanced around and was surprised when Lieutenant Culpepper spoke angrily. "If Billy the Kid was as smart mouthed as this runt, it's no wonder Cahill rode him."

He sauntered over to where Virginia was sitting and wagged his finger threateningly in her face. "Listen to me, boy, and you had better pay close attention . . . and it won't do you any good to run crying to the general either—he's been called to another fort. Stay out of my way. That little stunt you pulled yesterday got me a reprimand. If I catch you

215

spitting on the ground the wrong way, I'll have you hauled to the guardhouse." His face darkened with anger. "Did you understand, or do you need me to repeat it?"

Virginia, glaring at him, wiped her mouth on her shirt sleeve. "No, *Lieutenant,* you don't need to repeat nothin'."

Chapter Fifteen

"That pompous mushhead," Virginia grumbled under her breath as she angrily stomped back to her wagon. "I wish I were a foot taller and weighed one hundred pounds more! Why, I would show that smart-aleck lieutenant how it feels to be picked on! He's nothing but a bully, throwing his weight around, making threats!"

Virginia climbed into the wagon and tripped over something lying in the narrow walkway. Knowing the wagon had been left neat and tidy, she quickly lit the lantern hanging from the center rib that supported the canvas covering. Her eyes widened and she gave a sharp gasp of dismay. The contents of the wagon had been rifled!

While she slowly looked around, her hoarse whisper broke the silence. "Who could have done such a thing?" Then, remembering the look of hatred on the lieutenant's face, she realized he was the most likely suspect, though he would have had to have acted quickly, for he had left the saloon only about ten minutes before she had. By the appearance of her wagon, it seemed a person could do a lot of damage in ten minutes' time. Racks of ribbon and bolts of cloth had been unwound, the harnesses had been jumbled together, and a stack of blankets had been strewn about in chaotic disorder.

Her gaze fastened on her wooden keepsake box lying open on the bed. Her personal treasures had been few, and at one glance she realized that her long braid and the pendant watch that had belonged to her mother were gone. Many different emotions coursed through her: anguish, uneasiness, and a scalding feeling of rage.

Angrily, she rushed from the wagon to report the theft at the commander's office. Yet, as she hurried along, a sense of caution overtook her impulsiveness. The general was not what she might call a friend, although he was a fair man, yet he was out on patrol and Lord only knew when he would return. There was no way of knowing who had been left in charge. If the officer was a friend of the lieutenant's, probably nothing would be done, especially if there were no witnesses. And if she accused him without proof, it would just give him further cause for vindictiveness. Then too, the braid and pendant watch were the only items she definitely knew were missing. A female would be upset over losing such mementos, but not a young boy. However, if the lieutenant was the guilty culprit, and she did not report the theft, he might become suspicious simply because of the nature of the items he had taken. But she had to file a complaint. If the theft was not reported, her silence might raise suspicions too — unless she made light of the incident. Yes, that was the only possible solution. As for the braid, it was unimportant. Hair eventually grew back. But her decision would mean the pendant watch would probably never be recovered.

"Damn that lieutenant's sorry hide!" she muttered

angrily. "I certainly would like to show him a thing or two!"

Upon reaching the company headquarters, she found the door open, so she stepped inside. A young soldier sat at a desk behind an oak bannister.

"Yes? May I help you?" he asked, looking up from a stack of papers.

"Y — Yes, sir, I hope you can. I need to report a robbery, and my wagon was rifled too."

"Was anyone injured?"

"No, sir, wasn't nobody there when it was robbed."

"I see. Please take a seat while I inform the officer of the day. What is your name?" he asked, pushing back his chair.

"Jimmy Branson."

The soldier rapped on a door, entered a private office, and a few moments later he returned to his desk and told the boy to go on inside.

Virginia had always made it a point not to take off her hat in public, feeling it helped conceal her female identity. However, she realized that under these circumstances it would be too impolite not to remove it. She slipped it from her head, but deliberately took a chair just outside the soft glow of the lamp in hopes that the officer would not be able to see her too clearly.

"I'm Sergeant Hendrix," the man said, picking up a pencil and reaching for a clean sheet of paper. "My aide said your name is Jimmy Branson." He peered at her curiously. "Are you the same young man who recently arrived from New Mexico?"

"Yes, sir." Good Lord, she thought. Does everybody here at the fort know Jimmy Branson's life story?

The sergeant nodded. "I thought so. General Crook mentioned something about you." He leaned forward. "My aide tells me you need to report a robbery."

"Yes, sir, and my wagon was rifled too."

"What all was destroyed or stolen?"

"Well, wasn't nothin' really destroyed. Some ribbon and material was messed up a bit and a stack of blankets scattered. I figure whoever was doing it must have been scared off."

"Then what was stolen?"

Virginia frowned and shook her head. "Just a few keepsakes that belonged to my ma; a pendant watch that didn't keep good time and a wiglike hairpiece she used to pin in her hair. It really ain't all that important, Sergeant . . . it's just that. . . . Well, shoot fire, I figure an Injun or maybe one of their younguns got a little nosy." She noted by the sergeant's expression that he was relieved by her resigned acceptance of what had happened.

"It really ain't nothin' to make a fuss about, 'specially since there's already so much Injun trouble going on, but I thought I better report it just in case whoever it was decided to come back." She grinned and threaded her fingers through her shaggy hair. "I'm a bit more partial to this hairpiece and I shore would hate to lose it."

The sergeant settled back in his chair. "Then you don't want to file a formal complaint?"

Virginia shrugged. "It would probably do more harm than good. If I filed one, you'd probably have to search the Apaches' wickiups, and that would probably make 'em mad, then they'd probably go off and kill somebody. And that old hairpiece and a watch that don't work good ain't worth it. O' course, if you were to keep your eyes peeled and spotted 'em somewhere, I would like to have 'em back 'cause they did belong to my ma." She stood and walked to the door. "And it might not hurt if you passed the word around that I will be sleepin' with my old double-barreled shotgun and if I hear anybody messin' around my wagon, I won't hesitate one doggone minute to fill 'em full of buckshot."

In the days that followed, Virginia tried her best to avoid the lieutenant, but he took great delight in finding fault with everything she did. His horse's stall was never cleaned correctly, his horse was never fed or watered to suit him, and he used any excuse to complain. Cyrus noticed how unfairly the lieutenant rode Jimmy and even offered to say something to him, but Virginia refused, saying it would only make things worse. Finally, one day when the young officer was being overly cruel and callous, Cyrus told him in no uncertain terms that if he had any complaints he should take them to headquarters, but if he did, *he* might have a few complaints of his own. Although the lieutenant continued to make snide remarks, he stopped complaining about the care his horse was receiving.

Virginia threw herself into her work. By doing so, she found a mindless activity that helped camouflage her deep loneliness. But at night, when time hung heavily on her hands, she fell into the habit of taking her evening meal at the saloon where there was noise and laughter, even though she was usually the butt of that laughter. That did not bother her, because it was good-natured teasing, and it helped keep her mind off her loneliness and feelings of helplessness — helplessness because she believed she had no control over her life. Much like a marionette, she was being made to dance and move by someone else's command. If only the freighters would come and she could be on her way again, perhaps she might not feel such a gnawing ache. But at night, as she lay in her lonely bed, deep down inside she knew that Stephen Slade was the real reason for her despair.

Even her dreams were tortured by the memory of being held in Slade's arms. Many times Virginia awoke to find herself reaching for the man who was not there, who would never be there. Then her despair would start anew, because as illogical as it seemed and as badly as she dreaded to admit it, she was in love with a man she hated. When he had left her, he had destroyed a portion of her heart that could never be repaired.

"Jimmy?" Cyrus called out. "Where are you?"

Hurriedly tucking her shirt into her trousers, Virginia stuck her head out the back flap of the wagon. "Here I am, Mr. Cyrus. Help yourself to the coffee. It should be brewed by now." She jumped down from the wagon, filled the wash pan full of water, and splashed it over her face. While vigorously drying off with a rough towel, she said, "Sorry, I'm running late this morning. Guess I overslept a bit. It won't happen again though, I promise."

"You're not late. I'm just a little early," Cyrus said jovially, glancing at the still-darkened sky. "Do you have an extra cup though? I've brought someone with me."

She slowly lowered the towel and a lump formed in her throat when she saw a man standing beside Cyrus who strongly resembled him. He must be the nephew, she thought. I guess this means the end of my job.

"Jimmy, this is my nephew, Emery Jones." Cyrus

filled two coffee cups and handed one to Emery.

"Howdy," she said slowly. "You shore look like your uncle."

"Yeah, that's what folks tell me."

Pulling up a short, three-legged stool, Virginia sat across from the men who had taken a seat on a bench. She peered at them over the rim of her coffee cup. "I reckon you won't be needin' me anymore."

"Don't jump to conclusions so fast, Jimmy," Cyrus stated. "Me and Emery have been talking. I told him what a good hand you've made, and we decided we can make a place for you if you want to stay." Seeing the boy start to shake his head, Cyrus held up his hands to silence him. "I remember what you told me about wanting to go to California, but you can have a future here with us if you want it. Of course, the trouble with the Apaches won't last forever and the army won't be needing men like me and Emery. But when it is over, we plan to work our land up in the Graham foothills, and we'll make a place for you there too." Obviously at a loss for words, he cleared his throat and added, "I guess what I'm trying to say is . . . you can be a part of our family if you want to stay."

Virginia's conscience stabbed painfully. Apparently Cyrus had grown more fond of her than she had suspected. She foolishly had thought no one would be hurt by her deception, but now she had been proven wrong. Why did it always seem that the nicest people were the ones taken advantage of most often? And nothing ever seemed to touch the more cruel, callous people. It wasn't fair. Even though she had been more or less forced into her deception by circumstances she could not control, it still was not fair to a good man like Cyrus.

Mistaking the boy's silence for indecision, Cyrus

stood and tossed the dregs from his coffee cup onto the small fire. "Just think it over, Jimmy. That's all I ask. If you decide to stay, good. If you decide to go, there will be no hard feelings. And if that is your decision, don't worry about your job. It'll last until you leave." He glanced at the sky. "Well, men, we had best get to work before dawn catches us without any chores done."

The pungent aromas of spices, roasted coffee beans, and raw leather pleasantly assailed Virginia's keen sense of smell as she entered the general store. In a hurry, and having been sent to the store on errands by Cyrus before, she went directly to the leather goods and selected three long strips of rawhide Cyrus needed to repair worn bridles. She then walked to the counter, but her haste had been in vain. A woman claiming she had been overcharged for certain articles was meticulously going over her bill, item by item, with the proprietress, Mabel Sutton. From the shopkeeper's expression, it was obvious she was furious that her honesty was being questioned.

Realizing this transaction could take longer than she wanted to wait, and knowing Cyrus was urgently in need of the rawhide, Virginia stepped up to the counter. "Excuse me, please. Ma'am, can I go ahead and pay . . ."

Mabel slammed her pencil down on the counter and glared at Virginia. "Young man, can't you see I am busy!"

"Yes, ma'am, but I thought—"

"I don't care what you thought!" she snapped angrily. "You can wait your turn like everybody else!"

Virginia angrily whirled away from the counter.

She made a face and stuck out her tongue, wanting fervently to do it to the rude woman's face. Then she glanced up, startled, upon hearing a throaty chuckle.

Although Virginia had never seen the famous "Dovie" up close, she recognized her immediately. From top to bottom, the woman appeared to be dressed in a filmy pink cloud. Her vivid red hair, bobbed short and tightly curled, was covered with a broad-brimmed, dark pink straw hat. Her tight pale pink dress was form fitting, its neckline plunging scandalously low, and around her shoulders was a fluffy boa the same color as her hat. Hanging on her forearm was a pink lace parasol.

"I've felt like doing the same thing myself, only I never had the nerve," Dovie said in a low whisper. Chuckling, she added, "I'll give you two bits if you turn around and do it to her face."

Virginia grinned. "I'd do it for free if my boss didn't need this here rawhide in a bad way." She glanced over her shoulder at the proprietress and shook her head. "Mrs. Sutton has got to be the most mean-mouthed woman I ever heard."

"That's an understatement," Dovie remarked dryly. Then her brow lowered into a frown. "I could have sworn me and my girls have been visited by every male sixteen to sixty, but I haven't seen you around, kid. You just get here or don't you like girls? Or, do you even know who I am?"

Virginia could feel her face flushing from the woman's questions. "Oh, no, m—ma'am, I know who you are, M—Miss Dovie, and I—I . . . like girls . . . just fine," she stammered with embarrassment. "And . . . I . . . uh . . . I've been h—here for s—several weeks now. I've been working for Cyrus Jones until the freighters come through again, then

I'll be headin' over toward Phoenix with 'em, then on out to California." Virginia's face suddenly paled. "That is . . . if they let me join up with 'em." That was a possibility she had never considered.

Dovie tilted her head curiously. "Did you come through New Mexico by yourself?"

Virginia shoved her hands into her pockets. "Well, yeah, partways I did."

Dovie nodded. "Then I've heard about you. I just didn't think you would be so . . . little. From everything I've heard, I figured you would stand at least ten feet tall."

Virginia smiled. The woman certainly knew how to flatter a person. It was easy to see there were more reasons than one why the men all thought so highly of her. Remembering her boy's role, she toed the floor sheepishly. "Good Lord, I ain't done nothin' special. 'Sides that, size ain't got nothin' to do with what a fellar has to do."

Dovie's eyes narrowed. "Tell me, boy, are you handy with a gun?"

"Not very, but I got a double-barreled shotgun that don't require much skill to shoot. All you gotta do is aim it in the general direction."

The madam gave a thoughtful nod. "I'll tell you what, kid. Me and my girls are pulling out first thing in the morning for Fort Thomas. Then in a couple of weeks, we'll leave for Fort McDowell, which is close to Phoenix. Even though I pay three men to provide an armed escort, we can always use an extra gun. If you think the freighters might not let you accompany them, you're welcome to ride along with us."

"Well, I don't know. But my doubts ain't nothin' personal," Virginia was quick to add. She knew it was an offer she seriously ought to consider, because the freighters might object to taking on the responsibility of a boy's traveling with them. But Slade's parting taunts rang through her mind. It seemed so strange, almost as if he had foreseen the future.

The woman patted Virginia on her shoulder and smiled. "You think about it, kid, and if you decide to join us, bring your wagon to the back of the saloon before dawn, because we'll be leaving shortly after."

"Young man, yoo hoo, young man," the proprietress called in her shrill voice. "I don't intend to stand here and wait all day long. If you want to purchase those rawhide strips, then get over here to the counter!"

Intent on her conversation with Dovie, Virginia had not noticed that the other woman had left. Rolling her eyes scornfully, she slowly sauntered over to the counter and slammed down the correct change. Turning, she started for the door, but the woman stopped her.

"Wait just a minute, young man! How many rawhide strips do you have?"

Virginia glared at her and held the strips up so she could count them. "Three! They are a nickel apiece, and there's fifteen cents on your counter."

The look in the proprietress's pale blue eyes quickly turned to glittering rage as she grabbed the money and furiously jabbed buttons on the cash register.

Muttering under her breath, Virginia turned to leave again, but she stopped when she heard Dovie's indignant voice.

"What do you mean, my money's not any good in here? What in the hell is wrong with it? It happens to be United States currency and that makes it good in any territory!"

Mabel Sutton planted her hands on her hips and shook her head so hard, her mousy-brown-colored bun came unpinned and the hair straggled down her back. "I don't care if you have money signed by the President himself. It's still not any good! Not in my store, it isn't!" she sneered belligerently.

"And why not?"

"Oh, you know the reason why! It is tainted money, earned by sinful ways! And I would thank you to leave my store immediately, you shameless hussy! My husband and I do not need customers like you!"

Dovie's eyes narrowed coldly and her lips curled into a contemptuous sneer. "Maybe not, but I have customers like your husband. If he hasn't visited me and my girls, it's his loss, because I'm sure the last time he reached between your legs, he grabbed nothing but a fistful of cobwebs, you damned old bitch!" With that, Dovie threw her purchases on the counter, spun on her foot, and marched haughtily out of the store.

Outside, Virginia quickly caught up with her. "Ma'am, Miss Dovie, wait a minute. Here's the two bits I owe you." She removed a quarter from her pocket and pressed it into Dovie's hand.

Puzzled, Dovie frowned and asked, "Wha . . . what's this for?" By her expression it seemed she wondered if the boy were insulting her.

"For stickin' your tongue out at her." Virginia grinned impishly. "Only thing is, you did it better than I ever could have!"

Dovie blinked her eyes, then threw back her head and laughed heartily.

That night, Virginia went over to the saloon for

228

supper after she finished work. Taking her usual place at the end of the bar, she saw that the saloon was more crowded and noisier than normal. George was rushing back and forth between the customers, refilling beer mugs and opening new bottles of whiskey.

Finally noticing the boy sitting at the end of the bar, he hurried over to him, panting for breath.

"Busy tonight, huh?" Virginia remarked with a grin.

"Yeah, it's always like this the night before Dovie and her girls leave."

"Hey, George," a loud voice called above the din. "How about some service over here?"

George took a deep breath, and flinging a white cloth across his shoulder, he asked, "Jimmy, since I'm so busy, why don't you go on back to the kitchen and help yourself? It's steak and creamed potatoes tonight. I put your plate in the warming oven on top of the stove so it wouldn't get cold."

"Sure thing, Mister Adkins. I don't mind a bit. Do you want me to eat back there so somebody else can have my place at the bar?"

"Naw, just come on up here and eat," he said, giving an indifferent wave of his hand. "That stove has made it hotter than hell back there."

Carefully weaving her way through the crush of men so as not to spill her milk or drop her plate, Virginia did not see the foot that was suddenly thrust in front of her. She fell, sprawling across the floor, as food and milk flew everywhere. Amidst a chorus of loud guffaws, Virginia quickly scrambled to her feet and her mouth compressed into a thin white line when she saw Lieutenant Culpepper smirking at her.

"What's the matter, boy?" he gloated. "Can't you

stand on your own two feet? Of course, if you cleaned some of that horse manure off your boots, you might be able to walk better."

Furious, Virginia clenched her hands into fists. "You did that on purpose!"

"What?" he asked innocently.

"You deliberately tripped me!" Her voice rang throughout the now quiet saloon. Realizing that in anger she had spoken in her normal tone, Virginia added in her fake boyish drawl, "But what else could a body expect out of a ill-mannered, snot-nosed lieutenant, whose brains wouldn't even fill an eye of a thimble!"

Someone hollered, "Don't you mean an eye of a needle?"

"No, an eye of a thimble, 'cause it's littler!"

The lieutenant sprang from his chair and grabbed Virginia by her shirtfront. "Come on, you little brat!" he muttered between clenched teeth. "I'm taking you outside to teach you a few manners! Something your pa neglected to do!"

The man casually leaning against the bar timed his movement right. When Culpepper roughly shoved Virginia toward the door, the man turned and stuck out his foot, which sent the lieutenant sprawling on the floor. He tipped over a spittoon, spilling the contents all over himself.

"Oh, excuse me," the man said, his voice heavily laced with sarcasm.

Virginia stiffened at the sound of the man's familiar voice. Whirling about, she looked at him, then quickly lowered her head. The man was *Slade!*

"You son of a bitch! Why don't you watch what you're doing?" the lieutenant shouted as he unsuccessfully tried to get to his feet. Instead, he kept sliding in the putrid mess from the spittoon.

230

Slade reached down and grabbed him by his shirt and none too gently assisted him. "And why don't you pick on somebody your own size?" he asked coldly.

"I suggest you mind your own business." The lieutenant had fear in his eyes as he tried to step back, but Slade had too tight a grip on him.

"Any time a man—and I use that term loosely—throws his weight around by bullying kids, I figure it is my business." He released his hold and shoved the lieutenant backward. Slade splayed his legs in an easy stance and his hand moved dangerously close to his gun. "If you want to apologize to the kid, I figure our business is over. If not, then you can meet me out in the street."

Fear knotted inside Virginia. "Both of you, stop it!" she shouted, unshed tears choking her voice. "Ain't gonna be no killin' on my account." She was grateful that the brim of her hat partly concealed her face.

"Don't worry about it, Jimmy." George spoke in a deceptively calm voice as he leveled his shotgun across the bar. "There's not going to be any more trouble—not in my place. Lieutenant, you get on back to the fort. You're not allowed in this saloon anymore. And you can rest assured I will report your behavior to your commanding officer." He glanced at Slade. "And mister, I don't know who you are, but you can finish your beer and leave. If you decide to come back though, leave your gun at home." He raised his voice. "All right, men, the show's over. Beer is on the house."

George looked at Virginia. "Do you want me to fix you another plate?"

"N—No, sir, I ain't hungry no more." She turned and ran from the saloon, wanting to get out of there

231

before Slade recognized her. Her stomach lurched sickeningly at the thought of what would happen if he did. Her disguise was not the only thing at stake. How would her friends feel if they learned she was a young woman? What would Cyrus do if he learned her real identity? And George? Why, both men would be laughed out of the territory. And besides all of that, she knew she would never be able to face Slade's scorn again. It would simply be too much for her.

Following the youth outside, Slade called loudly, "Hey, kid, wait up."

She started to run but was afraid to. Instead, she stopped in her tracks and realized for the first time that her entire body was trembling violently.

Quickly walking up from behind, Slade placed his hand on her shoulder and turned her around. "Just a word of advice, kid. Grow up a bit before you go back into a place like that," he said softly.

The feel of his hand on her shoulder caused her to gasp. It was as though something hot, yet surprisingly gentle, had touched her. Her knees suddenly grew weak and her head began to spin. The urge to fling herself into his arms was overpowering. Virginia quickly realized that if she did not get away from him she would lose control of her emotions.

"Y — Yes, sir, I think I better," she mumbled. Then, wrenching from his grasp, she ran for the safety of her wagon as though a hundred devils were giving chase.

Upon reaching the wagon, Virginia leaned her head against the canvas-covered rib, gasping for breath. What was she to do? Either Slade had not brought his horse to the stable yet, or he had and just had not noticed the wagon. In the darkness, one Conestoga looked much like any other one, but come daylight, he would surely recognize it, and because he hated her so much, he would probably do everything in his power to humiliate her. But even if he did not publicly announce her true identity, she was certain Cyrus would learn the truth, and probably George too. She could not allow that to happen. Those men were her friends and they had treated her decently.

Suddenly an idea seemed to take root in her mind. Dovie had asked her to join her caravan. While she was not overly anxious to join a group of traveling prostitutes, at least it provided a solution to her dilemma.

Without taking time to think of the consequences, Virginia hurriedly began breaking camp and packing the wagon. Dovie had said they were leaving by dawn, and Virginia knew her only recourse was to go with them.

Two hours before dawn, Virginia harnessed the horses, hitched them to the wagon, and stealthily drove the huge Conestoga behind George's saloon, where Dovie and her girls were preparing to leave.

The area bustled with activity. The women were busy loading the last of the camp items into their wagons, while the three guards brought the horses over from a small, private stable and hitched them to the wagons.

Setting the brake and wrapping the reins around the lever, Virginia jumped down and hurried over to where Dovie stood beside George.

Dovie planted her hands on her hips and grinned. "Well, hello there!"

Virginia touched the brim of her hat. "Mornin', Miss Dovie. I decided to take you up on your offer."

"I'm glad you did—" Hearing an angry curse from one of her girls, Dovie rolled her eyes and gave an irritated sigh. "No, Hank. Those horses pull Egypt's wagon, not Rome's! And Tom, put that team of horses in back and the other team in front. You know they don't lead right!" Shaking her head, she tossed a glance at Virginia and George. "You all will have to excuse me or we won't get away from here until noon. I swear, sometimes they act like they don't have a lick of sense," she grumbled angrily, stomping off to set the guards straight.

Frowning, George stepped toward Virginia. "I didn't know you were planning on leaving so soon, boy. I thought you were going to wait for the freighters."

Virginia shoved her hands into her pockets and toed the ground with her boot. "Well, I was, but Miss Dovie asked me to join her . . . and then, there was that trouble last night with the lieutenant. I just thought it would be for the best if I got out of here before there's more trouble. Once you filed a complaint on the lieutenant, he would probably leave me be . . . but his friends might not."

"I suppose you have a point there," he said slowly. Then he looked at her sharply. "Did you tell Cyrus?"

"Heck yeah, I did. I woke him up last night and told him. He's been too good to me for me to sneak out without tellin' him anything." Her voice softened. "Just like you. I kind of figured you'd be here this mornin', or at least I was hopin' you would be. I just want you to know, I appreciate the kindness you've shown toward me."

George's face flushed. "Aw, it was nothing."

"Yeah it was too."

Even though George cleared his throat, his voice still sounded choked. "Tell you what you can do,

234

boy. When you get out to California, write me a letter from time to time and let me know how you're getting on. And if by chance you don't like it out there, hell, come on back here and I'll find something for you to do."

Virginia's heart wrenched at his kindness. "I appreciate the offer, George . . . and Cyrus told me 'bout the same thing. I'll keep it in mind." Unconsciously, her brow furrowed. "Say, George, you know that fellar who stood up to the lieutenant last night?"

"Yeah, what about him?"

"Do you know who he is?"

"No, I haven't ever seen him before last night."

"Oh, so he's a stranger in these parts."

"Yeah, he came back in and asked a few questions about a man. . . ." George squinted his eyes. "Can't really recall the name right off. He also asked questions about local ranches and who owned them. He was definitely looking for somebody in particular, though."

Nodding thoughtfully, Virginia asked, "Did he happen to mention how long he would be in these parts or where he was headin'?"

"No. Why?"

She shrugged her shoulders noncommittally. "Oh, I was just wonderin'. If you happen to see 'im again, tell 'im I said thanks for stickin' up for me."

Virginia jerked her head around when Dovie called loudly, "Hey, kid, if you're going with us, you had better get a move on. Pull your wagon over here behind Egypt's."

Thrusting her hand into George's and giving it a vigorous pump, she said emotionally, "You take care of yourself."

Turning, she ran for her wagon, but just as she reached it, she came to an abrupt halt, her mouth dropping open in surprise. "Good Lord Almighty!" she exclaimed, pointing to a huge, shaggy beast tied behind a wagon. "What in the world is that?"

Dovie, standing nearby, laughed, "Why, it's a camel, Jimmy. Bet you haven't ever seen one of those before!"

"No, ma'am . . . I mean, yes, ma'am. I've seen 'em in picture books . . . but what's it doin' here?" She walked slowly over to the camel and cautiously touched it.

Dovie shook her head as though unable to comprehend it all. "A prospector traded it to Egypt last night. He was on his way back east . . . and Egypt thought it would be an interesting feature, an added attraction. I've heard they are troublesome beasts though, onerous and stubborn, just like a cantankerous mule, or even worse." She shrugged her shoulders. I guess if he proves to be too much trouble, we can just turn him loose out on the desert somewhere."

Ben, the third guard, swung onto his horse and called to Dovie. "Any time you're ready, Miss Dovie."

Nodding, she clapped her hands together and shouted, "All right, people, let's move out!"

Virginia climbed into her wagon, took a deep breath, then reached for the reins, anxious to put miles between her and Slade.

Chapter Sixteen

Gray-black storm clouds hung heavily over the Gila Mountains, thunder rolled and reverberated through the distant canyons, and the sharp, pungent odor of ozone filled the air as lightning stabbed brilliantly across the sky.

Slade looked up warily at the threatening sky, then removed his rain slicker from behind the cantle and slipped it on. He bent down to tighten his cinch, put his foot into the stirrup, and swung into the saddle, then adjusted his broad-brimmed hat and gave one final look around the area in which he had camped. He had hoped to leave no sign of his passage, having dragged branches over the ground where he had lain in his bedroll, then scattering the camp fire ashes before brushing the area clean and covering it with pine straw. But with the storm approaching, the ground would soon be damp from the moisture in the air and it would be difficult not to leave a trail. That could prove to be dangerous, since he had seen Apache signs the previous day.

What he needed was a cave in which to take cover until the storm passed and the ground dried. Of course, weather in the high country was strange. It could rain hard enough in one canyon to cause a flash flood twenty miles into the desert, yet another canyon might not receive a drop of rain.

Knowing he would never be able to find a cave by sitting there, Slade nudged Blue in the flanks.

Two hours of riding through the misty rain and an occasional downpour brought Slade to a side canyon down which a gully, half a mile long and extremely rough and rocky, led into the deep gorge of the San Carlos River. Scanning the rocky ledge high overhead, he soon saw a dark shadow beside a huge boulder. Realizing the shadow was undoubtedly a cave but unable to determine how deep into the mountainside it ran, he spurred Blue up the rocky incline to investigate.

Approaching it cautiously in case it was a cougar's den, Slade found the cave unoccupied and exactly what he needed. The gully below had obviously been formed by flash floods, but the cave was high enough to be out of harm's way if one came roaring through. He hoped one would. A flood would wipe out all traces of his trail, enabling him to wait safely in the cave until the weather cleared.

After gathering wood for a fire, Slade placed some loose brush over the cave's opening, then built a small, smokeless fire and began brewing a pot of coffee. His earlier actions had merely been reactions for wilderness survival, but now, with time hanging heavily on his hands, his thoughts began to wander.

Ever since the incident with the smart-aleck lieutenant and the young boy back at Fort Grant, he had been troubled more and more by Virginia's memory. Why, he did not know.

Frowning, Slade shook his head. That was not exactly true. The memory of Virginia had haunted him ever since he had left her in New Mexico. And now, since leaving Fort Grant, questions had been nagging at him. Had her memory haunted him because of a guilty conscience? Or had he fallen in love with Virginia and been too stubborn to admit it?

Angrily, he forced that thought from his mind, pouring himself a cup of coffee and staring at the steam that rose from the cup. Before being sent to prison, he had known many women in his life, beautiful, warm, uninhibited women — women who knew exactly what he was and asked nothing more of him than he was willing to give. Freedom and sensual pleasure had always gone hand in hand with him, and he saw no reason to change that now, at least not until he had settled his past. He wanted no part of a woman who made more than a temporary claim on him, and no part of a woman who would ever try to touch his heart.

Why then did he wonder if he had fallen in love with Virginia?

Tightening his hand around the cup, he tried once more to drive such thoughts from his mind. Blast it, he thought angrily, how could he let one woman, a woman he hardly knew, a woman who was a treacherous schemer, worm her way into his thoughts and torture him like this?

He closed his eyes and visualized her: the dimples that were on either side of her pretty face when she smiled, that certain way she tilted her head when she spoke, the way her ebony eyes appeared to be darker than midnight against her tawny complexion and honey gold hair. Her hair . . . how stimulating it had been that last night when he had run his hands through the silken tresses and loosened it from the confines of that long braid hanging down her back.

Slade vigorously shook his head in an unsuccessful attempt to clear his mind. Why, he was pining for her like some gangly schoolboy and it was all for nothing! Even if he had fallen in love with her, it was too late now. He had no idea where she was and even if he did, after the way he had treated her, she had to hate him.

"Damnit, Slade, listen to yourself," he muttered aloud. "You seem to be forgetting what she did to you!"

But remembering what had happened did not soothe his conscience either. An expression of pain flicked through his eyes. If he could have stepped back into time, he would have handled it differently. It had been a mistake to direct his vengeance at her and not her father. He had blamed Virginia, but now that he could look at the entire situation more rationally, he could see that Carl Branson had been the real culprit. If Virginia was guilty, Branson had probably coerced her into doing what she had done. Only thing was, he thought sadly, it was too late to consider that now. When it came right down to it, he wasn't a damn bit better than that smart-aleck bully of a lieutenant back at Fort Grant.

Realizing he had to channel his thoughts in a different direction, Slade forced Virginia from his mind, although he knew he could never completely forget her. He could put her out of his conscious mind, but he could never bar her from his dreams. Lately, she had invaded them mercilessly.

He poured himself another cup of coffee, lit a cheroot, and walked over to the cave entrance and looked out. It troubled him that he knew so little about the Gila Mountains and San Carlos River area. His only knowledge of the region came second-

ACCEPT YOUR **FREE GIFT** AND EXPERIENCE MORE OF THE PASSION AND ADVENTURE YOU LIKE IN A HISTORICAL ROMANCE

Zebra Romances are the finest novels of their kind and are written with the adult woman in mind. All of our books are written by authors who really know how to weave tales of romantic adventure in the historical settings you love.

Because our readers tell us these books sell out very fast in the stores, Zebra has made arrangements for you to receive at home the four newest titles published each month. You'll never miss a title and home delivery is so convenient. With your first shipment we'll even send you a **FREE** Zebra Historical Romance as our gift just for trying our home subscription service. No obligation.

BIG SAVINGS AND **FREE** HOME DELIVERY

Each month, the Zebra Home Subscription Service will send you the four newest titles as soon as they are published. (We ship these books to our subscribers even before we send them to the stores.) You may preview them *Free* for 10 days. If you like them as much as we think you will, you'll pay just $3.50 each and *save $1.80 each month* off the cover price. *AND you'll also get FREE HOME DELIVERY.* There is never a charge for shipping, handling or postage and there is no minimum you must buy. If you decide not to keep any shipment, simply return it within 10 days, no questions asked, and owe nothing.

hand, from an old trapper he had chanced to meet a week after leaving Fort Grant. With Apaches on the prowl, being in an area he knew nothing about was dangerous, but the old trapper had mentioned hearing something about a man having a ranch near the San Carlos River. John Carlisle had often talked about settling on the San Carlos, and Slade had to find out if the rancher was the same man responsible for his spending five years in prison.

The possibility of finally being able to find John sent Slade into deep reflection about the past . . .

Slade supposed his life had started heading in a perilous direction when he lost his parents at age fifteen. For the next three years he was just a young kid without much common sense, the same as many other young men who were growing up in the aftermath of the Civil War.

He came close to getting into trouble, foolishly believing a fast gun was the only answer to the excitement he craved, but after one brief brush with the law, he realized there had to be a better way to find that excitement. That was when he joined the army. Then, within a few months, he was stationed at Fort Stanton in the New Mexico Territory.

There he met John Carlisle. John, four years older, was the epitome of what the eighteen-year-old Slade thought a man should be: adventurous, handy with a gun but not overly eager to use it, arrogant but not a smart-aleck, a dapper dresser with enough charm to nearly cause women to swoon if he smiled at them. They became friends and by the time their hitch in the army was over, they were inseparable.

As far as Slade could see, John's only fault was that he always had to have the very best, though he was not always willing to wait or work for it. His dream was to own a ranch—not *just* a ranch, but the *biggest* ranch in the Arizona Territory.

They wandered around New Mexico, Arizona, and even Texas for several years, gambling, prospecting, fighting Indians, herding cattle, and chasing women, lots and lots of wild, beautiful women. During that time, Slade's skill with his fast draw became second to none, although he never misused that skill. He had learned his lesson well from that earlier incident with the law.

And also during that time, Slade came to love John like a brother. He would have done almost anything for him.

Then, John betrayed him. They were prospecting in the Twin Buttes, in New Mexico, and doing rather well. Late one afternoon, hearing gunfire in the distance, they quickly investigated and discovered three soldiers under an Apache attack. Although they were able to drive off the Apaches, they found that two of the soldiers had been killed and the third severely wounded. They quickly buried the two men and loaded the other into the supply wagon so they could take him for medical help. It was then they discovered nearly thirty thousand dollars in the wagon; apparently one of the soldiers had been a paymaster on his way to Fort Defiance.

A small ranch was less than twenty miles away, and since the man's injuries were severe, they decided to take him there, then go to the fort for the doctor. They had to stop when the man started bleeding badly. After they had decided to wait until morning before continuing on to the ranch, John took the first watch while Slade slept. When he awoke, he was surrounded by ten soldiers. John and the money were gone, and neither were ever seen or heard from again.

The soldier eventually recovered, but he had faded

in and out of consciousness after being wounded and could not swear that another man had even existed. Slade was charged with the theft of a military payroll and sentenced to serve five years of hard labor at a federal prison.

Not one day passed during those five long years without Slade's renewing his vow to find John when he was released and to make him pay for what he had done.

His mother had had a favorite saying, which became meaningful to him as he served his sentence: "Behind every dark cloud, there is a silver lining." There was a slight chance that the friend he had made in prison would be the silver lining in his dark cloud—or a gold lining, depending on one's point of view.

Slade's cell mate had been a crusty old prospector who had taken him under his wing. He often lay in his bunk at night, talking about an abandoned gold mine located in a nameless mountain in Arizona. Supposedly, the gold had already been processed and placed into bags. The way Ed described it, there was enough gold to set up a man for life. He was always careful not to reveal too much information, however. He would only say, "The gold is in the *heart* of the mountain." Then he would cackle with glee.

A year before Slade was released and two years before the old prospector was scheduled to be discharged, Ed became very sick. The old man soon realized he was dying. He took Slade into his confidence and told him the entire story of his involvement with the lost Peralta gold, in Arizona's Superstition Mountains.

Old Ed's voice echoed through Slade's mind as clearly as if he had been standing beside him.

"On February 2, 1848, the Treaty of Guadalupe-

Hidalgo was signed. The treaty transferred thousands of acres of land to the United States, land that had been part of land grants held by wealthy Mexican families since the mid 1700's. Old Don Miguel Peralta knew about this treaty two years before it was signed. He also knew that after it was signed he would no longer be able to work the mines he owned since the land was being deeded to the United States Government. From the account I heard, the old Don brought several hundred of his peons up from Mexico and put them to work in the mines, taking out as much ore as they could — while they could — and the trusted members of his family began hauling the gold by mule pack trains back to Mexico. On the last trip back to the mine, the Peraltas were attacked by Apaches and all but one man were killed. That man was able to make it home, but he died soon afterward.

"Then, in the fall of 1865, I was prospecting in the Pinaleno Mountains and I stumbled across a young Mexican man — maybe twenty-five years old — who had been jumped by Apaches. He was dying and he knew it. I tried to make him as comfortable as I could, and, as some men do when they're dying — just as I'm doing now — he began to talk. Seems he was the son of the Peralta who survived the massacre. He offered to tell me where the Peraltas had stashed the gold they were going after on that last trip, if I promised to give his family half of it. Since I had heard the legend of the lost Peralta gold, naturally I gave him my word — and I meant to keep it too.

"After he died, I went directly to Tucson to buy supplies, but I got into a fight with a United States marshal. He died three days later, and I was sent to this hellhole and have been here ever since. At times, the only thing I think kept me alive was the thought of that gold, and how one day I would be able to find it. But that day will never come for me . . . However, it can for you," he had told Slade, "if you keep the promise I made to that dying man. I couldn't meet my Maker knowing I had betrayed his trust."

Slade gave him his word, and old Ed had talked way into the night, drawing a verbal map, describing landmarks, trails, then making Slade repeat it time and time again until it was thoroughly committed to his memory. Then, right before he died, he made Slade promise to drink a shot of good whiskey to his memory the day he was released from prison.

And Slade had . . . .

Two mornings later, Slade left the cave and scoured the region for the ranch the old trapper had mentioned, but after three days of hard searching, he decided to discontinue his efforts for awhile. He had a keen desire for survival, and there had been too many Apache signs for him to continue to stay in the area. It was too dangerous, and the tingling sensation that prickled about his spine told him there was plenty of trouble around. Besides, after waiting five years to find John, he could be patient for a few more weeks or months. Time had no real meaning for him now.

Glancing at the sky, Slade knew he still had several hours before dark. He could spend that time putting miles behind him, or he could search for a safe place to spend the night.

He studied the mountainous terrain with a more attentive eye. The mountainside was covered by a huge stand of fir and ponderosa pine. A few cotton-woods had somehow managed to grow beyond the upper valley floor, and their presence indicated a mountain stream was close by. He was pleased, for he needed water.

Listening carefully and hearing the telltale noise of running water, Slade nudged Blue in the direction of the stream. Finding it easily, he hesitated at the tree line because the stream was completely in the open, providing no cover except for some knee-high grass along the shore. Though he realized he should go downstream to a safer place, nevertheless Slade dismounted, walked over to the stream, and knelt to fill his canteen.

The odor of Apache — wild clover and wood smoke — assailed his keen sense of smell at the same time he heard hurried footsteps beating against the ground. Whirling and drawing his pistol in one fluid motion, Slade pulled the trigger just as the Apache screamed a warbling war cry and brought his rifle up to fire. Slade's bullet found its mark, as did the Apache's, but only Slade's shot was fatal. Ignoring the burst of pain coursing through his shoulder, Slade made a leaping dive for the ground. His first instinct was to whistle for Blue. The horse was well trained and would come to him immediately. But he would also reveal his location. Instead, Slade pressed his ear close to the ground and listened.

Except for muted, scrambling sounds in the dense underbrush and tall grass, everything was silent. Not even a bird trilled. Swallowing the bile that rose in his throat, Slade remembered that his rifle was still in the saddle scabbard and would be no help to him. And he would need help, or a lot of luck. There were at least two, or maybe even more, Apaches out there waiting for him to raise his head, which they probably thought he would do soon, for white men did not usually possess great patience.

Strangely, they did not wait. He could hear grass rustling as they crawled toward him. Realizing he would never reach the cover of the trees and underbrush a good ten yards away before they cut him down, Slade knew he would have to make his stand right there in the open. And judging from the way his shoulder was bleeding, he would have to do it quickly. Taking a deep breath, he rose to his knees and, seeing the Apaches inching toward him, he began firing. He shot one in the head. The other Indian rose to shoot and Slade shot him through the heart.

He pursed his lips and whistled for Blue, then slumped weakly against the ground. He felt an overwhelming urge to stand and look around for death in order to laugh in its face and gloat over the fact that he had won again. But Slade's relief was short-lived. Something made him look behind him and he saw another Indian on the other side of the stream. He raised his gun to fire, but the click of an empty cylinder echoed in his ears.

The Apache heard the click too. He grinned triumphantly, tossed down his rifle, and drew his knife, apparently preferring to kill the white man in that manner. Then his mouth opened in a bloodcurdling scream, but Slade heard no sound. He charged across the small, narrow stream that separated them, but the splashing water made no noise either.

Fear had magnified everything, blowing it completely out of proportion, changing reality with every thundering beat of Slade's heart.

Everything seemed to be happening so slowly, yet Slade's mind raced at a furious pace. His eyes were riveted on the rifle in the scabbard as Blue trotted toward him. But Slade knew the Indian would reach him before Blue did, and if he ran for his rifle, the

Indian would merely throw his knife, and Apaches were deadly accurate. However, he could not simply stand there; he would never be able to survive hand-to-knife combat. Suddenly spotting the half-filled canteen lying at the edge of the stream, Slade scrambled for it. He grabbed the leather strap, and drawing it back with his good arm, he waited until the Indian was almost upon him, then swung with all his strength, aiming at his head. The blow sent the Apache sprawling back into the stream, which gave Slade enough time to race for his rifle. Yanking it from the scabbard, he whirled and fired rapidly just as the Indian started toward him again. The bullets knocked the Indian back against a moss-tipped rock jutting upward in the water. His paint-streaked face froze in a death mask.

Not knowing if other Indians would soon burst through the trees on the other side of the stream, Slade grabbed hold of the saddle horn and, using Blue for cover, half ran, half staggered into the brush. He knew his shoulder was bleeding badly, but he also realized another attack could come at any moment. Grabbing the saddlebags that contained his extra ammunition, he swatted Blue on his rump and took cover behind a large tree. There, uneasily looking about, he quickly reloaded his guns before pressing a handkerchief over the wound in an attempt to stem the bleeding. Then he settled down to wait, wary and cautious, alert to every sound that rustled through the surrounding trees and brush.

His eyes kept darting to the two dead Indians lying in the tall grass. Had that one moved? he wondered. Instinctively, he tensed, his finger tightening ever so slightly on the trigger of his rifle. Were they just pretending to be dead, waiting until he relaxed his guard to jump him again? No, he told himself, he had shot one in the head and one through the heart. There was no way they could be alive.

Then Slade frowned. There was something nagging, eating at him, something he should have been able to put his finger on, but for the life of him, he couldn't. It caused a feeling of apprehension, but, strangely, he doubted it was connected to his predicament. The dead Indian in the mountain stream did not help matters either. His dead eyes stared in an accusing manner. Water from the stream had splashed on his face, wetting the war paint, and now it ran in watery paths to drip on his chest. The blood from the two gaping wounds mixed with the war paint, turning the crystal-clear water a murky red. Then, it gradually rippled away from the still body like a red tide.

Though alert to his surroundings, Slade went over the attack in his mind, step by step, trying to discover the reason for his uneasy feeling. Suddenly, all color drained from his face and his stomach balled into a hard knot. He felt cold, as if icy water had replaced the blood in his veins. His feeling did not stem from his wound; it was caused by something he had seen, or something he *thought* he had seen.

"I have to make sure," he muttered to himself.

Common sense told him if other Apaches had been about, they already would have attacked. Bearing that thought in mind and gritting his teeth against the pain that tore through his shoulder, he cradled the rifle in his arms and began inching his way over the ground, through the undulating grass, toward the first dead Indian. Retrieving the brave's ammunition and food pouch, Slade refused to look at it until he had returned to the safety of the trees.

Then, leaning against the trunk of a tree, he

249

unconsciously tightened his lips into a thin white line as he stared down at the pouch. Hanging from it was the tip of a honey-colored braid. He knew that Apaches seldom scalped people — their atrocities were much, much worse — but still, a brave could have been tempted. Slade's hand trembled as he raised the flap and removed the long braid that was so firmly etched in his memory. He swallowed hard, unaware of the tears that suddenly trailed down his cheeks. A sob caught in his throat when a pendant watch came loose from the braid and fell into his lap. It was the very same pendant watch he had seen around Virginia's neck.

How long Slade sat there thinking about Virginia, he did not know, but finally he remembered his wound. From the pain and the amount of blood still coming from his shoulder, he knew the bullet was deeply embedded and he would never be able to remove it by himself. And if it was not removed soon, he would probably die. Struggling to his feet, he left the braid where it lay, but he carefully put the pendant in his vest pocket and buttoned the flap. Then, using strength he did not know he possessed, he climbed onto Blue's back, and within minutes they disappeared into the approaching night.

Chapter Seventeen

The desert night was warm, but not unbearably so. Cicadas hummed noisily along the shallow-running river, the moon began its nightly climb, and stars studded the sky like glittering diamonds. Sounds of feminine voices and laughter drifted from the center of the eight wagons that had been drawn into a tight circle.

Since most of the troop at Fort Thomas had been on extended patrol, Dovie and her entourage had only entertained the soldiers stationed there for three days and nights before starting out for Fort McDowell.

Virginia had spent most of those three days sticking close to her wagon, just in case Slade suddenly appeared again. Since he was in the general area, she knew their paths could easily cross just as they had at Fort Grant, and she had come too far to be exposed now. And the thought of seeing him again was almost as distressing as her fear that he could reveal her true identity.

All too frequently his memory invaded her thoughts, and it seemed she was constantly in an emotional turmoil. Seeing him again, even so briefly, had stirred feelings she had hoped were dead. The question of how long she would have such feelings often nagged at her. A month? A year? Ten years? Or, would they curse her for the rest of her life?

The fort was a week behind them now, and that morning a wheel had broken on Dovie's wagon. The men had jury-rigged it well enough for them to reach the river, then Ben and Tom had set about repairing it properly, while Hank, having seen deer signs earlier, went hunting.

Just before dark, he brought back a white-tailed doe. Having field dressed it earlier, he cleaned it properly and placed half of it on a spit to cook over a low mesquite fire. Dovie made baking-powder biscuits, placed them in a huge Dutch oven, and covered the huge cast-iron pot with glowing coals so the biscuits could bake. And now, everyone was sitting around the camp fire, anxiously waiting for Hank to announce that the meat was ready.

"Do you need any help, Hank?" Virginia asked, leaning slightly forward and taking a deep whiff of the venison, which had roasted to a golden brown.

She had been pretending to be a boy for so long now, Jimmy's mannerisms and speech seemed like second nature, but it was a disguise she had grown weary of. Shudders of revulsion passed through her each time she had to rub ashes on her face and arms from the camp fire. And each time she jammed the smelly hat down over her hair, she longed wistfully for one of her starched, rose-scented bonnets that were kept well hidden beneath her bed. She looked forward to the day she would be able to walk, talk, dress, and act like a woman again.

Hank started to shake his head, then his lips compressed into a tight line. "Yes, you can take your friend back over with the horses where he belongs," he said, nodding toward the darkness behind her.

Virginia whirled about. The camel that Egypt had acquired had entered the wagons' circle, and it was now sitting, chewing its cud, not more than five feet behind her.

Egypt's interest in the shaggy beast had only lasted until he had nipped at her, the other women claimed he stank too badly to have anything to do with, and the men said they had enough chores to do without tending to an onerous, mule-headed beast. It came as no surprise to Virginia that total responsibility for the camel was quickly delegated to her. She really did not mind, having grown slightly fond of the homely beast, but at times like these, he sorely tried her patience.

Everybody was right; the camel did stink. It was not so much his body but the foul odors he unexpectedly produced from both ends that were terrible. And to make matters worse, he was cantankerous and stubborn. Virginia had named him Mule, and it fit the beast perfectly. However, after she started taking care of him, his disposition improved slightly, and he even began following her around—much to her chagrin and to everybody else's amusement—like a friendly puppy would follow its master.

Irritated, she picked up a small stick and hurried to where the camel was kneeling. "Mule! Get your filthy, foul-smelling, dadblasted hide out of here—right now! Get over there with the horses where you belong!"

He merely looked at her with those enormous brown eyes and twisted his mouth into a weird position. Grasping his bridle, she tugged, yet even though she waved the switch threateningly, she could not bring herself to use it on him. How could she strike a dumb beast simply because he was fond of her?

Just as she could have predicted, Mule emitted a terrible odor when he finally stood. The women held their noses and Hank cursed as she led him away.

Red faced, Virginia came back to the circle of the camp fire a few minutes later.

Now in a better mood, Hank grinned and winked at Ben. "Jimmy, that camel sure has been letting loose some stinkers here lately. What have you been feeding him, red beans?"

Virginia's shoulders slumped. She knew she was in for another round of teasing. She would have wagered her last dollar that Hank would be a polite, well-mannered man around women he considered proper ladies. But, with Dovie and her girls sometimes being a bit crude and slightly *risqué*, he was not particular about the things he said or how he said them. And, believing Virginia to be a young, innocent boy, he was always trying to embarrass her.

Knowing his teasing was coming, and knowing there was nothing she could do to stop it, she decided to get it over with as quickly as possible so he would leave her alone. "No, Hank, I don't feed 'im red beans."

Hank kept turning the spit, his grin growing even wider. "You know what else red beans are known as, don't you?" Two of the women, Paris and Rome, were starting to chuckle.

Virginia's face blazed. "Yeah, you done already told me . . . 'bout ten times now."

"They are called musical fruit," he said, ignoring her answer. He stroked his chin thoughtfully. "Now, let's see . . . there used to be a little poem about beans being musical fruit. Oh, yeah, now I remember: Beans, beans, the musical fruit, the more you eat, the more you . . ."

"And you've done already told me that poem too!"

Hank laughed. "And there's another little poem about beans being good for the heart . . ."

Virginia closed her eyes and cringed.

Dovie raised her brows and shot him a glaring look. "Good God, Hank, why don't you hush! That camel stinks bad enough without your reminding us of it all the time." She glanced over at Virginia. "Did you tie him up good?"

"Yes, ma'am," she answered quickly, relieved that Dovie had rescued her from Hank's nonsensical tomfoolery. "At least I tried to, but I thought I had 'im tied good before. I cain't help that he keeps chewing the rope in two. Maybe we can get some stronger rope at the next town."

"It would not be so bad if he didn't make those awful smells. But phew, my goodness!" Dovie said, waving her hand in front of her face. "I'm tempted to turn him loose out on the desert."

"That's the best idea you've had in a long time," Ben remarked dryly.

The suggestion distressed Virginia. "Miss Dovie, please don't do that. That old dumb beast cain't help how he is—or what he is. 'Sides, as tame as he is, coyotes would probably get 'im." She sighed heavily. "I promise to keep a closer eye on him."

"Well . . . see that you do."

Not wanting the conversation to continue in that direction, Virginia walked over to the spit and hungrily looked at the venison. It smelled delicious.

"Do you need any help, Hank?"

"Yes, you can take my hatchet and go cut down another mesquite bush. Not a big one either; one about five feet tall will do fine. I want to cook the other half of the venison tonight and I'll need more wood."

She pushed her hat back on her head and grinned. "That wasn't really what I had in mind. I was offering to turn it for awhile."

"I know," the big guard said with a chuckle, obviously not bothered by how Dovie had scolded him. "You wanted to turn the spit so you could sneak a piece of the meat."

"That's right," she bantered easily. "I'm a real good taster."

Hank appraised her critically. "For once, I will agree with you, Jimmy. As scrawny as you are, tasting is about all you have been doing here lately. I've never seen a boy your age have such a poor appetite," he said with a shake of his head. "Makes a fellow wonder if you're in love."

"Maybe it's 'cause I've been waitin' on you to bring fresh meat in," she retorted quickly, not wanting him to start pestering her again. Since they all took their meals together, the others often made remarks about her lack of appetite. But Virginia had never been a hearty eater, and with the weather so hot and Slade on her mind, she had just been picking at her food and it was starting to show on her already-thin body.

Dovie stood. "I'll go with you, Jimmy, to help drag the bush back. I need to stretch my legs for awhile. And you all had better not let my biscuits burn while I'm gone!" she cautioned.

As Virginia and Dovie walked past where the horses were staked, Dovie stated bluntly, "I have been wanting to talk to you in private for several days now, but I've never had a chance to get you alone."

"Oh? What about? Is it somethin' I've done?"

"Yes, I suppose you might call it that." She

stopped suddenly and grasped Virginia by her arms, not roughly, yet with a firm grip. "I want to know your name."

"M—My name? W—Why, it's Jimmy—Jimmy Branson," Virginia answered after swallowing the hard lump that had suddenly become wedged in her throat.

Releasing her hold, Dovie shook her head. "No, it isn't. Tell me the truth. Your name might be Mary, or Rebecca, or maybe even Anne, but it sure isn't Jimmy!"

Virginia wet her lips. She could try to brazen her way through this and still claim to be a boy, but what would be the point? Somehow, Dovie had discovered the truth.

Resigned, Virginia looked straight into Dovie's eyes, her voice soft, gentle, and feminine. "My name is Virginia . . . a few people used to call me Ginny . . . the similarity is why I chose Jimmy."

"How old are you?"

"T—Twenty."

Dovie nodded smugly. "That's about what I thought."

Virginia struggled to keep her features composed as she asked, "How long have you known? What did I do to give myself away?"

"Honey, I've suspected for several weeks now. In fact, I think I had a few doubts the first time I saw you. I remember thinking that you sure had soft features. But to answer your question, it was the way you sometimes talked—you occasionally forgot yourself and spoke like a nice young woman. Then too, there were your gestures, the way you tilted your head, mannerisms, how you sometimes walked. Mind you, though, it wasn't all of the time—just enough to make me suspicious. But you also have to

257

consider that I study women a lot more closely than most people do because of the business I am in. But I didn't know for sure until a few days back. You see, I keep close track of my girls' monthlies, and when I saw you washing your menstrual clothes . . . well, two and two finally added up to four."

"I see," Virginia said slowly.

Dovie reached out, removed Virginia's battered old hat, and ran her fingers through her shorn tresses. "You must have had beautiful hair, and you probably wore it long too. When you decide to be a woman again, just let your hair curl softly around your head until it grows out."

Virginia looked at her sharply with surprise. "You mean, you're not going to tell the others?"

"I really don't think it is anyone else's business," she answered and gave a shrug of her shoulders. "That is . . . unless your reason for disguising yourself as a boy could have an ill effect on my girls or the men. We're not going to wake up one morning and have an angry husband or lover raising hell with us, are we?"

Virginia thought of Slade and how he hated her. "No . . . no angry husband or lover."

Dovie frowned. "I don't particularly like the way you said that. I want you to tell me straight out, is there a man in your life? Is he the reason you are running away?"

Virginia began slowly, "There was a man in my life — very briefly though. I married him a few months ago, but . . . the marriage ended before it ever had a chance to begin. I assure you, I am not running away from anything or anybody . . . and the only possible trouble Slade might cause would be directed at me . . . only at me."

"Slade is your husband?"

"Y—Yes, he is the man I married."

Sighing heavily, Dovie said, "Look, honey, I'm not a prying person, but I do have a business to consider. To be frank, I don't like the answers you've given me. Let me repeat all of this back to you and I think you'll understand my position better. You claim not to be running away from anything, yet you have been traveling across the country pretending to be someone you're not . . . and you've gone to a lot of trouble to maintain your disguise. You say your husband won't cause any trouble if he finds you traveling with . . . well, let's not mince words . . . a flock of prostitutes, but he could cause trouble for you. Like I said, it's not my nature to pry, but unless you can give me some better answers, I'll give the order to turn around and we'll take you back to Fort Thomas."

Feeling foolish, Virginia stared at her hands. Dovie was right. After hearing the story from her point of view, she could well understand why the woman wanted more information. She began speaking in a voice that seemed to come from a long way off. "Slade and I were forced to marry . . . not because we did anything wrong. It was something my father did. But Slade thought my father and I were in on it together."

"What in thunderation did your pa do to make him think something like that?"

"He jumped Slade, robbed him, and left him for dead."

Giving an unamused chuckle, Dovie then whistled through her teeth. "I can see why that would make a man angry." Then she asked slowly, "Were you in on it with your pa?"

"No, ma'am, I was not!" she stated emphatically.

"All right, I believe you," Dovie said without a

259

moment's hesitation.

"You do?"

"Yes. I think I am a good judge of character, and I doubt you would do anything wrong unless there was no other choice."

A ragged pain tore through Virginia's heart. Why couldn't Slade have believed her as easily? If only he'd had a tiny bit more faith or even an ounce of love for her, how different things could have been between them.

Virginia pushed those thoughts from her mind and continued in an agonized whisper, "I told Slade I had nothing to do with what Papa had done, and I thought he believed me . . . but he hadn't. A few days later"—she closed her eyes tightly as though to block out the painful memories—"I found out that Slade had only pretended to accept me as his wife. In reality he was just trying to get even with me for what he thought I had done. He left me near a small town in New Mexico. I couldn't stay there, not with everybody gossiping about my father . . . and how Slade had treated me. So . . . I left."

"It must have been rough on you."

Now that Virginia was talking about what had happened, it seemed a great weight was being lifted from her breast. "Slade was the reason I decided to leave Fort Grant so suddenly. I saw him in George's saloon and I was afraid that if I stayed he would recognize me and tell everybody I was really a woman. As much as he hates me, he would have done it too," she added softly.

"But why did you disguise yourself as a boy?" Dovie asked, puzzled. "That's the part I don't understand."

Virginia met her eyes solemnly. "Just how far do you think I could have gotten as a woman? Don't misunderstand me. I did not want to travel by myself through Indian country. I knew for safety's sake I would have to join a caravan of some sort, and, logically, freighters or teamsters would have been my best bet." She shrugged. "However, I doubted they would allow a lone woman to travel with them, though I figured they would not object to a man. And since I couldn't pass for a man, I pretended to be a young boy."

It was a long moment before Dovie spoke. "Under those circumstances, I guess I can't blame you. But tell me, what are your plans now?"

"That depends on you," she said with a significant lifting of her brows.

"How so?"

"You mentioned something about sending me back to Fort Thomas. Are you still going to?" Virginia asked bluntly.

"No. I believe what you've told me and I feel reasonably certain there won't be any trouble from your husband. That was my main worry." She pushed back a wayward strand of red hair. "Honey, if you don't mind, let me offer you some advice — and if you do mind, listen to me anyway. Don't let on to my girls that you are a woman. Just keep on pretending to be a boy. Then when we get to within a few miles of Phoenix, pull out of our group and wait until we're gone. Then scrub your face, put on a dress and nice-smelling perfume, go on into Phoenix, and sell your rig and keep only what you can pack in a small trunk and carpetbag. Forget all about that man you married; get yourself a divorce. Then, when it is final, I suggest you buy yourself a stagecoach ticket to wherever it is you want to go. Once you get there, find yourself a man who adores you, marry him, and have his babies."

Virginia's voice broke miserably. "You make it all sound so simple."

"Maybe I do, but don't fool yourself, honey. It won't be easy . . . not if you love that man, which I believe you do." Seeing the expression that flitted across Virginia's face, she added, "You can argue that you don't love him until you are blue in the face, but you and I will both know you're lying."

"I'm not arguing with you," Virginia said sadly.

There was a bitter edge of cynicism in Dovie's tone. "If you don't take my advice though, don't be surprised if one day you don't wake up and find that you've turned into a woman like me."

Without waiting for Virginia to comment, Dovie forced a smile and said, "We had better get Hank's mesquite bush before he comes out here looking for us."

Chapter Eighteen

Virginia was restless. Although it was quickly approaching dawn, she still had not been able to sleep. Even the moonlight seemed villainous, shining its light through the space where the flaps had been tied back to permit the fickle summer breeze to stir through the wagon. Regardless of which way she turned or how many times she rearranged her pillow, the light seemed to shine directly in her face.

After tossing and turning for hours, she threw back the thin sheet covering her, lit a small lamp, and rummaged through the box of dime novels stored under the small bedside table, hoping to find one she had not read before. After a few minutes of flipping through them without enthusiasm, she shoved the box back under the table and blew out the lamp. She plopped down dejectedly on the bed and sat with her elbows on her knees, and her head resting on her hands.

How had all of this happened? she asked herself miserably. All she had ever wanted was a normal, respectable life filled with stability — not anything spectacular or fancy, just a common, everyday life!

Instead, what did she have? Her identity—even though it had been her own idea—had been stripped from her. She had a husband who hated and spurned her and a vagabond existence that offered no stability whatsoever. And comfort? That was something that did not exist anymore. Right now that little run-down farm in East Texas would have looked like a mansion to her. She was tired of the dust and the grit, the terrible heat, having to hide and sneak around just to take a bath, the sounds of horses plodding along, of creaking wagon wheels constantly turning, of never having fresh vegetables to eat.

I am sick of it! she screamed silently.

Virginia knew she could not sit there a moment longer. She had to get outside, to do something. The canvas seemed about to close in on her. "I know!" She said aloud to the darkness. "While everybody is asleep, I'll go to the river and take a cool bath. That should make me feel better. Then perhaps I'll be able to catch a little bit of sleep before dawn."

As she marched determinedly toward the river, deep inside Virginia knew the source of her discontent. Stephen Slade. Damn him, she thought. And damn me for allowing the memory of him to do this to me! Earlier, when Dovie had given advice—good, sound advice—she had acted as though I had a choice in the matter. Her suggestion to sell the rig and the contents of the wagon was a very good one, and I should do it even if I have to take a loss. With all of the Indian trouble out here, and not being able to travel safely to the outlying farms and ranches, it is senseless for me to try to keep the horses, the wagon, and the mercantile wares. I will simply have to think of another way to support myself until I can settle somewhere.

But what about Dovie's suggestion to divorce Slade? Virginia shook her head slowly. No, that was an entirely different matter.

Having removed her breast binding before going to bed, Virginia now stripped down to her pantalettes and camisole, waded out into the water, and vigorously began lathering herself. Yet while the bath was indeed refreshing, her thoughts continued to dwell on Slade.

Why did she abhor the idea of divorce? While her religious teachings had been against such practice, divorcing one man did not necessarily mean she had to marry another. *Marry another man?* That idea was too unnerving. How could she ever go willingly into another man's arms after being in Slade's? How could she ever endure another man's kisses after knowing the splendor of his lips? How could she ever allow another man to know her intimately? Could another man ever carry her to such lofty peaks of passion as Slade had? No, she did not think so, nor was the idea appealing. But love was more than passion, more than just the excitement of a man's kisses. It was a sense of closeness, of being completely committed to another human being . . . of sharing every secret of one's heart and soul. And that was what she could have had with Slade.

But he did not want her! He hated her!

Was there an unspoken hope hidden deep within her that he would one day come to his senses and realize he had been wrong, realize he loved her? But, even if that dream miraculously came to pass, what would she do? Could she trust him not to hurt her again? Could she recapture that romantic bliss she had known with him? After she had been hurt so badly, would her pride allow her to take him back? Could she ever forget his terrible accusations?

Virginia took a deep, sharp breath. It would never happen, and it was absurd to allow her thoughts to wander along such a ridiculous path. Her musings were as preposterous as those silly, fairy-tale romances she had read long ago.

Wading back to shore, she quickly toweled herself off and slipped on clean, dry clothes. Even though she still felt tortured inside, at least her body was clean. That was one small consolation.

Just as she was about to dry her hair, Virginia thought she heard a noise, an alien noise. She froze and listened closely. Although the sound was not terribly unusual, it seemed somehow different and very far off, yet she was aware of how sounds carried a great distance across the desert floor.

Then she heard the faint sound of a horse nickering, and a shod hoof clinking against a stone. Her eyes widened as sudden terror raced through her. All of their horses had been staked on the other side of the wagons. Someone was approaching, and no one traveled at this time of night! Good Lord Almighty, she cried inwardly, it had to be Indians! They were about to be attacked by Apaches!

Dropping her bathing items, she ran straight to where Hank had placed his bedroll underneath China Doll's wagon.

She searched in a hoarse whisper, "Hank! Hank! Wake up! God help us! A—Apaches! A—Apaches!"

He bolted upright, instantly alert, his hand already gripping his rifle. He brought a finger to his lips. "Shh, don't talk loud. And when I tell you to move, move quietly. If they think we're alerted, they will attack immediately. Now, from what direction did you hear them?" he asked in an urgent but quiet whisper, his gaze darting quickly about.

"On the other side of the river!" She glanced at

the soft glow of the camp fire and silently cursed the added light it provided.

"I'll get Tom and Ben. You go warn Dovie and tell her to help you warn the girls, then go get your shotgun and plenty of ammunition. Take cover over by Rome's wagon . . . and remember, kid, try to make every shot count."

"B—But . . . I thought they only attacked in the daytime?"

"You thought wrong. Now get a move on."

Crouching low, she hurried first to Dovie's wagon, then to Paris's, leaving instructions for them to help alert the other women. Surprisingly, none of the women reacted with hysterics. Apparently, having been in this area for so long, they all knew that at the first sign of alarm the Indians would attack.

.After retrieving her shotgun and ammunition from her wagon, Virginia took her place where Hank had indicated, then settled down to wait. Her eyes were trained on the river, alert and wary.

She heard a horse blow through his nostrils and her fingers tightened ever so slightly on the trigger. Then, suddenly, she heard Hank whisper a warning from behind her.

"It's me, Jimmy," he said, crawling forward on his stomach and elbows, stopping beside her. "Did you just hear a horse?"

"Yes, I did." Her voice trembled with fear and she nervously moistened her dry lips. The lines of concentration deepened along her brows and under her eyes.

"Something's not right then. An Indian trains his horse not to do that," he said, shaking his head, puzzled. "What exactly did you hear to make you think Apaches were out there, that they were about to attack?"

"I heard a horse nicker. Now . . . it was a l—long way off," she stammered. "But I'm positive it was a horse. And you know yourself, if someone friendly were out there, he wouldn't be trying to sneak in."

"You have a good point there, but did you hear anything else?"

"Yes, I sure did. It was like a hoof hitting a stone. No," she corrected herself slowly. "It was like a hoof *clinking* against a stone." Her eyes narrowed thoughtfully as it suddenly occurred to her that she might have made a silly mistake. "That would indicate a shod horse . . . and Indians don't have shod horses, do they?"

"Not usually, but don't ever stake your life on it. When an Apache steals a horse, he's not particular if it's shod or not." He peered intently into the darkness. "I'm going to see if I can get a closer look. Stay on your guard, but until we know who or what is out there, don't be too eager to shoot."

Turning slightly, she looked at him with huge eyes. "Are you saying it might just be someone who saw the remains of our camp fire and decided to ride in?"

By this time they could hear a horse splashing through the water as it crossed the river, but there were no screams or war whoops that should have accompanied that noise.

He shook his head. "No, you did the right thing, so don't worry about it. If it was just somebody riding in, they would have hailed the camp first. But it could be someone who is hurt . . . or someone the Apaches have caught and are using as bait—I've seen it happen before. So, if it is a white man or woman, don't reveal yourself too soon. Let me check it out first," he warned while he inched away.

When Virginia saw the strangely marked horse

with a man slumped forward in the saddle, she gasped as a wave of horror swept through her.

"Wait!" she shouted, scrambling to her feet without regard for her own safety. "I know that horse! And God have mercy . . . I know the rider too!"

"Stop, you little fool! Get back under cover!" Hank cried as she jumped over the wagon tongue and ran toward the horse and rider.

Grabbing Blue's bridle bit, she raced back toward the wagons, fully expecting an arrow or bullet to hit her in the back. She never stopped to look at the man; she simply knew he was Slade. Entering the circle where the wagon tongue was low, she brought the horse to a stop beside Hank.

"Please, help me get him off the horse! He's badly hurt!" Again, it was nothing she knew; it was merely logical reasoning from the sane portion of her brain that had taken command of her actions.

Crouching close to the ground, Dovie stealthily hurried toward them. "What's going on here?"

All in one motion, Hank swiftly pulled the injured man from the saddle while bellowing angrily, "That damn little fool almost got us all killed!" He called over his shoulder, "Ben, Tom, you women too, keep your eyes open! They might attack any minute now!"

"N—No Indians . . . out . . . there," Slade muttered falteringly as Hank laid him on the ground. His hand moved weakly toward his shoulder. "It's not a . . . trap. Got . . . this . . . in mountains."

"Mister, are you sure?" Dovie asked, gazing anxiously out into the night.

"Y—Yes." Then, doubtful recognition flashed through his eyes as he moved his head slightly and saw a woman who strongly resembled Virginia kneeling beside him. He opened his mouth to speak,

269

but instead he slumped into unconsciousness.

"Oh, Lord!" Virginia moaned. Fear like she had never known before welled in her throat. A raw, primitive grief overwhelmed her. She raised her eyes and looked pleadingly at Hank. "Is he . . . is he dead?"

He pressed his fingers against Slade's neck and waited a moment before shaking his head. "No, but his pulse is weak, and by the looks of him, he's lost a lot of blood. I'd say he is in pretty bad shape. I had better get him to a wagon and see what I can do for him."

"Take him to my wagon."

He eyed Virginia intensely, a questioning expression on his face. "All right," he said slowly. "I guess that's as good a place as any." Running his hands underneath Slade's arms, Hank locked his hands together around his chest and started dragging him toward the wagon.

Virginia's lips compressed in a tight line. Hank's treatment of Slade was entirely too casual. "Don't drag him like that. You'll hurt him. Can't you carry him?" she asked, her voice rising emotionally.

"Look, he's about two hundred and twenty pounds of dead weight. Have you ever tried to lift . . ."

Dovie sensed Virginia was near hysteria, and from what the girl had told her in confidence and by her behavior, she knew who the man was. "Tom," she called abruptly, "Come over here and help Hank get this man to a wagon."

"No, I'll carry him. Tom needs to stand guard." Hank grabbed hold of Slade's arm and, straining, hefted him over his shoulder.

Virginia shook her head. "But . . . Slade said there were no Indians out there."

Hank had already started for the wagon, but he

stopped and turned around. "If you want to trust your life to the ramblings of a delirious man, that's up to you, but I intend to remain alert until I know it is safe. I've seen what those savages can do!" he stated adamantly.

"All right! All right! Please . . . just take him to the wagon. It is ridiculous for us to waste time talking when he is badly injured and needs immediate help!" Virginia knew she was not really being fair; everybody had been thrown into a panic in the middle of the night and, naturally, confusion was to be expected. Yet, realizing that fact did not help, not with Slade hurt so badly.

Staggering under the injured man's weight, Hank climbed into the wagon and laid him as gently as he could on the bed. Virginia and Dovie followed close behind.

"You have any scissors?" he asked, feeling for Slade's pulse again. "It'll be better if we just cut his shirt off instead of jostling him around, trying to remove it. Then too, it's liable to be stuck around the wound."

"Yes, right here in my sewing kit." Virginia knelt and pulled a small basket from under the bed, then handed Hank a scissors. "Dovie, can you light the lamp?"

"No, don't do that," Hank said quickly as he began cutting the shirt away. "The man might have known what he was talking about, but like I said a minute ago, I'm not particularly anxious to find out. A lamp will light up this canvas-covered wagon like a beacon, silhouetting us inside. Now, if you have a candle and something we can use to shield the light, we can at least clean the wound . . . or wounds . . . and check the extent of his injuries," he suggested, stressing the fact that there could be more than one.

"I have an entire box of candles," Virginia said, already setting boxes aside in order to find it.

"I'll go put some water on to heat," Dovie offered.

"Be sure to bring plenty of clean cloths and a fresh bar of soap too," he reminded her.

Virginia caught herself glaring at Hank. She wanted to shout at him to hurry; his slow but steady pace was extremely discomfiting. It was as though he felt no urgent need to move more rapidly.

Worry strained Virginia's voice. "Will this dark woolen blanket be a heavy enough shield if we spread it over us like a tent?"

Hank paused in his work to glance at her. "Should work fine. Here, give me one end and I'll secure it up here."

Virginia had been able to mask her inner turmoil with deceptive calmness as long as she had kept busy. But now, as she sat under the blanket holding the candle while Hank carefully cut Slade's shirt away from the ugly shoulder wound, an emotional dam seemed to burst within her. In the dim candle-light, he looked much worse than when they had first taken him from the horse. Blood entirely covered his shirtfront. His face bore the stubble of a week's growth and it was gaunt and ashen. Severe pain had etched deep lines on his features. Just the sight of him lying so helpless, possibly only a breath away from death, was almost more than she could endure.

Virginia felt little surprise when she realized that regardless of how he felt about her, regardless of how he had treated her or what he believed about her, she had lost her heart to him, for better or for worse.

Suddenly, he began moaning and the sounds of his agony penetrated her mind. She planted her feet firmly on the floor of the wagon, then leaned back against the sideboards for support as a sickening dizziness swept over her.

"What's the matter?" Hank asked, glancing at her. "All this blood making you sick?"

"N—No," she murmured. It wasn't the actual sight of the blood that bothered her; it was the fact that it was Slade's blood. "What else do you want me to do?"

He flung part of the bloody shirt to the floor. "Nothing until Dovie brings that hot water. In places, the shirt is stuck to the wound. It'll have to be soaked off." He peered closely at Slade's shoulder. "I see the bullet is still in there too."

"How can you tell?" she queried, eager to keep her mind occupied. By asking questions, she could avoid the torture of wondering if he would survive.

"Very simple. There's no exit wound."

"It sounds like you know quite a bit about bullet wounds."

"More than I would like to know," he replied, giving a wry tilt of his head. "I was a medic during the war between the states." Then he measured her with a cool, appraising look. "You know . . . I think it's simply amazing what fear will do to a person."

Virginia inhaled sharply. "What do you mean?"

"For awhile there I could have sworn you were a man . . . or almost a man." Appearing indifferent, he continued to snip at Slade's shirt. "But now that you've had the hell scared out of you, and from the way you have carried on about this fellow here, I've noticed that you have lost that backwoods drawl, your grammar is good, and your voice has changed considerably. It makes me think you have been pulling the wool over our eyes, Miss . . . whoever you are."

She raised her chin defiantly, moistening her lips, then looked away. It was several long moments before she spoke. "That fellow there, as you put it, is my husband. His name is Stephen Slade. My name is Virginia."

"Does Dovie know?" Then he shook his head. "Never mind. Forget I asked that question. The way I see it, even though you fooled the hell out of all of us, your behavior as a young man was decent . . . and I imagine you had your reasons for doing what you did. And now that I know you are a woman, well . . . inside I guess you are still the same person."

"If it will make you feel better, Dovie knows who I am, but you are the only other one who does." It was obvious to Virginia that many questions were running through his mind, but he made no move to pry, for which she was grateful. She was not up to offering any explanations at that moment.

Hank glanced down at Slade. "We'll make him as comfortable as we can, then when it comes to be good daylight, I can check this wound further, and if he is strong enough, that bullet will have to come out."

Virginia could hardly lift her voice above a whisper as she asked, "Please be honest with me. Do . . . you think he is going to . . . die?" Her gaze was riveted to Slade's face.

He considered his reply carefully. "That's a question only the Big Man can answer. But, in my opinion, he should be all right as soon as I get this bullet out of him and he's had a few days' rest."

Dovie stuck a pail of hot water and small metal container through the opening. "Here. Sorry it took so long. I had to hunt for the medicine kit. What do you want me to do, Hank?" She started rolling up her sleeves.

"Come up here and hold this end of the blanket." He glanced at Virginia and a faint smile touched his lips. "*She* can hold the other end while I get her husband cleaned up and the rest of his shirt off him."

"So you know the truth."

"I know she's a woman . . . that's all."

"I'll wash him, Hank," Virginia said softly.

Hank eyed her warily. "Have you ever taken care of an injured man before?"

"No."

He cautioned her. "Even though he's unconscious, he could still feel the pain. His flesh is raw and the soap will burn. He's liable to thrash about when you start washing the shoulder. But you'll have to cleanse it good, or infection will set up in it. Now, do you still think you'll have the stomach for it?"

She jutted her chin bravely. "Probably not; nevertheless, I will do it anyway."

Recognizing her compelling need to help, he reluctantly agreed. "All right, change places with me."

Virginia poured some of the hot water into a shallow pan, then vigorously lathered a cloth with the fresh bar of castile soap. Then, after taking a deep breath, she gently but thoroughly began washing the dried blood and loosened what remained of the shirt from his chest. When his face contorted with pain and he writhed on the bed, perspiration glistened on her forehead, but she gritted her teeth and continued, knowing the ghastly chore had to be finished.

Finally, when she had his chest bared and thoroughly cleansed, she glanced first at Hank, then at Dovie. She smiled weakly, her face blanched, then her eyes widened and she clamped her hand over her mouth and bolted out of the wagon. A short while later, Dovie found her sitting on a stool, huddled within her own arms and staring miserably at the eastern sky as it gradually became light.

"Feel better now?"

Virginia nodded.

"Hank says after that bullet is out and with a few days' rest, he should be as good as new."

"I know. He told me."

"Want to talk about it?"

"There's really nothing to say," she whispered wretchedly. "Just because Slade has been injured, it will not change his feelings toward me. I doubt he will even be grateful for the small part I've played in helping him."

"Aren't you painting him awfully black?"

"Perhaps so, but I don't want his gratitude . . . I want him. But he has to want me too, and . . . I know that is something that can never be. He made his feelings very clear." She laughed bitterly. "I have always placed great value on pride and self-respect, yet I cannot help but wonder where mine is now? My head tells me to wash my hands of the entire affair—to forget him, to go on with my life. But my heart tells me that's impossible."

Dovie reached over and patted her hand. "Honey, nothing is impossible. And it sounds like you are just trying not to build your hopes too high so you won't be hurt again."

"And what is wrong with that?" Virginia's expression was strained.

There was a critical note in Dovie's voice as she said, "Unfortunately, we don't live in a perfect world. People make mistakes all the time—we are only human. And who knows? That man lying in your wagon might have regretted the mistake he made where you are concerned. But you'll never know if you take that attitude. Why not give him a chance to tell you he was wrong?"

She pressed her hands to her throbbing temples. "I don't know, Dovie. I just don't know."

"What is it going to hurt to try? You are miserable now, aren't you? Well, aren't you?" she asked again when Virginia did not immediately answer.

"Yes," she murmured sadly.

"Let's suppose you try to set things right with your husband and fail. You'll still be miserable. Right?"

"Yes."

"But if you try and you are successful. . . . Like I said a minute ago, what do you have to lose?"

"M—My pride."

"To hell with pride! It damn sure won't keep you warm on a cold winter night! And . . . I should know. I lost the man I loved because of my stubborn pride," she said pensively, her tone much softer. "If there is one chance in the world for you to be with the man you love, grab it, because you may not ever get another chance. I know I gave different advice to you earlier . . . but I should have kept my mouth shut because that was before I realized how much you love that man." She stared at the girl hard. "Meet him halfway, and for goodness sake, use your womanly wiles. I have a real pretty pink dress in my wagon that I haven't worn in ages. And ages means twenty pounds ago," she added, chuckling. "If we took a few tucks in it here and there, I'll bet it would fit perfectly."

Still not thoroughly convinced, Virginia chewed on her bottom lip. She glanced at the women sitting, drinking coffee, in front of China Doll's wagon. "What about them? I can imagine what they would say if I suddenly appeared wearing a dress."

"Don't worry about what my girls will say. Your husband is who you want to impress." Dovie stared at her anxiously. "Well, honey, what do you say? What about my pink dress? Or, are you a coward?"

Virginia stiffened at the challenge. "No, I am not a coward! If it will make you happy, I'll give it a try." She shrugged. "I suppose it cannot hurt anything."

It was difficult for Dovie to keep the triumphant smile from her face. "That's right, and who knows? It might just help!"

Virginia took a deep, quaking breath. "I only wish. . . ."

"What?"

"Oh . . . nothing. It was just a foolish thought."

"Tell me anyway."

Virginia attempted an uncertain smile. "I suppose it is silly . . . but I wish Slade didn't have to know I pretended to be a boy. I . . . guess I am afraid he will make fun of me." She could not bring herself to discuss all of Slade's accusations with Dovie. Yet she suspected that if Slade discovered what she had done, he would probably think she had used the boyish disguise to take advantage of people, and she reflected silently, as God was her witness, that was never her intention.

Dovie thought about it for a moment. "Maybe he doesn't have to know," she said slowly.

"How will I keep him from finding out? Right now, only you and Hank know I'm a woman, but the moment your girls and your guards see me wearing a dress, they'll know, and they are bound to talk. And once Slade is up and about, he'll know too." She shuddered inwardly at the thought.

"The only way he will know is if he overhears my people talking about it and if I ask them to keep their mouths shut, they will."

"A—Are you sure?" Virginia asked hopefully.

"Yes, honey, I am sure. In our business, we have to use discretion." She made a waving gesture with her hands. "Now, you hurry on over to my wagon."

"No, I want to see how Slade is doing first."

"All right, check on him, then go to my wagon. I'll go talk to my people and after I finish, you can rest assured that Jimmy will no longer exist."

Chapter Nineteen

"Be patient for just one more minute. I am almost through with your hair," Dovie said, winding the last uncurled tress around the curling iron. "I want you to look your prettiest when your husband sees you."

Virginia gazed worriedly out the back of Dovie's wagon. "I wonder what's taking Hank so long?" she muttered, nervously twisting her hands together.

"You don't remove a bullet just like that," Dovie said, snapping her fingers. "Now sit still. We're almost finished."

Virginia squirmed on the chair. "I should have insisted on helping him."

"If he had been foolish enough to agree, you probably would have fainted the first time Slade moaned or a rush of blood appeared. And quit fidgeting. Hank said he would call you the moment he was through."

Dovie tilted Virginia's chin upward and fluffed the hairbrush through her curls. Smiling, she placed her arms akimbo and admired her handiwork. "Now, I want you to stand up, close your eyes, and turn around and look at yourself in my full-length mirror."

"Really, Dovie, I feel so silly doing this," she protested.

"Humor me, honey. Please just humor me . . . that's all I ask. Now . . . close your eyes and turn around." She hurried to remove the covering from her mirror. "I think you are in for a big surprise!"

Reluctantly, Virginia complied. Then, she stiffened with surprise as she stared in awe at the woman's reflection in the mirror. Could that beautiful creature be her? Had she changed so much in the short span of a few months? What had happened to the young, naive girl? When had she become a woman?

Her gaze slipped downward, timidly, lured by the soft contours of a body that was already full and ripe. A slender waist — yes, as slender as the most fashionable woman, even without a corset to lace her in. But beneath the billowing skirt, her hips showed gently rounded curves, and firm young breasts, without their past restraints, strained the meager fabric of the bodice. And her skin, which had seemed too dark only the day before — how exotic it now looked, all bronzed and golden against the tantalizing glow of pink silk. Her hair, although unfashionably short, was even shorter still after Dovie had attacked it with her own scissors, but it now lay in soft, curly layers instead of the straggly, uneven lengths she had worn to enhance her boyish disguise.

When had all this happened? It was as though she was a beautiful butterfly that had just emerged from a dark cocoon.

Dovie beamed proudly. "I realize your Slade won't be too rambunctious for awhile, but if the sight of you doesn't make him sit up and take notice, then I don't know men as well as I think I do. And believe me, honey, I have known my share!" she said without a hint of shame. "Now, go over to the wagon and wait outside until Hank calls you in. He should be finished before too much longer."

Virginia did not acknowledge her suggestion with a reply. She merely stepped down from the wagon and hurried across the campground, heedless of the astonished women when they caught sight of her.

She reached the rear of the wagon just as Hank stepped down from the makeshift infirmary, drying his hands.

"*Jimmy?*" he sputtered, his eyes widening in surprise. "Is that you?" Her transformation into a beautiful young woman was almost unbelievable.

"Please, Hank," she whispered, craning her neck, trying to peer into the wagon. "I am Virginia now."

"I certainly won't argue with that!"

"How is he?" she asked, her attention on the man lying so still inside the wagon.

His expression grew evasive. "As much laudanum as I gave him, he'll sleep for at least another hour."

"That did not answer my question. *How is he!*"

Hank flipped the spent bullet into the air and caught it, then held it out so that Virginia could see. "All I can say is, he is a very lucky man. The cartridge this bullet came out of had to have been packed wrong, or it lost some of its gunpowder or something, because he was hit at fairly close range and it should have damn near tore his shoulder off. He will be all right though, so you can quit worrying about that."

"There is something else, isn't there?" Virginia pressed. "I can tell by your expression that something is wrong."

Hank shuffled his feet and avoided her eyes. "He is going to have a stiff arm for awhile . . . and truth is, it might always be stiff."

"Do you mean . . . paralyzed?" Her face blanched at the thought of what that would do to Slade.

"No, I said stiff, and that is what I meant." He chewed on his bottom lip for a moment, trying to find the words to explain himself better, then he paused and sighed heavily. "You are putting me in a bad spot here."

"I don't see how!"

"I know he is your husband, but there are certain things a man . . . doesn't tell a woman." He rubbed the back of his neck, wondering how he had ever gotten into this mess.

Placing her hands on her hips, Virginia stepped closer. "Look, Hank, the fact remains, I am his wife. He has been badly injured and you are withholding information from me. I demand that you tell me the truth about his arm!"

"All right!" he conceded, throwing his hands up in the air. "To be blunt, he will have use of his arm and hand, but his arm will be stiff."

Angrily, she stamped her foot. "Hank, you've already told me that!"

He flung the towel to the ground and glared at her. "Damnit, what I am trying to say and you are too female to understand is, I doubt he will ever be able to use his gun again . . . not the way he is accustomed to using it!"

Pressing her hand against her heart, Virginia breathed a deep sigh of relief. "Good Lord, Hank, you had me scared half to death. You have no idea what all I was thinking."

He shook his head, concern filling his eyes. "And you have no idea what I just said. I don't know your husband, but I do know, from the way he had his holster strapped on and from the calluses on his hand, he was fast with a gun. If he has a reputation, word will soon get around and every snot-nosed kid in the territory will be gunning for him, circling around him like a vulture around a wounded mountain lion, hoping to build a name as a fast draw." He wagged his finger at her. "I don't know what your problem is with him, but I suggest you get it straightened out. Then I suggest you convince him to open a general store, or start farming, or maybe buy a little ranch somewhere. You'll live a much more peaceful life that way . . . and maybe a hell of a lot longer one."

For a moment, Virginia could only stand there and gape at him. It had not occurred to her lately just how little she knew about Slade. The memory of how he had stood up to Lieutenant Culpepper flashed through her mind. No doubt he was a dangerous, volatile man, and perhaps he was a notorious gunman, as Hank had implied. But considering how he felt about her, how could she hope to persuade him to change his way of life? He would probably ignore any suggestion she made—out of spite, if for no other reason.

"Will you tell him what you've told me?"

"Do you think he would listen?"

"Perhaps." She tried to shrug indifferently but was not quite successful. "At least he would come closer to listening to you than to me."

Hank stared hard at the beautiful young woman. "I doubt that, but if it will make you feel better, I'll talk to him."

Devils were chasing him, blood-red devils with long, pointed tridents. He could hear their pounding footsteps growing closer and closer. Then he heard a whooshing sound and felt an excruciating stab of pain rip through his shoulder. With heart pounding, legs churning, arms flailing, he tried to run faster but found himself becoming mired in a sticky substance on the ground. In terror, he glanced over his shoulder to see how close they were. One devil had John Carlisle's face, and the others were those Apache braves he had killed in the mountains. He tried to run faster, but the harder he ran, the slower his steps became, and the more entrapped he became in the sticky muck, until it held him like clutching hands.

Then, almost miraculously, the devils disappeared when he felt a hand gently stroking his brow. His vision blurred, then an angel on a pink cloud appeared through the mist. She was waving a wing over him, which produced a cool breeze.

"Lie still. You will tear open your wound," the angel murmured in a soothing voice as she pressed a wet cloth against his dry, parched lips.

"Where . . . am . . . I? Am I . . . dead?" In his pain-fogged mind, he thought he must be. But devils were in hell. Why then was an angel present?

"No, you are not dead. You are safe . . . You have been badly wounded though. So, please, just lie still. You have been thrashing about on the bed and I am afraid you will tear open your wound. Are you thirsty? Would you like a drink?"

"Y—Yes . . . thirsty," he mumbled. There was something about the angel's voice that was disturb-

285

ingly familiar.

The angel carefully slid her hand underneath his head and raised it slightly, enabling him to take a sip of water from the glass.

Sagging back weakly, he opened his eyes wide, then blinked them rapidly. "I . . . can . . . hardly see. E—Everything . . . is so blurry."

"You're weak." Her voice sounded like it was coming from a long way off. "You have lost a lot of blood, and the laudanum could be partly to blame."

"L—Laudanum?" The rational portion of his brain realized this was why he was so groggy and disoriented. Laudanum had that effect on him.

"Hush now," the angel crooned. "Go back to sleep, and when you wake again, I will give you another drink of water."

"Yes . . . sleep . . . sleep," he mumbled softly, closing his eyes.

Hank leaned against the tailgate and peered inside the wagon. "How's the patient doing?" he asked, taking note of the fact that the girl was fanning her husband to make him more comfortable.

Virginia turned her head and smiled. "He's resting easily. He awoke once thrashing about, but when I gave him a drink of water and placed a wet cloth on his forehead, he went back to sleep almost immediately." With her free hand, she brushed an errant lock of hair from his brow.

"He should be waking up before long, and from the way I had to dig around for that bullet, he'll probably be in a lot of pain. I left a small bottle of laudanum over there on top of that crate. And if he tries to get up, don't let him. Back during the war, any time I had a patient I figured would want to get up before he was physically ready, I simply told him to stay in bed for five days, knowing full well he'd get up in three, which was what I really wanted all along." He chuckled in remembrance. "That system seldom failed."

"How long do you want Slade to remain in bed."

"Tell him I said five days."

She gave him a conspiratorial wink and touched her thumb and forefinger together. "Five days it is."

"I realize you will want to talk to him for awhile in private, but after you are finished, I want to talk to him too. I want to find out exactly where he was when the Apaches jumped him and how many signs he's seen lately." He scratched his brow. "Guess I had better see if Dovie has any chores for me to do. If you need anything, just holler. Oh, and by the way, I have something for you." Reaching into the wagon, he handed her a book.

"What's this?" she asked, turning it over to see the title.

"It's a book on Apaches. I figured after that fiasco last night, you ought to know more about them. And what better time to do it than when you're sitting by a sick bed. It tells about their culture, superstitions, and their general way of life. Of course, it was written by a white man, so you will have to take some of it with a grain of salt, but a lot of the book is very accurate."

Virginia's lips twisted upward in a smile. "Thank you, Hank, but why do I have the feeling that I have been nicely insulted?"

Bantering in a relaxed manner, Hank replied, "Because you should. I am getting on in years and I doubt if my heart could take another scare like the one I had last night. Why, your false alarm scared me out of at least ten years of drinking whiskey and chasing wild women! Well, I have to get busy. Remember, holler if you need me."

After Hank left, she glanced down at Slade and her smile quickly disappeared. Her feelings although understandable, were very confusing. She desperately wanted Slade to hurry and awake, yet she dreaded it as well. Sighing deeply, she pushed such thoughts from her mind. It was senseless for her to torture herself unnecessarily with conjecture. She would discover soon enough his reaction to her presence.

Slade was trapped in a deep, dark hole. Looking upward, he could see a hazy shaft of light piercing the darkness, and he sensed if he could somehow reach the source of that light, he would find safety and comfort.

Carefully feeling his way around the edge of the walls, he was dismayed to find they were as smooth as glass. He had to get out! He had to! Then, a faint ray of light revealed a small notch on the wall. Was the notch deep enough for a foot or a hand to take hold? If there was one indentation, could there be two? Instantly, he was standing at the notched wall, and his heart began beating faster and faster as he discovered hundreds of notches, some small, some large enough to slip his entire foot into. Then, miraculously, pegs appeared above the notches. There was a way out! All he had to do to make good his escape from the pit was to ignore the pain and climb! Climb!

Slade slowly opened his eyes to a swirling grey

mist. He was somewhat confused by his surroundings, but he knew he had reentered the world of reality. He lay perfectly still for a few moments while he regained his bearings. Having trained himself to think rationally whenever faced with an illogical situation, he turned his thoughts to the last clear thing he remembered and began retracing the steps that had brought him to this place. Water . . . ! That was the key factor. He had been filling his canteen when Indians had attacked and wounded him. But how badly was he injured? And why was the memory of Virginia nagging at him? Had she been with him when they had attacked? No, he had left her in New Mexico. What was it, then, that troubled him? Then the memory of her braid's being in the Indian's pouch filled his mind. No! No! No! She couldn't be dead! She couldn't be!

Virginia glanced up sharply from the book she had been reading when she heard Slade moving. Quickly placing it on the small table, she moved from the stool and sat down on the side of the bed. "Slade? Slade? Can you hear me?"

His eyes flew open and his brows drew together in a dumbfounded expression. "Virginia . . . ? Is that you?" he questioned incredulously, his voice sounding extremely weak, even to his ears. She was dead, wasn't she? He had seen the proof. But she looked so real, like a living flesh-and-blood woman, not a mere vision! A jumble of confused thoughts and feelings assailed him. Was his mind conjuring up more hallucinations simply because he wanted her to be alive?

When Virginia's eyes met Slade's, her tongue suddenly seemed to stick to the roof of her mouth, her mind went blank, and she could think of nothing to say, even if she had been able to speak. This was not the reaction she had expected of herself.

"You *are* real . . . aren't you? I'm not hallucinating?" he pressed, his brow wrinkling in a deep, bewildered frown.

Her voice trembled with ill-concealed emotion. "Y — Yes, of course I am."

"Then you are not . . . dead," he repeated, more to help convince himself than to state a fact. After taking her braid and pendant watch from that dead Apache, he naturally had assumed she had been murdered. Thank God his assumption had been wrong. She was very much alive, and looking more beautiful than he had remembered. How he longed to crush her in his arms. But, he realized with a sinking feeling, after what he had done to her, she would probably recoil from his touch.

Turning her head toward him, she lifted her chin with just a touch of defiance. "No, I am very much alive. Why? Are you disappointed?" she queried a bit too sharply. Virginia could feel her stomach tightening into a hard knot. She had every reason in the world to be angry, but to sound so cold and bitter, to deliberately antagonize him, would not help matters any. She quickly looked away, afraid he would see the raw emotion of her love reflecting from her eyes.

"No, that's not it at all," he murmured weakly, reaching out to gently stroke her arm, in part to reassure himself she was real and also to see if she would recoil from his touch. His gaze traveled over her face and searched her eyes. "Your hair . . . what happened to your hair?"

Her heart lurched and her pulse pounded at the feel of his hand on her arm. His presence was disturbing in every way, but then, she had known that was how it would be. "I cut it," she murmured simply.

"When?" he asked, his voice sounding stronger.

Her back stiffened. Why was that important? Was it possible he thought she had cut it because of him? Because of what he had done, perhaps as a way to signify her loss? No, surely he was not that arrogant. She shrugged to hide her sudden rush of hostility. "I—I don't think that is important. And I'm not sure it is wise for you to be talking so much. You need to rest. Try to go back to sleep."

"No, I have too many questions." He reached out and gently touched the hollow of her throat. "Didn't you used to wear a pendant watch on a chain around your neck?"

"Y—Yes, I did. It was my mother's, but why . . . ?" Then her features softened as she realized he was babbling incoherently. "It was stolen."

"Along with your braid," he said slowly, as the pieces started to fit together.

"Yes, but how did you—"

"The Indian who shot me had your braid and pendant in his war pouch. When I found them, I naturally assumed . . . well, let's not talk about what I assumed. But I do remember putting the pendant in my vest pocket . . . so you can have it back." He tried to assess her unreadable features.

Virginia remembered what she had told that officer back at Fort Grant. So that's what had happened! she reflected. I thought I was being so clever by telling him I believed Indians had looted my wagon—and, in reality, at least one was guilty.

His offer cheered her. "Thank you. I would love to have it back. My mother's pendant meant a great deal to me." Being so near to Slade was discomfiting, for his appeal was devastating. Squaring her shoulders, Virginia decided she would have to remain aloof until she could learn whether or not his feelings had changed. At least hatred did not shine from his eyes. But then, he was now lying flat on his back, helpless. He needed someone to nurse him back to health. That fact alone could make a huge difference in how he would treat her. She moistened her lips. "But we can discuss pendants and cutting hair and Indians later. Right now, you need your rest."

He caught her hand, ignoring the frightened look she gave him. "No . . . I promise to rest if you will answer my questions first."

"All right, but just a few." Trying to hide her reluctance, she slowly pulled her hand from his grasp.

He tilted his brow, looking at her uncertainly. "Is this the first time I've come to myself?"

Virginia tightly gripped her hands together so they would not tremble so badly. "No, you awoke a little while ago and I gave you a drink of water."

"Ahh, that must be it, then." His mouth curved into an unconscious smile. "I thought I was dreaming, or hallucinating. You are the pink angel."

"P—Pink angel?"

"Yes, there was a pink angel fanning me," he murmured, a glint of wonder shining in his eyes.

Her gaze lowered, as did her voice. "I—I . . . you were burning up. I had to do something." Nervously clearing her throat, she said, "That was one question. I will answer two more. Then you will have to get some rest or Hank will have my hide."

"Hank?"

"Yes, Hank is the man who removed the bullet from your shoulder. And you could not have been in better hands. He was a medic in the war." Standing, she placed her arms akimbo and could not prevent the teasing smile that parted her lips. "Now, you only have one question left."

Even though his shoulder hurt badly, a glimmer of amusement danced in his eyes. "That's not fair. You tricked me." The moment he said it, he felt like biting his tongue. He quickly tried to smooth over his poor choice of words as Virginia's tentative smile disappeared from her lips. "I've lost track of time. How long have I been here?" He glanced about the wagon. "And where am I?"

It was as though a mask had descended over Virginia's face as she moved abruptly from the bedside and spoke icily. "You rode in before dawn this morning. As to where we are, I'm not sure of the actual miles, but we . . . the caravan consisting of eight wagons left Fort Thomas a week ago." Wary of looking at Slade, she stared at her hands. "Hank said he wanted to talk to you after you regained consciousness, but before I go, is there something I can get for you? Perhaps a drink of water?"

Slade did not want her to go. He would never be able to rest without finding out first if there was a chance she would forgive him. He had to stall her.

"Yes, there is. I sure am thirsty . . . and I'd appreciate another pillow for my head if you don't mind. I never could lie this flat on a bed."

Not trusting herself to comment on that particular disclosure, Virginia removed a spare pillow from the storage area beneath the bed. Hoping her voice sounded cool and remote, she said, "If you'll lift your head, I'll put the pillow underneath it."

Her brows drew together doubtfully when he tried to raise himself, then slumped against the thin pillow on which he lay.

Shrugging weakly, he managed a helpless smile. "I thought I had enough strength to raise myself . . . but I don't. I guess you will have to help me." He reached his hand toward her. "Slip your hand underneath my head and I'll wrap my good arm around your waist for leverage.

Her brow creased with skepticism. "It is amazing how your strength suddenly comes and goes," she remarked dryly.

"That thought crossed my mind too," he said, running his arm around her waist. Lord! How good it felt to touch her.

There was a sudden tingling in the pit of her stomach, and her legs felt as if they had turned to jelly when, as he leaned forward, his forehead brushed against her breasts. She quickly slid the pillow under his head, removed his arm from around her waist, and stepped back abruptly. Her heart fluttered wildly in her breast as she searched his features for a clue to his thoughts, but she saw nothing but a blandly innocent face.

"Now, I'll . . . get you a . . . drink," she said in a hoarse, trembling whisper. Deliberately presenting her back to him, she turned to the small table and stood for a moment to regain control of her ragged emotions. Taking a deep breath, she turned back to him, and tilting his head forward slightly, she held the cup to his lips. Her hand started trembling violently when his hand encircled hers on the cup.

"No, Slade, please . . ." Her voice broke.

"Let's stop this shilly-shallying, Virginia. I have to talk to you about that day. I have to tell you—"

"No! Not now, Slade. Please . . . not now!" Clamping her hand over her mouth to silence a sob, she whirled and ran from the wagon.

Chapter Twenty

The afternoon was so hot, shimmering waves of heat reflected from the desert floor, and what breeze there was seemed like a furnace's sweltering breath.

Virginia sat in the shade of the cottonwood trees lining the bank of the shallow river, grateful for a few minutes respite from all the questioning glances Dovie's girls had given her since she had left the wagon. As usual, the camel had chewed through his ropes and within minutes after she had sat down, he had ambled over and settled his huge body right beside her.

Naturally, Dovie's girls were curious, Virginia mused. That was to be expected. But she was too troubled about her conversation with Slade to worry about their curiosity. She would simply have to place her trust in Dovie and hope she had given them a reasonable explanation. Later, she would ask Dovie what she had told them, and if they still proved to be too curious, perhaps then she could explain her motives for impersonating a boy without having to reveal too many details.

But for now, Virginia thought with a heavy sigh

as she absentmindedly stroked the back of Mule's long neck, she was fighting her own battle of personal restraint—and it was a battle she was certain to lose.

Talking with Slade again had made her realize just how deeply she loved him—how she wanted to share her life with him, to have his babies, to grow old with him. And those feelings came from a place in her heart and soul that was beyond reason or logic, because she knew he did not want her.

Why did she continue to love him when, deep inside, she believed that her love was futile? The realization hung over her like a heavy weight.

"Are your thoughts worth a penny, little girl? If so, I'm buying," Hank said, squatting on his heels beside her. When she turned to face him, her expression was so pitiful, so heartrending, he briefly wondered if he had made the right decision to join her. "Surely it can't be that bad," he challenged.

"I think perhaps it is," she murmured softly. Looking away, she quickly wiped her eyes, feeling shame that someone had caught her crying.

Hank picked up a small stick and began scratching on the dry earth. "I take it your reunion with your husband did not go too well."

She shook her head, a tremor touching her smooth, tawny face. "It wasn't what happened between us earlier. It was what happened months ago. Our marriage was a mistake . . . my falling in love with him a mistake," she choked out miserably.

"How's that?"

"Because Slade does not love me. He never has and he never will." The spoken admission sent sharp, stabbing pains through her heart.

He rubbed his chin and his brows creased in a

heavy line. "That's not the impression I got when I talked with him. Seems to me, he is more moon-struck over you than that wily beast." He nodded toward the camel.

Attempting to smile, she scratched Mule behind his ear. "Oh, he's a wily beast now? What happened to cantankerous and stubborn?"

"Any time a creature can get a pretty little gal like you to scratch his ears, he has to be wily. The way I see it, ol' Mule is not as dumb as I thought."

At that precise moment, Mule stretched his neck, turned his head, and looked at Hank with his big doe eyes and made a sound much akin to laughter.

"See!" Hank exclaimed. "That damn thing is laughing at me now."

Virginia was conscious of a quickening pulse in her temples, a wild pounding of her heart against her breast, as it suddenly dawned on her what he had just said. "Hank . . . I must have misunder-stood what you said a few moments ago." Her con-fused tone did little to conceal the mixed emotions she felt. "What did you mean, that was not the impression you got when you talked with Slade?"

Tossing the stick aside, he picked up a few small pebbles and started throwing them into the water, one by one. "Oh, every time I asked him a question about that Indian trouble he had been in, he would answer, then he would fire back a question about you. Weren't nosy questions either. He was more concerned about *how* you've been doing than *what* you've been doing. For what it's worth, I figure the two of you have patched up your differences . . . only you just don't know it yet."

Her black eyes widened excitedly and her heart leapt in her chest. "You aren't just . . . making it up to make me feel better, are you?" she asked hesitantly, almost afraid to believe what he had just said.

He looked at her with the innocent face of a cherub. "Now, little girl, do you really think I would do something like that?"

Afraid he was merely teasing her again, she scolded, "Hank . . . please be serious. This is very important to me." If there was a chance Slade had had a change of heart, she had to know. But then, she should not let her hopes rise too much. How well she knew from past experience that Slade did not always mean what he said or implied. Her broken heart was proof of that.

"I am serious." He looked at her from beneath craggy brows. "I want you to listen to me, little girl, and I want you to listen good. Your man has had at least two hours' rest since I left him. And I know from experience, two hours can work wonders on a man like him. Now, if his pretty little wife decided to take him a bowl of that venison stew Paris has been cooking, I'm sure he would be extremely grateful—"

Virginia interrupted him. "A bowl of stew!" she snorted disgustedly. "I realize he should be getting hungry before long, but a bowl of stew will not solve our problems . . . and I thought you were going to offer me some helpful advice." She started to rise. "Excuse me. I need to be by myself for awhile. I have to think."

Hank caught her by the arm and pulled her back down beside her. "No, not so fast, little girl. I'm not finished yet." His voice had depth and authority. "I want you to hear me out, then I promise never to mention this again. I don't know which one of you has a burr under your saddle blanket and I don't want to know, but it is my intention to give you some advice, and if you have any sense between those pretty little ears of yours at all, you will listen to me. I have been giving "Jimmy" and "Virginia" a lot of thought today, and I have reached the conclusion that you are a very proud person. You can go back to that wagon with your hackles up . . . and you'll probably leave with them up. But if you can leave all your hurts and angry feelings in the past, where they belong, you just might be able to come to terms with that young man, even if it means swallowing your pride — and, I've never heard of anyone choking on pride yet." His countenance was immobile. "If that man is who you want, and I believe he is, then give a little bit if you have to. Bend, but don't break. Are you familiar with that tale about the little sapling and the mighty oak tree?"

His forcefulness commanded her attention. She stammered, "N — No, I don't think so."

"Well, I won't take the time now to tell you the whole story, but let me ask you something. If there was a small sapling standing next to a big oak, which one do you think would be standing after a fierce wind storm?"

"The sapling, I suppose."

"That's right, and when troubles threaten a young marriage, if the people will only bend, they'll still be standing when or if the next storm comes, but if the people stand firm and stubborn, refusing to bend, they'll break, and broken wood will eventually rot." He shrugged as his face flushed with color. "I never meant to lecture you, girl, but I'm not the sort of man who can stand by and see someone — whom I think a lot of — ruin her life out of sheer stubbornness. I'm going to say one more thing, then I'll leave you alone."

He took a deep breath. "You've shown you have grit and determination. Not many women would have sacrificed what you have — and I'm referring to your womanhood. You were faced with being stopped in your tracks or taking the necessary steps to continue — and in my opinion pretending to be a boy was about your only choice. You are a fighter — you've proved that fact. You've done everything from cutting your hair to shoveling horse manure. But what confuses me is, if you are in love with this man, why aren't you willing to fight for him?"

"I am willing!" she protested hotly.

"Then act like it! You've gotten yourself all fancied up, but instead of sitting by his bedside batting those big black eyes of yours and charming him out of his socks, you're down here by the river, feeling sorry for yourself and looking as miserable as I have ever seen anyone look."

"Are you suggesting I . . . I . . . seduce him?" she asked, lowering her head, embarrassed that Hank would suggest such a thing to her.

"Hell, yes! If that's what it takes!"

"That just . . . doesn't seem . . . quite fair. I want him to love *me* . . . not what I can give him!"

Hank muttered a curse under his breath. "Who said you had to fight fair?" He got to his feet. "Well, I've said all I'm going to say. It's now up to you, little girl."

Virginia stared dejectedly at the water. Letting her eyelids close, she mulled over what Hank had said, and she felt a chill deepen in her heart. He was right. She was allowing her stubborn pride to stand in the way. But, when that was all one possessed, it was difficult to carelessly toss it aside, especially since Slade had destroyed it once before. Nevertheless, Dovie had told her basically the same thing about her pride, that it would not keep her warm on a cold winter night. The fact remained, though, that neither Dovie nor Hank had seen the hatred shine from Slade's eyes as she had. He had not listened to reason then; why should she think he would listen now?

Then, she sat up abruptly. Her heart began beating a staccato rhythm against her chest. When Slade had left her in New Mexico, she had been powerless to stop him. But now that he was lying practically an invalid in the wagon, it would be impossible for him to walk out on her again without giving her a chance to deny his accusations. He would have to listen to her! Why, she *had* been behaving like a little whipped puppy running around with its tail tucked between its legs. No wonder Hank's eyes had been filled with disgust. He had seen she had made up her mind that it would be useless even to try to resolve her problems with Slade.

Virginia slammed a fist into her hand with determination, and fiery lights shone in her eyes. She would prove Hank wrong. She would go to that wagon and, if necessary, sit on Slade until he listened to what she had to say. Maybe he wouldn't believe her, but at least she would not give up without a fight.

Perspiring heavily from the heat, Slade flung off the thin sheet that had been covering him and pulled one corner over his nakedness for modesty's sake. Pursing his lips, he blew his breath downward to cool his perspiration-drenched chest, then upward to cool his forehead. Judging by the length of the shadows penetrating the opening at the rear of the wagon, he calculated he would have to endure at least another hour of stifling heat before the afternoon breezes began. Where was everybody? Had they forgotten him? Were they planning to leave him in the wagon to roast while they took refuge under the cottonwood trees that lined the river's edge? Even some of the tortures the Apaches devised were not as bad as how they were treating him.

I'll bet Virginia is behind this, he thought sourly. It's probably her way of getting a taste of revenge. God, am I glad she wasn't the one who dug around in my shoulder for that bullet. Hell, she probably would have cut my shoulder off . . . or maybe even worse.

A rivulet of sweat dripped into his ear and Slade swiped at it angrily. He had had enough! He glanced about the wagon, looking for his trousers, but they were nowhere in sight. "Hell, she probably took them out and burned them," he grumbled to himself. "I'll wait ten more minutes, and if somebody does not show his face, I'll get out of this bed even if I have to crawl . . . naked . . . over ground glass and burning coals!"

It was almost as if Virginia appeared on the steps at the back of the wagon in response to Slade's threats.

Surprised, she exclaimed, "Oh! You are awake." Then she quickly averted her eyes, embarrassed to see him with only the corner of a thin sheet covering his nudity.

Slade reluctantly pulled up the sheet to cover himself, not out of modesty or to put Virginia at ease, but out of fear that if he did not, she would leave him to swelter in the sweatbox the wagon had become.

After he had covered himself, Virginia stated uneasily, "I thought you would still be resting." This spoiled her plans. She had hoped to make a good impression on him by being at his bedside when he awoke. Now, she would have to change her tactics.

"Yes, I am awake, and no, I am not resting!" he stiffly replied.

Wanting him to be as comfortable as possible, she quickly offered, "You must be hungry. I'll get you something to eat."

"No! Don't leave!" he gruffly commanded.

A frown creased her brow when she noticed his grim expression and the way his eyes glinted with anger. "Is something wrong?"

"I never thought you would be the sort of person to take your vengeance out on a dying man!" he snarled.

"I . . . what? Who is dying?" Her voice reflected her bewilderment at his incoherent accusations.

The words ripped from his mouth. "I am! I think it is ironic that I escaped an Apache attack only to be tortured to death at the hands of supposedly civilized people!"

Believing Slade had suddenly become delirious, Virginia was not sure whether to summon Hank immediately or to see what she could do to help. She did not know much about medicine, but she did know delirium indicated a fever, and a fever meant that an infection had set in. Then, realizing he could possibly hurt himself if he became violent and started thrashing about, she decided she could not chance leaving him alone. Squaring her shoulders, she quickly climbed into the wagon, but the wall of heat she encountered made her gasp for breath.

"Good Lord! It's like an oven in here!"

"That's what I have been trying to tell you!" he accused angrily.

"Slade I didn't know. . . ."

"Like hell you didn't!"

Biting her lower lip, she felt tears welling in her eyes. Bless his heart, no wonder he was complaining so bitterly, she reflected silently. She had had no idea that the heat settled in the interior of the wagon like this, but then, ever since the weather had become so hot, she had never entered the wagon during the heat of the day. She realized she would have to do something to cool Slade off immediately.

He continued to rant. "I thought when I rode in here, I would receive humane treatment . . . but hell no! It's a torture chamber! When I get back on my feet, I'm going to march everybody out into the desert and stake them out . . . just like the Apaches do! I'll dig a hole in an anthill and bury everybody in it! I'll fasten them to spits and roast them over an open flame. . . ."

Grabbing some towels, she started to wet them in the wash pan, but the water was as hot as if it had been sitting on a stove. That would never do. Ignoring Slade's venomous threats, she rushed to the back of the wagon and stuck her head through the opening.

Seeing Hank standing near Dovie's wagon, she called to him. "Hank! Hank! Bring a bucket of water from the river—and please hurry!"

"Now what do you plan to do, drown me?" Slade muttered with dark sarcasm.

Whirling about, she placed one hand on her hip

and brandished a towel at him. "No, but if you don't keep quiet, I am going to stuff this down your throat!"

He blinked and looked at her in astonishment.

"It so happens, I had no idea it was this hot in here and I'm sure neither Hank nor anyone else in this caravan knew either! For that, I am sorry. But if you don't like the treatment you're getting here, then pick someone else's camp to come to when you're half dead!"

Hank, breathing heavily, lifted the bucket of water over the tailgate and set it on the wagon floor. "What's wrong, Virginia?"

She turned at the sound of his voice and muttered pitifully. "Oh, Hank, no one considered how hot the wagon would get at this time of the day. It's like an oven in here and Slade has nearly roasted alive. Will you please hitch a couple of the horses to the wagon and move it over by the river where it is cooler? Either that or call the other men to help carry him and his bed out under the trees."

He shook his head. "They are out scouting the area right now. I'll just move the wagon." Looking at Slade, he paused. "Sorry about this, man. I never even stopped to think how hot it would get in here." Then he was gone, not waiting for, or expecting, a reply.

Not intimidated by Slade's glowering visage, Virginia quickly dipped a small towel in the bucket of water, wrung it out, and spread it over his brow. She then dampened another cloth and deftly ran it over his face, throat, and upper torso.

Almost immediately, Slade felt relief, but he was too resentful to admit it. They had left him to suffer and, by damn, he was not through complaining, not by a long shot. "Why don't you just pour the entire bucket of water over me? I'll bet that would cool me off."

"It would also get your bandage wet," she replied matter-of-factly.

He parried with contemptuous sarcasm, "Come to think of it, the water would probably start boiling!"

Feeling the wagon lurch forward, Virginia dauntlessly met his black scowl. "I told you I was sorry. What more do you want?" Her sharp words were cushioned by a softening tone. Without a doubt the sweltering heat had made him miserable, but there was no reason for him to continue to carry on so.

"You could at least pretend you meant the apology." If his shoulder had not been bandaged so tightly, he would have crossed his arms and glared more fiercely at her.

Why, the big baby, she thought, biting her bottom lip to prevent the smile that threatened.

Slade's pouting reminded her of the time her father had slipped on some ice and sprained his foot. He had become almost completely helpless and she had run herself ragged nursing him, taking him countless glasses of water, cups of coffee, trays of food, straightening his bed, listening to his painful moans, his numerous complaints. It had seemed endless. Yet on another occasion, when she had been called to help Mrs. Matthews, she had seen the woman suffer through a most difficult labor for over thirty-six hours with scarcely a moan. Could it be that men had little pain tolerance? Or was it just their nature to behave like spoiled infants when a woman was around to take care of them?

Her eyes narrowed slightly. Perhaps she should take advantage of this opportunity to pamper him, even baby him, if necessary. It would give her a logical excuse to stay right by his side — a task she did not find the least bit disagreeable.

"Poor man," she crooned, removing the damp cloth from his forehead and smoothing back an errant lock of hair, ignoring how the feel of his skin made her insides tremble. "I can imagine how badly you suffered in this horrible heat, thinking we had forgotten you — and with your painful wound, no wonder you are angry. As soon as Hank unhitches the horses from the wagon, we'll raise the canvas on the side facing the river where you can catch what breeze there is stirring, and I'll even give you a sponge bath. That should make you feel better."

His bottom lip protruded ever so slightly. "Well . . . it might."

Chapter Twenty-one

"You stay right there. Don't move," Virginia admonished Slade when the wagon came to a stop. "I'll ask Hank to help me roll up the canvas on the side facing the river."

"Don't worry," he remarked dryly. "Since I barely have the strength to move, I'm not about to go traipsing off across the desert without my trousers or my boots. You never did tell me where they were," he called after her, but Virginia left the wagon without answering.

The moment he was alone, his scowling expression miraculously transformed itself into one of cunning amusement. It had been rather obvious that what Virginia and Hank had claimed was true. Apparently, they had not stopped to think how hot the wagon would be during the heat of the day. At any other time or place, he would have waved it off good-naturedly; after all, it had not been intentional. But Virginia did not have to know his feelings. Since she had refused to talk to him earlier, he realized he would have to do something to keep her by his side, and if he goaded her enough, she might stay out of sheer stubbornness if nothing else, even if it meant unfairly accusing her of mistreating him, or pretending to be an obnoxious patient, or feigning helplessness. Later, if he was able to persuade her to forgive him, he could always claim to have made a remarkable recovery.

Slade slid his unbandaged arm under his head and grinned. Yes, the next few hours might prove to be very interesting — very interesting indeed.

Puzzled, Virginia calculated the distance from her wagon to Dovie's caravan; it was a good fifty yards. Also, she mused, noting the way Hank had parked the Conestoga, as long as Slade was confined to bed, it would be impossible for him to see the path that led from the wagons to the river. In her opinion, if his wound or the heat did not kill him, monotony soon would.

"Hank, why did you place the wagon so far away from the others?" she asked when he climbed down from the wagon seat.

"Shh," he cautioned, raising a finger to his lips. Taking her by the arm, he walked several feet from the wagon before he explained, "I talked to Dovie a while ago and told her Slade needed several days of bed rest before he could travel again. With all of the Indian trouble, we couldn't very well leave an injured man behind. And knowing you wouldn't leave without him, she agreed to stay. So, little girl, you have two more days to iron out your troubles before we hit the trail again. That's all the time I could buy you."

"Thanks for talking to her for me. I had intended to speak to her myself. But still, why did you park the wagon way down here? And in this particular direction?"

"You're not using your head, little girl," he scolded gently. "The way I figure it, Dovie and her girls are seven out of eight of the most beautiful females west of the Mississippi—it goes without saying who I think the eighth one is—and the less distraction your husband has, the better chance you have of making up with him. I know Dovie's girls, and the minute they find out Slade is a handsome young man, why they would wear that path to the river clear down to China. If they didn't have a reason to go, they would invent one." He squinted one eye and smiled. "I've been accused of having a fanciful imagination, and I'd hate to think what might happen if just about the time you and he were to patch up your differences, one or more of those little lovelies decided to take a bath in the raw. He's only a man, and there's no need tempting any male human that way."

She drew in her lips thoughtfully. "I . . . see what you mean. And you're right. I wasn't using my head." The warmth in her sudden smile echoed in her voice. "Thanks again, Hank."

"My pleasure. Now, let's get that canvas rolled up so he can get a breath of fresh air."

"My, it is much cooler in here now," Virginia cheerfully observed.

Slade admitted reluctantly, "Yes, I guess it is . . . a little." He shot her a sullen look. "Now that you've changed your mind about roasting me alive, I suppose you've decided to try to starve me to death."

"Are you hungry?"

"No, I passed that a long time ago," he muttered sarcastically. "And I also have pressing personal needs."

"Personal needs . . . ?" Then her mouth formed a silent "oh" as she realized what he meant. "I'll ask Hank to help you while I get you a bowl of stew."

"And don't forget the coffee."

Her features softened at the memory of the first day she had seen Slade. "No . . . I won't forget the coffee. I remember how much you like it," she murmured huskily.

After Virginia left the wagon, Slade's expression hardened in reflection. "I know how much else you remember too, sweetheart . . . I only hope I can make you forget."

When Slade claimed to be too weak to feed himself, Virginia eagerly volunteered, but by the time he had finished his meal, she was gritting her teeth. Never had she seen such a difficult, more temperamental man. She realized he was uncomfortable and his shoulder hurt dreadfully, but it almost seemed as if he were deliberately trying to test her patience. He complained that the stew was too hot and the coffee too cold; and she was either too fast or too slow in offering him a bite or a sip of coffee, yet not one single morsel or drop of coffee remained.

But through it all, she had somehow managed to keep her irritation to herself.

Virginia was painstakingly aware of how Slade critically scrutinized each item she set out for his bath: a pan of clean water, a facecloth, a bar of delicately scented castile soap, a fresh towel, and a tin of bathing powder.

"What is all of that for?" he demanded in a voice that was whipcord sharp.

312

"Why, it is for your bath," she replied in what she hoped was her sweetest tone.

He took a deep whiff through his nose. "I can smell that soap from here . . . smells too much like a woman. And what's in that tin? Bath powder?" He shook his head indignantly. "You are not about to put powder on me! Men don't wear such as that." A glimmer of a smile teased at his lips when he saw her shoulders stiffen with indignation.

Virginia quickly suppressed her anger under the guise of acquiescence. This was proving more difficult by the minute. Apparently the scoundrel did not know powder would help keep him cooler and enable him to rest better while he was confined to bed. But instead of arguing, she merely placed the powder tin aside and removed another bar of soap from a wooden box, deciding to use a different approach.

"What's that?" he demanded, craning his neck to see.

"Soap," she answered nonchalantly, all the while seething inwardly.

"I know. There's nothing wrong with my eyes. I meant, what kind of soap?"

"Lye soap. It is the only other kind I have."

"Lye soap! Isn't that awfully harsh?"

"A little, but I used to use it to wash my hair all the time." She smiled and her eyes narrowed. Two could play his game as well as one. "It usually left it soft and shiny."

"Usually?" he queried with a raised brow.

She wrinkled her nose. "Yes, unless I miscalculated and used too much lye when I made it. That happened once to a lady I knew. Bless her heart . . . At least her husband was kind enough to buy her a wig." Sighing, she shook her head. "Last I heard, she

313

still had to wear it though. Seems her hair never did grow back on the crown of her head. Needless to say, that's when I stopped using it for that purpose." Virginia wanted to laugh. She could have sworn that raw terror had briefly flared in Slade's eyes while his back had burrowed a foot into the bed.

"Well . . . I suppose that bar of castile soap will do this time." Even though he had tried to sound reluctant, his tone of voice had indicated differently.

Now that Virginia had cleverly discovered a way to get him to do what she wanted, she picked up the tin of powder and again sighed heavily. "It's such a shame . . ."

"What is?"

"Your refusal to let me use this on you after your bath. When a person is confined to bed during hot weather—even for just a few days—he tends to get bedsores . . . big, gaping, painful sores. Powder usually prevents them, but if you'd prefer I didn't use it . . ."

His expression was that of pained tolerance as he conceded, "Well, since you are determined to use that female soap on me, I suppose female powder won't hurt either! But if I hear anything about how I smell . . . !"

"Don't worry, I promise no one will say a word," she interjected quickly while briskly rubbing the soap over the facecloth to raise a lather.

When she sat on the bed beside him, his gaze caught and held hers. His eyes momentarily gleamed with bold assertiveness, which contradicted his obstinate behavior. Yet with his bold gaze, there seemed to be a thinly veiled plea.

A pulse beat and swelled at the base of Virginia's throat, as though her heart had risen from its usual

314

place. She realized there was a deeper significance to the visual interchange, and this discovery left her with a sense of bewilderment. At times, she had had the feeling that Slade was merely pretending to complain. If he was, why? Why did he have that pleading look in his eyes? And what did he expect to gain by acting like an obnoxious buffoon? Unless it was only his way of showing his contempt. And if that was the case, there was no hope for them. Still, she had to make this one last attempt. She simply had to!

Struggling to maintain her composure, Virginia began the task of giving him his bath. However, when she touched the cloth to his face, she could not prevent her hand from trembling.

"Ouch!" he yelped the moment the cloth touched him. "That's my face you're scrubbing."

Virginia looked at him in surprise. She had scarcely touched him. "Do you want to do it yourself?" She found it difficult to keep the animosity from her tone. That in itself was irritating because her feelings were as changeable as a swinging pendulum. One moment she was angry; the next, she was melancholy; and still the next, she was in a strangely euphoric mood. There was no logic to her emotions, unless logic could be found in the emotion called love.

"No," he said with a pitiful sigh. "I'm too weak."

Worrying her bottom lip, she doubted his words but did not say anything. Instead, a diabolic gleam shone in her eyes as she spread the facecloth over her entire hand, plopped it on his face, and vigorously scrubbed. That would teach him to gripe and complain, she thought, greatly amused.

When she finally removed the cloth, her lips were

parted in a satisfied grin. "Now, was that better?" she asked smugly, her tone warranting no argument.

"Mmm, much, but . . . I think you missed a spot behind my ear." Slade wanted to laugh, but he did not dare. And a moment later when she attacked his ear with the cloth, that particular desire quickly left him. He had to force himself to resist the urge to check to see if the ear was still there when she finished.

Virginia used the same procedure to wash the rest of his body. She had to. If she had washed it at her leisure, the sensuality emanating from his body would have driven her mad. Mentally, she placed a barrier around her emotions as she bathed his broad, heavily furred chest and taut, muscular stomach. She deliberately kept her eyes averted from the dark line that ran from his navel to the maleness concealed under the sheet.

Then, still listening to Slade's complaints, she methodically washed, rinsed, dried, and powdered his unbandaged arm, legs, and feet, deliberately avoiding the part where the sheet covered his male nudity. Each time she washed a different section of his body, she pitched the water out the back of the wagon, then reached through where the canvas had been raised and refilled the small pan from the barrel strapped to the side. After finishing, she expelled a deep rush of air and wiped the perspiration from her brow.

It took a moment to steel herself against the criticism she knew would be forthcoming. "Now, I'll wash your back," she muttered tersely.

Slade squirmed uncomfortably on the bed. He had been sorely affected by her ministrations, having to plant his foot on the bed and bend one leg so that

Virginia could not see his body's reaction to her touch. He discovered he had to clear his throat before trusting himself to speak. "Shall we use the same method as when you put the second pillow under my head earlier today?"

She tried to shrug with indifference but failed miserably. "I suppose so. It seemed to work well."

Slade hesitated for an instant, then he wrapped his good arm around her waist. He hoped she would not yank him up into a sitting position. Any sudden moves could hurt his shoulder. But apparently Virginia had put a limit on her roughness, refusing to do anything that might possibly cause him real pain. Once Slade realized that, he breathed a sigh of relief and rested his chin across her shoulder, his arm still wrapped tightly around her waist.

Virginia froze as her senses leapt to life and her heart started hammering wildly against her chest. His corded muscles beneath her hands were so strong, so masculine, so much a part of the man she loved, that she bit her lip to stifle an outcry of delight. Then, a sobering thought swept over her. Physically they were near, but in reality they were a million miles apart.

She managed in a strangled voice, "H—How do you expect me to wash your back when you are holding me so tightly?"

He nuzzled his face against her hair and deeply inhaled the pleasant scent. Was it such a short time ago that he had thought he had lost her for good? "I don't know," he murmured huskily, "but I can't let you go."

"W—Why not?"

Blinking, he realized how his words must have sounded. "Uh . . . because I'm too weak to sit by myself. I'd probably fall back on the bed and make my shoulder start bleeding again."

Virginia was not eager for him to let her go either, but if their somewhat unorthodox embrace did not end soon, she more than likely would make a fool of herself. She shuddered at the thought. He had made a fool of her once and now she was openly inviting him to do it again. If she had simply given him the wet cloth and let him do his own bathing, she would not be in this predicament now.

"I — I'll never be able to wash your back like this," she stammered. Removing herself from his one-armed embrace, she cupped her hand around his neck to hold him steady and moved behind him. Then she quickly ran the soapy cloth over his back, and rinsed, dried, and dusted it with powder before gently easing him down on the bed.

After dabbing at her brow with the corner of the towel, she placed her hands on her hips and breathed a heavy sigh of relief. "I'm glad that's finished."

"B — But, you're not." He gestured helplessly to the part of him that was covered by the sheet.

Adamantly, Virginia shook her head. "Oh, no. You can wash that part!" Handing him the wet cloth, she presented her back to him, but not before she saw an amused gleam shining from his eyes.

So, he has been making fun of me all along, she thought with a sudden rush of anger. I thought he was acting like a buffoon and he was trying to make one out of me! Why, I'll show him two can play that game!

"Let me know when you are through," she said in a syrupy tone.

A few moments later, his voice trembled weakly as

he announced, "You can turn around now. I'm decent." He moved his head slowly from side to side. "I see right now, it's going to take a while for my strength to return. Just the task of washing my . . . myself has left me very weak. I guess you are stuck with me for several days . . . maybe even longer."

Having already decided on her course of action, Virginia turned around and moved within arm's reach. She could not help but comment, "You mean a *little* chore such as that left you exhausted?"

Slade shot her a dark look. Was her remark intended as an insult?

Reaching over, she sensually trailed her fingers along his jaw and pretended to study him closely. "Now, all you need is a shave for your toilette to be complete," she announced, deliberately sliding her fingertips over his whisker-roughened neck.

His brow creased. Suddenly he was not so sure he wanted her to come at him with a razor. "Uh . . . I think I can shave myself," he offered quickly.

She looked at his shoulder, noting how Hank had immobilized the arm by putting it in a sling. "Now, how can you do that when you only have the use of one arm? Besides, you are too weak. You just said so yourself." Glancing about the wagon, she mused aloud, "Let me see, where did I put those razors? I think I have three left, . . . but do I have any strops?" She shrugged indifferently. "Oh, well, no matter. I'll simply make do with the razor as it is." She could have sworn she heard Slade give a strangled cry.

"There's no need to trouble yourself. I'm sure Hank won't mind shaving me."

"No, I believe he mentioned something about going hunting . . . and there is no telling when he will return." She began searching through a small crate.

Sensing no amount of protest would deter her, Slade reluctantly said, "Since you are determined to shave me, use my razor. I always keep it sharp. It's in my saddlebag. If you'll hand it here, I'll get it." Worriedly, he glanced up at her. "Have you ever shaved anybody before?"

"No," she replied with wide-eyed innocence. This was not true, for during the past few years the only way she had been able to persuade her father to shave was by offering to do it for him.

"Then you must have watched your father shave?"

"No," Virginia answered more truthfully. "My papa and the razor were never on very friendly terms after he started drinking heavily." Not wanting to dwell on the subject of her father, she asked quickly, "Aren't you supposed to use hot water though?"

"The water straight out of the barrel will do fine. I shave with cold water quite often." He held up a shaving brush and soap. "I prefer that you use these too."

Virginia slapped a wet cloth on his face to wet his whiskers thoroughly while she worked a heavy lather onto the brush. Then she quickly whisked the brush over his face, taking a great deal of satisfaction in the fact that he grimaced and wiped his mouth when she accidentally got soap in it.

Noting the sharp gleam of the blade, she picked up the razor and leaned toward him, but he caught her wrist and held it with a strong, yet gentle, grip. His gaze locked with hers and she could see questioning doubts in his eyes.

Finally, his voice strong and sure, he said, "That's not how you hold it, sweetheart. Let me show you."

320

As he placed it in her hand properly, his eyes never left hers.

She stared at him defiantly, and her mouth curved into a bemused smile. Then, with a flick of her wrist, she began to shave him.

The moment the razor started gliding over his face, he knew Virginia had lied. Her strokes revealed self-assurance that could only have come from experience. Almost before he knew it, she had finished with his face and was tilting his chin for easier access to his throat.

Leaning his head back, Slade waited until she had placed the blade at his throat before saying softly, "Now is your chance."

There was a spark of some undefinable emotion in her eyes as she paused, the razor resting below his ear. "My chance for what?"

"Revenge, if you want it." His expression was a mask of stone except for the tensing of his jaw.

Virginia frowned uneasily as her mind reeled in confusion. She was unwilling to face him and unable to look away. "I am happy to know you realize how difficult you have been. I have never heard so many complaints in all my life! In fact, I almost dumped a bowl of stew over your head a while ago."

Slade's eyes were compelling, magnetic, and a huskiness lingered in his tone. "That's not what I meant, sweetheart, and you know it."

She swallowed back the lump that suddenly rose in her throat. Without warning, sarcastic words rushed from her mouth. "Oh, are you referring to deliberately breaking my heart and riding off that morning? Why, what makes you think I have any ill feelings about something as insignificant as that?"

"I'm sorry," he uttered softly, a slight catch in his

voice. "And I think you are the only person I have ever said that to."

"You're sorry!" she echoed, her low, seething tone giving evidence to her pent-up fury. A cold, congealed expression settled on her face. "That doesn't quite set things right!" She slammed the razor into the wash pan and folded her arms miserably across her breast. "There go all of my . . . or what I thought were my good intentions."

"Oh?" His jaw visibly tensed.

She glared at him. "You wouldn't lie there so calmly if you knew what I had planned to do!" Her golden curls clung damply about her face as she lifted her chin in haughty defiance, and her small but firmly rounded breasts heaved with indignation as they swelled above the edge of her bodice.

There was an imperceptible tightening of Slade's features, but he did not hesitate for a moment as he said, "Sweetheart, if you think I'm calm, you're badly mistaken."

Tears brimmed in her black eyes and she averted her face so Slade could not see them. "I had planned to hold you down on the bed with the razor across your throat and force you to hear me out, force you to believe that I was innocent of what you accused me of." She threw up her hands. "But what's the use? You didn't believe me then, so why should you believe me now?"

Reaching out, he cupped her chin and urged her to face him, then he tenderly smoothed her hair away from her brow. He took a deep, steadying breath, but his eyes were raw with longing. "Why don't you try me?"

She moistened her lips nervously as her heart seemed to leap from her chest. "Y—You mean . . .

322

you're willing to listen to me now?"

"No," he murmured huskily. "I don't have to. I know the truth. I think I knew it that morning, but I was just too damn big a fool to listen to my heart." Gently grasping her silken shoulder, he pulled her to him, expertly guided her mouth to his, and devoured its softness.

Chapter Twenty-two

Inside Virginia's head a diabolic voice laughingly mocked, *Do you honestly believe his feelings toward you have changed? What's that, Virginia? Oh, Slade said he was sorry, and maybe he is, but just because he apologized, you can't necessarily expect it to mean anything. People apologize all the time and never mean it. He might be playing you for a fool again, just like he did back in Barkersville. Has he ever said he loved you? No, never — not even once. Remember how he used you? How he tricked and deceived you? How he used your body to satisfy his own carnal lust? Perhaps all he wants right now is a woman — any woman — and you are available. And really, you shouldn't have expected anything else, not with the impression you have given him. Look at you, parading around in front of him dressed like a shameless hussy — the bodice of your dress is so scandalously low, he can almost see your breasts. Why shouldn't he think he can amble right in and take up where he left off? You were naive then and really didn't know any better, but what is your excuse now? Ha! You are a silly, love-struck fool, Virginia. A fool! A fool! A fool!*

Virginia, her eyes wide, her face ashen, pulled from Slade's embrace and vehemently wiped off his kiss with the back of her hand. Her heart was pounding so thunderously, she knew he had to have heard it. Excruciating anguish ripped through her, and she clamped her hand over her mouth to keep from screaming her despair.

Slade stared numbly at her as his mind reeled from the knowledge that he was responsible for the abject misery reflecting from her eyes. He reached for her, rasping hoarsely, "Virginia, don't turn away without—"

Glaring at him, she slapped his hand aside. "No! You can't do this to me again! I won't let you! Did you honestly think you could whisper a few words of regret and make me forget what you did to me back in Barkersville?" she bitterly accused. Much to her chagrin, tears began streaming down the satiny smoothness of her cheeks.

She looked about frantically. I have to get out of here, she thought. I cannot let him see me cry! I refuse to give him that satisfaction!

Realizing she was about to flee and he would be powerless to go after her, Slade clamped his hand around her wrist and pulled her down to the bed beside him, wincing and sucking air between his teeth as pain stabbed through his shoulder from the sudden movements. Then, gritting his teeth, he struggled into a sitting position, feeling less vulnerable by doing so.

The bronzed, chiseled planes of his face appeared quite rigid, yet behind his stern demeanor was a silent plea as he commanded her to look at him. "Listen to me, Virginia, because I will only say this once; I *won't* grovel at your feet. When I told you I was sorry, I meant it. And, like it or not, that is all the apology you're getting out of me. What happened in Barkersville shouldn't have . . . but it did. However, that was then, and this is now. Even though I have denied it, tried to ignore it, and have fought against it, I have feelings for you . . . I love you. And I am reasonably sure at one time you loved me too . . . and I hope you still do." His piercing gaze searched her face for some clue to her feelings but saw only her trembling countenance and tear-misted eyes.

Releasing his hold on her, Slade let out a long, audible breath and dragged his hand through his hair. "Maybe I'm not saying this right . . . I don't know. Being able to express myself well has never been one of my attributes. But I am laying myself wide open to you, Virginia . . . and that's something I've never done before either. I had hoped you would be willing to put all of what's happened behind us and start over again—the right way this time. However, if you're not . . . I guess there's no point in my continuing. I was wrong, and I admit it. But I am not going to beg you."

Virginia stared through the blur of her tears at her hands, which were knotted together on her lap. Slade sounded so sincere. She wanted to believe him—oh, God, how she wanted to believe him. But when she had thought he was being sincere before, her heart had been broken. His confession had taken her by surprise and she had not been emotionally prepared for it. She had, in fact, been prepared to humble herself before him. Now though, it seemed too easy. The skeptical side of her said it was nothing but a ploy, another way to hurt her further for something she had not done.

But what if it isn't a ploy? a rational voice deep inside her asked. What if he is indeed sincere? You have acknowledged that you love him. Are you willing to risk losing him forever just because of your stubborn pride, your inability to forget the past? If you are willing to do that, perhaps you do not love him as much as you claim.

She slowly raised her head, and there was a pensive shimmer in the shadow of her eyes as she looked at him. "I *want* to put all of what's happened behind us. I *want* to believe you . . . but how can I when you've done nothing but lie to me?" Slade started to answer, but Virginia stopped him. "No, please, let me finish." She set her chin in a stubborn line, determined to have her say. "I think I fell in love with you the first time I saw you . . . and I still love you. But you have come back into my life after cruelly walking out on me once. I have to wonder what's to stop you from doing it again? I love you, Slade, but that doesn't mean I trust you — and love without trust leaves me feeling cold and empty." She shook her head in dismay and pressed her hands against her throbbing temples. "So many questions and doubts keep running through my mind. I can't even think rationally anymore."

His expression was tight with strain. "Maybe I can answer some of your questions."

Virginia's face glowed with uncertainty. "Maybe you can . . . If you will answer them truthfully," she added.

"I'm certainly willing to try," he said, flinching inwardly at being called a liar, though he knew that as far as Virginia was concerned, he deserved every despicable name she could think of to call him.

Taking a deep breath of determination, she squared her shoulders and lifted her head proudly, staunchly steeling herself against the love she felt for this man. But, in spite of all her bravado, her voice trembled when she asked, "Tell me, do you still believe I was my father's cohort when he attacked you and left you to die?"

"No."

An emotional dam broke inside her with his simple but straightforward answer. "Then why in Heaven's name did you believe it before? You had no reason to think I would do something like that! And you had no right to treat me the way you did. Even a . . . criminal is given an opportunity to defend himself!" Virginia turned her gaze away as tears of frustration abruptly filled her eyes.

Slade gently grasped her chin and urged her to look at him. His voice was low and strained. "You say I had no reason, but I thought I did. A minute ago, you mentioned something about trust. Did you ever stop to consider that I might have had no reason to trust anyone outside of my family?" He tilted his head slightly as a possible way to explain his actions occurred to him. "Do you remember telling me your observations about that woman you used to work for occasionally?"

Virginia nodded wretchedly. "Yes . . . that was Mrs. Matthews."

He regarded her with a speculative gaze. "I can't pretend to know the workings of a human mind, but it seems reasonable to assume a person's past experiences sometimes affect that person's actions in the future. You saw what Mrs. Matthews's life had become, and you began to fear that all men were like Mr. Matthews, or your father. I remember once—I guess I was about four—I burned my hand on the fireplace, and months later, each time I walked by it, I was afraid it would burn me again . . ."

"Are you saying you were *burned* once when you placed misguided trust in someone?"

The muscles in his jaw tensed and his eyes clouded with memory. "Yes, I suppose you could put it that way."

She clutched his hand tightly. "Then tell me about it, Slade. Help me to understand why you walked out on me."

He shrugged and flashed a reluctant grin. "It's a long story."

A glimmer of hope brimmed in her eyes. Suddenly,

328

a future with Slade did not seem as impossible as it had a few moments earlier. A ghost of a smile brushed her lips as she attempted a touch of levity. "The last time I looked at my social calendar, there were no plans penciled in." Then she groaned and shook her head. "I'm sorry, Slade. That was a pitiful attempt at humor and this is not the time for it. Please . . . tell me what happened to you."

The rich timbre of Slade's voice slowly cut through her agonizing doubts and the thousands of questions that had been tormenting her for so long as he told her about his past. He explained everything, from the trouble he had gotten into as a young man, to that fateful day he had ridden into her camp seeking a cup of coffee. He also told her how he had reached the conclusion that she and her father had intended to rob him from the very beginning, how miserable the past few months had been, how he had not been able to put her from his mind, and how he had felt when he thought she had been murdered by Apaches.

When he finished, tears were streaming down Virginia's face, but they were happy tears, because as he related his life's story, she understood. And with that understanding, she knew she could forgive and forget. Slade was her husband, a man she loved, a man with whom she could spend the rest of her life, a man whom she could trust with all her heart and soul.

Trembling, Virginia reached out and gently touched his face. "Oh, Slade, if only you had told me all of this at the beginning, so much heartbreak would have been—" Her voice broke. "But then, I suppose you couldn't have."

It was as though as great weight had been lifted from his shoulders, and he pressed her hand against his lips and tenderly kissed it. "No, I never intended to tell anyone how I feel about John Carlisle . . . not even you. But I couldn't stand by and allow you to walk out of my life without doing something."

Not able to stand it any longer, Virginia threw her arms around Slade's neck and cradled his head against her breasts. His arm tightened around her so tightly, she thought her ribs would break. But she did not care. She was in the arms of the man she loved more than life itself. Then, suddenly, his lips were on hers and she could feel herself responding with wild passion, her own mouth parting to welcome him eagerly as he plunged his tongue into the honeyed recesses of her mouth. A thrill shot through her entire body — a familiar sensation that Slade had produced within her before — and it licked through her veins like wildfire, igniting her with feverish desire and blazing out of control. At that moment, she wanted nothing other than to remain in his arms, with their lips locked together in blissful ecstasy until they could divest themselves of their clothing and join as one. But surprisingly, Slade, breathing rapidly, pulled from their embrace.

He ran his hand caressingly over her jaw and cheek, then through her hair, and his eyes shining with adoration as he seemingly memorized each and every detail of her lovely features. Swinging his head from side to side, he spoke, his voice rasping with huskiness. "No, Virginia. I want you — God only knows how much I want you — but we can't, not right now."

"Oh, yes, your . . . wound," she said, swallowing hard with disappointment.

He took a deep, steadying breath. "No, sweetheart, my shoulder has nothing to do with it. I want you so much, and tonight, when I am lying here, burning with desire, I'm sure I will regret this decision. But I'm not going to make love to you until we can do it right."

She managed a timid smile. "You mean when we made love, we did it wrong?" Then she giggled impishly. "Ooh! Do you mean it is going to be even better?"

Slade grinned, and resisting the urge to crush her in his arm, he kissed the tip of her nose instead. "You are twisting my meaning. I was referring to a way to prevent you from having doubts about my sincerity."

Virginia grew serious. "I have no doubts now."

"No, perhaps not now, but you may tomorrow and I don't want to take any unnecessary chances where you are concerned. A while ago, you said you loved me, but you didn't trust me. Well, I intend to earn your trust. Except for the love we share, I want us to wipe the slate clean and start all over. I want to court you properly . . . then, I intend to ask you to become my wife."

"B—But, I am already your wife."

"Maybe so, but that farce in Barkersville was no wedding ceremony, not the kind that should bind a man and woman together. I want us to get married again, and the next time we will do it right."

Her heart soared with joy such as she had never known. "I—I'm deeply touched, my love. I—I never dreamed I would ever be this happy," she murmured, reaching out to embrace him again.

Slade caught her hand. "No, we mustn't," he said determinedly, his jaw flexing. "I am a man, sweetheart, and you are a beautiful, desirable woman. If a kiss or an embrace lasted a little too long . . . and if I ever put my hands on your body . . ." Shaking his head, he gave a long sigh. "I might forget all of my good intentions." Then he chuckled. "Might, hell! I know I would! I'd have your clothes off so fast it would make your head spin."

"Oh, Slade, be serious!" Averting her eyes, Virginia flushed, in part from embarrassment, but a shiver of delight ran through her at the mere thought of Slade's making love to her.

He replied solemnly, "Sweetheart, I've never been so serious in my life." He did not look forward to the long, unfulfilled days and weeks that loomed ahead, but still, it was something he felt he had to do. His tight expression relaxed into a smile. "Now, sweetheart, if you will get me a pair of trousers and help me up . . ." Slade started to swing his legs off the bed, but Virginia stopped him.

"What do you think you are doing?" she demanded.

"I'm getting out of bed."

Barring his way, she stood quickly with arms akimbo. "Oh no, you're not! You are not going anywhere! You are going to stay right here!"

Slade glanced about at the cramped quarters. "But I can't take your bed." He admitted rather sheepishly, "Even if I slept on the floor, I'd probably be in bed with you before morning, so I don't think I should even stay in the wagon with you."

"Hank gave me strict orders to keep you in bed and that is exactly what I intend to do!" She gave an indifferent wave of her hand. "I'll sleep outside on a bedroll."

"Oh no, you won't! I'm not about to let you sleep outside on the ground while I'm in here on this soft bed." He started to rise again, but Virginia placed her hand against his chest.

"Then I will ask Dovie if I can share her wagon."

His brow furrowed questioningly. "Wouldn't Hank have something to say about that?"

"Why should he?"

"Aren't they married?"

"Dovie and Hank? No, they're not married. Hank works for her."

"I see." Then he looked at her quizzically. "I thought Hank was in charge of this small wagon train."

"No, Dovie is . . ." Virginia caught herself before she said anything further.

Turning suddenly to prevent Slade from seeing her expression, Virginia nervously moistened her lips. How was she going to explain Dovie and her girls to Slade without his getting the wrong idea? And when she told him about Dovie, she would also have to tell him how she had traveled across the country disguised as a boy. Slade was a very smart, observant man. More than likely he would ask when and where she had joined the caravan, and if she told him the truth, how long would it take for him to connect "Jimmy" with that near brawl in George's saloon? Then, after learning she had deliberately fooled those people at Fort Grant, how long would it take for him to start having doubts about her honesty again? Somehow, Slade had convinced himself she had been innocent of those terrible accusations he had made against her. But the truth could raise his suspicions all over again. What was she to do?

The truth, Virginia, you must tell him the truth. You cannot build a firm foundation on lies. He will understand. You have done nothing wrong. You meant no malice whatsoever when you misled those people.

Swallowing hard, she turned back to face him. Her voice was shakier than she would have liked as she slowly began, "Slade, there is something you should know about Dovie—" Then, she gave a startled cry and jumped backward as the camel ran its head through the rear flaps and snorted ferociously.

333

Everything seemed to happen simultaneously.

Slade twisted his head around at the strange noise and his eyes widened in surprise. "What in the hell is that?"

Virginia slapped her hand against her chest and took several deep breaths before she could find her voice. "Darn it, Mule, you scared me half to death!" She stepped forward, waving her hands to shoo him away from the wagon.

Slade bellowed. "Mule, hell! That's a camel!" His voice betrayed his astonishment. Seeing Virginia move toward the ugly beast, he shouted a warning as he struggled to get off the bed in an attempt to protect her. "Don't get too close; he might bite you!" He was aware that the cavalry had at one time tried to use camels for military purposes in the deserts of Arizona. But when it proved to be an unsuccessful venture, the army had turned them loose. The few that remained roamed wild over the countryside, and most of them had become extremely mean.

The moment Slade tried to stand, his knees buckled, for he was still weak from loss of blood. If Virginia had not quickly swung his arm over her shoulders and grabbed him around the waist, he would have slumped to the floor of the wagon.

Virginia's hand trembled as she pulled the sheet up on Slade's chest after helping him back to bed and checking to see if the near fall had made his shoulder start bleeding. She had been so frightened, she was positive her face would be as ashen as Slade's, though for an entirely different reason.

"You could have ripped your shoulder wide open. Please, Slade, promise you won't try to get up again until Hank says you can."

It was obvious he was in deep pain as he muttered

through clenched teeth, "I was afraid he would attack you. I—I had to do something."

"Bless your heart, I was in no danger," she said, smoothing his hair from his brow. "Mule . . . the camel belongs to someone in the wagon train. And the silly thing has more or less adopted me. Ever time we make camp, he follows me around like a little lost puppy."

Slade tried to laugh, but his voice was wracked with pain. "That's some 'puppy.' An animal that size has to weigh at least a ton."

Virginia's heart wrenched at how Slade attempted to hide his pain. She reached for the laudanum and poured a spoonful. "Here, take this and it will ease you."

"What is it, laudanum?" He shook his head. "No . . . I'll be all right in . . . a few . . . minutes."

"Now, Slade, please don't be stubborn. Take this. It will help ease you and allow you to sleep."

He managed a feeble grin. "That medicine makes me see strange things."

She jutted her chin determinedly. "Maybe so, but it is better to have bad dreams than to be miserable. If you want to get well, you have to have your rest. Now, if you refuse to take it willingly, I'll pour it down your throat. If you think I won't, you are wrong!"

He threw her a sour look. "Has anyone ever told you that you are a hardheaded, stubborn female?"

"Yes, you just did." She tilted his head forward and put the spoon to his lips. "Now take this."

He swallowed, grimacing at the taste, and settled back down on the pillow. "I'll probably dream I'm being attacked by a thousand camels," he grumbled, shaking his head. "You have no idea what ran through my mind when I saw that camel. I guess I thought he

335

was trying to climb into the wagon. After all, you just don't expect to see something like that . . . not here in the middle of Arizona."

Noting with relief that Slade's pain was easing, she chuckled and said, "I know. That's what I thought when I first saw him."

"Will you hold my hand and sit with me for awhile?" he asked, his speech starting to slur.

She took his hand and pressed it to her lips. "I'll be right here when you wake. A thousand camels couldn't drive me away."

Closing his eyes, he muttered dazedly, "Camels . . . camels. There's even a mountain near . . . Phoenix shaped like one."

Virginia smiled lovingly when he drifted into a deep sleep. Still holding his hand tightly, she laid her head across his chest and closed her eyes.

Chapter Twenty-three

Dark, angry clouds hung low over the surrounding mountains, partially obscuring the towering peaks. Jagged streaks of lightning stabbed across the distant sky and the ensuing thunder rolled across the arid valley floor in undulating waves.

Virginia stood outside the wagon holding a wicker basket filled with freshly laundered clothes while she stared at the majestic sky with awe.

When she had first come to this western land, she had detested it, the jagged mountains, the barren sand and rocky terrain, the overwhelming spaces, which at times appeared to stretch into infinity. But now it seemed she had found a tranquil serenity here, a peacefulness like none she had ever known. But then, she supposed her growing fondness for this land could stem from her own personal happiness. She and Slade had been back together for two days now — two of the most wonderful days she had ever lived.

The only dark cloud that loomed over her horizon was the fact that she had not had an opportunity to tell Slade about what had happened during the past few months. It was not that she had been deliberately withholding the information; it just seemed as if she could

337

never find the right moment to tell him.

Virginia shook her head pensively. That was not true. She could have made an opportunity, but the simple fact of the matter was she was reluctant to tell him. Not because she was guilty of any wrongdoing; instead, the past two days had been so near perfect — aside from Slade's being wounded — she did not want anything to blemish the memory of this enchanted time. If only that blasted camel had not interrupted her when she had had her courage built up, it would have been over and done with instead of hanging over her like a heavy weight. And now, she had no other choice. When Hank had changed Slade's bandage earlier that morning, he had informed Slade he could sit up for awhile, and if he felt strong enough later that afternoon, he could even walk around a bit. Slade had to be told or he would soon see for himself that Dovie and her girls were prostitutes. And once he learned that, he would have to be told about her boyish disguise.

"Does it look like rain?" Slade asked from inside the wagon. He was lying on his stomach with his head propped on his hand, watching the many different expressions flitting across Virginia's face as she stared at the sky.

Pulled from her reverie, she shook her head. "Only in the mountains." She glanced up as a huge white thundercloud scudded overhead. "All of the clouds here in the valley are as white and fluffy as freshly picked cotton."

Slade's gaze devoured her beauty. How any woman could look so lovely wearing a simple blue calico dress was beyond him. But then, he had never seen her not looking beautiful, and he doubted he ever would. He grinned at his thoughts, suddenly grateful that no one could hear them. He was behaving like a love-struck

338

young kid, and he wouldn't have had it any other way.

"Where's your friend?" he asked, craning his neck in an attempt to see around the corner of the wagon.

"My friend?"

"Your camel. He's usually here by this time of the afternoon, trying to mooch a lump or two of sugar." Although he did not particularly like the meddlesome beast, he was impressed by how easily Virginia handled him. From what he had heard about camels, they were usually cantankerous and mean, and balked more often than mules. That was why the army's venture with them had failed; the soldiers simply could not manage them.

"Mule is staked out with the horses. And don't worry, if you are leading up to inquiring about Blue, I checked on him before I took the clothes off the line," she explained, referring to the makeshift clothesline Hank had erected between two of the other wagons.

She stepped closer to the wagon. "By the way, Slade, since you mentioned Mule, I have been meaning to ask you something. The other day when I gave you that dose of laudanum after Mule scared us half to death, just as you were going to sleep, you said something about a mountain near Phoenix shaped like a camel. Is it really there, or was it merely the effects of the medicine talking?"

"No, it wasn't the medicine. There really is a mountain shaped like a camel lying down. In fact, it's even called Camelback Mountain." He added rather dryly, "It looks just like Mule does when he parks his stinking carcass here behind the wagon."

Thoroughly amazed, she shook her head in wonder. "Well, my goodness, who would have thought it. Can you see the mountain from Phoenix?"

"Yes, I think so, and it's quite possible that we'll pass close by it."

"If not, will you take me to where I can see it?"

"Sure . . . that is, if you agree to leave Mule at home. We can't have him thinking it's his girlfriend."

She laughed infectiously.

Slade appreciated her sense of humor. "Seriously though, this land is a mighty strange place. It's beautiful too." He peered at her intently. "Have you ever seen the desert floor a day after it rained?"

"No." Her eyes widened to give added emphasis. "I haven't seen a drop of rain for so long now, at times I wonder if I would know what it looked like."

He chuckled, fully understanding what she meant. "Seeing the desert after a rain is well worth waiting for. Dormant seeds burst to life overnight and by the next day, the entire land looks like it had been carpeted with multicolored flowers and green plants."

Virginia set the basket on the ground, propped her arms on the tailgate, and sighed wistfully. *"Green!* What I wouldn't give to see something green! That's what I miss most about East Texas. Regardless of the time of year, there was always something green — something alive. I've even had dreams about tall pine trees, their fragrant scent, and how the wind whispers through them late at night."

Slade pretended indignation as he peered outside.

"That's strange. I could have sworn those cottonwoods were trees. And I guess I'm getting color-blind, because I thought their leaves were green . . . Guess they must be purple."

Virginia picked up a towel and threw it at him. "You know what I meant," she playfully chided.

"If you want trees, just wait until we reach the next valley," he boasted. "There is a forest of trees . . . as far as the eye can see."

"Really?" she asked excitedly, then a puzzled frown creased her brow. "I thought the area over there was even more of a desert than this, and with much less vegetation." She gave a wave of her hand.

"It is. "

"Then how can there be a forest in the desert?" she asked, placing her hands on her hips. "You really must think I am a greenhorn."

"They are Arizona trees."

She flashed a doubtful smile. "I've never heard of an Arizona tree." Seeing a grin twitch at his lips, she tilted her head and asked, "Slade, are you teasing me?"

He burst out laughing. "Arizona trees are really saguaro cactus. They are the ones that sometimes reach sixty feet in height and have arms coming out of them."

She mused aloud, "I don't think I have ever seen one of those before. Or if I did, I didn't know its proper name."

"No, I doubt you have. I think I read somewhere once that the only place they grow in the world is in that desert. And, if you are interested, I'll tell you the reason they are called Arizona trees. There is a local legend that God made a saguaro, intending it for a tree, but he had never seen one before so he did not have the right pattern."

Teasing, she gave an awed whistle. "My goodness! I had no idea you knew so much."

Completely caught up in the playful mood, he boasted haughtily, "Why, of course I do. I know just about everything. All you have to do is ask me and I'll tell you." His expression became deadly serious. "But just in case there is something I don't know—now mind you, I said *just in case*—you can ask one of my relatives and he will tell you the answer."

"Why, you braggart!"

He gestured grandly. "Like I always say, if you've got it, spread it around! And sweetheart, I am full of it!"

"You'll get no argument out of me over that!"

Suddenly, Slade winced, but obviously still in a playful mood, he began hollering, "Ouch! Ouch! Ouch! I have a pain!"

"Where?" she asked doubtfully.

"Right here." He pointed to his lips. "It needs to be kissed." If anyone had told him he would actually enjoy tomfoolery such as this with a woman, he would not have believed it. But somehow it was different with Virginia. Not only was she beautiful and loving, but she had other qualities most young women her age did not possess. Maybe that was why he had fallen in love with her.

Chuckling heartily, Virginia climbed into the wagon, and Slade, anticipating her, rolled over on his back and clutched her in a tight embrace the moment she knelt by his bedside. Then his lips touched her mouth, pliantly, almost tentatively. He seemed to seek with infinite patience, gradually pressing her lips apart, and his tongue began its dancing possession of her mouth. He seemed to kiss her forever, tasting and discovering her lips as though for the very first time.

Her senses reeled under his loving assault, spinning her into a wild vortex of pleasure. At last his mouth left hers to cover her cheeks and neck with faint kisses, and his hot breath feathered against her skin.

Slade knew he was playing with fire. Each time he took her in his arms it became more and more difficult to release her. How he yearned to feel her firm breasts beneath his hands, to ply her nipples with his tongue until they became taut with desire, to stroke her velvety skin until it tingled with passion. Drawing air between his teeth, he remembered the euphoric sensation of thrusting his sword into her hot, tight sheath, and he trembled at the memory. It was as though his body had suddenly taken control of his mind. It would be so easy to push aside the vow of abstinence he had made, and from the way Virginia responded to his embraces and kisses, he could tell she wanted him as badly as he wanted her. Groaning inwardly, he tensed. Their love was still so fragile, he did not want to gamble a few minutes of pleasure against a lifetime of togetherness. He had to stop this lovemaking now, while he still possessed a glimmer of willpower.

"I love you," he whispered hoarsely in her ear. "And do you know what else?"

"No, what?" she murmured, the sound much like that of a cat purring its contentment.

With all of the sincerity he could muster, he whispered, "I would love you even more if you'd get my boots."

Her warm glow of passion was shattered by his request. It was as if he had doused her with cold water. "Slade!" she cried, pulling from his arms. "That was cruel! You did that deliberately."

"No," he answered slowly, shaking his head. "That, sweetheart, was either bravery or complete stupidity, and from the way I am aching inside, I'm more inclined to opt for the latter." He swatted her playfully on her bottom. "Now, get my boots for me. And I still think you ought to be staked out on an anthill for hiding them from me!"

"Now you know that was the only way we could make you stay in bed," she retorted with a haughty toss of her head.

"Maybe so, but you didn't have to keep my pants too."

"You have trousers on." She allowed her gaze to travel over his length, openly admiring how snugly the blue denim fit him, and after their aborted lovemaking, how the evidence of his desire strained against the fabric.

"Yes, but only since this morning when Hank said I

could sit up," he commented tersely. Then his expression stilled and grew even more serious. "Sweetheart, if I don't get out of this wagon and breathe some fresh air, I will lose what little sanity I have left."

She sighed. "All right, I'll get your boots . . . but first I want to talk to you about something." Whether she liked it or not, he would have to be told about her life as "Jimmy."

He shook his head adamantly. "No, we have been talking, and if this is another one of your little delaying tactics, it won't work." An irritated tone had crept into his voice. "I have been patient, I haven't complained, I have followed yours and Hank's instructions to the letter. He said there was no reason why I couldn't walk around for awhile this afternoon. Now I want my boots!"

From his tone, Virginia knew he would not stand for any more excuses. "All right, I'll go over to Dovie's wagon and get them . . . Then we can talk? I'm not teasing or trying to stall. There is something important you should know."

"That will be fine with me, as long as we do it outside this damned wagon!" He glanced about at the close confines and shuddered.

As Virginia returned from Dovie's wagon, she could see a large cloud of dust rising in the distance and could hear a dull, roaring sound. Not knowing what it was, she hurried to her wagon.

"Slade, do you hear that roaring noise?" she asked, climbing inside. "And there is also a huge cloud of dust coming from the northwest. Do you think it is a dust storm?" Her brow creased with worry. She had heard dreadful stories about such storms and how much damage they could inflict on people and on livestock.

He quickly put her fears to rest as she helped him put on his boots. "No, it isn't a dust storm, it's wagons.

If you listen closely, you can hear the jingle of the riggings along with the roar of the wheels." He nodded affirmatively and grinned. "That's good. Now maybe we can find out what has been going on with the Apaches." Standing somewhat unsteadily, he took a few hesitant steps to test his strength.

Virginia's features were grim as he stepped around her and started for the rear of the wagon. "No, wait, Slade. You promised we could talk."

He waved aside her protests. "It'll keep, sweetheart. First, I want to hear what those people have to say. Since they are coming this way instead of over the mountains, they just about have to be teamsters and they always seem to have inside information about the Indians." Then he frowned when he heard women's pealing laughter and excited squeals. "What in the world . . . ?" He knew the noise could not be coming from the other wagons; they were still too far away.

Tightly holding onto the corner of the wagon for added support, he stepped down and immediately his gaze jerked toward the main section of the camp.

Virginia's heart seemed to flip over inside her chest when she saw a scowl crease his brow. Hurrying after him, she stopped short when she saw Dovie and her girls through Slade's eyes.

They all stood in a single line like birds perching on a fence, watching as the teamsters approached. From their manner of dress, it was plain to see what they were. Dovie was wearing her usual vivid pink garb; Paris wore only a pair of lacy black drawers and a matching corset, with a red boa flung around her shoulders; Egypt's working costume was a filmy yellow sari; Rome's vestment was a sheer, pale blue toga; China Doll was attired in a brocade silk kimono; Mexico wore a wide, flaring skirt with a matching bolero jacket—no blouse; and 'Frisco's raiment was a golden-colored gown that did little to conceal her body.

"Good God Almighty!" Slade swore underneath his breath. It suddenly occurred to him why Hank and Dovie were the only other people he had seen from the other wagons, why few men's and no children's voices had been heard, and why Virginia had skillfully avoided answering many of the questions he had asked. This was a traveling *whorehouse!*

His face was etched with vivid rage as he whirled about to glare at Virginia. He clenched his hands — even though one was still tightly bound — into white-knuckled fists.

Virginia, her ebony eyes stricken with horror at his furious demeanor, offered in a small, choked voice, "T— This is w — what I wanted to t — talk to you about." Panic was rioting within her.

"You damn sure did — you suddenly decided to tell me the minute you knew I'd walk outside and see those . . . those whores!" he accused with raw, impotent fury, then glared contemptuously at the expression of stunned disbelief that quickly flashed over Virginia's face.

Virginia's breath burned in her throat when her eyes met his smoldering gaze. "No!" she chokingly protested. "I tried to tell you before that! Remember the other day when Mule stuck his . . . ?" But her protests went unheeded. Instead, Slade was riveted with horrified fascination to the spectacle that was beginning to unfold.

The men started jumping down from their wagons after pulling them to a halt. Their boisterous male laughter mixed with women's shrill giggles. Then there was a flurry as the women-starved men raced to be the first to grab a woman. One huge, burly bear of a man came up empty-handed, then after looking around frantically, he spied Virginia standing alongside Slade.

His mouth split into a wide grin and he spread his arms grandly as he ran toward her.

"Here I am, sugarcakes! Big Jake's gonna make you smile!"

It was as if Virginia had frozen to that very spot. She could not speak, nor could she move, as he lumbered toward her with an awkward gait.

Just before the man reached her, Slade stepped between them and met the man's face with his tightly clenched fist. Slade, weak and unsteady on his feet, staggered from the force of the jarring blow. The teamster, however, not expecting such an unwelcome greeting, went sprawling backward in a powdery cloud of dust. He sat there for a moment, stunned. Cupping his whiskered jaw, he looked up at Slade, then shook his head as if to clear it.

"You mangy son of a bitch! *Sugarcakes* happens to be with me!" Slade shouted angrily, roughly yanking Virginia to his side.

Her eyes widened in alarm and she cringed inwardly as his intonation. Why hadn't she made a clean breast of the past few months? This would not be happening if she had not been such a silly fool.

The man made a low, growling noise in his throat and started to rise. He had lost out being first with the other women, but he would rot in hell before he lost out on this pretty little bitch. Murder gleamed from his eyes. Virginia saw it and stepped in front of Slade to bar the man's way, but Slade pushed her aside. She fell to the ground.

"No, mister, please, don't hit him!" she cried. "He's been badly injured."

The man hesitated. "Who?" he asked, rubbing his jaw again. "Him or me?"

"Shut up, Virginia!" Slade ordered bitterly as he hunched his body forward slightly, assuming a warrior's stance.

Ignoring him, she turned imploring eyes toward the man and pleaded for leniency. "It's his shoulder, He took an Apache's bullet and nearly bled to death. Please don't hit him! He's my husband!"

The man stopped in his tracks. "Hell-fire, why didn't you jest say so in the first place? Don't want to mess with no married woman . . . my ma was one." He gestured toward the other women. "Dallying with one o' them and dallying with a man's wife is two different thangs," he drawled. "Ain't hankerin' to git my head blowed off . . . or knocked off, neither, for that matter." He swung his lower jaw from side to side, checking to see if it was still hinged properly. Then he turned and marched jauntily toward one of the wagons where a short line had formed, already rocking with a carnal rhythm.

Breathing hard, Slade turned and stared at Virginia, his jaws flexing angrily. Then, compressing his lips into a grim white line, he spun unsteadily on his foot and stalked toward where the horses were staked.

Having the sensation of reliving a terrible nightmare, Virginia scrambled to her feet and ran after him. She tried to grab his arm, but he flung her hand aside. "No, Slade, I can explain. Please . . . just listen to me . . ."

"I don't want to hear anything you have to say," was his terse reply as he unfastened Blue's tether and started leading him to the wagon where his gear was stored.

Unbeknownst to Virginia, tears streamed down her face. "Slade, please don't let your stubborn pride do this to us again. That's what I was trying to tell you earlier. I was going to explain about Dovie and her g— girls . . . and how I came to be traveling with them, honestly I was."

He stopped abruptly and nodded in the direction of the wagons. "When? In between customers?" Just the thought of her being in another man's arms made his blood run cold.

Virginia gasped, stricken with renewed horror, as she realized what he was thinking. "No, Slade . . . I'm not one of Dovie's girls! I never have been either!"

He stopped her with a raised hand. "I don't want to hear your lies!" The angry retort hardened his features. "The way I see it, if you were not a member of their little group, you would have told me about them sooner. Not that it would make much difference — a decent woman would never travel with a bunch of whores!"

"But that is what I've been trying to tell you . . ."

"Stop lying! If you'd had an explanation, it damn sure wouldn't have taken two days for you to get around to it!" The knowledge of what she was twisted and turned inside him.

Virginia watched miserably as he climbed into the wagon to get his saddlebags and guns. She had to reason with him, and he had to understand. She could not lose him again. "You're not being fair . . ."

He bristled with indignation as he grabbed hold of the wagon's edge for support and lowered himself to the ground. "*I'm* not being fair? Lady, you don't know the meaning of the word!" His face was a glowering mask of rage as he dragged his hand through his hair. Suddenly, he felt drained, lifeless, hollow. He loved her so much and he had thought she loved him. He had been living in a fool's paradise. But one thing was certain — it would never happen to him again.

She grabbed his arm, frantic to make one last, desperate attempt to force him to listen to reason. "Are you angry because I'm traveling with Dovie, or are you angry because you think I'm one of her girls?"

349

"Sweetheart, you don't have to draw a picture for me. I *know* what you are . . . and that man recognized you for what you are too." His lips curled with disgust. "Hell, if the truth were known, he was probably one of your regular customers." He knew his words were cruel, but he wanted to hurt her as badly as she had hurt him. He had loved her so much—no, God help him, he *still* loved her.

Complete dismay washed over her as she realized the intensity of his contempt. She could only stand there and watch helplessly as Slade struggled with his saddle. This was her fault. She did not blame him for being so angry. If the situation had been reversed, she would have been furious too. She knew he did not mean his ugly accusations. He was merely lashing out because, deep inside, he was hurting so badly. If she could only make him listen to reason. . . . As he was about to climb on his horse, she touched his back. "Slade, please, I *can* explain."

He tensed. "As far as I'm concerned, there's no explanation possible." Then slowly turning his head, he looked back over his shoulder at her and muttered contemptuously, "I'm curious, Virginia. Tell me, how long did you wait before you took my advice?"

"A—Advice?" A dark shadow of misery crossed her face. She knew what he was about to say.

"Yes, remember? I suggested that you join a group of women like this."

Virginia dropped her hand from his back as though she had been burned. She squared her shoulders and gave a proud toss of her head. Then, jutting her chin, she muttered bitterly, "Go to hell, Slade!"

He tipped his hat, and his blue eyes seemed as cold as sharply honed steel. "Thanks to you, I'm already there."

Chapter Twenty-four

Hank hunched his shoulders against the driving force of the wind and hurried toward Virginia's dark wagon. Slipping his kerchief from his mouth, he shouted above the gusting roar, "Little girl, are you in there?"

Not sure if he had heard a muffled sob, he untied the flaps and climbed into the wagon. Taking a match from his pocket, he raked his thumbnail across the head, removed the globe from the lamp, and lit it. One quick glance confirmed his suspicions; Virginia was alone, and she was obviously in distress. Where's Slade?" he asked, his tone cautious.

"He's gone, Hank . . . He's gone," she muttered wretchedly. She sat huddled on the stool, head bowed, arms crossed over her breasts.

Muttering a curse, he sat down on the bed across from her. Lines of contemplation deepened along his brows and under his eyes. There was a long, cold stretch of silence, then he cleared his throat and began softly. "Do you want to talk about it?"

"N—No . . . yes . . . no." She spoke in a low whisper, twisting her hands in her lap, still keeping her head bowed. "I just want to be left alone."

By her tone, he doubted it was so. "Now, little girl, you know I can't do that. You said Slade's gone . . . Do you know where?"

"No. After the teamsters arrived, he just . . . rode off." She gestured helplessly.

"Was he angry?" Even as Hank asked it, he knew it was a ridiculous question.

"Angry?" She laughed bitterly. "No, I don't think I could call it angry. I doubt that word would do justice to how he felt."

Hank's jaw tightened. That low-down bastard had run off and broken the little girl's heart again! He had suspected as much when he had come back from hunting and had found the teamsters being entertaind by Dovie and her girls, Slade's horse missing from the other horses, and Virginia's wagon dark and deserted looking. Cursing himself for being a sentimental fool, Hank nonetheless felt a twinge of regret for his part in Virginia's distress. He should have let the son of a bitch bleed to death.

He knew if she kept her misery bottled up inside, it would only make her feel worse, and if he could get her to talk, it might help.

"Have you had any supper yet?"

"No, I'm not hungry."

"I noticed someone made a fresh pot of coffee. Would you like a cup?"

Tears suddenly welled in Virginia's eyes, a blinding, stinging heat brought on by Hank's innocently mentioning coffee. Waves of fresh pain and wretchedness crashed against her. How long would simple words like that be a constant reminder of what she had lost?

A sob rose in her throat and lodged there as she struggled to regain control of her battered emotions.

Finally, she murmured in a pathetic voice, "Hank, please, I would rather be alone right now. I'm really very tired . . . and I have so much to think about."

Stubbornly, Hank shook his head. He was not about to leave her like this. He had been with Dovie long enough to know how a woman's mind worked. Whenever men had painful hurt deep inside, they preferred to crawl off and be alone with their misery. Regardless of what women thought, if the hurt was bad enough, men did cry, but their pride wouldn't allow anyone else to see their vulnerability. However, women were different. His experiences with Dovie's girls had taught him that females occasionally needed a strong shoulder to cry on and a sympathetic ear to listen to their troubles. But it was even more than that. He had grown so fond of Virginia, it was upsetting to see her this way.

"Why don't you just go ahead and cry?" he suggested kindly. "Get it out of your system. It usually makes women feel a lot better."

Her lips and chin quivered. "I've tried to, but I can't—at least, not the sort of tears you are talking about. The only thing that would help would be the ability to turn back the clock to yesterday. A mere twenty-four hours might have made all the difference in the world," she added sadly.

Hank's eyes were hooded. "I'm not sure I understand. Why would a day make a difference?" That's the way, Hank, he told himself. Take it slow and easy, and get her to talking. If you can ever get her started good, she'll be all right. But be careful and don't let any of your questions sound accusing.

"Because I . . . I never told Slade about Dovie . . . and when those teamsters came—" Her voice broke. "I suppose he thought I was one of her girls. If only I had told him the entire story—not only about Dovie, but how I pretended to be a boy—maybe he would have understood." She let out a long, audible sigh. "It wasn't like before, Hank. I saw the betrayed look in his eyes. He left here hurting . . . hurting badly. I . . . broke his heart!"

Unconsciously, his brow furrowed. Now it was beginning to make sense. But why hadn't she told Slade earlier? That was foolish. No wonder he got mad. Those teamsters were a rowdy bunch and it wasn't likely they came politely into camp with their hair slicked down, holding their hats in their hands, like they were attending Sunday school. They probably drove in like half-crazed wild men. And with Slade not knowing about the girls, it was easy to see why he had become riled. If he had been in Slade's boots, more than likely he would have felt the same way. He shook his head. Poor little girl. It seemed like with every step she took toward happiness, something happened to yank her backward.

"Well, you stop fretting," Hank drawled. "He's probably sitting out there a few miles from camp thinking about what you told him and once he gets—"

Her face paled at his suggestion, and she shook her head forlornly. "No, Hank, you don't understand. He never gave me a chance to explain." Then she breathed a deep, shuddering sigh. "That's not true. I had two days in which to tell him, but I kept stalling and stalling . . . . It's all my fault. If only I had told him sooner, none of this would have happened." Biting her bottom lip, she looked away.

"So he rode off still thinking you were one of Dovie's girls?" Now he understood completely.

All she could manage to do was bob her head.

Taking a deep breath, he stood, crammed his hat on his head, and firmly snugged it. "Well, looks like some-

354

one has to find him and make him listen to the truth. I'll see if I can find his trail . . ."

"No, Hank," she said softly, staring outside dejectedly.

"Any trail he might have left behind has long since been obliterated by the wind."

Hank knew she was right, that the dust storm had been raging for the past three hours, but it would make her feel better if he tried. "Maybe so, but the least I can do is search for a few hours. We'll be pulling out at the break of dawn. I'll look for as long as I can. If I find him, don't worry, I'll set him straight. He paused in the wagon's opening. "And, little girl, even if I don't find him tonight, when we reach Fort McDowell, I'll take time off and find him for you then. You have my word on it. If he loves you half as much as I believe he does, after he hears the truth, wild horses won't be able to keep him away from you." The beginning of a smile tipped the corners of his lips. "I believe I ought to warn you though, I do expect something for the trouble I'm going to. I want the privilege of naming the first boy." He clenched his fist to give added emphasis. "I think James Henry Slade has a good, strong sound to it — a name like that will help give the boy character."

"I hope so, Hank. I certainly hope so."

They both knew she was not referring to a child she might have sometime in the future; instead, her thoughts were on the man she loved.

The sweltering weather that had encompassed the land for months abated during the night after the wind died. When morning came, the scorching sun was covered by low-lying gray clouds that held a promise of rain and gave the desert a brief respite from the searing heat. But any beauty the land might have held had vanished. Instead of a sandy-taupe color, the desert now appeared drab gray, dotted with even grayer scraggly plants and grotesquely twisted ironwood and mesquite trees. Even the cottonwoods had lost their luster under the many layers of filmy dust. But then, that was how Virginia saw it. Hank had returned just before dawn without finding a trace of Slade's trail.

Mid-morning found wheels turning, horses straining against harnesses, as the small, white topped caravan moved northwestward, following close to the river, while the teamsters headed in the opposite direction.

As the day slowly passed, Virginia kept scanning the horizon, desperately hoping for some sign of Slade; however, she saw nothing but barren wasteland, an occasional glimpse of the shallow river, and rocky hills and mountains. By late afternoon, even the threat of rain had passed, and the land was even hotter than before, more arid, more desolate — as desolate as Virginia felt.

The next day turned into another and another until they all seemed the same. Virginia would rise in the morning, pick at the food that was placed before her, harness the horses, hitch them to the wagon, and drive the team until Hank gave the order to stop. It was the same process at night, only in reverse.

As the tiny caravan pushed onward, the travelers were plagued by a rush of mishaps. Wheels constantly broke, a horse came up lame, water was scarce, and time after time, they were delayed by what would have been minor problems at a settlement, but which proved to be major ones on the trail.

Virginia gradually began to feel they would never reach their destination. It was as if time had no meaning and they were caught in some gigantic spinning vortex, going around and around in endless circles. She tried so hard not to think about Slade, but it was useless. She would have had the same difficulty if she had tried to stop breathing. One was as necessary for life as the other. The only thing that gave her strength to continue was Hank's promise to find him. It was a hope she clung to desperately.

The sun grew hotter, the women became more weary, and the days, seemingly endless, slipped by. Hank first led the small caravan down the trail they usually traveled, but finding the water holes almost dry, he decided they should stay close to the river, even though it meant going miles out of the way. Yet once they reached the river, it was so shallow, only murky, stagnant pools could be found, if anything. The water level in the barrels ran dangerously low and the liquid became brackish and sour tasting. Everyone's patience wore thin and tempers constantly flared among the girls. It was as if a nightmarish hell existed on earth.

Hank spurred his horse down the line of wagons. He gave a shrill whistle and swung his arm in a circular motion. "All right, ladies, let's get a move on it! This is the minute we've been waiting for! I've scouted up ahead and Apache Springs is right around the next bend. It has the sweetest water in all of Arizona Territory! Let's move it!"

Not wanting her hopes raised again only to have them dashed, Virginia hesitantly flicked the reins and slowly urged the horses on. Twice before, Hank had mentioned water holes, only to find they had either dried up or turned into pools of alkali water. But as the caravan rounded a huge red clay knoll, her mouth fell open in surprise. For a moment, she thought she was seeing a mirage. Not only did Apache Springs seem to be a good water hole, it was virtually an oasis paradise, and it lay less than two hundred yards ahead.

She eagerly flicked the reins and a scant twenty minutes later she was standing at the edge of the delightfully cool, fresh water, having drunk her fill. The horses had been unhitched, watered, and were hungrily cropping on the abundant grama grass.

It was a mystery to Virginia how the oasis had come to be. It was shaped something like a huge footprint, at least fifty feet wide at its largest point. Surrounding the heel were a jumble of rocks and boulders that had somehow been thrust up from the desert floor. Or, if one had a fanciful imagination, one might say it looked as though a giant child had filled its pockets with hundreds of stones and pebbles, stacked them in the middle of a sandbox, then toppled them, letting them scatter wherever they fell. Around these boulders, an underground spring forced its way upward within the rocks, then burst through to form a waterfall. In turn, the water cascaded into the deep, heel-like depression below, then flowed out to the more shallow sole. Yet there was no outlet, and since the water was not stagnant, Virginia assumed it merely disappeared into an underground stream only to resurface again elsewhere in the desert.

Beautiful green trees, cottonwoods, willows, oaks, and sycamores, as well as plants, grapevines, and flowers bursting with brilliant color, grew densely around the sole portion of the oasis. But the density of growth only extended about thirty or forty feet from the water before the desert reclaimed the land. It truly looked like a magical place.

As soon as Virginia had finished with the horses,

she had hurried to the water's edge, and now she re-moved her shoes and stockings, then, raising her skirts to her knees, she waded into the water. It was sheer heaven! Every so often, she wiggled her toes in the sandy bottom, which forced the mud up between them. It was something a lady would never think of doing, but these were not normal circumstances and at that moment, she was no lady—she was a child again!

Dovie and her girls, wearing only their camisoles and drawers, squealed with giggling laughter as they raced by Virginia and jumped into the water. Soon they were swimming, splashing, and dunking each other in the deeper area of the pool. When the men finished with their immediate chores, they also took a revitalizing dip, although they only stripped to their trousers.

A short time later, Hank waded over to where Virginia was now sitting with her feet dangling in the water, washing her face and neck with a cloth.

"Feels good, doesn't it, little girl," he said as he splashed through the water, a wide grin on his face.

"It surely does!"

"Why are you sitting over here by yourself? Why don't you join us? Do you know how to swim? If not, I'll teach you how . . . just like my pa taught me." He grinned mischievously.

Smiling, she shook her head. "I've known how since I was five years old, thank you . . . and besides, I have a good idea your method is probably the same one my father used to teach me."

His laugh was a low chuckle. "He threw you in the water and told you to sink or swim, huh?"

"Yes," she stated adamantly, remembering the inci-dent well.

"Since you know how, then why not join us?" he

invited again.

Staring wistfully at the enticing water and at how everyone was romping and frolicking like playful children, Virginia reluctantly shook her head. "No . . . not now."

"And why not?" Hank demanded.

"I can't swim in my dress . . " Blushing, she lowered her gaze. "And I can't swim in my undergarments like they are . . . not in front of you men. I'll go in after it gets dark.

Hank gave an understanding nod. He should have realized she would be too modest to do what the girls had done. He started to wade off, but stopped suddenly, turned around, and pretended to count on his fingers. His gaze caught and held hers. "Little girl, I just want you to know it's good to see a smile on your face again. By my count, it has been eighteen days . . . and that's too long."

"I know. Perhaps soon I'll *really* have something to smile about though." Then she became serious again. "Where are we, Hank? I know the directions, but I'm lost. How far are we from Phoenix now?"

As it was his habit to judge distances by time instead of miles, he replied thoughtfully, "I'd say about five days if we don't run into any more trouble. We won't have to plan our route by the water holes anymore though. We'll be able to continue on a straight course. We'll empty out what water is left in the barrels, let them air overnight, then fill them before we leave in the morning. They will hold enough water to see us through to Phoenix . . . and I have a good idea that's where we will find that mule-headed husband of yours."

She gave a long, audible sigh. "I hope so, Hank. Oh Lord, how I hope so!"

Virginia assessed the western sky and estimated there were about thirty minutes left before sundown. Wrapping her clean clothes and toilet items in a towel, she left the camp and made her way through the trees to where the rocky incline began. Glancing back over her shoulder every so often, she continued on until the camp could not be seen.

"If I cannot see them, it stands to reason they cannot see me," she mused aloud, sitting down to remove her shoes and stockings. Then, from where she sat, she noted a dark shadow near the waterfall. Was it a cave? Worrying her bottom lip, she glanced at the direction of the camp. Although the girls were friendly — and, in their own peculiar way, nice — their behavior and bawdy sense of humor was still too unprincipled for her taste. It would not surprise her if they tried to sneak up on her while she was bathing and hide her clothes or take them back to camp, especially since she had been too modest to join in their swimming party earlier in the day.

She decided to check quickly to see if it really was a cave. If so, it would be the perfect place in which to hide her clothing.

Slowly and cautiously, Virginia climbed over the rocks and around the huge boulders to the partially concealed shadow, which she soon learned was not actually a cave but a deep indentation in the rock. Virginia smugly decided it would be an ideal hiding place from anybody intent on making mischief. Believing it was too dark to be seen, she quickly removed her clothing, and clutching soap and a facecloth tightly in her hand, she dove headlong into the water.

She came up gasping for breath. The water was so

cool in the deep end of the pool, it felt almost icy, yet it was extremely refreshing and invigorating after days and days of scorching heat and having to bathe with a small cloth and water from a wash pan. Treading water, she scrubbed herself fiercely from top to bottom before swimming over to the rocks and placing the soap and cloth on a tiny ledge. She then took a deep breath and curved nymphlike back into the water.

When Virginia resurfaced again, a frown overtook her features. Had that been a scream? It was difficult to hear over the roar of the waterfall. Then, sounds penetrated Virginia's mind that would live with her a lifetime. Guttural yet shrill war whoops mixed with the thundering hooves of many horses. Screams and gunshots echoed from the surrounding boulders. Her eyes widened with horror as she realized that the camp had been caught by surprise. They were being attacked by Indians!

Run! Hide! Flee for your life! Those were the words that hammered through Virginia's mind.

Instinct for survival swept over her like a shroud. She quickly filled her lungs with air and dove under the water's surface and swam for refuge behind the waterfall. There, the sounds and the screams of the brutal attack were muted by the roaring water, but terror and horror filled her heart and soul. The roar muffled her cries of anguish. She was badly torn by indecision. Her affection for Hank, and yes, even for the others, demanded that she try to help them, but the logical portion of her brain screamed the futility of it. She had heard the thundering hoofbeats and knew the sounds had been made by many horses. She was not a coward, but what could she do, unarmed, against a savage horde? By frantically racing back to camp, she would only succeed in getting herself killed.

If only she had had a rifle or her shotgun, it would have been a different matter entirely. She never would have hesitated for a moment. But Hank and the others would not expect her to sacrifice her life for nothing. And deep in her heart, she knew they were beyond any mortal's help.

Tears streamed down Virginia's face as she made the grim decision to remain hidden behind the waterfall, though, in truth, it was the only decision she could have made.

Finally, as darkness settled over the land, the icy cold drove Virginia from the water. Shivering, she crouched low against the rocks and made her way to where she had left her shoes and clothing. There, she quickly dressed. Then forcing herself to remain perfectly still, she listened intently, fervently hoping it had been some horrible nightmare, desperately yearning to hear Hank calling her name.

Silence has no sound, but it virtually screamed at her. Except for the roar of the waterfall, there was no noise—no screams, no moans, no bloodcurdling cries—not even the musical trill of a bird cutting through the night air. But there was the distinct odor of burning wood and cloth, and an occasional flame licked at the darkness from the site of the camp. Without her realizing it, tears streamed down her face and deep, rasping sobs tore from her throat as she slipped, crawled, and climbed over the rocks.

Then, a slim thread of hope budded in her heart as it suddenly occurred to her that her friends might have been able to drive the Apaches away. With that thought in mind, she hurried along, though self-preservation forced her to approach the camp cautiously.

Virginia stared at the charred remains with dull, glazed eyes. Inside her head a raging scream whirled around and around, while some strange, alien noise tried to creep past her lips. Her mouth stretched wide, but her throat closed and would not allow the scream of anguish and horror to spew forth.

Ben was lying face down on the ground, his back riddled with arrows. A woman was lying dead by his side. Was that bloody, lifeless creature really Egypt? Laughing, carefree Egypt? Virginia pulled her horrified gaze away, feeling somewhat like an intruder, an intruder guilty of invading their privacy.

She was afraid to look for the others, but she knew she would have to make the attempt. She stumbled blindly around the charred skeletons of the wagons, searching for remains but desperately hoping for survivors. Except for the two bodies, the camp seemed completely deserted, yet Virginia could not bring herself to search underneath the wagons. If there were bodies there, she did not want to find them.

Then Virginia realized something was amiss. All of the horses, and even Mule, were gone, and two wagons were missing. It seemed logical for the horses to be missing, but why the wagons? Had they been used to carry goods back to the Apaches' camp? Or could they have been used to transport prisoners? Could the others still be alive? Did the Apaches even take prisoners? Or, had they merely been taken to another place to die more tortured, agonizing deaths? An image of her friends, especially dear, sweet Hank, flashed before her eyes. With great sorrow, she understood that wherever they were, on this earth or in some better place, they were now beyond her help.

Raw, burning tears slid down Virginia's face as she

slumped to the ground. There she sat for hours, rocking to and fro as she slipped further and further into the depths of despair.

Chapter Twenty-five

The sun eased over the horizon, pushing away all traces of night. Then it hung momentarily on top of the distant mountains, shimmering and red, apparently gathering energy for the day's assault.

It was as though Virginia had formed a barrier around her heart, disassociating herself from the grief and pain, as she placed the last stone on Ben and Egypt's common grave. Those pitiful creatures were not the people she had known; they were merely shells of the friends who had once laughed, loved, and lived.

Virginia mumbled a brief but reverent prayer, then stepped back and wiped the perspiration from her brow. "Now what should I do?" she wondered aloud as a surge of renewed apprehension welled up in her heart.

Realistically, there were only two choices: she could remain there and hope for rescue, or she could strike out on foot. Swallowing hard, she turned her gaze toward the desert, which was already shimmering from the heat. How long could she last out there? But how long could she survive here? Neither choice was too appealing.

Numb and dazed, Virginia methodically weighed

her options. The Apaches knew this land the same way she knew the back of her hand. This oasis was probably the only good water hole for miles around. If the Indians who had attacked them did not return, others surely would. If they only stopped for water, she could probably hide until they left, but if they set up camp, it was highly unlikely she could go undetected. In the book that Hank had given her, it had stated that Apaches were experts in torture, and that the squaws were even more cruel than the men. If the Indians captured her—and that was almost a certainty if she stayed—how long would they torture her before she died? The book had stated that depending upon an individual's stamina, some prisoners lived a week to ten days before dying an excruciatingly painful death.

Drawing a quivering breath, Virginia stared once again at the desert. Like it or not, that was really her only option. Out there, she might stand a chance, a slim chance at best, but it would be better to die of thirst than to sit passively waiting for the Apaches to return.

How far had Hank said it was to Phoenix? Five days? That meant ten, probably fifteen, on foot. Glancing at the charred canteen she had found in the aftermath of the carnage, Virginia estimated it might hold enough water for three or four days, perhaps five if she was very careful. Then what would she do? That left five to ten days of having to rely solely on her wits to keep her alive.

Her jaw tensed and her eyes narrowed thoughtfully. Even the most skilled could not do the impossible, and it was doubtful she could reach Phoenix. But as long as she did not panic, it might be possible to reach some outlying ranch, or perhaps even a trading post.

Her confidence spiraled upward as courage and determination surged through her. Adversity would beat her only if she allowed it to. Although this was a harsh land, it teemed with life that had adapted itself to the arid climate over the centuries. So that meant survival was possible. But the desert was only capable of sustaining so much. Thus the strongest, most cunning, or the most resourceful of any species were destined to endure. All species of life, from the lowly desert rat to the majestic golden eagle, shared two common enemies: the sun and the scarcity of water. While the animals had had the benefits of evolution, she would have to rely on her brain and common sense to survive.

One thing was certain; she would have to travel by night. It would be foolhardy to try to cross the desert on foot during the heat of the day, and she should carry nothing with her that was not absolutely necessary.

With that in mind, Virginia began her preparations, always wary and alert in case the Apaches decided to return. After working loose a small piece of steel from one of the wagons, she searched until she found a small piece of iron pyrite, knowing these items would enable her to build a fire if necessary.

Hungry, Virginia ate her fill of the wild grapes, then gathered what remained, even the ones that were not ripe, and a few willow branches on which to chew if she was in need of a painkiller, wild onions, and several stalks of cattail, which grew along the shallow edge of the pool. She also selected a few round stones, having heard they produced saliva if placed in the mouth and worked about. She folded the dress she had worn the previous day, laid her meager supplies in the center, tied it, and ran a rigid stick through the bundle, believing that would be the easiest way to carry it.

Since her bonnets had been in the wagon, she made

368

a mud paste and soaked her towel in it, believing the mud might provide natural protection against the heat if she was not able to find shelter during the day. Then she climbed into the rocks and waited for darkness to fall.

Three days later, early in the morning, Virginia stared bleakly at a mountain looming ahead. Panther black in the pale light, it gradually turned to a tawny lion color as dawn broke across the sky. It seemed to be crouching like a great sleeping beast, head on forepaws, weary of the hunt. Its massive flanks wrinkled, folded, aged by countless centuries, weathered by merciless elements. Along the mountain's western extremity, gigantic spires thrust from the desert floor, beckoning the sky above. From the maps she had examined, she knew this was what the Indians called Crooked Top Mountain, though it was known to the white men as the Superstitions.

Without warning, a cold chill rippled through her spine, for she suddenly had the feeling that something was uncannily wrong with that piece of land. It looked forbidding, yet strangely compelling, as though it contained many unexplainable mysteries.

How far she had traveled, Virginia did not know. It was becoming more and more difficult to judge distance and time. The muscles in her legs and back were cramped and there was an aching soreness all through her from the long hours and grueling miles she had walked. The ruffed collar of her bodice was stiff with dirt and dried perspiration, and the scratchy weight of her skirt seemed to smother her skin. Wisps of hair trailed wetly along the sides of her face, but she was too exhausted to push the tendrils of hair aside. Besides, it did not seem important enough to waste the energy.

Perspiration burned her eyes and Virginia raised her arm and used the sleeve of her dress to blot at the moisture beading on her brow and upper lip. Her throat and mouth were parched and the salty taste of her own sweat only increased her thirst. Her chin trembled and a wetness gathered in her eyes. She blinked and forced her mind to focus on anything that might help her.

"Shelter, I have to find shelter," she mumbled.

She looked slowly about, searching for a place to rest. It was as Slade had once said, a forest of saguaro cactus. They also gave her an eerie feeling, as though with their arms thrusting upward they stood like sentries at their posts, guarding the reigning monarch, the mountain.

Pushing those thoughts aside, she stumbled over to where a giant saguaro had fallen apparently having been blown over during a fierce windstorm, and she scraped enough of the dried pulp away from the carcass to enable her to crawl inside. The body of it was much like that of a hollow tree and would provide excellent shelter.

Her stomach rumbled from hunger, and her mouth and lips were dry, parched from thirst. What grapes remained had soured, but she ate them nonetheless and saved the two bulbous cattails to eat late that afternoon before she began her trek again.

As she shook the canteen, her face paled at the sound. Her supply of the precious liquid was getting dangerously low and she had not seen one sign of water. Swallowing hard, she resisted the overwhelming urge to tilt her head back and drink her fill or drink until the canteen was empty. Instead, she took only a small sip of water, knowing her thirst would be greater when she awoke. Then she carefully put the lid back in place, crawled inside the cactus, wound the charred canteen strap around her hand, and fell into a restless sleep.

Virginia came awake with a start. Dazed, she struggled to collect her wits. Hoofbeats! Had she been awakened by hoofbeats? Then her sudden rush of fear quickly dissolved into a feeling of immense relief as she heard a familiar sound and recognized the lumbering gait. Mule! It was Mule! How had he found her? Where had he come from?

Crawling out of the cactus and struggling to her feet, she could not contain the wide smile that split her cracked lips as the camel trotted toward her, groaning and snorting. If Mule had been a person, she would have sworn the sounds were squeals of delight.

Laughing, she threw her arms around his neck, and salty, happy tears trailed down her face, stinging her lips, but she did not care. Her tongue automatically flicked out to taste the moisture. Then, hearing a gurgling sound, she frowned in puzzlement and looked down. Her eyes widened with horror as she realized the brittle canteen strap had broken and Mule had stepped on the canteen, crushing it. The precious water was being hungrily devoured by the sand.

"Oh, no! No! No!" she cried, frantically reaching down to save what she could. But Mule stepped forward, nuzzling her, and his hoof kicked against the canteen, sending it sprawling across the ground. She desperately scrambled after it, but each time she almost had it in her grasp, Mule kicked it away in his eagerness to sidle close to her. Finally, she managed to clutch it to her breast, then, horror-struck, Virginia realized the canteen was almost empty. Though she quickly pressed it to her lips and tilted back her head as far as it would go, she was able to catch only the last few remaining drops of water.

She slumped to the ground and stared mutely into the vast wasteland, too beaten, too disheartened, even to cry. All of her careful planning, all of her strict rationing, all of the times she had longed for just one satisfying drink of water, had been in vain. Mule moved beside her and settled in the sand. His short, shaggy tail beat a staccato rhythm against the earth and he tried to run his head underneath her hand like an overly friendly puppy.

Suddenly jerking her head about, Virginia glared at him with burning, reproachful eyes. She was breathless with fury as the realization of what had happened fully dawned on her. Her nostrils flared with rage and her hands clenched into fists. Never had she wanted to strike another creature so badly.

"You . . . stupid . . . stupid . . . !" Anger permeated her for a moment, invading her like a fierce maelstrom, but she could not hold on to it, and all too soon it ebbed away, leaving her with nothing but that terrible, debilitating fear she had felt when she had first realized the canteen had been smashed.

Then Virginia gulped hard, bottom lip trembling, hot tears brimming in her eyes, and she slipped her arms around the camel's neck. "Oh, Mule, what am I going to do now? I am so thirsty and hungry . . . and I am so tired. Tell me, please tell me, what am I going to do?"

Shadows started to fall, and still Virginia sat there, too beaten to move. The battle had been lost; she had no will to continue. It was as if the land had reached inside her with long tentaclelike fingers and had plucked all of her strength and willpower.

Her thoughts became morose. Faces of those she loved flashed before her eyes: Slade, her mother, Hank, and even her father as he had once been. Her mother and Hank were gone, but Slade and her father . . . would they remember her? Would her father ever wonder what had happened to her, and perhaps feel a pang of regret that he had not been a stronger man? And Slade . . . A sob caught deep within her chest. It would be easier to face death if she could hope that somehow, someway, he would learn the truth about her. But that was impossible. There was no one alive who knew the truth but her.

And her legacy . . . She was leaving none. Not one soul would be aware of her passing. Except for Slade's bitter memories, it would be as though she had never existed, that she had never left a mark on the world. No one would mourn her; no one would shed a tear. Perhaps years from now—if the shifting sands did not conceal her forever—someone would stand over her bones, bleached by the sun, and wonder who she had been. Maybe that person would even feel a moment of sadness.

Darkness fell and stars brightened the sky. Still, Virginia sat there, her heart heavy with grief for the life she would never live, for the children she would never have, and for the joys she would never know.

Suddenly skittish, Mule stood, his flanks quivering. He bellowed a frightful cry. Virginia blinked uncomprehendingly and glanced about, gradually becoming aware that she had been in a dazed stupor and that it was now dark. Where had the hours gone? Then, as Mule became more agitated, she realized he was frightened, that his animal instinct detected danger.

Grasping hold of his leg, she pulled herself to her feet, then she heard a distant snarl that made her blood run cold. Cougar!

Unconsciously reacting to the danger, Virginia quickly grabbed the stick from her bundle of meager possessions and drew it back like a club. It felt so puny in her hands. This will never do, she thought. It won't drive off a ferocious cat! Think, Virginia, think! Don't panic or you will die! Her fear mixed with fury—only this time the rage was directed inwardly. How could she have allowed herself to wallow in self-pity? How could she have given up? As long as there was a breath left in her body, she had a chance to survive!

The cat snarled again and Virginia realized the sound had come from several miles away, but this did not lessen her fear. Wild animals survived by attacking the weak, and no doubt it had sensed she would be easy prey. Or had the cat merely caught Mule's scent? It did not matter. If the cougar was after Mule, it would probably kill her too.

But, perhaps it would be frightened of humans. Maybe her scent would deter it long enough for her to . . . to do what? Scare it off with a flimsy stick?

A fire! If she could only build a fire before the beast attacked, the flames would probably frighten it away. Ripping through her bundle, she groped for the iron pyrite and the piece of steel.

Her mind raced. Tinder! I have to have tinder. The dress! It should burn.

Quickly, she held the pyrite and steel over the fabric and began striking the rock against the metal. Sparks flew, but only a few smoldering circles appeared on the material, then they quickly disappeared. A frightened moan escaped her lips and her hands trembled. Then Virginia took a deep, steadying breath. She knew her life depended on her ability to remain calm. Pursing her lips and blowing gently, she struck the metal again, hoping her breath would help feed the sparks, but something seemed to be preventing the sparks from catching hold.

Virginia could feel herself growing frantic again. Why wouldn't the material burn? Could it have too much sand mixed in with the fibers? Surely there was something else she could use.

Then, remembering the dead saguaro, she broke off a piece of the dried carcass, and holding the rock and steel over it, she frantically struck the steel, knowing she was in a desperate race against time. Using only the tiniest bit of imagination, she could feel the cat's eyes hungrily watching her.

A spark fell on the dried pulp, flickered, and dried. She struck it again and again, but each time the spark merely smoldered for an instant, then disappeared. Her spirits sagged, but she could not give up. Striking it again, she quickly cupped her hands around the tiny ember and blew ever so gently. The spark caught and burst into a tiny flame no larger than the flame from a candle wick. Tearing tiny strips from the brittle cactus, she methodically fed the flame until it blazed with enough strength to allow the addition of larger pieces.

It was only after the flames lit up the night that Virginia ripped the dress apart and wound pieces of it around the end of the stick to make a torch.

Lighting the torch and brandishing it triumphantly, she taunted, "Now, Mr. Cougar, if you are still intent on having me or Mule for supper, come ahead . . . only I have a surprise for you! You will not get either of us without a fight!"

She stood guard, listened for any sounds the cougar might make if he decided to attack, and kept a watchful eye on the fire, heaping more fuel on it each time the flames looked as thought hey were starting to diminish.

For how long Virginia kept a constant vigil with the fire and torch, she did not know. It could have been minutes or hours. The one thought that kept her going, was that if she ever relaxed her guard, she would die.

Finally, Virginia slumped exhausted to the ground, realizing she was on the verge of using her last ounce of strength. Why should she keep torturing herself this way? She was on foot in the middle of the desert, no food or water, surrounded by hostile Indians, miles from civilization, at the mercy of wild animals with only a fire for protection. Maybe it was time for hysteria, but what good would that do? It would not ease her thirst, or satisfy her hunger, or take away her fear.

Then, hearing a noise from the desert floor, she swallowed hard and her eyes grew wide with renewed fright. Dear God in Heaven! What else was going to happen to her? Was that a horse she heard? Yes, yes it was! Oh, Lord, no! After all that she had suffered, the Apaches had found her!

Virginia knew it was useless to run. To show that kind of cowardice would only make her death more painful. Yet she could not bear to watch the face of death descend upon her. Grasping her knees with her hands, she curled forward, lowered her face, and took a deep, shuddering breath and held it.

The horse blew air through his nostrils and she could hear the Indian dismounting. She tensed, expecting at any moment to feel the sharp pain of an arrow tearing through her back and ripping through her breast.

Instead of an Apache's arrow, Slade's angry voice cut

through the night as he started stomping out the fire. "Goddamn it, Virginia, what are you using for brains? What in the hell possessed you to build a big fire on such a dark night? Don't you know it can be seen for miles around? I though you, of all people, would have had better sense than this!"

Momentarily dumbfounded, she could only raise her head and stare mutely at him. Then the earth started spinning and Virginia could feel herself falling . . . falling . . . .

Chapter Twenty-six

A prodding hand started the painful agonies all over again. Virginia struggled to remain in the darkness where there was no pain, no thirst, no torturing memories. But the hand shook again, more determinedly this time.

"Sweetheart, you have to wake up," the familiar voice said. "Come on now," he urged gently. "There is water, plenty of cool, sweet water."

Virginia groaned. She slowly raised her heavy eyelids halfway, until a soft, flickering light filled her vision, then it was blocked by a huge, dark shadow of a man. She was disoriented and for a moment had trouble focusing her eyes. Where were the stars, the open sky? What . . . how . . . ? What had happened? Was she dead? Had the Indians killed her? No, Slade had appeared . . . or had he? Was his presence merely a figment of her wishful imagination? Could this man be the dark specter of death in disguise?

"Here, Virginia." Slade spoke softly, lifting her head slightly and holding a cup of water to her mouth. "Drink this . . . slowly now, slowly . . . not too much at one time!"

As the water slid down her parched throat, a cry of

relief broke from her lips and her heart leapt with a surge of emotion. It was Slade! Thank God! But why wouldn't he give her more water? Why was he torturing her so? She clenched her jaw to stifle a sob. "Water, please, more . . . I am so thirsty," she pleaded, desperately grasping at the cup that he had so cruelly yanked away.

"I know, sweetheart, I know." His heart twisted at her pitiful condition and he could feel his insides tremble at her misery, but he steeled himself against her pleas. "If you drink too much at one time, it will make you sick." He held the cup to her lips. "Just drink it slowly, and in a few minutes I'll give you a whole cupful. I promise."

There were many questions he wanted to ask her, but they would have to wait for a little while longer. She was in such a bad way, she could not have lasted much longer without water. He hated to think what would have happened to her if he had not followed his instincts.

Mustering all of the willpower she possessed, Virginia struggled to sit up, then forced herself to take tiny little sips until the cup was empty. "May I please have more?" Hands trembling, she pushed the cup toward him. She was torn between wanting to throw her arms around him in an eager embrace and waiting for more water.

"In just a minute." Slade removed a handkerchief from his saddlebag and started wetting it from the canteen.

Virginia's eyes widened with alarm as she grabbed frantically for the canteen. "No, no, please, don't! The water is spilling on the ground! Please don't waste it!"

Shaking his head, he continued to dampen the bandanna. "There is plenty of water here, sweetheart.

There is a natural spring running through one of the nearby chambers. Just suck on this wet handkerchief and it will help quench your thirst until it's safe for you to drink more water. Trust me now, I know what I'm doing."

Glancing about, Virginia finally understood that they were in some sort of cave. The flames from the small, flickering fire made eerie shadows on the surrounding walls. But how? How did had they gotten here? What had happened to the desert and all of those reaching saguaros?

"Chamber? How . . . what chamber? How did we get here? What happened to the desert?" She was so confused.

"Shhh." He smoothed back her hair from her brow. "Try not to talk too much." With the tips of his fingers, he traced the gauntness of her cheeks and his heart wrenched at how pitiful she looked. God, how she must have suffered.

His touch felt so good, and Virginia longed to press his hand against her lips. She thought he had been lost to her forever, and maybe he still was, but she was safe with him and, for now, that was all that mattered. She studied his face, the dark stubble of whiskers, and the thick sweep of his lashes that hid his eyes from her. "But . . . how . . . did we get here? How did you find me? The last thing I remember, you were stamping out my fire."

"That's right, I did stamp out your fire. Suck on the handkerchief and I'll explain."

Virginia pressed the cloth against her mouth. Slade was right. Not only did the wet bandanna help her thirst, but it felt so good, so refreshing, against her dry, split lips.

He patiently began, "You were in the desert . . .

380

about an hour's ride from here. You fainted . . . or lapsed into unconsciousness. I brought you here." He glanced about. "This is where I have been camping. We are in the mountains, in a maze of ancient Indian ruins."

She felt momentary panic as her mind jumped on the words *ancient Indian ruins*. Did he mean Apaches? Dear God in Heaven, all of this time she had done everything within her power to avoid the Indians, and, now Slade had brought her right to them! Had he lost his mind?

Seeing her panic and realizing the reason behind it, Slade quickly explained. "Don't be frightened. These are not Apache ruins. They are centuries old and were built by an ancient tribe that disappeared long ago. A friend of mine told me about them and he said these ruins would be safe to hole up in because the Apaches fear this place. I've been here for over a week now and I've yet to see any in this canyon. But they do have a stronghold in this area, so we have to be careful."

"I see," she said, breathing a sigh of relief. "B—But how did you find me?"

Slade poured more water into the cup and handed it to her. "When I left the caravan . . ." His mouth settled into a grim line and he looked away abruptly, not wanting to talk about the day he had left her. "When I left, I needed time for my shoulder to heal before I started looking for John again, so I decided to do a little prospecting. I've been here for nearly two weeks now."

"Two weeks," she mouthed. Such a short time, yet so much had happened.

Slade had not told Virginia about the buried treasure and he saw no reason to mention anything specific now. "Earlier today I ran across two Apache *rancherias* — strongholds — and I decided the prospecting could wait for a little while longer. I waited until dark before I left, figuring it would be safer. But as I was leaving the mountain, I happened to see your fire. I started to go on, but I got to thinking that whoever it was might not know how many Apaches were in the area, so I decided to warn. . . . Anyway, when I saw it was you . . . I guess I went a little crazy. I shouldn't have yelled at you the way I did, but you scared the hell out of me. The Apaches could have seen your fire the same way I did."

Virginia leaned her head back and gazed into his blue eyes. "I realized the danger of a fire, and I certainly knew better than to build one . . . but there was a cougar." She shuddered at the memory. "I heard it and was afraid it was going to attack me and Mule . . . where is Mule?" she asked suddenly. "You didn't leave him . . ."

He chortled. "No, don't worry, I didn't leave him. I doubt if I could have even if I had wanted to. He is staked in another chamber with Blue."

"I see."

Slade hesitated, measuring her for a moment, then when he spoke, his eyes were hooded and his voice was unsteady and troubled. "Virginia, why were you out there in the desert all alone? What happened to the others?"

A shimmer of tears glittered in her ebony eyes when she slowly lifted her gaze to his face. The wrenching mental anguish reflecting in them spoke of horrors she would never be able to forget.

"They are . . . dead . . . all dead. Oh, Slade!" she sobbed miserably. "We were attacked and I just let them . . . die! I hid in the rocks like . . . a coward instead . . . of trying to help!"

The guilt, desolation, and despair of the past few days washed over her, and she cried bitterly. The tears she had not completely shed during this whole ordeal flowed freely, while she wept for all of the times she had felt pangs of guilt, or anguish, or rage that had had no release. When the emotional storm abated, she realized Slade was now holding her in his arms, and his stamina gave her the strength to continue.

She breathed in deeply, sniffing at her runny nose, and lifted her head. She then told him everything that had happened: the caravan's desperate search for water, finding the oasis, the Indian attack, her hiding among the rocks, and her attempt to walk out of the desert.

Slade sat holding her tightly, listening patiently, knowing she had to talk, to rid herself of this grief and terrible sense of guilt. His own anger, hurt, and feelings of betrayal seemed unimportant. All that mattered to him now was Virginia and her safety. Through his own stubbornness he had almost lost her, and regardless of what had happened between them in the past, the future looked bleak and hopeless without her. But he would have to come to terms with such feelings and make a decision later.

"No one will ever know how I feel," Virginia added softly, blinking through a haze of tears. "The guilt I feel because I did nothing is something I will have to live with for the rest of my life."

"I understand your feelings, but what could you have done though?" Slade asked. "You said yourself you had no gun, no weapon of any kind. They had those things and were still unable to save themselves. Do you honestly think Hank and the others would have wanted you to sacrifice your life for nothing?"

"No . . . but Hank would not have hidden while

they killed me. He would have done something."

"Maybe he would have," Slade agreed. "But more than likely all he would have succeeded in doing would have been to get himself killed. I know he was your friend . . . as were the others, but there was nothing you could have done. I didn't know Hank that well, but I am sure this is how he would have wanted it. He wouldn't have wanted you to have sacrificed your life for nothing."

"My rational mind has told me the same thing time and time again, but my heart . . . my conscience . . ." She bit her lower lip and looked away.

Slade took a deep breath. "You said you only found two bodies . . ."

"Yes, Ben and Egypt. Oh, God," she murmured in prayer at the ugliness of that memory. "I assumed the others were underneath the burned wagons . . . but . . . I couldn't look to make sure. I just couldn't."

"I'm sorry." Slade gathered her in his arms and rocked her against his length, his head bent and his mouth moving against her hair. "It was horrible, I know."

Slade started to say something else but changed his mind, knowing what he had been about to say would not be comforting. It might be easier on Virginia if she thought the others were dead. Two wagons missing, no signs of other bodies, added up to their having been taken prisoner. He knew for a fact, depending on how badly the Apaches needed weapons, they sometimes took prisoners to trade for weapons when they were warring. Women were sold into bordellos, and the men were sold to work in mines down in Mexico. Finding them after this much time had passed would be next to impossible. If they had been taken prisoner, they might be at one of possibly thirty Apache *rancherias* either in the immediate area or below the border. No, if they were alive, it would take a miracle to find them. Still, as soon as they reached Phoenix, he would report their possible capture to the cavalry, and who knew, maybe miracles did happen.

Wanting to get her mind off the unpleasant memories, Slade asked in an even, conciliatory tone, "Do you think you could eat something now? And before you start thinking how cruel I am, I had to make sure you could keep the water down before offering you something to eat."

Hungrily, Virginia licked her lips and her whole face spread into a smile. "Oh, yes! I know I could eat something. It has been days since I've had a decent meal." She sat crossed-legged and watched as Slade began removing food from his saddlebags.

"Well, I doubt if one could call this a decent meal—I haven't been able to hunt, but I have snared some quail, which I cooked to take with me, and I have a quart of cold-flour and three of these." He smiled and brandished an apple proudly. "I couldn't believe my good luck when I found an apple orchard over in the next canyon."

Virginia's mouth watered as she bit into the roasted quail. She fought the urge to tear into it ravenously and forced herself to chew it slowly so that her empty stomach would not repel it.

"Let me mix you a cup of cold-flour and warm water. It's very easy to digest after going a long time without food."

"What is cold-flour?" She peered at the mixture curiously while savoring the delicious taste of quail in her mouth. Whatever it was, it certainly smelled good.

"Ground-up parched corn mixed with cinnamon and a little sugar. It's nourishing and filling too. I've known of men living on a quart of it for a week at a time. You shouldn't eat a raw apple though. It might tear your stomach up. But I'll bet you could manage it cooked." He placed one near the fire and raked hot coals over it to bake.

Virginia hungrily sucked on a leg bone. "Aren't you going to eat?"

"No, I had supper before I left. You go ahead." He lit a cheroot and settled back to watch Virginia eat. It seemed as though a sense of strength had come to her and her despair had lessened. It made him feel good to see her enjoying her meal so much. He only wished it were more. She had never been very heavy and her weight loss was evident, but a few weeks of good food would change that. Staring at her, he caught in his breath. Even though she looked like a homeless waif, she was still beautiful. He doubted anything could ever destroy the beauty that surrounded her like an aura.

Finally, Virginia wiped her mouth on the damp handkerchief and took a deep, satisfied breath. Her body vibrated with new life. "I think I had better stop now. I'm so full, I doubt I could hold another bite." She offered apologetically, "I'll have to eat the apple later."

Slade smiled to himself and nodded. She had only eaten one tiny quail and had drunk one cup of the cold-flour mixture, but considering what she had had to eat for the past few days, he did not doubt she was full.

Love for Slade swelled Virginia's heart and she suddenly found it difficult to swallow. The powerful muscles that rippled beneath his dark blue shirt stirred her pulse beyond belief. The weak feeling that suddenly swept over her had nothing to do with her recent tribulation. He behaved as though no problems existed between them, as though no shadows hung over their past. Could it be that he regretted not listening to her explanation? Could it be that after having had time to think, he had realized why she had kept silent about Dovie and what had happened during those months they had been apart?

"S—Slade . . . can I talk to you . . . about what happened?" she suddenly asked. Right before her eyes, his mood seemed to change. It was as though some invisible weight suddenly dragged at him and pulled him down.

A dark shadow flickered over his features and he spoke without emotion or inflection, as though callously dismissing her. "I thought we had been talking." He stood and stretched, feigning a yawn. "But now I think we should try to get some sleep. I know you are bound to be tired." He pointed to his bedroll. "You can use my blankets and I'll stretch out by the fire."

Virginia did not like the hard set of his jaw, the sudden blaze of light in his eyes; she remembered the temper that boiled behind them. But she held her tongue, hoping for the right opportunity to talk to him later. She halfheartedly protested, "I can't take your blankets. What will you use for cover?"

He gazed at her with a half-bland smile and spoke firmly. "I insist you use them. You need the warmth more than I do. Like I said, I'll just stretch out here by the fire." He turned away and began preparing her bed.

Her eyes were dark and unfathomable as her expression stilled and grew serious. She steadfastly refused to look at him, concentrating all her attention directly on the fire, looking neither to the right nor the left. How could he suddenly treat her so coldly? After all, they *were* husband and wife. Maybe their marriage was a farce, but did he find her so revolting that he could not

387

bear to be close to her? She felt her stomach knot with apprehension. Maybe he did find her that revolting; after all, he thought she had been one of Dovie's girls, and if that didn't tear his guts out, he wasn't much of a man. Then, as a thought struck her, her blood ran cold. Even if she could persuade him to listen to the truth later, that didn't mean he would believe her. He had no reason to believe her without proof, and she had no proof to offer. Whether she liked it or not, the best thing she could do was just keep her mouth shut about the past.

Then, an idea suddenly began to form in the back of Virginia's mind. It was devious, cunning, and underhanded, but she had lost this man twice before and she would be damned if she lost him again without a fight.

Before she had a chance to lose her courage, she spoke quickly. "Slade . . . wait a moment. I hate to put you to any more trouble, but I doubt if I could get a moment's sleep like this." She was pleased and a little surprised at how nonchalant she sounded.

"What's wrong?" he asked, turning from his kneeling position and looking at her. He wondered if she had any idea how sensuous her voice was.

Virginia wrinkled her nose and ran her hand over her arm. "After three days of walking in the desert . . . I feel dirty and gritty . . . and I have perspired so much, I smell terrible. You mentioned something about a spring running through another chamber. Do you think I could take a bath . . . or at least wash some of this stench off?"

He shrugged noncommittally. "I don't see what it would hurt, but the water is cold, so I wouldn't tarry long if I were you." He dug in his saddlebag and handed her a bar of soap. "Sorry, I don't have a towel to offer you. But I suppose you could wrap a blanket around you, then dry it by the fire before you go to bed."

"I can make do without a towel." The warmth of her smile echoed in her voice. "Soap and water are what I need most." She shuddered visibly. "Anything to get this grit and awful smell off me!"

"Follow me and I'll show you the spring." He lit two torches, handed one to Virginia, then picked up the nearly empty canteen. "Be careful to duck your head when we pass through the doorways though. The people who built these dwellings were much shorter than we are."

Virginia stood and glanced about cautiously. "Slade, I realize this may sound like a silly question, but are you sure it is safe to light these torches? Is there any danger of Apaches seeing the light?"

He grinned. "No, it's not a silly question. If it will help put your mind at ease, I've checked the ruins thoroughly. Light can't get in or out. I've made sure by lighting torches and going outside to see. Whoever built this settlement built it to last. They used hardwood lintels to support the doorways, and they layered the roofs with hewn logs. Reeds were used as a caulker, and a layer of mud and grass was placed on top to seal it all. The walls were put together with carefully chosen rocks, fitted together and mortared with mud." He touched one of the walls. "This place has been here for hundred of years and I imagine it will still be standing a long time after we're gone and forgotten."

Virginia paused and looked at the doorway. For a moment, she wondered in awe about the people who had once inhabited this place. Then, realizing Slade had walked on ahead, she hastened her steps, not wanting to fall too far behind him as he wound his way through a maze of stout walls. Finally, they reached the chamber where the spring bubbled from the center of the rocky floor and formed a stream that ran not more than five feet before it flowed back into the floor.

"How many rooms are there?" she asked curiously, looking around, noticing several old pottery bowls sitting on shelves that had been carved from the rock.

"I've counted eighteen, but there are a few more toward the back. They're not safe though. I suppose earthquakes have caved them in." He quickly refilled his canteen, then gestured toward the small spring. "Well, there it is. I'll wait in the other chamber until you are through. You might get lost trying to find your way back." The beginning of a smile tipped the corners of his mouth.

Confidently, she rejected such an idea as absurd. "You don't have to wait. I remember the way."

His raised brows suggested his doubt.

"All I have to do is go through those two doors, turn left, go through the next four, then turn right . . . no, left again, and we are camped in the chamber three doors down. Is that not correct?" she asked just a little smugly.

"I see you are a very observant lady," he conceded. "Just yell out if you need me for anything." His grin was a little more brazen. "Like maybe washing your back?"

Virginia could feel herself blushing. "Thank you. I'm sure I can manage just fine."

"Well . . . in case you change your mind . . ." He spoke in a jesting way.

"I'm sure I won't," she said, lifting her head proudly.

He shrugged and walked away, his expression one of faint amusement.

Virginia stared at his retreating form. His blustering words had not fooled her for a moment. It was as though he had deliberately tried to make her angry by his thinly veiled innuendos — as though he was afraid to get close to her. Well, she would show him a thing or two. After tonight, if he could turn away from her, then maybe there wasn't anything between them that could be salvaged.

Chapter Twenty-seven

Although the water was deeper at the base of the spring, Virginia deliberately chose the more shallow part where it flowed back into the ground, so as not to soil their water supply. She briskly rubbed the bar of soap into a frothy lather, scrubbed vigorously, then quickly rinsed off. It took several soapings before she felt completely clean. Chilly bumps had popped up on her skin when she finally stepped from her invigorating bath.

After wrapping the blanket around her shoulders, Virginia laundered and rinsed her dress and undergarments. Then, spying several sticks lying on the floor, she draped her tattered clothing over them so that she could later hang them in the corner near the camp fire, enabling the clothes to dry faster. However, if everything went according to plan, she would have no need of her clothing this night.

Holding the torch in one hand and her clothes in the other, she hurried back to the chamber where Slade was waiting.

Seeing Virginia with only a blanket wrapped around her, Slade quickly averted his eyes, and selecting a rock beyond the fire, he fastened his gaze there. He did this not to be a gentleman, but quite the opposite. Just knowing what beauty lay beneath that scant blanket had sent his thoughts reeling and his pulse pounding. He wanted her. God, he wanted her! He wanted to crush her in his arms, ravage her lips, and explore her body as he had done before. But he was afraid to make a move. His pride would not let him. If she refused his advances, what would he do then? Force her? No, he could never do that . . . not to Virginia—not to any woman. Besides, what would he do if he took her in his arms and the image of another man holding her the same way flashed through his mind? Would he suddenly be rendered impotent? No, it was best just to ignore the passionate heat thudding through his body rather than risk such humiliation.

"That bath felt marvelous!" Virginia murmured as she wedged the sticks holding her wet garments in the corner. "Of course, the water was cold, though I can't say I wasn't warned. Nevertheless, it was worth it. I can't remember when I've felt so refreshed." She knew she was babbling, but the mere thought of what she had planned for later was extremely unnerving. She had never behaved like a seductress before and it was going to be a new experience, yet it would be worth it if it brought them closer together.

Walking over to the fire, she sat down on a large rock and began ruffling her hair to help dry it. "I wish I had a hairbrush," she mused aloud, staring intently at him while slowly wetting her lips with her tongue.

"I have a—" Slade paused when his voice broke like a young schoolboy's. He cleared the thick lump that had formed in his throat and continued. "I have one. You are welcome to use it." Removing it from his saddlebag, he gritted his teeth and beads of cold sweat

393

popped out on his forehead when he caught a glimpse of her silken shoulder and the slight swell of her breast as she reached for the brush.

A delicious shudder heated Virginia's body as his fingertips barely grazed hers. For a brief moment, alarming thoughts raced through her mind as Slade nonchalantly moved to the other side of the fire, sat back down, and looked away. He seemed so disinterested. What if he ignored her advances? What if he found her attempt at seduction amusing? No, surely he wouldn't. He was an extremely virile man and he did have feelings for her. They might be buried underneath his stubborn pride, but he had to feel something for her; *he simply had to!*

Before she lost her courage, Virginia rose and slowly walked toward him.

Slade's eyes were riveted to her face, for he did not trust himself to look at the creaminess of her skin where the blanket had slipped from her shoulder. "Is there something else you want?" he asked, his voice sounding strained to his ears.

"Yes."

"What?"

"You," she murmured huskily, wantonly staring at him. With tantalizing slowness, she allowed the blanket to drop around her waist as she stepped forward and placed her hands on his shoulders.

For a brief moment that seemed to last an eternity, silence fell awkwardly between them, strangling them with its choking grip as memories of the past flooded their minds.

Virginia finally found her voice. "Slade, life is too short to dwell on the pain we've inflicted on each other. Our future lies before us. Whether our future together is just for this one night or for the next fifty years . . . I love you . . . and I want you."

Slade slowly reached out and encircled her waist with his large hands, then, placing his head on the soft swell of her stomach, he wrapped his arms around her waist tightly, as thought half afraid she was a vision that would slip from his grasp the moment he reached for her. She had done so too many times in his dreams.

Then, in one fluid motion, he rose to his feet to embrace her. He could feel sobs shaking her body as she buried her face against his broad chest, just as he could feel the rivulets of her tears soaking through his shirt. He held her close and lovingly stroked the silky softness of her skin.

Slowly, he twisted her countenance up to his. "My God, sweetheart," he muttered huskily, all of his fears and reservations suddenly disappearing. "What have we done to each other?" he asked before his hands tightened in her honey gold hair and his mouth took hers with a passion she had not thought possible.

Eagerly, Virginia parted her lips for him as she felt the tip of his tongue begin to seek her out. It shot deep inside her waiting mouth to explore the sweetness within as though he had never known it before. Gently, so gently, his tongue caressed hers, twining hesitantly at first, then swirling with a more insistent pressure when he met no resistance. But then, he had known she would not resist, that she was offering herself freely, willingly, and with an eagerness that was truly sincere.

It seemed as though they kissed forever. In every way a man's tongue could know a woman's mouth, Slade's discovered Virginia's once more, teasing, tantalizing. Then, her tongue darted swiftly, boldly, between his lips to probe his mouth in kind.

Later, much later, Slade cast away his clothing to

reveal his nakedness to Virginia as she had shamelessly done to him.

Slade's hands touched satiny skin as he scooped her into his arms and laid her on the blanket. His hands stroked her skin, trailed down her face, throat, and shoulders to her breasts, where they lingered tantalizingly.

Time flew by, but the lovers paid it no heed, for their world was timeless, endless, the moments measured only in each other's desire and need.

His eyes darkened into deep blue pools until they became nearly as dark as ink as he pressed her against the blanket. Her arms crept up to tighten around his neck. She kissed him eagerly, wanting him, shivering slightly as she felt the demanding pressure of his mouth on hers. His muscles quivered and rippled beneath her fingers and she felt the sheer power and strength that swept the length of him.

Virginia's nipples flushed a dusky rose and hardened into taut little peaks that nuzzled at Slade's palms enticingly, invitingly. He lowered his head and kissed them both gently, and each one in turn grew even more rigid between his lips and tingled beneath his lightly nibbling teeth and slowly circling tongue. Rapturous waves of delight raced through her body as his tongue swirled about her nipples and breasts.

She lost her hands in his shaggy mane of black hair as she urged him on with tiny moans of pleasure and drew him closer against the soft mounds that swelled upon her chest, round, full, and ripe for his taking. His hands swept down to gently probe, to passionately explore, the core of her femininity, stroking slowly at first, fondling the sweet, velvet length of her.

His fingers played her flesh as they might a classical violin, creating melodious music in the shimmering gold light reflecting from the fire. The headiness of her eagerness filled him, enveloped him, enticed him with a siren's song from which he could not escape, even if he had wanted to. He captured the essence of her love, eliciting its haunting melody over and over until he knew every single cord and heard at last that dulcet, trilling note he sought. She joined him in a harmony that made him gasp from the sheer beauty of their desire, before the rhythm of her lips, tongue, and fingers made his heart pound with an intoxicating heat and his loins throb to some primitive never-to-be-forgotten beat.

Virginia cried out softly as the crescendo of his music crashed through her veins over and over, then diminished to soft, melodic strains before rising again and again.

Then, at last, Slade was on his knees between her thighs, towering over her briefly before his hard masculinity penetrated her swiftly with a deep thrust that took her breath away. He gasped and pulled away from her, righted himself, and plummeted once again into the very core of her being.

Fiercely, he took her, and just as fiercely, Virginia gave herself to him, wildly, wantonly, locking her legs around his back to draw him even farther into herself. He thrust into her again and again, gripping the soft curls at her temples as he drove her to the heights of rapture and beyond. Down, down, down, into the velvet honey of her, he plunged faster and faster, until for one glorious, triumphant moment she was his, all his, as she arched her hips against him wildly and dug her nails into his back. As ecstatic as she, Slade joined her, and together they soared upon the wings of rapture as a thousand galaxies exploded, blinding them with the fiery brilliance of shooting stars.

Ever so slowly they relaxed, their minds and their senses returning from the far-flung stars, and they divided into two people again. Slade sank back against the blanket, and the sweat on his bronzed skin glistened, then cooled on his body. It seemed a conscious effort to breathe. He pulled Virginia into the crook of his arm and held her tightly. He was aware of a hundred sentiments crowding his mind that he wanted to express, but he was incapable of uttering any of them. So they lay side by side in silence, flesh touching flesh, their souls retaining the oneness they had just experienced. But the longer they lay there, the more tortured Slade's thoughts became.

Later, much later, Virginia awoke slowly, stretching like a well-fed cat. For just a brief moment, her memory was blurred, and she wondered why there seemed to be such a tight, restricting bond around her. Then she gradually became aware of Slade's arms still wrapped around her and her memory came crashing back. She purred contentedly and snuggled closer to him. One of his strong hands rested upon one breast that peeked from under the blanket. Then, as she desperately tried not to think about it, she felt her nipple tingle and harden beneath the slight pressure of Slade's fingers and her loins quickened, as though molten heat flowed through her veins instead of blood. She found it to be utterly amazing; after his thorough, satisfying loving, she still wanted him. It was as if her passionate appetite had only been whetted, not sated.

Slade only pretended to be asleep when Virginia started stirring in his arms. He felt if she knew he was awake she might say something and he was in no mood to talk, not now, not with such haunting images crowding his mind.

Where had Virginia learned so much about love-making? Even worse, who had taught her how to satisfy and please a man? Who had rid her of her inhibitions? Back in New Mexico, her lovemaking attempts had been shy and hesitant, but a short while ago, when she had given herself to him with such wild abandon, had it been another man she was making love to? Had another man's face flashed before her eyes when he had entered her and possessed her completely?

Groaning miserably, Slade unwound his arms from Virginia, sat up, and reached for a cheroot. Taking a deep draw, he ground his teeth together. Why did he torture himself this way? Why couldn't he just accept their relationship as it was? Why should he condemn Virginia. Hadn't he known other women intimately?

Yes, you have, but there is a big difference and you know it, an inner voice argued. He had not known another woman since he had been with Virginia that first time, and what's more, he'd had no desire to make love to another woman. She and she alone had been the only woman to occupy his thoughts and mind. It was as though she had been a conquering invader, driving away all other desires and longings.

Virginia rose up on her knees and, pressing her bared breasts into his back, wound her arms around his heavily furred chest. "What's wrong, my love?" she murmured, kissing the corded muscles of his neck.

"Nothing," he muttered, closing his mind to how it felt as though her breasts were burning holes in his back like two glowing coals. "It's just now coming daylight. Go on back to sleep. You need your rest." Slade's voice sounded tense, and strained.

"I'm not sleepy, and I'm not tired either," she whispered huskily. Caressing his flesh with subtle hands and reclining on her haunches, she trailed tiny nipping kisses around the back of his neck to where his broad shoulders met in the center of his back. Feeling his supple muscles tense, she queried hesitantly, "What's wrong, Slade?"

Abruptly, he stood and started yanking on his trousers. "I'm in no mood to talk right now."

"But, Slade . . ."

"Just leave it alone! Let it lie!"

Virginia bit her lower lip and her brows drew together in an agonized expression. She had hoped their lovemaking would ease the tension, but even after the magic they had shared, the tension was still there, hanging like a heavy curtain between them. Not knowing what else to do, she rose and began dressing.

Slade looked at Virginia standing in the corner of the chamber with her back to him. His heart lurched at the sight of her pulling her pantalets up over her rounded hips. His mouth became dry as desire surged through him. If only he had the power to go back and change the past, there never would have been other men in her life and he wouldn't have a reason to be saddled with the heavy weight of jealousy.

As though sensing his gaze on her, she glanced over her shoulder and was suddenly furious at his behavior. One moment he was kind, loving, and considerate, and the next he was the most arrogant, insufferable, exasperating man she had ever known, almost heartless in his treatment of her. Still, he loved her—she *knew* he did—and she loved him! If he weren't so obstinate, he would admit it and they could sit down and talk and clear the air between them. But no, he had to behave like a thickheaded, stubborn jackass!

Remembering the old adage about catching more

flies with honey than with vinegar, Virginia gritted her teeth to keep control of her temper. "I refuse to argue with him," she muttered to herself. "And I won't give him a reason to become angry with me, no matter how grouchy he gets."

Slade's voice was gruff with anxiety. "You shouldn't be up. You should stay in bed and get your rest. You'll need it. You've taxed your strength to the limit. We'll have to pull out tonight as soon as it gets dark."

Slipping her camisole over her head as slowly and seductively as she knew how, Virginia turned and smiled. "But I've already said I'm not sleepy, sweetheart, and I'm not tired either. However, after last night—"

Slade held up his hand to silence her. "Listen," he commanded in a ragged whisper.

The sound of unshod horses trotting through the canyon just outside the ruins filled the chamber. Virginia's eyes suddenly widened with fear.

"Is it Apaches?" she asked in a fearful whisper.

"I don't know. Stay here and be quiet . . . but go ahead and get dressed just in case we have to make a run for it," he ordered, moving stealthily to the outer chamber so that he could see what was happening outside.

A few minutes later, he returned, grim faced, and led Virginia into another chamber to lessen the danger of their voices' carrying. After the ordeal she had been through, he knew she was not a typical hysterical female and saw no reason to mince words with her. She deserved to hear the truth. "There are about thirty or forty Apache braves not more than fifteen feet from the entrance of the ruins."

Swallowing hard, Virginia tried to remain calm as she digested that frightening bit of information. "Are they . . . do you think they are looking for us?"

Apprehension was evident on his features. "I don't know, but from what I was able to hear, they're looking for a man. But I just don't know if it's me they're looking for or not. Damn!" he swore bitterly. "I've tried not to leave any signs of my presence in these mountains." He chuckled without humor. "Looks like I didn't try hard enough."

"Then you understood what they were saying?"

Slade shook his head and sighed with disappointment. "Only a word every now and then. There was too much noise for me to hear them very clearly. He then grasped Virginia by her arms and stared at her intently. "If it's me they're after, they may not know you are here. I want you go back to the farthest chamber, and for God's sake be quiet and stay there . . . regardless of what you might hear."

She listened with rising dismay. Why did the past constantly seem to repeat itself? She gulped hard and found it impossible to hold back the hot tears that slipped down her cheeks.

Seeing her tears, he murmured, "Please, sweetheart, don't cry. And don't fall apart on me now. When it's safe . . . I'll come for you." He drew her into his arms and kissed her hard, then abruptly released her. "Now go, sweetheart, hurry!"

Tossing her head in a gesture of defiance, she swallowed hard, lifted her chin, and boldly met his gaze. "No," she whispered staunchly.

Slade's eyes darted anxiously toward the other chamber. Along with the trampling horses' hooves, he could now hear war whoops. "Damnit, Virginia, don't argue with me! Get the hell out of here!" he hissed.

"No! I'm not leaving you to face them alone! You have two pistols and a rifle . . . I figure I'll do more damage with the rifle."

"Damnit, Virginia . . ."

She stubbornly shook her head. "No, Slade . . . I'm not going. A few days ago I hid like a coward while my friends were murdered . . . and I am not about to do the same thing again. You are my husband and I love you . . . and I don't want to live if you're not with me." The image of Egypt's and Ben's brutalized bodies flashed through her mind. "The only thing I ask is . . . don't let them take us alive."

Slade raked his hand through his hair. Time could quickly be running out. "All right then, but stay here while I go after the guns and the canteen."

Shaking her head, Virginia followed closely behind him. "And have you rush them while I am safely in here? Give me credit for being smarter than that. I'm not about to let you sacrifice yourself for me."

Slade shot her a glaring look over his shoulder, but the look instantly softened into one of awe and wonderment.

Being as quiet as possible, Virginia scooped up the blankets, canteen, and saddlebag, while Slade kicked sand over the embers of the camp fire and fastened his gun belt around his waist. Grabbing the rifle that was propped against the wall, he then flung the saddle over his shoulder.

Shaking his head, Slade gave one last quick glance around as Virginia hurried toward the rear chambers. He knew the abandoned chamber would not fool the Apaches. If they ever walked inside, they would know someone had been there recently. If only Virginia had not been so stubborn, he could have removed all traces of her being there. Now, she would have to take her chances with him.

Still looking behind him, Slade hurried through the

doorway and ran right into Virginia, who had stopped suddenly. "Damnit, sweetheart, go on!" His pet name for her was no longer one of endearment.

"I . . . we . . . can't! Slade, look!" she said, her voice breaking with fear.

Standing just inside the next doorway was an Indian holding a torch, a seven-foot Indian who menacingly towered over them.

Chapter Twenty-eight

The giant Indian, whose face seemed carved from granite, beckoned them to follow. *"Shee-dah nejeunee. Pindah lockoyee, ish-tia-nay, das-ay-go dee-dah tatsan. Shee an-han-day anah-zon-tee, nah Reavis, inju ostin."*

Fear, stark and vivid, glittered in Virginia's eyes as she grasped Slade's arm. "Wh—What did he say? Is—Is he going to kill us?" She began to shake as fearful images built in her mind.

Slade's eyes were sharp and assessing as he slowly shook his head. Even though the Indian had spoken Apache, his features were those of a Pima Indian, and they were friendly toward the white men. "I don't think he means us any harm. In fact, I think his intention is to help us. Roughly translated, he said he is a friend and wants us to follow him. He wants to take us to a safe place to see a good old man named Reavis."

Her hand tightened on his arm. "Do you think we can t—trust him?"

Slade chortled without humor. "I'd rather trust him than stay and fight those Apaches. Go on," he urged. "Do as he says, follow him, and I'll bring up the rear."

The Indian turned and, ducking his head, hurried through the doorway. When they were several chambers away, Slade called softly to him. *"Nejeunee, tash-ay-ay* horse, *tash-ay-ay ish-tia-nay's* beast."*

Although Virginia did not know any Indian words, she realized Slade had said something about his horse and her camel. Knowing him, she concluded he did not want to leave the animals behind, not if he could help it.

The Indian nodded and headed directly to the chamber where the animals were staked. Obviously, he had already known about them. With gestures and a few spoken words, he intimated that Slade should saddle his horse. But Virginia noted that his stoic features relaxed slightly when he handed Mule's reins to her. It was as though he felt awe that she could readily handle such a strange beast. Virginia unloaded her burden of blankets and canteen onto Blue and followed the Indian as soon as Slade had cinched the saddle.

They finally reached the area where a long-ago earthquake had partially caved in the walls. Virginia's mind raced as she frantically looked about. They could go no farther. Her gaze rested on Slade. Even though she said not a word, her eyes spoke her fears. How could they be safe here in this impasse? Had the giant Indian led them into a trap?

The Indian disappeared behind a huge boulder, but when they did not immediately follow, he turned back and impatiently gestured for them.

Frowning doubtfully, Slade stepped forward and peered behind the boulder. There, he could see a black slit on the far rock wall. Apparently it was a passageway into a cave that led into the mountainside. Hearing grunting voices coming from the other chambers, he realized the Apaches had pushed aside their superstitions and fears concerning the ancient ruins and had followed them.

"Pronto, neustche, pronto!" the Indian said urgently, gesturing for them to follow.

Neither Slade nor Virginia needed further urging. Although it was close, she squeezed Mule through the dark opening and Slade followed close behind, leading Blue. They had not walked more than five feet when the passageway opened into a huge cavern. The Indian handed the torch to Slade, doubled back, and with his enormous strength lifted a huge slab of rock and fitted it over the opening, thus sealing them inside the cavern and, hopefully, concealing them from the dread Apaches.

The cave was about thirty feet across and nearly eight feet high. Its length was indeterminable as it led away from the passage and disappeared in darkness. The floor was sandy, with rock underneath. There were a few pieces of pine knot lying about, and on an eroded shelf by Slade's shoulder was a pack rat's nest. From the appearance of the place, it could have been a day or a hundred years since anyone had been there.

Slade gave Virginia a dubious look when he saw a single light emerging from the long corridor of darkness. Someone else was approaching, but who?

Her heart hammering against her chest, Virginia reached for Slade. As soon as she touched the warmth of his arm, she felt safer, more reassured. "Slade . . who . . . ?"

Intrigued, he muttered, "I don't know, but we'll soon find out. Whoever he is, I have a feeling we owe him and his tall friend here our lives."

Fascinated, Virginia gaped at the wiry man who soon stood before them. He held a Winchester rifle in one hand as though it was an extension of himself, and a flaming torch in the other.

He curiously sized up Virginia and Slade as they.

407

stared at him.

She judged that the man could have been anywhere from forty to sixty years old. His face was leathery, obviously from spending many hours in the harsh sun, and his small eyes would have pierced even the strongest man or woman. His nose was crooked, as though it had been on the wrong end of a well-directed fist, and it appeared that not one tooth remained in his head. She wondered when he had last trimmed his hair or beard. Both hung long, covering the front and back of his shirt, and on his head was a small, dilapidated hat.

"Well, Thursday, I see you got them out in time," he said to the Indian. Then he turned to Slade and explained, "My friend says as little as possible, so I doubt he introduced himself properly. His name is Thursday . . . leastwise that's what I call him. I stole the idea from Daniel Defoe, the man who wrote *Robinson Crusoe,* and since he died in 1731, I seriously doubt he will be lodging a complaint against me." He extended his hand. "Among other things, I'm known as Caleab M. Reavis. What's your moniker?"

Heartily, Slade grasped his hand. "I'm Stephen Slade. This is my wife, Virginia."

Caleab's small eyes narrowed thoughtfully. "Pleasure to meet you, ma'am." His expression did not change when he turned back to Slade and said, "My folks taught me it was impolite to pry, so later on, if you decide to tell me why you have been digging and poking around in these mountains for the past few days, then had to go running down to the desert floor to rescue your wife and her . . . camel"—he threw a curious glance toward the unusual animal—"I figure that will be entirely up to you, because it's not my nature to pry." For the first time a flicker of amusement touched his leathered features. "My folks also taught me that it was impolite to stand around in a damp cave making small talk when there was a fresh pot of coffee just waiting to be drunk." He motioned with his head and started walking. "Come along, folks. Just in case you didn't recognize it for what it was, that was an invitation." Thursday fell into step behind him.

Slade watched their retreating forms, then glanced at Virginia and shrugged before pressing his hand against the small of her back. "You heard the gentleman; he has coffee on. And I for one have seldom turned down a cup of that brew."

Virginia had no intention of declining his hospitality, but many unanswered questions gnawed at her. "Slade, how did he know about us? How did he know you rescued me? How did he know where we were, and how—"

Slade silenced her with a raised finger across her mouth. "I don't know, but I am sure he will tell us in his own good time. That is . . . if they don't run off and leave us," he added, noticing how the old man's torch was growing dimmer in the darkness that lay ahead.

The passageway became more narrow and dark, and seemed to stretch endlessly. Slade did not like it, but from the fast pace the old man and the Indian were setting, it seemed they knew the passage well and evidently there were no hidden obstacles or drops. But Virginia was unaware of this and she proceeded more carefully, which slowed Slade's progress since he was bringing up the rear.

The old man stopped and asked, "Are you coming or not?" Then, realizing the woman was the apparent reason for their lagging behind, he handed his torch to Thursday and waited for Virginia to catch up to him. "Ma'am, no offense intended, but if you keep taking those teeny-weeny steps, we'll be in this cave all day and the dampness makes my rheumatism hurt powerfully bad. You walk on ahead with Thursday and I'll pass the time with your husband."

Although Virginia was still a little afraid of the towering giant, she did as the old man requested after Slade nodded reassuringly.

Reavis fell into step with Slade. "This passageway wasn't always like this. Thursday and I cleaned it up a bit. Never know when a body might have to get going in a hurry, and when I take to running, I don't want nothing in my way." He pointed to a tunnel leading off to his right. "And just in case you haven't noticed, this corridor isn't the only way in or out. This entire cave is nothing but a series of catacombs. I figure the Salados had a lot to do with it though."

"The Salados?"

"Yes, the people who built those ruins you were holed up in. Or, it could have been the people who were here before them. Who knows?"

A quarter of a mile more found them emerging into a much wider room where a little light filtered in from some cracks above. Several passages trailed off in different directions.

"Well, folks, we're nearly home. I can almost smell the coffee brewing," Caleab happily declared. "You, young man, stake your animals right over there and Thursday will feed and water them in a bit. But there are a few things he has to check on before he joins us."

Again, Thursday moved a huge slab of rock, which revealed a small tunnel. Virginia glanced at Slade in amazement. The slab had seemed a natural part of the cave, completely indistinguishable. Caleab motioned for them to follow him though the tunnel. They walked ten feet before reaching an adobe wall. The old man pulled on a handle, and as though by magic, the wall opened and they entered a small cabin.

"This is where I hang my hat," Caleab said with a sweeping gesture. "You folks have a chair and I'll pour the coffee. Ma'am, you'll have to excuse the untidiness. I wasn't expecting company."

She smiled. "Please don't apologize. Your home looks very comfortable."

The cabin was surprisingly neat for what she had decided was a hermit's abode. Two neatly made cots, one much longer than the other, lined one wall, with a chest of drawers separating them. A crude table and two chairs were in the center of the room, and a massive fireplace and hearth, on which many iron pots and skillets hung, completely filled the wall to her left. Beside the door leading to the outside was a washstand and a battered kitchen safe. However, it was the wall behind them that intrigued Virginia. The hidden door was actually a bookshelf, and on it were at least a hundred books. In front of the shelf was a rocking chair and a small table holding a kerosene lamp and a candle. Although far from fancy, it was comforting to the eye and had a homey feel about it.

"You must love to read," she stated softly, her voice filled with awe. This old man was truly a paradox, and Virginia realized she should not be surprised by anything she learned about him.

"Yes, ma'am, I surely do." He beamed proudly. "Good books help to pass the time when I'm snowed in during the long winter months." He pulled a chair back from the table and held it for her. "Come on and sit down. Your coffee will get cold."

Leaning his rifle on a stand built especially for it, he walked over to the kitchen safe, removed a venison roast, a loaf of bread, a bowl of apples, a large hunk of

411

cheese, and placed them on the table along with several plates and eating utensils. "Figured the two of you might be hungry." He pulled up the rocking chair and joined them at the table, then reached for his rifle and placed it on the worn arms of the chair.

Conversation remained at a standstill as Virginia and Slade ravenously attacked the food. It was only after they had shoved back their plates and Caleab had refilled their coffee cups that Virginia ventured to ask hesitantly, "Mr. Reavis, I realize this may be a foolish time to ask such a question, but are we safe here?"

"Safe?"

"Yes, from the Apaches."

"You are safer here than any place in these mountains," he boasted with good reason. "The Apaches don't bother me and I don't bother them . . . leastwise not anymore. They used to, but I haven't had any trouble out of them for more than three years now."

Confused, Virginia frowned. "But . . . why not? I thought when an Apache was on the warpath, he tried to kill every white man he saw."

Caleab chuckled as he reached for his calabash and tamped the tobacco in his pipe. "That's not entirely true. The Apaches are smart, wily devils. If they're outnumbered, they have sense enough to leave it be."

"But you don't outnumber them."

"That's right, I don't. However, there is a very good reason why they leave me alone."

Slade wisely settled back in his cane-bottomed chair and listened. Apparently Reavis did not object to answering Virginia's questions, but the old man might react differently if he started asking them.

Thoroughly interested, Virginia leaned her elbow on the table and rested her chin in her hand. "Do you mind telling us the reason why?"

"No, of course not." He tried not to act too pleased. It had been several months since he had been out of the mountains and regardless of the fact that he had grown tired of civilization, he still liked to talk whenever he had a willing audience. He puffed vigorously on his pipe and began his story.

"Even though it happened over three years ago, I can see it in my mind just like it was yesterday. If I hadn't been setting out some cabbage plants, they wouldn't have caught me off guard . . . but they did and that was my fault. They jumped me, and through a hail of gunfire, I made a beeline for my cabin." He gestured excitedly and his voice rose and fell with emotion. "After the shooting died down, I peered through the gun slits and could see their camp fire — they had attacked just before dark," he added. "I knew I had hit three of them with my faithful old Winchester, but there were at least ten left. I also knew I was seriously outnumbered and if they decided to rush me I would be a goner. Then I remembered an old story about Indians and hit upon a scheme. If I could convince them I was crazy — something folks in these parts have been claiming for a long time now — they might leave me alone. It was an act of desperation, but I figured I was a dead man anyway so I had nothing to lose. I stripped off all my clothing, grabbed two butcher knives, and rushed, screaming and hollering, directly into the Apache camp."

Caleab laughed at the memory. "The Apaches heard, then saw, the screeching "white devil" racing toward them. My scheme worked. They must have thought I was crazy, because no sane man would run naked, armed only with two knives, into a camp of ten heavily armed warriors. All I could see was Indians scattering, and they've left me alone since then . . .

except to steal my apples from time to time." He glared at Slade. "Which, by the way, that reminds me, young man, you owe me" — he rubbed his chin thoughtfully — "I figure about four bits for those apples you helped yourself to."

Suddenly red faced, Slade grinned. "Yes, sir, I'll be happy to pay for them, but for the record, I didn't know that orchard belonged to anyone in particular."

Caleab squinted one eye at him. "Now you know differently. That's how I make my living — that and growing vegetables. I have little vegetable gardens all over these mountains close to the water holes." He grunted. "Surprised you didn't see any of them while you were blundering around looking for the Dutchman's gold."

His lips parted in surprise. "Looking for whose gold?"

"The Dutchman's. You were looking for his mine, weren't you?" Even though Caleab had presented it as a question, his words were more a matter-of-fact statement.

"No, sir. I'll admit I was doing a bit of prospecting, but I have no idea who the Dutchman is." Slade felt a tingle of apprehension. Stories about gold mines here in the West had a way of being blown out of proportion. Still, he wondered if they were referring to the same mine. If so, someone else might have already found the Peralta gold.

Caleab eyed him doubtfully. "You mean to tell me you've never heard of Jacob Waltz, otherwise known as the Dutchman? Why, everybody in these parts has heard of him!"

Slade shook his head. "No, not everybody. I've never heard of him. But it's been years since I've been anywhere near this area and never in these mountains."

He drew in his lips thoughtfully. "Just who is this Jacob Waltz?"

"He's a crazy old codger just like me. Only where I like to grow things, he'd rather spend his life burrowing in a mountain searching for a hidden bonanza. And from what I've heard down in Phoenix, he's shown enough gold to the merchants to give people the idea that he's found something up here. He comes up here every few months and there is always a whole pack of men trying to follow him, but so far, he's been able to give them the slip—"

Virginia, not knowing Slade's interest in the Superstitions' gold mines, interrupted the old man. "Mr. Reavis, that is all very interesting, but I'm more curious to learn how you knew we were here, and how you knew the Apaches had found us."

Caleab looked at her through a fog of tobacco smoke. "Well, ma'am, to be truthful, there's not much that goes on in these mountains that I'm not aware of. I can tell you within a few hours when your husband arrived in these mountains. And, I might add . . . I find it strange that he hasn't been in these mountains before, but he knows exactly where he's going." He glanced at Slade curiously. "You must have a very good map, young man."

Slade shrugged noncommittally, aware of the thoughtful expression that suddenly flickered over Virginia's face.

Caleab, figuring the young man would keep any information he had about gold mines to himself, looked at Virginia. "To answer your question, I keep well informed about exactly where the Apaches have their *rancherias*. That way, I'm not faced with any sudden surprises in case they get a tad too brave. I have little hidey-holes all over these mountains; then there are the tunnels . . . I manage to keep abreast of what's going on. I figured if I knew you were here, the Apaches did too, only they must have decided to wait until daybreak to roust you out of those ruins. They are a superstitious lot."

Virginia reached out and grasped Slade's hand and squeezed it. "I know I speak for my husband as well as myself when I say we're extemely grateful to you for saving our lives."

Caleab rubbed his face sheepishly. "Well, I have to be honest with you. You were not in that much danger of being killed . . . not unless you had put up too much of a fight. Of course, if they had captured you, you might have preferred being dead."

"I'm not sure I understand." The tone of Virginia's voice revealed her obvious confusion.

"Why, the Apaches are gathering as many prisoners as possible—men and women alike. There must be at least thirty of them scattered among the *rancherias.*"

"You mean they are holding that many white men and women!" The idea was very disturbing to her.

"Whites and Mexicans." Caleab nodded his head. "I figure something big is about to happen. Like maybe another swapping of prisoners for rifles." He slowly brought his rifle around and leveled it at Slade. His small eyes narrowed cautiously. "I've been sitting here doing a lot of talking and you've been keeping your mouth shut. If I don't hear what I figure to be a reasonable explanation of your presence and the mysterious way this young woman—who *claims* to be your wife—arrived here, I'm liable to think you are in cahoots with that low-down varmint who has been trading rifles to the Apaches for prisoners. I might add,

I'm not a patient man and my trigger finger tends to get a little heavy at times when I don't hear the right answers."

Chapter Twenty-nine

"Take it easy, old timer. You have it all wrong," Slade said, watching him warily. He carefully placed his hands flat on the table so Reavis would not have a reason to think he was going for his guns.

Virginia's clenched hand flew to her mouth. What Caleab Reavis suggested was unthinkable. "Slade would never do anything so heinous as to sell guns to the Apaches! Never!" she protested hotly.

Grimly, Slade set his chin in a stubborn line. "Stay out of it, sweetheart. I'll handle this."

"But . . . Slade . . . I'm not about to sit still and let him say those things without—"

Caleab interrupted forcefully. "No disrespect, ma'am, but I think you should do as your man says." He turned his attention to Slade but still kept Virginia under scrutiny out of the corner of his eye. "And I also think you ought to try to convince me that I'm wrong . . . before my mind starts to dwell on those poor souls the Apaches are holding. And in case you suddenly get any fancy notions, stand up, put your guns on the table, and slide them, real easy, over here in front of me." To give himself added insurance that Slade would do as he had ordered, he leaned forward and positioned the rifle barrel right at Virginia's throat.

The cords stood out on Slade's neck and his jaw was rigid with tightly controlled emotion as he complied with the old man's request, being very careful not to make any sudden moves. "I have not been selling guns to the Indians, but I don't know how I can prove it to you. Just like I told you a while ago, I've been prospecting in these mountains and that's all," he said after he had eased back down onto his chair.

"No you haven't," Caleab challenged, his finger tightening minutely on the trigger. "And you had better let that be the last lie that comes out of your mouth. I've seen no picks, no shovels, and no mining supplies of any kind. A man doesn't prospect with his bare hands."

Slade's eyes narrowed thoughtfully. So, the old man had been watching him. That left the strong possibility that he was interested in the gold for himself and his accusations were nothing but a ploy to get him to reveal the gold's location. He quickly decided to find out just how interested the old man was. "He does if the gold has already been mined."

Caleab's head remained cocked at a listening angle for a second longer, then he stirred. "Keep talking," he said with a significant lifting of his brows.

"Have you ever heard of Don Miguel Peralta?"

It was a long moment before Caleab answered. "Yep, I've heard of him, and I've also heard the rumors that . . ." He grinned. "Well, it appears to me that if you know of Don Peralta, then you've heard the rumors too. It might interest you to know, there has been some speculation that the Dutchman's gold and the Peralta gold are one and the same."

Remembering the old man's story about his charging the Apaches armed only with two knives, Slade decided the Indians might have had good reason to believe that the old codger was crazy. And he was not about to risk his or Virginia's life over gold that might or might not exist. It was not worth it.

He breathed in deeply. "I might as well level with you. I have been looking for the gold, not in a physical sense, but, instead, I've been trying to locate the landmarks. I have no map; the directions to the cached gold are in my memory. A friend of mine was dying, and he told me where I could find the Peralta gold, but I had to agree to share it equally with the family that remains in Mexico. Over the years, the landmarks have changed some, so I really don't know how accurate his directions are. But then, you've lived in these mountains long enough to know that one or two landslides and a flood can change the appearance of the terrain."

Slade spread his hands and shrugged in mock resignation. "Now, I suppose the next step of this little scenario is to sit back and let you rough me up, because if I tell you the location of the gold right now, you won't believe me; it would be too easy. Then, when you can't get the information out of me by force, you can threaten to hurt Virginia. Since I'm not about to let you hurt her, I'll be forced to tell." He jutted his chin forward. "Come on, let's get this over with."

Caleab eyed him skeptically. "You seem awfully eager to tell me where the gold is."

Slade uttered a curse under his breath, then said, "That's what I just got through explaining. The way I see it, I don't have much of a choice; the deck is stacked against me. You're holding the rifle, there's no telling when your friend will return—and I've seen a demonstration of his strength—and the Apaches are turning over every rock looking for us. So what else do you think I should do? Our lives are not worth the gold—even if it exists. You should know as well as I do how these lost gold mine stories are blown out of proportion."

Not answering, Caleab glanced at Virginia, although he was careful not to let his attention stray too much from Slade. That young man was as dangerous as a coiled rattlesnake, and if he gave him one opportunity, he would take advantage of it. "Suppose you tell me what you were doing down there on the desert all by yourself."

"I can assure you it was *not* to sell guns to the Indians! Neither Slade nor I would ever do anything like that!" She was conscious of the bite in her voice and of the old hermit's observing eyes.

"That's your story," he bantered, staring at her warily. Even though he knew for a fact that someone was selling guns to the Apaches, and their sudden presence here in the Superstitions was awfully suspicious, he had a gut feeling that the two youngsters were good people. But still he had to be sure. Too many lives, now and in the future, were at stake for him to rely solely on a hunch.

"Since you've been keeping him under observation and since I only arrived here last night, where are the guns? Answer that question for me!" she demanded angrily.

"I've never claimed he was the only one involved. As far as I'm concerned, he could have a partner."

Even though the situation was serious, Slade focused his attention on Virginia and saw her in a different light. He was thoroughly impressed with the way she was handling herself under fire, how she had kept her wits about her, and how she had come to his defense.

"Let me ask you something, Mr. Reavis," Virginia

challenged. "If Slade has been involved in selling guns to the Apaches, then why were they searching for us a while ago?"

"I don't know . . . maybe he double-crossed them." He had to admit, the young woman was making good sense.

"You should know the definition of that word very well!" She glared at him vehemently.

Caleab blustered right back, "You still haven't offered me any reasonable explanation as to why you were in the desert alone and he was here in the mountains—pretending to look for gold. I don't see a ring on your finger either. It's awfully easy just to *claim* to be a man's wife without it's being legal!" He became more threatening with his rifle, knowing how people's tongues loosened with fear.

Virginia swallowed hard as it suddenly dawned on her that they were completely at this man's mercy—a man who had readily admitted he might be slightly crazy. He could very easily decide to kill them. Helplessly, she looked at Slade and swallowed hard. One man wanted an explanation and the other man refused to listen. Maybe she should tell the entire story. At least Slade could hear her side of it. Determination washed over her and her heart lifted. Yes, that was exactly what she should do. She might never have another opportunity. If the old man decided to kill them, at least Slade would know the truth.

She lifted her chin, meeting Caleab's narrow gaze head on. "All right, I'll tell you anything you want to know. Where should I start?"

Shrugging indifferently, he shook his head. "Doesn't matter to me, just as long as you are able to convince me that neither one of you is involved."

"T—Then I guess I should start at the beginning."

Her voice was shakier than she would have liked. "I met Slade several months ago in the New Mexico Territory—"

Slade interrupted. "Sweetheart, I doubt he meant for you to start that far back."

"No," Caleab drawled slowly, his eyes glinting speculatively. There might be a viable reason the young man didn't want her to tell him how and maybe even why they had met. "Don't pay him any attention. Go on with your story . . . from the beginning."

Suddenly feeling unsure of herself and not quite so brave, Virginia twisted her hands in her lap. "Mr. Reavis, I am not going to bore you with unimportant details. The point of the matter is, when I first met Slade, I fell in love with him immediately. If the circumstances had been different, he might have realized he had fallen in love with me too. But the circumstances were such . . . they were extremely . . . difficult. You see, my father was a very unscrupulous man . . . and he forced us to marry. Papa left right after the ceremony, and a few days later . . . Slade and I had . . . a disagreement and he left too. He thought I was as unscrupulous as my father . . . but I wasn't, I swear I wasn't!" She raised her chin haughtily, and her black eyes pierced the distance between her and Slade.

"I hated that place and did not want to remain there, yet I knew a woman traveling alone would never be allowed to cross through Indian country . . . so I cut my hair . . . and disguised myself as a young boy."

"You did what?" Slade asked, leaning forward in surprise.

"You hush!" Caleab said, pointing a finger at him. He did not want him influencing what she had to say. Then he peered at Virginia. "Why didn't you just catch a stage?"

"Because I had very little money, and at that time I felt the wagon and goods were my only security and I could not abandon them."

"You lost me there, ma'am," Caleab said with a shake of his head. "What wagon?" Had it been used to run guns? he wondered.

She was keenly aware of the old hermit's scrutiny. "My father purchased a Conestoga back in East Texas and filled it with mercantile goods that would be in demand on outlying farms and ranches. It was our intention to settle in California," Virginia explained patiently.

"All right, now I see what you meant about not being able to catch a stage," Caleab muttered. "Go on with your story," he urged.

Virginia spoke with deceptive calmness. "I made it as far as Fort Grant before I was forced to stop. Even though I was eager to continue on to California, there were so many rumors and reports of Indian trouble, I knew a lone wagon would be asking for an attack. Before my father left, someone had told me that when we reached Arizona we should join a group of teamsters or freighters for safety. So that's what I decided to do. But when I arrived at the fort, they had already left and were not expected back for weeks . . . so I was forced to stay there for awhile."

She took a deep breath and tried to maintain her curtness. "I went to work at the stables helping to take care of the cavalry's horses. I tried to stay out of everybody's way and not draw any unnecessary attention to myself, but there was a smart-aleck lieutenant who had it in for me. He did everything he could to make my life miserable. Then, one night, I went over to the saloon for supper . . . and he caused some trouble . . . and a nice man came to my rescue." She glanced at

Slade and the expression of astonishment in his eyes told her he remembered the incident. "I assumed the camp commander would question me — and possibly even the man who had come to my rescue — about the lieutenant's ugly behavior, and I felt if there was an investigation, my true identity might be revealed. And . . . I could not allow that to happen."

"Because they wouldn't let you go on, you being a woman and all," Caleab concurred.

"Well, there was another reason too." She could hardly lift her voice above a whisper. "Slade had accused me of being unscrupulous, and I started thinking about how those people who had befriended me would feel if it became common knowledge I was a woman. The bartender and the man who owned the stables were my friends . . . and if people learned I had fooled them, they probably would have been laughed out of the territory. And it was never my intention to hurt anyone, I swear!"

Slade felt as though he had been hit in the stomach with a heavy log. That boy in the saloon had been Virginia! No wonder the memory of her had haunted him so after his departure from Fort Grant. It must have registered in his subconscious mind that, in reality, *he* had been *she!*

"Before anyone could start asking questions, I left the following morning with a small caravan. It was . . . they were . . ." She struggled to find the right words. "The women . . . I believe out here they are called "soiled doves." They had in their employ three guards, so there was protection. And, I might add, I still pretended to be a boy. They didn't know I was a woman until later."

Caleab was intrigued by her story, and, what's more, he believed it. It was too farfetched to be any-

425

thing but the truth. If her husband was involved in gunrunning, there was no doubt in his mind she was an innocent victim. Still, a question nagged at him that had nothing to do with his suspicions. Clearing his throat, he asked, "I'm curious about something. How did you come by that camel?"

"He belonged to one of the women, but she didn't like him—really, no one else did either—and his care was soon delegated to me." Aware of how closely Slade was watching her, she wanted to continue quickly. "But to go on with my story, we were camped by the river one night and I couldn't sleep, so I went to the river to take a bath. I heard a noise and thought we were about to be attacked by Apaches. I raised an alarm, and Hank, one of the guards, gave the order to wake the entire camp. But it wasn't Apaches; it was Slade. He rode into camp badly wounded, a breath away from unconsciousness. We found out later that he had been shot by Apaches."

"Where did this happen?" Caleab asked, the lines of concentration deepening along his bushy brows and under his narrowed eyes.

"In the Gila Mountains," Slade replied. His voice was thick and unsteady as a broad spectrum of emotions flashed over his face.

"And we had left Fort Thomas a few days before," Virginia said in a low, composed voice. "I would like to add that everybody still thought I was a boy—except Dovie. I wasn't able to fool her. But with the arrival of my husband, I dropped my disguise. I knew it would be senseless to keep up the pretense. And I really didn't want to anymore, because . . . I had missed him so much."

She reached across the table and took Slade's hand in hers. It was as though no one was in the room but them. Tears blinded her and choked her voice. "When you left me like you did there in New Mexico, I was hurt so badly . . . at times I thought I hated you . . . but I didn't. I loved you. I—I tried to convince myself differently . . . but it was a truth I could not deny. I loved you and I wanted to spend every day of my life with you. Then, it seemed almost like a miracle when you came riding in . . . even if you were half dead from loss of blood. T—Then . . . when you regained consciousness and told me that you loved me too, I was ecstatic. I knew whatever problems we had, we could work together to solve them."

Slade's blue eyes showed the dullness of guilt and regret. He grunted with self-disgust, "But, as usual, I insisted on being a thickheaded fool."

"I didn't blame you for feeling the way you did. But . . . do you remember when Mule interrupted us that day?" She bit her lower lip to keep it from trembling when he nodded slightly. "I was going to tell you everything then, but after we were interrupted . . . I lost my courage and I kept putting it off. Don't you see, Slade, I was afraid to tell you . . . and I was afraid not to. Because of what had happened in New Mexico, I was afraid you would think I had disguised myself merely to take advantage of people. But without the explanation, you would think I was one of . . . Dovie's girls. And I really didn't know which was worse." She closed her eyes tightly and tears spilled down her cheeks. "I can imagine what you thought and how you felt when those teamsters came tearing into camp and that . . . horrid man mistook me for one of Dovie's girls. It broke my heart to see such . . . such pain in your eyes."

Slade tipped the chair over in his haste to reach Virginia. In one forward motion, she was in his arms and was clasped tightly to him, her soft curves molding to the contour of his lean body. No words were needed to express their joy and their love; just touching each other was enough. He exhaled a long sigh of contentment, as though a heavy weight had been lifted from his heart. Virginia was his and his alone! And, God as his witness, he would never do anything to hurt her again.

She locked herself into his embrace and buried her face against the hard muscle of his chest. A muffled cry of relief escaped her lips. Her tears were gone, as if evaporated by an onrushing wind.

Caleab squirmed uncomfortably in his chair and cleared his throat, more so to remind them of his presence then to remove any lump that might have formed. When he spoke, his voice did not hold the threat that it had before. "I hate to interrupt such a tender scene . . . but, young man, I want you back in that chair. So far, I've heard nothing that proves my suspicions wrong. And I still don't know why she was alone on the desert."

Slade glared hard at Reavis, then glanced at the rifle. Reluctantly, he righted the chair, but instead of placing it where it had been, he moved it beside Virginia and sat down, wrapping his arm around her shoulder.

"Mr. Reavis, Slade thought I was a . . . was a . . ."

"I already figured that from what you said."

"He left the caravan very angry . . . no, not really angry; he was more hurt than anything else."

Caleab supposed that was how he would have felt too, but instead of commenting, he waited for Virginia to continue.

"But I suppose, in a strange way, it was a blessing in disguise."

"How's that?" Caleab wanted to know.

"If he had been with us, he might have been killed too," she said, her face solemn. "You see, we ran short of water and had to take a different route; therefore we were running way behind schedule. It was, I think, five days ago . . . I'm not really sure. So much has happened since then. We were attacked at Apache Springs." She looked at Caleab through a sheen of tears. "I don't want to talk about that. B—But I was the only one left. I knew I couldn't stay there, because I was afraid the Apaches would return at any time . . . so I struck out across the desert, and Slade found me last night." Slade's arm tightened around her shoulders in an instinctive gesture of comfort.

The old man scratched his whiskers, stalling for time. Finally he spoke. "What would you say if I told you I was inclined to believe you?"

"I'd say you should, because everything I said is the truth. And if you believe me, you have to believe Slade, because my story confirms what he has told you all along—that he has not been selling guns to the Indians."

"How do you figure that?"

She touched her chest in a gesture that emphasized the sincerity of her statement. "Other than the fact that I *know* he is innocent, it has been years since he has been in this part of the country. I don't know that much about Apaches, but I doubt that a person can walk into one of their camps—*rancherias*—and offer to sell them guns without their knowing something about that person. It seems to me, whoever the gunrunner is, he would have to know his way around and be free to travel about without raising questions. Doesn't that seem logical to you?"

A muscle flicked in his jaw and he stroked his beard

thoughtfully. "Yes, I suppose it does." He lowered his rifle and stood it on the butt of the stock. Then he looked at Slade. "If you are riled about my drawing down on you, speak your peace now. If not, then let's put it behind us." He offered his hand for a shake.

Slade stared at the proffered hand. He felt no animosity toward the old man. He supposed he might have had the same suspicions if the situation had been reversed. Besides, if the old timer had not been so insistent with his accusations, he might not have learned the truth about Virginia until it was too late. "All right," he said, removing his arm from Virginia's shoulder and firmly grasping Caleab's hand. "I have no hard feelings."

Realizing they would probably want to be alone, Caleab stood. "I need to go find Thursday—figure it will take me two, maybe three hours, just in case you younguns want to catch up on your smooching. Then, when we get back, we all need to sit down and discuss what we're going to do to help those poor people the Apaches are holding captive."

Chapter Thirty

Virginia lifted a checkered oilcloth hanging over the cabin's single window and pretended to gaze out at the rugged terrain. The window had been placed in a strategic spot, enabling anyone in the cabin to have a clear view of most of the vantage points of the canyon, but they held little interest for her. Caleab had just left, using the passage behind the bookshelf. And now, the small room was immersed in a deafening silence.

She could feel Slade watching her, yet, strangely, she was reluctant to turn and face him. He had embraced her and acted as though he loved her more than anything in the world, but she wanted to give him a moment to think about their relationship, to be absolutely sure, because she doubted she could take another disappointment. Also, though it seemed somewhat childish, since she had made her revelation a short while ago, she felt it was time for him to make the next move.

With Virginia's back presented to him, Slade was forced to move slightly in order to study her profile. Although her smooth brow, her tiny, uptilted nose, and the stubborn jut of her chin had been permanently etched in his mind, he felt he would never grow weary of watching her. A gamut of emotions coursed through him. He felt relief that at last he knew the entire truth and it was nothing like he had thought; he experienced despair, for he had caused her so much pain, and he was overwhelmed with happiness because she still loved him, though he should have known that from the love they had shared the night before. It amazed him that this wonderful, magnificent woman could endure his stubborn stupidity time after time, yet still love him. At that moment, he wanted to hold her in his arms and never let her go.

A spasmodic trembling started deep within Virginia when she heard his footsteps on the rough-planked floor, and she clenched her hands until her nails bit painfully into her palms in order to resist the urge to fling herself into his arms.

Tenderly, Slade placed his hands on Virginia's shoulders, turned her around to face him, and lowered his lips to the long, slender column of her throat. He murmured softly, "A man's mind can be cruel, sweetheart. He can imagine all sorts of things, especially when the woman he loves is involved." His voice was gentle and held a tinge of self-reproach. "I'm not going to ask your forgiveness, because I feel you already have forgiven me." Even though he believed his statement, a wave of relief washed over him when she nodded her head. "Nevertheless, I will say this: I realize my promise will do little to erase the past, to make you forget all the pain I've caused you, but, as God is my witness, I swear I will never abandon you or willingly hurt you again."

She felt as if her breath had been cut off and her heart would burst. Then, slowly, she lifted her eyes to his. Her heart jolted and her pulse pounded. "I love you, Slade," she whispered adoringly. "I love you with all my heart and soul. I think I always have, and I know I always will."

His gaze was as soft as a caress. "And I love you, sweetheart, more than you'll ever know." He cupped her face in his large hands and held it gently, then his lips claimed hers possessively, hungrily.

Virginia clung to him and artlessly responded with intense yearnings. Her head spun wildly at his nearness and masculine scent. Then, abruptly coming to her senses, she murmured breathlessly, twisting from his arms, "No, Slade, please. I want you so much, but not now, not here."

Immediately, he searched her eyes for signs that bitterness or reluctance had been the reason she had pulled from his embrace. Instead, when he saw only the heartrending tenderness of her gaze, he queried softly, "And why not?"

"T—That man, Mr. Reavis. He might return."

His gaze roved and lazily appraised her. Then, breaking into a devilish smile, he cajoled, "The old man said he would be gone for two or three hours . . . and besides, he gave us permission to smooch."

"Slade, please, don't tease." She rubbed her arms uneasily. "That old recluse is just a . . . little strange and even though he said he would be gone for several hours, he might come back sooner than we expect, and if you kiss me once more like that"—she looked up at him with a glint of wonder in her eyes and shrugged slightly—"I doubt I could be held responsible for my behavior . . . and I would hate to be caught in an embarrassing situation. Our love is much too precious for that."

"I think I've turned you into a shameless wanton, sweetheart," he said, a wide, teasing grin breaking across his handsome face.

"I think so too, but not shameless enough to make love to you at the risk of someone's seeing us."

The thought of making love to her sent waves of excitement through him. Squinting one eye, he grinned lecherously. "That problem can be easily solved," he muttered huskily, lacing his fingers through hers and leading her to the bookshelf.

"Where are you taking me?" she asked, not out of protest but with the thrilling hope that she might soon be in his arms again in a passionate embrace. He was right. He had turned her into a shameless wanton, and she would not have had it any other way.

"You'll see, but first I had better get a candle." Spying the one on the table, he quickly lit it and handed it to Virginia. Then, removing a book from the shelf as he had seen Caleab do earlier, he found the handle and opened the door concealing the passageway.

Once they were inside the cavern, Slade took the candle and quietly cautioned Virginia to stay where she was until he came back. A few minutes later, he returned and led her into one of the narrow tunnels.

She gasped with surprise when she saw his bedroll spread neatly over the ground.

He placed the candle on a stone ledge and gently took her into his arms. "My apologies that this isn't a fine hotel with a bottle of chilled wine by the bedside and a huge bouquet of roses on the night table, but it's the best I could do on such short notice. One day though, sweetheart, I swear we'll have a proper honeymoon."

The smile in her eyes contained a sensuous flame as she made a sweeping gesture with her hand. "This is lovelier than the Taj Mahal!" Then she slowly wound her hands around the back of his neck and ran them up his corded muscles until she reached the shaggy lengths of his hair. "And do you know why it is lovelier?" she breathed huskily.

"No, suppose you tell me." His voice sounded thick with desire as he ran his hands down the length of her back and cupped her buttocks.

"Because when I am with you, I feel the effects of heady wine, I hear the soft strains of violins, I smell the delicate fragrance of roses, and the smallest hovel magically becomes a palace. I love you so, my darling." Her whisper was as light as a baby's breath.

Slade needed no further urging. He lowered his mouth to hers, gently at first, then his kisses became more demanding, more insistent. Slowly, lingeringly, his tongue outlined her alluring mouth, and he felt it tremble beneath the pressure of his questing lips.

Nothing mattered to the lovers anymore, not the threat of Apaches, the dangers the mountain presented, or Slade's hatred of a man in his past. Their circumstances, their surroundings, made their future uncertain, but they did not care. The only thing that was important was now, this precise moment, and the fact that they were in each other's arms, where destiny had decreed they belonged.

Slade unbuttoned her bodice and slipped the garment from her shoulders, allowing it to fall unheeded to the ground. He lovingly scooped Virginia into his arms and, kneeling, placed her on the blankets.

His lips sought, then found, hers again. Urgently his tongue compelled her mouth to part, then it shot deep between her lips to pillage the sweetness within. Thoroughly, almost savagely, he ravaged the dark, moist recesses of her mouth, leaving no crevice unexplored.

Virginia's head reeled at the feel of Slade against her. Even though she had known him before, it was

435

like a new experience, and one she would never grow weary of. The candle flickered, making their skin appear tawny colored as limbs entwined with limbs. The silken strands of his furred chest pressed into her soft, heaving breasts.

When had he removed his shirt? She didn't know; she didn't care. She was too caught up in the magic and the delicious passion he evoked in her as his lips continued to hungrily devour hers.

Again and again, her lips met his; her tongue intertwined with his until she was panting for breath like a magnificent cat after a great chase, even though, in actuality, the race had not yet been run.

He rained searing kisses on her eyelids, her cheeks, her temples, the curls of her honey gold hair, until she felt as if she were being showered by the fiery sparks of falling stars. His loving assault left her highly excited and breathless, and greedily longing for more.

He buried his face in her hair and gently teased her ear with his tongue, his breath hot against her skin. Exquisite pleasure attacked her mind and senses, and eternally conquered her. Fiery lights danced before her passion-dazed eyes as sweet rapture enslaved her. She shivered with delight.

Fervently, Virginia flung back her head in exultation as his mouth coursed hungrily down the column of her slender throat, nibbling, tongue flicking, kissing. Her hands caressed the corded muscles of his back, then she moaned and writhed beneath him, and dug her nails into his flesh when he carried her to loftier heights as his tongue assaulted the valley between her breasts.

With a sharp, ragged gasp, she felt her pink nipples stiffen against him, as did he. His fingers teased the taut peaks to even greater fullness before he lowered his mouth to envelop one rosy tip between his lips. His tongue traced tiny, swirling circles about the bud, sending shivers tingling from its center in all directions.

She could feel her warm, wet desire for him on the insides of her thighs when he began exploring her innermost secret. His fingers stroked her satiny fold and his thumb flicked and teased the tiny button that would send her passion soaring past all limits of her endurance.

Then, his hand clasped hers and guided it down . . . down.

Her fingers curled around the velvet hardness of his manhood, then danced upward to the tiny bead of moisture on the tip.

With a muffled snarl, he rose to his knees, then lowered himself onto her, penetrating her swiftly, completely, with a clean, sharp thrust that made her gasp aloud with delight and cling tightly to his broad back as she held onto him. His powerful muscles flexed and she locked her legs around his as though to prevent him from escaping. Over and over he plunged into her, faster and faster, until their lovemaking became like a mass of rumbling clouds that had built to a thundering peak, and as their bodies unleashed their fury, a blaze of lightning stabbed tempestuously, shattering them to the very depths of their souls.

"I wonder what could be keeping Mr. Reavis and his Indian friend," Virginia remarked for the third time in the past hour as she moved the cloth covering the window a tiny bit and peered outside. Nothing. There was not a sign of a living soul; not even an animal or a bird stirred. She resumed pacing, something she had been doing off and on since washing the few dirty dishes and sweeping the floor.

"I don't know, sweetheart," Slade replied, breaking down his gun-cleaning rod and slipping it back into his saddlebag. He too was starting to worry. It had been at least six hours since the old man had left, and the possibility of Apaches' attacking had been creeping more and more into his mind.

Casually, Slade blew out the lamp and set it on the hearth so the table would be clear in case it had to be tilted over. Although he could see that the cabin had been built like a small fortress, if attacked, he believed they might need additional cover, and while the kitchen table would not be much protection, it might stop a bullet.

"Aren't you worried?" she asked abruptly, her brow drawn in a troubled frown.

He started to say he wasn't, then caught himself. Virginia was very astute and she would probably know he was lying the moment he opened his mouth. Why insult her intelligence? Still, he could be diplomatic about it. Shrugging as though it really did not matter, he said, "Worried? No, not really. I'd say I am more concerned than anything else."

"Do you think the Apaches . . . ?" Then she exhaled a deep rush of air and gave a wave of her hand. "I'm sorry, Slade. You have no way of knowing that any more than I do. It's just . . . he's been gone so long and there is no telling how many more Apaches joined in the search."

Sliding back his chair, he quickly crossed the room and gently grasped her by the shoulders. "Look, sweetheart, there's no doubt in my mind; if anyone can survive out there, that old man can. He's been doing it for years. If he did run into Apaches, he's probably holed up somewhere waiting for dark before he tries to make it back. Why don't you go sit down and maybe read a book? It might help take your mind off things."

Sighing, she wrinkled her nose and shook her head. "I doubt it would hold my interest."

"Then will you please sit down and quit pacing! It's beginning to get on my nerves." His voice was much sharper than he had intended and he was instantly sorry.

"I knew it! I knew it! Now you are snapping at me for no reason at all," she declared adamantly, tossing her head and placing her hand on her hips. "You *are* more worried than you've been letting on."

Slade was spared an answer when he thought he detected a noise coming from behind the bookshelf. "Listen!" he hissed, instinctively grabbing his rifle and raising it to his shoulder.

The Apaches were not supposed to know about the secret passage, but he had to consider the possibility that they had followed the old man. Quickly, he tilted the table over and crouched down behind it. Seeing Virginia just standing there with a surprised expression on her face, he grabbed her hand and none too gently yanked her down beside him. He gave her the rifle and filled his hands with his two pistols, then waited, warily, as the door started to slide forward.

"Don't anybody get any itchy fingers in there. It's me, Caleab Reavis," the old man said, slipping his thin body through the narrow opening. Pretending not to hear the young couple's sigh of relief, he nodded with approval at the overturned table, then swung the door wide open so that Thursday, who was carrying a man over his shoulder, could enter. "You," he said to Virginia, "build a fire to heat some water. And we're going to need more light in here. This man has an arrow in his leg and he has other injuries that need to be tended."

"I'll get the lamp," Slade offered quickly, stepping aside so that Thursday could lower the injured man onto one of the cots.

Caleab immediately started cutting away the man's trouser leg so that he could get a closer look at the wound. "Sorry it took so long, folks, but we had to rescue this fellow from the Apaches. And it appears that we made a mistake when we assumed they were after the two of you. Evidently, they were after him and another man."

"How's that?" Slade asked, blowing out the match and placing the globe back on the lamp. He was curious as to who the injured man was and what had happened out there, but he figured the old hermit would tell him in due time. Then he felt a kick of discovery go through him when he caught a glimpse of the man's face. Slade's eyes widened with recognition, even though the man scarcely looked like himself.

"Virginia . . . come here. It's Hank . . . he's alive!"

Virginia dropped the block of wood she had been about to put in the fireplace. Hank? Here? How could that be? She must have misunderstood him. "S— Slade, did you say Hank?"

Not trusting himself to speak, Slade merely nodded his head. He would have given anything in the world not to have her see her friend in this condition.

Hank tried to raise himself on his elbows but was unsuccessful. "Little girl? Is that you?" He squinted his eyes, yet he could not focus them clearly.

Pushing her way past Thursday, Virginia ran to the cot and knelt by the bedside. Finding Hank alive had been beyond her wildest dreams, yet she was unable to mask the horror she felt when she saw his face. Then

440

her gaze slowly swept the length of his body. It was obvious he had been brutally tortured; his face was badly bruised and swollen, one ear was missing, only tatters remained of his shirt, which did little to conceal the welts and cuts on his chest, and his poor, pitiful feet were nothing but bloody, blistered pulp.

"Oh, Hank!" she cried. "What happened to you?"

"If you think I look bad, you ought to see what the other guy looks like." He attempted a smile, but it fell short. His expression grew serious. "Like a fool I let my guard down and I . . . no, *we* paid the price. Those Apaches were on us before we knew what hit us. We never had much of a chance." He reached out and brushed away one of many tears that spilled down Virginia's cheeks. "God, little girl, I've worried about you! I didn't know if they had captured or killed you. You have no idea how it makes me feel to see that you got out all right. How did you escape from them?"

She lowered her head and tears fell freely to her twisting hands. "I — I didn't. I d-didn't have to. They never caught me. When I heard them a — attacking . . . I — I hid in the pool and in the rocks."

"Good for you!" he exclaimed through swollen lips. "That was using your head!"

"For h — hiding in the rocks like a c — coward?"

"No," he rasped. "For being smart enough to stay alive. There wasn't anything you could have done to help. The minute they attacked, we were goners."

His words helped lift her heavy burden of guilt. "The others, Hank, what happened to the others?" She moved out of the way when Slade offered him a drink of water.

Caleab signaled Thursday to tend the man's leg wound while he stood back and listened. He realized the young woman was obtaining as much pertinent information from the man as he could hope to get. No doubt the man had suffered at the hands of the Apaches, but the cuts and bruises would soon heal, and the arrow in his leg was just a flesh wound. It was his feet that concerned him. Apparently those heathens had made him walk barefoot over hot coals.

Hank wiped his mouth with the back of his hand and leaned back against the pillow. After he had taken several deep breaths, his voice seemed stronger when he continued. "I'm not sure what happened to all the others. The Apaches split us up when we reached the first camp — why, I don't know, unless they were wary of having too many captives in one camp. I do know one thing though; I'd gladly give everything I own to see Dovie right now."

"Yes," Virginia murmured softly, smoothing Hank's hair from his brow. "Bless her heart."

"Bless her heart, my ass!" he snarled viciously. "I'd like to get my hands around her neck! That bitch — sorry about the language, little girl," he muttered, cutting his eyes up at her. "But she sold us out . . . every last one of us! She's been selling guns to those savages!"

Virginia could not believe what she was hearing. "Hank, are you sure?" she anxiously inquired, noticing Caleab's interest had been piqued.

"Yes, I'm sure," he muttered, his lips tightening bitterly and his eyes glazed with some unmentionable horror. "There was a false floor in the bed of her wagon filled with guns. That's why her wagon and yours were the only ones taken after the attack."

"But there were no weapons in my wagon."

"No, but they needed room to carry the prisoners, and, too, there were a lot of goods in your wagon. That's why they took it." He glanced at Caleab, then at Slade. "The only consolation is, something went

442

wrong. Apparently she didn't bring them the guns they were expecting, because now they are holding her prisoner too. I don't understand the Apache language very well, but from what I was able to gather, they're trading the prisoners in two or three more days to a band of marauders that work around the Mexican border. We have to do something to help them. If it was just Dovie, I'd say leave her to the hell she's going to, but they are holding a lot of innocent people who never asked for anything like this."

Woodenly, Virginia shook her head. It was so difficult to believe, yet what Hank had said made sense. She declared to no one in particular, "When we were talking a while ago, the fact that Dovie could be the gunrunner never crossed my mind. But now that I think about it, Dovie had the perfect opportunity. Her caravan could come and go to each fort with no questions asked. And I wonder how much information she was able to get from the unsuspecting soldiers?" Virginia shuddered at the thought.

Hank frantically clutched at Slade's arm. "You have to do something! Someone has to go for the cavalry at McDowell. If those savages leave this mountain as heavily armed as they are, this territory will run red with blood."

Slade stared intently at Caleab. "He's right. I'll leave as soon as it gets dark."

"You'll never make the fort."

"I'll have to try," Slade said adamantly.

"Trying is not good enough . . . not with this many lives at stake. And I didn't say it couldn't be made; I said *you* couldn't make it."

"What makes you think that?"

Caleab shrugged. "Whoever goes needs to leave as soon as it is good and dark or he'll never make it through. And during this particular phase of the moon, that Appaloosa horse of yours is just too light colored. The Apaches would be able to see him coming from two miles away. Thursday has a horse, but I doubt any other man could ride it besides him. Oh, you probably could if you worked with him, but we don't have that much time. I'm sure you have seen horses like that before; fact is, I believe you own one."

Slade nodded. He knew exactly what the old man was talking about, especially since Blue was a one-man horse. "Will you go?"

"I can't. I'd never get there in time. All I have is a burro, and she isn't fast enough."

"I guess that leaves your friend." He motioned toward Thursday.

Caleab scratched his head and twisted his face into a grimace. "I don't think that is a good idea either. To some people, one Indian looks just like another, and somehow it's hard to visualize the cavalry taking an Indian's word about other Indians' riding the warrior's path."

"Then I suppose it is up to me to go," Virginia said softly. "If someone could fashion a makeshift saddle for Mule, I could ride for help."

Slade started shaking his head before she even stopped speaking. "No, Virginia, it's too dangerous for a man, let alone a woman."

Resentment flared through her. She tossed her head and glared at him. Didn't he realize too much was at stake for him to be concerned with manly pride? "Being a man or a woman has nothing to do with it!" she finally said.

"You're wrong. A man might be able to escape if jumped by three or four Apaches, whereas a woman couldn't. You are not going, and that is final!"

Virginia was not sure that that was his only objection, but it was not the time to argue about personal differences. She squared her shoulders and jutted her chin stubbornly. "Someone has to do it, Slade, and the only logical person to go for help is me."

Seeing Slade about to protest again, Caleab spoke up. "Wait, young man, don't be so hasty. What your wife suggested makes sense. A camel is just as fast as a horse, considering you don't have to stop and rest it as often. Thursday could lead her through the mountains and they could be at Fort McDowell by mid-morning tomorrow, all safe and sound. Besides . . ." Motioning for Slade to follow him to the other side of the cabin, he spoke in a hushed tone. "It might be best that she gets out of here while she can. Those Apaches are swilling mescal, and they might decide to test their bravery by trying to kill a crazy old man. I'll admit, the trip to Fort McDowell will be dangerous, but if they make it — and they should — at least she will be out of harm's way. Now you think about it for a minute before you say no again."

Slade could feel cold sweat popping up on his brow. He did not need the old man to draw him any pictures. And as reluctant as he was to admit it, he knew that considering the number of Apaches out there, if they did decide to storm the cabin, they could do so in minutes. And if they got their hands on Virginia . . . He did not want to think about that possibility.

Before he could change his mind, he spun on his foot and walked toward Virginia. His expression was that of worried reluctance as he tilted her chin up, commanding her to look into his eyes. "I guess . . . maybe you're right . . . maybe you are the only one who can go, but . . . sweetheart . . . damnit, promise me you'll be careful."

445

Not trusting herself to speak, Virginia merely nodded and gave what she hoped was a reassuring smile. There was so much she wanted to say, yet she could not, not with everyone watching them.

Hank had been lying quietly, listening, while Thursday tended to him. He reached for Virginia's hand. "You'll make it, little girl, I know you will. And if you find yourself losing your courage, just think of Dovie. There's no telling how many deaths she has been responsible for. I know of three for sure: Ben, Egypt, and Carl, the man who tried to escape with me. But there is no telling how many more there will be if the cavalry doesn't arrive in time to stop them."

The heavy lashes that shadowed Virginia's cheeks flew up and she gasped. "C—Carl? Did you say Carl?" No, the thought going through her mind was ridiculous. Many men were named Carl, and her father was probably hundreds of miles from this godforsaken place.

"Yes." His eyes misted. "I owe my life to him. He was a very brave man. And, you know, it's odd, but you sort of remind me of him."

She exchanged a troubled look with Slade and he gripped her shoulder comfortingly. The attribute of bravery certainly did not sound as if it would describe her father, at least not the father she had known over the past few years; still, she could not just let it lie. She transferred her gaze to Hank. "Did . . . did he tell you his last name?"

"No, not that I recall. Why do you ask?"

"Carl was—" She corrected herself for using a past tense. "Carl is my father's name." She gave a nervous, yet humorous laugh and asked a little too eagerly, "I realize I'm probably being foolish, but is there anything else you can tell me about him?"

Attempting to remember, Hank frowned. "Let's see, I know he never mentioned any names, but he did talk about his wife and . . . his . . . little girl . . ." His voice trailed off and he watched Virginia anxiously. "And he talked about being a ship's captain on the Cypress River in East Texas . . ."

Virginia's lungs suddenly felt tight, her mouth dry. Acute pain stabbed through her chest, as if her heart were screaming in protest. Her father was dead! Dead!

Suddenly, her mind was besieged by memories from the distant past: how she had sat with her father on the top deck of the riverboat, mesmerized, listening to his stories; how he had occasionally tucked her into bed at night, brushing a kiss across her brow; and she recalled his gentleness, his kindness. Yes, he had changed when her mother died, but even those miserable years that followed would never make her forget the man he had once been. And it was that man for whom she would sorely grieve. A deep sob caught in her throat.

"Sweetheart," Slade whispered softly, "I'm sorry." He gently wrapped his arms around her and pressed her head against his chest. "Regardless of what happened between me and him, I would have moved heaven and earth for it not to have ended this way."

"I know," she cried, seemingly unaware of the tears that trailed endlessly down her cheeks.

"That man, Carl, was her father," Slade explained to Caleab and Hank. Then he continued to hold and comfort Virginia as her muffled sobs echoed forlornly throughout the small cabin.

Chapter Thirty-one

Later, Slade and Thursday went to the cavern to rig a saddle that would fit Mule. Caleab gave Hank a large dose of laudanum for pain before he finished cleaning and bandaging his wounds. After Hank went to sleep, Caleab settled down in his rocking chair with a book, leaving Virginia sitting at the table, alone with her memories.

Every so often, Caleab peered worriedly over his wire-rimmed spectacles at Virginia. Her eyes were red and puffy, but it was obvious she was trying not to cry anymore. Finally, he laid his book in his lap and said, "Don't hold your grief in; let it out. Tears won't bring shame on you."

"I think I have cried until there are no more tears left, Mr. Reavis," she replied sadly.

"Why don't you call me Caleab, like all of my other friends do?"

She tried to smile, but it was a pitiful attempt. "All right . . . Caleab it is, then."

"You have to let your grief out, young lady. You can't keep all that hurt inside." He paused for a long moment, his thoughts painful. "If I had taken that advice years ago, my life might have been different. I know if my little girl had lived, I wouldn't have wanted her to grieve for me —" His voice broke off, as though squeezed by some long ago memory that had been buried in his past.

"It's not just my grief, Caleab . . . it's a combination of so many things." Frustrated, she slammed her hand down on the table. "I — I *hate* the Apaches! Why do they have to kill? Why do they have to torture people? Look at poor Hank — why did they do that to him? How can human beings be so cruel? Why can't they live in peace with us?"

Caleab could understand her feelings but not her reasoning. He knew that the questions she posed had been the same ones people had been asking throughout the ages, in all civilizations, about various races of people, and no one had ever come up with a suitable answer. When men became tired of tyranny and oppression, they either packed up and went elsewhere or fought back. And that's what the Indians were doing now, he mused, fighting back, because they had no place left to go. After the birth of the nation, whenever its shores were threatened by foreign powers, Americans defended their country, and that's all the Indians were doing. Only they were making their last stand. Some knew it, but Indians like Geronimo, Victorio, and Nana didn't . . . or maybe they did.

Even though he was guilty of calling them "savages" and "heathens" at times, it was wrong to do so — very wrong. It all seemed a matter of one's point of view. If the Indians struck against the white men, whether their victims were men, women, or children, it was called a massacre; but if the cavalry rode into an Indian village, killing men, women, and children, it was termed a well-directed battle against the hostiles. It seemed to Caleab there was no logic behind that.

Maybe the Apaches were more brutal and ruthless than other tribes of Indians, but that was how they had lived for centuries. Perhaps they had to be more ruthless in order to survive in this harsh land. And Caleab's intuition told him the young woman would understand all of these things if she did not have such a powerful hurt twisting deep inside her. Perhaps he could later find the right time to talk with her and explain the Apaches' side of the story.

Virginia walked over to the window and looked out over the vast expanse surrounding them, the dry heat ever present, the thorned and spiny plants bristling, and the scorched earth out there just waiting for some poor soul to make a mistake. The warring Indians, snakes, scorpions, thorny cactus, lack of water, and blistering heat made this a hostile land. But maybe this wasn't a land; maybe it was hell and they were all too stupid to realize it.

"I also hate this land, and I hate these mountains," she muttered wretchedly. "Before Slade found me, I remember thinking how evil these mountains looked . . . and I was right, they are evil!"

Caleab repacked his pipe and lit it before speaking. "You are entitled to your opinion, but I have a different feeling about this place. It is a sanctuary to me. But, you know, several people have made the very same statement about these mountains' producing an evil feeling, so you might have a point, yet there might also be a logical explanation. Fact is, there's an old Pima legend about Kakatak Tamai, the Indian name for Crooked-Top Mountain, which is where we are. The legend might surprise you. It tells of good and evil, and walks hand in hand with Bible teachings." He stroked his beard thoughtfully. "Sit back down and let me tell you about it; then you decide for yourself if there is truth in the legend or not. And believe it or not, it might make you feel better.

"The Pima legend says, The Maker of the Earth, or 'Earth Maker,' came from beyond the planets and the stars. He moved his hand over the land and molded the Crooked-Top Mountain. It was he who also formed the blue cliffs of the Rio Salado, Salt River, and from his sweat created all men and animals.

"As the men grew in numbers, they became greedy and selfish. And, as the situation on earth worsened, Earth Maker decided to drown all of the evil men, but not without warning. He asked for all men to listen to the North wind as it called to them to be honest and live in peace. But few listened to the North Wind.

"The next night another warning echoed from a distant thunderstorm in the east. When the prophet Suhu spoke, he was called a fool, and the people continued to ignore the warning of the wind.

"On the third night, the wind came from the west. They were cautioned again to listen to the voice of the prophet Suhu. And still, they did not listen.

"On the fourth night, the wind came from the south, and only Suhu heard its mournful cry. 'Suhu,' said the Earth Maker, 'take your people who are good to the summit of Kakatak Tamai, for all of the land will soon be covered with water, and all of the evil will perish.'

"The prophet Suhu gathered the good people from all corners of the land and led them to the top of Crooked-Top Mountain. Then lightning and the roar of thunder enveloped the land. From the east the rains came, and for two moons it fell. All of the land except for Crooked-Top Mountain was covered with water.

"Earth Maker spoke once again from the thunder-clouds: 'All good men will return to the desert valley to till the fertile soil, and all evil men will be turned to

451

stone,' he said. And so it was."

Virginia spoke in awe. "Why, that is a combination of the story about Noah and the flood and the tale of Lot and the people turning to pillars of salt."

"That's true," Caleab readily agreed. "As the legend goes, all the evil ones who were turned to stone by Earth Maker still silhouette the skyline high above Fremount Pass. Those stone formations should serve as a reminder to any evil ones who enter the mountain, but, unfortunately, the Apaches don't believe the legend and the whites have never heard it. Even if they did hear it, it probably wouldn't do any good. It didn't back in Noah's day."

"So it's not the place; instead, it's the people who make a place good or evil," she said softly.

"Yes, and one of these days—my bones may be in the ground then and long forgotten—this land will know peace." Then he shrugged sadly. "I don't know though; since old Jacob Waltz found gold up here, men will be scouring these hills as soon as the threat of Apaches is over. More gold might be found, but mark my words: long after it is gone, there will still be people out there who will refuse to turn loose a dream, who will still believe there's more gold here and will never stop searching for a treasure that will be forever elusive." His eyes watered and he gruffly cleared his throat. "Come to think of it, I doubt this mountain will ever know peace."

She started to reply, but Slade pushed open the bookshelf and called to her. "Virginia, we—" Concerned, he paused, "Are you all right?"

"Yes, Caleab and I were just talking."

He nodded, obviously relieved. "We have the saddle finished. You need to see if it fits so we can adjust it if we have to." A touch of humor glinted in his eyes.

452

"Neither Thursday nor I have ever made a camel saddle."

Virginia and Caleab followed him into the cave, now brightly lit with torches. Mule was sitting on the ground patiently chewing his cud. Virginia agilely climbed on his back, but from her expression they could see that something was not quite right.

"I tried to figure out a way for you to ride sidesaddle, but considering some of the terrain you'll be traveling over and Mule's shape, I decided that wasn't too good an idea." Slade's voice did little to conceal his feelings of apprehension about her making the long, dangerous ride to Fort McDowell.

"The saddle is fine. I prefer to ride western style anyway. It's just. . . ."

"What?"

She smiled somewhat sheepishly. "I wish I had a pair of trousers to wear. I never did like to ride wearing a dress. In my opinion, trying to ride wearing a long skirt is nothing but a nuisance."

"I think I have something that might remedy that. I'll be right back," Caleab said, hurrying to the cabin. A few minutes later, he returned carrying a small bundle. "A couple of years ago I bought a new pair of denim trousers, but I never could wear them, and here's a clean shirt." He handed the bundle to Virginia. "You can go down to one of those small tunnels to change."

When she left, he turned to Slade. "You need to get that worried look off your face. She'll be all right. Thursday will take good care of her."

The tensing of his jaw betrayed his deep frustrations. "If I thought differently, I wouldn't let her go," he stated matter-of-factly, then his tone softened. "It's just . . . she's more important to me than life itself."

Caleab's respect for Slade increased a hundredfold with his statement. There were too many men who were ashamed to admit such deep feelings for their wives, believing it to be the mark of a sissy, and that was one thing no one could ever accuse Stephen Slade of being. "All the more reason for her to get out of here while she can."

"That's what I keep telling myself."

Slade's eyes narrowed when he saw Virginia hurrying toward him, still tucking the tail of the shirt inside her trousers.

"Now doesn't this look much better?" she asked, spreading her arms, then planting her hands firmly on her hips.

"No, the pants are too tight and the shirt is too loose." Slade reached out and buttoned the two top buttons on the shirt, then stepped back and looked at her appraisingly. "Turn around." His eyes swept up and down her backside as she did a slow pivot. He expelled a deep rush of air. "Sweetheart, I hate to disappoint you, but you are going to have to put your dress back on. Those trousers will never do."

"Why?"

Splaying his legs in a stubborn stance, he glanced once again at how the pants clung to her body. "Because they are too tight . . . they're too revealing," he stated adamantly.

"Not as revealing as a dress if we get caught in a windstorm, or have to ride through bramble bushes."

"That wasn't all I meant. I don't want those soldiers looking at you dressed like that. I know how army posts are. You'll have to beat them off with a club."

In spite of the grave situation, she laughed. "Why, Slade, I do believe you are jealous."

"Damn right I am!" he said, folding his arms together. "I don't want other men looking at my wife with that particular gleam in their eyes!"

Caleab turned his head, grinning from ear to ear.

"If that's your only argument," Virginia retorted, "then give me the money to buy a new dress when Thursday and I get there. That should solve the problem."

Caleab guffawed. "She's got you there, son! You walked into that one with both eyes open. Never seen a woman yet who wouldn't jump at the opportunity to buy a new dress."

Virginia, not knowing just how serious Slade was, slipped her hand in his and stubbornly met his gaze. "Sweetheart, joking aside, the trousers are really much more comfortable, and if you will only admit it, they're more practical than a dress. If I had a riding skirt, I would gladly wear it . . . but I don't."

His mouth worked wordlessly and he propped one hand on his waist and shifted on his feet. Then, finally sighing with resignation, he glanced at Caleab. "Does a married man ever win an argument?"

"Very seldom, son, very seldom," he replied, chuckling. Then his face instantly grew somber as Thursday said something to him. "He says it's time to be going." Seeing the intense look that passed between the couple, he knew they would want to be alone for a few moments. "I'll go help Thursday get the canteens and the gear you'll need."

When they were alone, Slade wrapped one arm around her waist and gingerly drew her to him. His large hand took her face and, tilting it upward, cradled it gently. Each experienced a deep physical awareness of the other, yet it went much further than mere sensuality. "You'll never know how much I've dreaded this moment."

455

Virginia smiled sadly and her dark eyes seemed extraordinarily bright. She suddenly wished there were some other alternative, but the lives of all those poor people being held captive were in her hands. Still, why did she and Slade have to be so deeply involved? Why couldn't it be someone else? Instantly she felt ashamed of her thoughts. What if she or Slade were being held captive? Their lives would depend on someone's willingness to help.

Slade wondered why he had never noticed the small dimple in her right cheek that appeared when she smiled. Or, maybe he had; maybe it just wasn't a conscious memory. There were so many mysteries about her and he prayed he would have a chance to explore them all. He studied her features, as if burning them into his memory.

Not surprisingly, his kiss was gentle when his lips touched hers. Then he stepped back and murmured huskily, his hand still caressing her face, "Remember, be careful. Please be careful. I don't want to lose you."

"Why, I'll be fine," she reassured him. "Thursday will take good care of me, I know he will. And I want *you* to promise to be careful. If I know you, you'll be right in the middle of the rescue when the cavalry arrives."

"You're not going to tell me not to, are you?" His tone indicated defiance.

"No, I doubt it would do any good . . . besides, I don't intend to start our marriage by placing a demand like that on you. Just promise that you'll be careful and that you'll hurry to Fort McDowell for me as soon as possible. I'm anxious to get on with our lives."

"I am too, sweetheart." He threaded his fingers through her hair and gently kissed her again, only this kiss hinted of what would follow when they were reunited.

456

Breathless, she pulled away slightly, her expression one of concern. "Love, I—I have one request. After the cavalry comes, will you t—talk to Caleab and Hank and find out where . . . where my . . . father is and see to it that he is . . . properly buried? I can't stand the thought of him . . . just lying out there somewhere." She gestured helplessly.

Slade nodded. "I'll see to him. I give you my word." Then, hearing Caleab and Thursday returning, he crushed Virginia in his arms and gave her one last kiss.

Mule stepped high and tossed his head, catching the eagerness that Virginia felt as they rode into Fort Mc-Dowell. Thursday's big horse easily kept pace with the camel, although when they had first started out, he had shied away from the unfamiliar animal. Yet under the big Indian's masterful hand, he had soon settled down.

As they rode into the quadrangle, Virginia quickly noticed their presence had garnered considerable attention. A group of young boys, not more than ten years of age, stared in openmouthed astonishment, and a few of the soldiers who had come out of their quarters did also, only most of them tried to act less obvious about their curiosity. A bemused smile tugged at her lips. It must be a rare sight indeed to see a woman wearing pants, riding a camel, and being escorted into the fort by a giant Indian. Maybe it would give them something to tell their grandchildren on a cold winter night while sitting before the fire.

Stopping in front of the headquarters, Mule knelt, then settled on his belly so that Virginia could dismount. With as much dignity as she could muster, she swung her leg over the make-shift saddle and slid to the ground.

The bravest of the boys — or the most curious, Virginia did not know which — ran toward her. "Is that really a camel?"

"Yes, he is."

He glanced over his shoulder and yelled to his friends, "Yep! It's a camel all right. I told you it was!" Then he looked at Virginia with a passing glance, his rapt attention on the strange-looking beast. "What's his name?"

"Mule."

"That's sure a funny name for a camel."

"That's because he is as ornery as one." Anxious to see the camp commander, she tried to step around the boy, but each time she moved, he darted in her way. "Son, please, I have urgent business with the camp commander."

"But . . . ma'am, I just want to look at him."

"I know, but he's ornery and he might bite you."

"Really?" His hand inched around to the pocket holding his slingshot.

Virginia's lips tightened. She knew that the minute she stepped inside the building all the boys would swarm around Mule. Without a doubt they would make him nervous, he'd probably bite them, then they would clobber him with stones from those silly slingshots. It stood to reason, if one boy had one, they all did. She could leave Thursday to guard him, but that could present problems too.

Her dilemma was solved when Thursday stepped between Mule and the boy, his arms folded and his face set in a glowering scowl. Slowly, the boy's gaze traveled up the entire seven feet of the Indian's height. Thursday reached down and plucked the slingshot

458

from the boy's pocket and placed it on the saddle. He then touched his knife, and turning so all the boys could see him, he made a slashing motion across his throat. The implied threat was obvious and the boys scattered as though the devil himself were chasing them. He looked at Virginia, and for the first time she saw him smile.

"Come on, Thursday, let's go see the commander."

Walking inside, she noticed the front office was much like the one at Fort Grant, only larger. The young clerk glanced up from his papers when they entered, his brow arching with surprise as he saw the huge Indian.

"General, I need to see the man in charge, right now," she said, leaning on his desk.

"W—Why, I'm not . . . a general . . . and that's impossible, ma'am," he stammered, looking at Thursday with wide, almost fearful eyes.

She slammed her fist against the desk top. "If the commander is out on patrol, he had to leave someone in charge and I must see him, immediately!"

The clerk gulped. "The commander is here, but . . . he is in a conference and left . . . strict orders not to be disturbed. You may wait if you like, but it will be at least two hours."

Virginia was not about to wait that long, not if she could help it. Seeing the commander's nameplate on the closed door behind him, she squared her shoulders determinedly and pushed open the small swing gate that separated the waiting area from the clerk's office. The clerk scrambled to his feet and barred the way.

"Ma'am, I said he can't be disturbed, and . . . and if you insist upon creating a disturbance, I'll be forced to call the Officer of the Guard!"

"But . . . I have to! Lives are at stake! And every

minute we waste haggling is important!"

"Yes, ma'am, I know, but I have my orders." His voice softened. "Lives are at stake all over the territory."

Sagging her shoulders in apparent defeat, Virginia turned away. When the clerk started to sit back down, she darted forward, but he caught her arm, stopping her. Suddenly a massive dark hand clamped over the clerk's. The young man's eyes widened with terror and he swallowed hard. Thursday grasped his upper arms, lifting him two feet off the floor, then he stepped inside the office area, set him back down, and followed Virginia, who had just burst into the commander's office.

Six uniformed men sat around a conference table, and she immediately recognized General Crook from Fort Grant.

Half rising from his chair, the officer at the head of the table demanded, "What is the meaning of this intrusion?" His expression revealed no intimidation from Thursday's presence. "Corporal!" he shouted. "Please remove these people from my office!"

"I tried to stop them, sir, but . . . they forced their way in!" the corporal explained, red faced.

"Lives are the meaning of this intrusion, sir!" Virginia shouted, angry that they did not want to listen. "And if you do not hear me out, more lives than you ever thought possible will be lost!"

The commander's eyes became hooded. "Ma'am, I think you should explain yourself."

"That's what I've been trying to do." She gestured frantically. "I have just come from the Superstition Mountains, and the Apaches have gathered there to go to war against the whites—and I'm speaking in terms of days . . . maybe even hours. They are holding a countless number of people prisoners . . . and what's even worse, they have recently acquired a large number of rifles and ammunition!"

General Crook stared intently at the commander. "This confirms my field report that something big is about to happen. However, I didn't believe it would be this soon."

Excited but concerned voices filled the room as questions were rapidly fired. Finally, the commander's voice rang out over the others. "Gentlemen! Let's have order! She can't answer us all at once." As soon as the room was quiet, he asked, "Now, ma'am, this is very important. Can you tell us who the chiefs are?"

"I—I'm not sure." She swallowed hard as she saw their anxious faces. "But Thursday might be able to. He knows much more about it than I do. He speaks the Apache language. Perhaps if you called an interpreter . . ."

The commander glanced at one of the men. "Lieutenant Carlisle, go get Nah-kah-yen, the Apache scout. Also, give the order for the men to get outfitted and mounted. We'll probably be pulling out within the half hour."

General Crook had been watching her, puzzled. "Ma'am, excuse me," he said, leaning forward. "Don't I know you from somewhere? You look very familiar."

Virginia wet her lips nervously. She did not want him to remember her as a boy, not now. They might tend to disregard her story if they knew she had lied before. An explanation could be offered later, if it was necessary, when he found out about Dovie. "I don't think so, sir."

"Who are you?"

"My name is Mrs. Stephen Slade."

She did not see the lieutenant stiffen and pause at the door, and the general's attention was soon directed elsewhere as the officers heatedly talked among themselves, occasionally asking her a question.

A short time later, the scout, wearing bandages on his arm and leg, was brought in and the officers gathered around so he could translate their questions to Thursday — all the officers, that is, except the lieutenant who had been sent out. He sidled close to Virginia.

"Excuse me, Mrs. Slade, but I am curious. Why did you come with this news instead of your husband? Has he been injured . . . or captured?"

"No, he is with Caleab Reavis, an old mountain hermit, but an injured man is with them. Slade doesn't know I overheard him and Caleab talking about the uprising," she lied, intent on protecting her husband's reputation. "He sent me here because they were afraid the cabin might be stormed by Apaches, and even though the journey was dangerous, they knew I would be safer with Caleab's Indian friend."

"Slade . . . you call him Slade?" he asked, pursing his lips thoughtfully.

"Yes." Something nagged at the back of her mind, but she could not seem to put her finger on it, and her train of thought was interrupted when the commander abruptly strode from the conference room.

"Let's go, Lieutenant, and pass the order to the men that we are to proceed at double time."

A wave of immense relief swept over Virginia as she followed the men outside. At last, help was on the way. Now all she had to do was wait for Slade, though she knew that would be more easily said than done. Without a doubt, the next few days would be the longest she had ever lived.

Leaning wearily against the porch post, she watched with misty eyes as the men gave hasty good-byes to their ladies. Everyone knew that probably some men would not return. An order was given, the men climbed on their mounts, and in a cloud of rising dust, the clanking of bridle chains, and the groaning of saddle leather, they were off.

Chapter Thirty-two

"Mrs. Slade? Are you Mrs. Slade?"

Virginia turned to see a large-bosomed, matriarchal woman with silver hair rapidly fluttering her fan. "Yes, ma'am, I am Virginia Slade."

Smiling pleasantly, the woman extended her hand. "I am Amanda Riley, the colonel's wife, and also the unofficial welcoming committee. Since there are no civilian accommodations here, my husband suggested that you might need a place to stay until your husband can come for you. The colonel and I already have guests, so I shall make arrangements for you to stay with the wife of one of the younger officers . . . unless you have friends here or have made different arrangements." She waited expectantly.

"No, ma'am, I don't know a soul . . . and I thank you for your generous hospitality."

Mrs. Riley's eyes sparkled with interest. "Do I detect a Southern accent?"

Virginia smiled, very pleased at the woman's friendliness. "Yes, I suppose you do, at least a partial one. I am originally from Northeastern Texas."

With a regal swish of her skirts, Mrs. Riley turned, taking Virginia by the arm. "Then come with me and I

464

shall introduce you to Maggie Carlisle. She's about your age, and I am sure she will be delighted to have you for company." Amanda stopped short. "That is . . . if you don't mind keeping late hours. Maggie is new to army life and she has difficulty sleeping whenever John is out on maneuvers or on patrol." She clicked her tongue in droll sympathy. "Poor dear, I sometimes wonder if she will ever adapt to the rigors of a military life."

"Oh, no, I don't mind at all. . . ." Virginia's smile vanished as though whisked away by a gust of wind. That name was what had nagged at her earlier.

Virginia's steps slowed as her thoughts raced. John Carlisle was not a highly unusual name. But it was the name of the lieutenant in the commander's office who had expressed an interest in Slade! Why him and no one else? Could he be the same man Slade had been searching for? If this John Carlisle was the same man, when Slade arrived at the fort, could he put the past behind him and forget the hatred that had been eating at him for all these years?

Her face paled when a frightening question loomed in her mind. If indeed this was the man, and even if Slade was willing to walk away without seeking revenge, would John Carlisle do the same? She did not think so. Slade was the only man alive besides him who knew the truth, and as long as Slade remained alive, he posed a threat to the lieutenant's freedom, his career, and perhaps even his bride. *And she had told him where Slade was!*

Even if Carlisle did not personally know Caleab, someone in the unit probably did—or at least knew of him—and a few innocent questions would gain him the general location of Caleab's cabin. After the cavalry had the Apaches under control, it would be so easy for him to slip away from the other troopers and lie in ambush for Slade. She shuddered at what would happen then.

Virginia's nails bit deeply into the palms of her hands. *Stop it! You're letting your imagination run wild,* she told herself. The lieutenant probably isn't even the same man. Before you start making reckless accusations or do anything foolish, ask a few questions first.

In Virginia's mind her attempt to sound jovial and nonchalant fell flat. "Mrs. Riley, you said Maggie Carlisle was new to army life. I suppose she and her husband have just recently arrived in this part of the country?"

"She has, but John has been here for awhile," Mrs. Riley offered readily. "They met lat summer when she came out to visit with a recently widowed aunt who lives in Phoenix."

"I see." I think I am beginning to see all too well! she thought, apprehension twisting her insides into a hard knot. "You mean . . . the lieutenant has been in the cavalry for a long time?"

Mrs. Riley laughed. "Well, if you consider four years a long time, yes." Then she frowned as though suddenly uncertain, an emotion Virginia doubted the woman experienced often. "But now that I think about it, I believe he served at another fort when he was younger. Of course," she added pointedly, "he was not an officer then. The lieutenant was awarded a field commission two years ago." She dismissed it with a casual wave of her hand. "I declare, it is becoming more and more difficult to keep up with all these minor details. The names and faces all start to run together after awhile. I'm afraid Maggie will have to answer any other questions you might have."

Virginia heard a loud roaring sound and her knees felt like they had turned to jelly. Everything the woman had said confirmed her suspicions; in all likelihood this John Carlisle was the same man who had betrayed

Slade. And, without a doubt, he had ridden out of the fort with murder in his heart. It was a realization that left her mind reeling. She looked about frantically. John Carlisle had to be stopped! Slade had to be warned!

"M—Mrs. Riley, please, you'll have to forgive me. There is something I must attend to immediately." Desperately hoping Thursday had not already left the fort, Virginia whirled and ran, leaving the commander's wife with a most astonished expression on her face.

A deep feeling of relief swept over Virginia when she saw Thursday at the hitching post, apparently standing guard over Mule until she returned. Thursday's usually stoic visage suddenly showed concern when he noted her obvious distress.

"Thursday, you have to take me back!" she gasped breathlessly, jabbing her finger to her chest, then pointing to the mountains, hoping to make him understand.

Frowning, he shook his head from side to side.

Her mouth was tight and grim. How could she convey to Thursday how serious this was? She had no idea how much English he understood. Yet if she got an interpreter, he might be friends with John Carlisle. Perhaps sign language and drawings would do, she decided.

Setting her chin in a stubborn line, she dropped to the ground on one knee and in the sand drew a rough sketch of the mountains and the fort. Thursday had knelt too, and when he nodded, she added a man in the mountains and a woman in the fort. She placed her hand flat on her chest, then pointed to the drawing, indicating herself. He nodded again with understanding.

Virginia clasped a doubled fist against her chest and let her features go soft, then she pointed to the man figure in the mountains. "Slade," she murmured dreamily.

Bobbing his head, Thursday pointed to each figure and muttered in a guttural tone, "Slade . . . you." He looked at her expectantly.

Encouraged, she quickly drew a picture of a man at the fort and with a waving motion of her hand indicated he had left. "Soldier . . . bluecoat . . . yellow leg," she muttered hopefully.

"Ahh, soldier."

Virginia twisted her face into an ugly grimace and slammed her fist against her chest. "Soldier . . . hates Slade!" Then, acting as though she were lying in ambush with a rifle, she made a shooting sound and again whispered, "Soldier will kill Slade." By his expression, she knew Thursday understood. She pointed to herself, to him, then made a waving motion with her hand toward the moutains.

He slowly shook his head and gestured that only he should go. "You . . . here."

"But, Thursday," she muttered fearfully, using sign language with her spoken words, "you don't know what the soldier looks like, and I do. If I don't go, the soldier will kill him."

Thursday studied her for a moment before rising to his feet. Silently, he nodded, then took their mounts' reins and led them toward the stables. The animals would have to be fed, watered, and rested for several hours before they could start back to the mountains.

"Do you have a pick and a shovel I can use?"

Caleab glanced up from the trousers he was patching and, for a moment, stared hard at Slade before he asked in an amused tone, "Plan on doing a bit of prospecting?"

"No." The muscles in Slade's jaw tightened. "I promised Virginia I would bury her father."

"Don't you think it can wait until tonight when it's safer?"

"He's been out there a day already. With the heat, wild animals, and buzzards, if it's not done soon, there won't be anything left to bury . . . and I gave her my word."

Sighing heavily, the old man placed his trousers aside, cautiously opened the front door of his cabin, and looked about before going out to his gardening shed. He returned a few minutes later with pick and shovel in hand. "I still think you are making a mistake. There are Apaches close by. I can almost smell them."

"I'll be careful." He smiled. "I'll take Blue with me. He is better than a watchdog." It was a statement of fact. A good horse would prick his ears at the first sign of a strange scent. "Now if you'll tell me where the body is, I'll get this over with. It's not a chore I'm looking forward to."

After Slade left, Hank awoke and asked to speak to the younger man. Caleab told him where Slade had gone.

Hank's eyes narrowed and became hooded with concern. "I wish you had stopped him. It gives me an uneasy feeling to know he's out there alone."

"I know," Caleab said, shrugging and taking a long pull on his pipe. "But he's in love and a body can't reason with a man when he's like that."

Slade's stomach lurched when he found Carl's body lying in a crevice on the back side of a knoll, partly screened by brush and boulders. If he had not known the pitiful remains was Carl Branson, he never would have recognized him.

Blue shied away from the odor of death, so Slade tied him to a creosote bush twenty yards beyond the crevice to calm him, then he removed his shirt to prevent the stench from permeating the material. He tied a handkerchief around his mouth and nose, and set about his grim task, being careful to keep his rifle within easy reach.

Alternating between the pick and the shovel, Slade worked at a furious pace to finish quickly, yet dig the grave deep enough to that animals could not get to Carl's body. He piled the larger stones he removed beside the hole, intending to use them to cover the grave after filling it with dirt. So intent was he on completing his grisly chore, he never heard the four Apaches until it was too late.

Leaving Fort McDowell, Thursday and Virginia forded the Verde River and in less than an hour they had passed through the rich grasslands surrounding the river and were well into the arid stretch of desert that separated the fort from the northwestern slopes of the mountains. They set a rapid pace in order to reach the cabin before the cavalry reached the Apache *rancherias*. Before long, they started to thread their way through the higher, more rugged country.

The sun was beginning to dip low in the western sky when they finally stopped to rest. Thursday gestured for Virginia to eat and sleep, and indicated that he would take care of their mounts. Wearily, she climbed off Mule, stretched her aching muscles, then sank onto the soft sand under a desert laurel tree and leaned back against the slender truck. Too tired to be hungry, she removed an apple and a *tortilla* from her food bag and ate anyway, knowing she might need every ounce of strength she could muster before the night was over.

Trying to keep her thoughts off Slade, she munched on her apple and casually glanced about the tranquil setting. A feeling of awe slowly drifted over her. Long purple shadows danced on the canyon walls and the sun bathed the mountain peaks in colors of rusty red and burnt orange. For a brief moment she could see why many people had fallen so deeply in love with this land and were willing to fight for it. Then, remembering her father, she tore her mind from such thoughts. She closed her eyes and soon fell into a fretful sleep.

It seemed she had just fallen asleep when Thursday gently shook her, but it was now dark except for stars glittering in the ink black sky. Feeling too tired, sore, and stiff to move, she wanted desperately just to lie there, but the thought of Slade and the danger he was in gave her strength to stagger wearily to her feet and climb back on Mule.

The mountains towered higher, at times almost obliterating the sky; the trail became steeper, seemingly impassable, but Thursday and his horse carefully picked their way while Mule followed, frequently balking when the trail became too rugged. Virginia knew from reading, and Thursday knew from some innate sense, that camels had never been intended for travel over such rugged, mountainous terrain. Whenever he balked and refused to move, they dismounted, and with firm but gentle prodding, they were able to continue. Eventually, the trail wound through sandy *arroyos* and it became easier to follow.

At times, Virginia wondered if she would make it. After traveling all night long the previous night, and not having had a chance to recover from her ordeal on the desert, she was beyond exhaustion. And the rocking motion caused by Mule's plodding gait did not help matters any. Often, she caught herself drifting off to sleep, then she would come abruptly awake when he stepped into a shallow spot or reached a small incline. Still, she uttered not one word of protest.

However, Thursday knew the woman had reached the limits of her endurance. He also knew they would make better time if she rested for awhile. When he reined in his horse, Mule stopped without any urging and immediately bellied down in the soft sand of the dry wash.

"What are we stopping for?" Virginia asked groggily. "We have to press on! We have to get there before the cavalry does!"

Thursday only recognized the word cavalry, but he had understood the urgency in her voice. Effortlessly, he lifted her from the camel's back and carried her over to the steepest part of the bank and laid her down, propping her against it.

"Rest," he grunted, then quietly moved away. But she did not hear him. She was already asleep.

Sheer black fright swept through Virginia when she was abruptly awakened by a large hand clamped tightly over her mouth. Panic rioted within her and she struggled frantically, but upon hearing a soft, shushing sound, she realized it was Thursday who had awakened her. After she bobbed her head and gently touched his hand to let him know she was aware and understood, he slowly removed his hand from her mouth. Her eyes widened with fear when she heard horses approaching and the whispered, guttural sound of an Apache's voice. Even though the night was now pitch black, she remained perfectly still, knowing movement could be detected in the darkness, especially by a practiced eye. Suddenly her heart lurched and the taste of bile rose in her throat when four Apaches rode by on the ledge above them. Hot tears filled her eyes and a deep, searing pain such as she had never before felt swept over her. But still, she sat there, frozen in anguished silence, her expression that of mute wretchedness.

How much time passed, Virginia did not know, but she slowly became aware of Thursday's hand on her arm. Although it was too dark to see his eyes, she looked at him and realized he had seen it too. One of the Apaches had been riding Slade's horse.

Knowing Blue had been stabled in the passageway, Virginia and Thursday assumed the tunnels had been discovered, and they rode directly for the cabin, not stopping, not pausing. Virginia's anguished thoughts were on Slade, and Thursday's were centered on his old friend, the man who had saved his life many years before.

They arrived at the first light of dawn, and instead of finding smoldering ruins, they were puzzled to see that the cabin and surrounding area appeared serene and peaceful. After Thursday scouted about and found the area clear, they approached the cabin, wary and cautious, acutely aware they could be walking into a trap. But at that point, Virginia really did not care, because she feared the worst. She knew something terrible had happened; otherwise the Apaches never would have had Blue.

Crouching low, rifle ready, Thursday suddenly bolted for the cabin, kicked at the door, and burst inside. Virginia followed close behind, both hammers pulled back on the shotgun Caleab had lent her.

Caleab was at the table cleaning his Winchester and Hank was sitting up in bed filling shotgun shells with buckshot.

Caleab, ignoring the relieved expression on Thursday's face, remarked wryly in the Indian's native tongue, "Guess I must be getting old. I never heard you coming." Having been together for so long, that was all the greeting they needed.

"Where's Slade?" Virginia urgently asked, holding her breath until he answered.

"The Apaches jumped him while he was burying your father." He eyed her warily. "Now don't fret and don't blame yourself for asking him to do it. I told him to wait until dark and he should have known better, and for God's sake don't go getting female-hysterical on me. He's alive and well, or at least he was two hours ago. I became worried when he didn't return . . . so I went looking for him." Anticipating her next question, he added, "They're holding him in the largest *rancheria*, about three miles from here."

She wanted to feel relief but couldn't find it in her to do so.

Caleab continued to clean his rifle. "We're going to have to get him out of there and we'll have to act mighty fast. Once that camp starts stirring, the bucks might decide he is too strong and dangerous to hold captive and turn him over to the squaws. If that happens, they'll kill him, or make him wish he were dead," he stated matter-of-factly.

"How many Apaches are in that *rancheria* where they're holding him?"

"Oh, I'd say . . . about thirty, maybe forty, warriors, not counting the war women, squaws, and children."

Swallowing her dismay at those numbers, she asked softly, "What did you intend to do, attack the camp by yourself?"

"I'm really not sure." Then he frowned, his eyes level under drawn brows. "What are you doing here? You're supposed to be at Fort McDowell."

Virginia quickly explained the entire story, and when she finished, Caleab leaned back in his chair and slowly released a deep rush of air. "That boy has gotten himself into a hell of a mess!" He stroked his whiskers,

474

searching hard for a way to help Slade, short of charging into the Apache camp almost single-handedly.

Desperate for a slender thread of hope to hang on to, Virginia paced the floor, also trying to think of something to do. Then she paused and spoke, but the tone of her voice suggested that she was trying to convince herself as much as anyone else. "M — Maybe it isn't as grim as it seems. The cavalry should arrive soon and it's very possible they can save Slade. And where John Carlisle is concerned, it's also possible he will be sent with another detachment of men to a different camp."

There was a rapid exchange of words between Caleab and Thursday before Caleab turned back to Virginia. "Young lady, I don't want to sound cruel . . . I feel you want me to be honest with you . . . so, don't delude yourself by thinking that way." Her agonized expression was too distressing to watch, and he pulled his gaze from hers. "The Apaches usually kill their captives at the first sign of trouble — the cavalry knows this, but they'll charge anyway. Getting the rifles and the renegades will be their first concern, and the captives their second. And since this *rancheria* is the main one, it will be their primary objective. I doubt they will split the men into separate detachments . . . so, in all likelihood, this enemy of Slade's will be in on the attack. And from what you've told me, if the Apaches don't kill him first, then this man will. With bullets flying, you'll never be able to prove anything." When he heard her strangled sob, he mumbled, "Sorry . . . but it's best you know what we're facing."

She rigidly tried to hold her tears in check, but inside her emotions were in turmoil.

Softly, a voice came from the other side of the room. "I may have a solution." Hank had been listening and thinking.

"For God's sake, what?" Virginia rushed to his side,

as did Caleab, and even Thursday.

"Little girl, do you remember that book I gave you about the Apaches?"

She nodded.

"Did you read it?"

"Yes."

"Do you recall the chapter about their superstitions?"

"Y — Yes." She wondered what he was getting at.

"I have an idea . . . but it will be very dangerous. You'll be taking a great risk."

"If it's a chance to save Slade, I'll take it."

"Even at the risk of your own life?"

"Yes, even that!" she said without a moment's hesitation.

"All right then. I can help too. I may not be able to walk, but I can shoot. If our big friend here will carry me, this is what I have in mind. I know from first hand experience that the chief and several of his warriors speak English, so communicating won't present a problem. Men, we can take cover above the *rancheria* . . ."

Slade had been in some tight situations before, but he was starting to get worried. His hands, bound with rawhide straps, thudded with pain from being tied too tightly, and because he had been forced to stand, bound to a tree, since he had been captured, his legs felt like soft mush, but those were the least of his worries.

He had overhead two bucks talking; one had suggested putting an arrow through him and the other was in favor of turning him over to the squaws. He might have known the buck wanting to let the squaws torture him would be the one whose teeth he had kicked out when the Indian had tried to climb on Blue. Fortunately, a different Indian had claimed the horse before the nasty-tempered one had been able to kill him.

In spite of his determination not to show fear, sweat beaded on his forehead when he saw the women dragging bundles of firewood toward him. The toothless buck had won. Slade knew what the squaws were going to do; he had seen the results of their favorite form of torture before. They would hack the firewood into small pieces, sharpen them into splinters, then they would take their own sweet time until every inch of his body had been pierced by them. Then, when he finally looked like a human porcupine, they would set him on fire. He swallowed hard and wondered what he could do to get them angry enough to kill him now.

Slade was so intent on his thoughts, he did not hear the commotion stirring on the far side of the camp. Finally, the noise penetrated his mind and he glanced up. He wished he hadn't. *Virginia was riding boldly into camp on that damn camel!*

When she pulled back on the reins, Mule stopped, went to his knees, then to his belly. Virginia climbed off, gave a haughty toss of her head and arrogantly planted both hands on her hips. "I want to talk to the chief!" she stated bravely, never blinking an eye.

The chief, whom the Apaches called Goyathlay, but whom Slade knew as Geronimo, stepped forward, his expression reflecting curiosity, wariness, and a slight touch of admiration.

Extending her arm, she pointed directly at Slade. "I have come for him! You and your people have made the Maker of the sky, the earth, and the water angry by taking him prisoner!"

Geronimo stiffened and his lips curled into an ugly snarl. "I have seen no visions of this. You are a foolish woman to come here. Now I will take *you* prisoner!" His tone was deep and guttural.

She kept her voice strong and her manner brave and unwavering, knowing her charade would be over at the first sign of fear or hesitation. "The Maker gave Goy-athlay the power of visions and in his anger He has removed that power. It will be returned when the man is released." She could hear their words being interpreted among the ones who could not understand English.

Geronimo's face became expressionless, but Virginia knew he had to be considering the ultimatum. Hank had told her that even though Geronimo was a war chief, his ability to have visions earned him deeper respect among the Apaches, for they valued such power greatly.

His gaze fell on the camel. "You ride a strange beast."

"He is from the earth. The Maker breathed life into the nostrils of the mountain near the town that the white-eyes call Phoenix. I rode the mountain here to get that man!" Again, she pointed adamantly at Slade. "Have two of your bravest warriors cut him loose and put him on the beast-mountain. Then we will go, but do not follow, for we will disappear into a secret place in the earth. It will be then that your powers will return.

The Apaches respected bravery from men and women alike, and Virginia was counting on this fact. Also, her standing up to Geronimo would not cause him to lose face in front of his people; it was possible the confrontation would increase their esteem. Few Apaches could boast of meeting a messenger from the Maker and coming face to face with a beast-mountain.

Geronimo turned to the warrior standing by his side, made a swift gesturing motion, and within moments Slade was released and placed on the camel's back.

"*Anah-zont-tee!* Begone!" Geronimo grunted. Then he turned and stalked to his wickiup.

Taking Mule by his reins, Virginia led the way from the *rancheria*. Hank had cautioned her not to look back or say a word until they were well away from the

478

Apache stronghold. Her heart slammed against her chest when she caught movement out of one eye, then felt relief when she realized it was her friends pulling back from their vantage points. It seemed to her that hours had passed, though in reality, it took them less than ten minutes to reach the dark slit in the rocks that concealed a tunnel.

Suddenly they were inside and she was in Slade's arms, sobbing quietly, but the tears were an outpouring of blessed relief.

"Oh, Slade . . . Love . . . I was so scared! I thought . . . I thought . . ." Her words were smothered by a torrent of fervent kisses.

Slade murmured huskily, his tone a mixture of love and anger, "Sweetheart, I wanted to wring your neck when you came riding in like that! Didn't you know you could have been tortured to death?"

In the faint light, she gazed deeply into his eyes and saw adoration shining from them. "No, the men had positioned themselves in the rocks . . . and if it had come to that . . . they were going to shoot us both."

For an instant his countenance tensed, then the most incredible expression softened his features. "Looks like I married one hell of a woman . . . and will you please explain what you're doing here? You are supposed to be in Fort McDowell where it's safe!"

Wrapping her arms tightly around him, she told him what had happened, about John and all she had discovered, leaving nothing out. As she talked she felt his body grow tense and his breath come in short, impotent rasps. Terror ripped through her that rivaled the horror she had felt when she had seen the Apache riding Blue. Then, slowly, his tension eased and his arm tightened around her in a loving embrace.

"Don't worry, sweetheart. It's over. If he comes out of this skirmish alive, I'll let the law handle it." His voice broke with huskiness. "Early yesterday morning, Hank and I were talking and he told me about a valley in Colorado. He said there were green trees all year round and that it was the best location for a ranch he had ever seen. He asked me to be his partner. Only thing is, the winters are awfully cold. We'd have to snuggle most of the time." He looked at her and grinned. "What do you say?"

Virginia could not say anything. Tears of happiness had choked her voice.

Just before Slade's lips met hers, he realized that he had come to these mountains seeking gold and he had found the richest treasure in the world.